SUMMER SEASON

Darcy Drummond

Published by Saron Publishing in 2018
Copyright © 2018 Darcy Drummond

Summer Season is a work of fiction. Names, characters,
places, events and incidents are either the products of the
author's imagination or used in a fictitious manner. Any
resemblance to actual persons, living or dead, or actual
events is purely coincidental.

ISBN-13: 978-1-9999871-0-7

Saron Publishing
Pwllmeyrick House
Mamhilad
Mon
NP4 8RG

saronpublishers.co.uk

Follow us on Facebook or Twitter

DEDICATION

For my father
Somewhere over the rainbow

ACKNOWLEDGEMENTS

It goes without saying my heartfelt thanks go to my lifelong show business friends, for their talent, success and love and on whom absolutely none of these characters is based. They are entirely fictional and although parts of this story are accurate portrayals of my own experiences, I have used much dramatic licence. I must thank Penny Reeves, a special lady who reignited my passion for writing after a series of unfortunate life events. Her help throughout has been invaluable and I hope we shall continue to collaborate for many years to come. To my husband, who lost me to this project for much of our spare time together, thank you for your support darling. Finally, my unending love and gratitude to my mother, she knows why.

PART ONE

'THIS IS YOUR HALF HOUR CALL, LADIES AND GENTLEMEN, HALF AN HOUR'

CHAPTER ONE

Present Day

The smell of backstage is unique. It shrouds the unseen areas of every theatre in the land. An essential ingredient in the narcissistic anodyne cocktail called show business.

An addict relishes that first shot of stimulating aroma as they step through a stage door. They are the performers and the high they crave is applause. Loud, enthusiastic, vindicating applause. And vindication is important, for they stand in the brilliant, dust mote-ridden illumination of the footlights at the cost of all else. That crucial rapturous sound from the auditorium at the end of a performance is their absolution.

But when Doug Delany arrived for his weekly slot on a national radio station, it was for another reason.

He raised a hand in acknowledgement to the receptionist and hit the lift button with the heel of his hand, standing silently looking up at the glowing red numbers as they fell in accordance with the lift's descent. Doug's tall frame was slightly hunched, a little thinner than it used to be and, dressed in jeans and polo shirt, far removed from the image he'd left behind.

Once an A list celebrity. A talented quickfire comedian with snappy suits and an act to match. A man with a Midas touch during his long illustrious career. Now, instead of the bright lights, grease paint and TV cameras, Doug hosted a chat show from a small glass booth. Surrounded not by nubile dancing girls, nor facing his once-staple diet of adoring audiences in the darkness beyond the stage or studio floor. No, in his windowless studio, Doug interviewed other 'happening now' celebrities about their lives, away from the daily pursuit of the press, the very piranhas that had brought today's guest to his show.

They occasionally said a few words about him, here and there, on a slow entertainment news day but Doug was no longer the hot material he once had been. Because Doug had made it that way.

Doug Delany had a secret. Actually, he had several, but this one was a big, nasty, festering secret. Behind this new persona he had created, was a very different man. One he never wished to meet again. Within the new structure he had built around his life, it was possible. But for how long?

This rare but briefest of visitations to his most private domain was ended by the ping of the lift arriving. Upon entering, Doug realised he had been joined by several other people, some oblivious but one lady with a visitor's pass eyed him discreetly. He knew the look. It happened a lot now. Was it him? Yes, it was. Hasn't he changed? And so on. It would have mattered years ago but now, Doug shrugged it off like an irritating mosquito.

Seated in his tiny studio, glancing quickly over the last-minute adjustments to the show's script, he knew he was living each day at a time. He had been for the last few years. Like his guest, a recovering alcoholic, Doug knew he might fall off the wagon at any time, but not if he could help it. He also knew there were only a handful of people who were party to his secret and they wouldn't talk. Unlike much in his life, that was certain. The rest, well... the rest was up to Doug, and would be for as long as he lived.

Why he was having these bouts of reminiscence, he wasn't sure. Something must have triggered them. Maybe in the way a dormant volcano occasionally spits steam and ash to relieve the pressure, so Doug's carefully protected state of mind needed a release. Whatever. Right now, he had an interview to do. It was probably one of the most newsworthy for a while and Doug had to be on top form.

Bob Welsh stood outside the studio, looking in at Doug through the soundproof glass, and smiled somewhat hesitantly. Doug smiled back and beckoned him in like an old mate, but Bob was beaten to it by his agent and manager, Cynthia Hersh. A brash, slightly masculine woman, not how Cynthia used to be at all.

'So, Doug, how are you?'

Like she cared.

'Great, just great. Yourself?' Doug responded politely, though he felt more like telling her to piss off. He knew what was coming.

'Peachy. Now listen, Doug, this is Bob's first live interview since the story broke. He's fragile, okay?' She shot a quick look at her client still standing in the doorway. He was blankly observing the studio, not really listening. 'Just keep to the agreed questions and...'

'Cynthia, please. You know my format. It's not *Hard Talk* on News 24, for Christ's sake. I like Bob at lot...' Doug smiled at his nervous guest, their eyes connecting, but Bob remained silent. 'Give me a break, "okay"?' he said, emphasising her own patronising enquiry.

She bristled at the sarcasm.

'Oh, you've had your fair share of those, darling. I'd say more than you ever deserved, right?'

Her look could have frozen Hell over. Bob raised an eyebrow but pretended he hadn't heard their verbal fencing match.

Doug regarded the agent and slowly smiled. Or was it a smirk? 'Well, you know what they say, love.'

Biting down on the urge to ask him not to call her 'love', Cynthia turned to Bob and indicated for him to take his seat, which Bob did like an obedient child. As she reached the studio door, Cynthia turned back and looked deep into Doug's eyes. 'Just what do they say, Doug? Not much these days, is it, "love"?' And on that note, she closed the door behind her before he could reply.

Cynthia detested Doug Delany and everything he now stood for. This new, caring family man crap just didn't wash. In fact, it made her feel quite sick. As arse holes went, Doug Delany should have trophies for it. She wished she could have spilled the beans long ago, when he was that much-acclaimed star who could do no wrong, even when he did, and was quietly known in the business as 'Teflon'. But Cynthia was making her own, rather unexpected life change at the time.

Having been a fairly successful dancer, Cynthia had begun to take on small acting roles and was enjoying the challenge immensely. She landed a meatier role in a courtroom drama as a witness and she was finally getting noticed. At the same time, she realised quite by accident that she had a good nose for sniffing out other talent, often having a bet with herself who would land the part at auditions and finding out that they had. So when an event occurred that took away her will to carry on as a performer, and very nearly finished her off altogether, she set herself up as an agent, with the help of friends and colleagues in the know, concentrated on a new career and discovered her true forte. It was a time she needed her signings to trust their agent. And they could still trust Cynthia Hersh, but maybe one day...

One day when she had packed herself off to a retirement villa in Marbella, and just didn't give a shit anymore, she might just delve into an unsolved mystery that doggedly sat in the back of her mind every day. Cynthia had no doubts it would lead her to Doug.

Bob Welsh adjusted the table mike and put on the headphones. He was an actor who had achieved a place in the heart of the nation through his role as Jimmy Newgate in a long running television soap. The loveable rogue who ran the local greengrocers and bedded most of the new female characters as they arrived in the show. Short and stocky with a friendly round face, he was happily married, or so it had seemed, with two small children. Now here Bob sat, two days after the *Mail on Sunday* had called Cynthia with the story they were about to run - and did Bob have any comment to make? Bob had plenty but left it to his agent to retrieve his life and career, something she was renowned throughout the industry for doing with much sang-froid.

For reasons only really known to himself, Bob's fairly hefty social drinking had slowly developed into lengthy solitary bouts, all deftly kept from the studio heads. Then, the now-infamous scene in the nightclub, at which, it just so happened, a reporter was present.

Doug waited for a signal from his producer and then began his usual cocky banter to open the show. '... and without further ado, I'm delighted to have Bob Welsh with me today. Morning, Bob.'

'Morning, Doug.'

Bob's voice was wedged somewhere between his real voice and that of Jimmy Newgate. It was a comfort zone, one of many he would be forced to call upon in the much-changed future ahead of him.

'No doubt you've all read the papers and seen the pictures, and Bob's asked to come on the show today to tell his side of the story, haven't you, Bob?'

Bob didn't much recall 'asking' to be on the show, more like being presented with a *fait accompli* by Cynthia, but he said, with a smile he hoped made its way through the air to the listeners, 'Yes, and thanks for having me at such short notice. I'd like to put a few things straight, if I may.'

'So, let's cut to the chase, Bob. Would you class yourself as an alcoholic?'

It was a question buried deep within the approved script but Doug had deliberately asked it in its most basic form. Certainly not as Cynthia would have wanted him to. After a moment's surprise, Bob replied candidly. Not quite how Cynthia had drilled him.

'Yes, I am. A recovering alcoholic. That may shock a few people but it's the truth and that's what's important here, Doug. I want people to know the truth.'

'That's something we strive for on this show, Bob, I think the truth gives us freedom.' It was a perfect response to his guest but stirred something cold and dormant within Doug.

'I should also like to thank my wife for being so supportive and sticking by me. She's been wonderful through all of this. Thanks, Sandra.'

'And I have indeed met the lovely Sandra. You're a lucky man, Bob.'

'I know.'

Doug sensed that perhaps his guest needed a few seconds to collect himself again. He browsed through the question list provided by Cynthia and skipped down to one he felt worth getting into.

'So, I presume Jimmy Newgate won't be departing our screens then?'

Joking laughter all round, Bob taking it all in his stride, when what he really needed was a stiff drink, or two. Just the thought brought a rush of saliva and his stomach heaved in futile anticipation.

'My producers have been unbelievable, Doug. I owe so much to their generosity.'

Steady on, thought Doug. *Let's not get too carried away here. They're only waiting to see if the public will still accept you, mate. If not, Jimmy Newgate will be written out of the show at the speed of light. Probably get crushed to death by a sack of potatoes.* 'Well,' said Doug, 'you've been in the role for how long, eleven years now? You're an integral character, and just where would they all go for their fruit and veg?'

Doug cast a glance at Cynthia, knowing full well he had overstepped the mark. She simply regarded him with icy, unreadable eyes.

'Even so, Doug, I've been less than professional and let a lot of people down, not least my family. It's great to know the show still has faith in me to turn things around.'

Doug was getting a little bored with the schooled answers. Cynthia was present in every word. Time for a break and a track. 'I'm sure they're grateful you've acknowledged that, Bob. Now, I think it's time we played your first request. What'll it be?'

While his slightly sweaty guest got up to go to the toilet

and no doubt have a chat with his agent, ever-present on the other side of the glass, fag drooping from lips adorned with bright pink lipstick, Doug sat listening to the track Bob had chosen.

As Frank Sinatra sang *I've Got You Under My Skin*, he closed his eyes and realised what the trigger had been for his earlier thoughts. Unlike his subconscious, Doug hadn't paid enough attention to Bob's request list. If he had, Doug would have somehow changed this one. The words from the chorus drifted from the headphones into his senses and sent a shiver down his spine. His throat suddenly constricted, and he reached for his usual jug of water, always ready during a broadcast. Doug poured a long glass and gulped most of it down, though his shaking hand caused most of it to spill.

The song drew to a close as Bob settled back into his chair and replaced the headphones. Doug tried to conceal the ragged tear that had just ripped across his heart. So unexpected but no less painful.

It had been a long time and he wished they would all go away. All the memories. Images that dragged him kicking and screaming back to the past. A former interlude in time that had been his loveliest, and yet darkest, hour.

CHAPTER TWO

Some years before...

'Hiya,' gushed Sara Harmsworth, giving her friend a big theatrical hug and air kisses.

'Hello, you old tart,' replied Amanda Jacobs as she extracted herself and gave Sara a surreptitious once over. *Damn it, she's in good shape,* thought Amanda. Even Sara's cascading Raphaelesque auburn curls looked recently and expensively attended to. Perhaps the thighs were a tad heavy but despite that minor detail, Amanda knew she should have gone to more classes.

Petite next to her friend, Amanda's bleached blond hair scraped back into a short ponytail, she envied Sara to some extent. Vivacious, her forceful personality got Sara into many shows, though not for a while. Amanda wondered whether the stint as company rep for Equity, the show business union, while working in Eastbourne the previous summer, had played a part in Sara's failure to get into anything notable since. There were rumours that Ms Harmsworth had been rather zealous in her extra role, and the production grapevine had been buzzing. As it was prone to do.

'Wonder who else will be here?' said Amanda. 'Looks like the usual cattle market.'

'Yep, it's a big show,' Sara responded, while scanning the ever-increasing crowd of hopefuls. A diverse spectacle of attire, fitness and beauty. Some of the men were prettier than the girls. *Such a waste,* mused Sara as she smiled to herself. Many of the male dancers would be gay or swinging both ways. That being so, two of her best friends were a gay couple. Carl and Richy 'with a y' had been together for years and were Sara's most loyal companions. She trusted them in a way she would never trust any female counterpart. But God forbid you should cross them, or they might cross themselves. Even the great David Attenborough hadn't seen a cat fight like it. They had a special talent for spite that no other living thing possessed.

'Looks like we're in for a long one today,' Amanda commented as she began stretching exercises. Not that she needed to. The gym earlier had loosened her up and got rid of some of her nerves. Nevertheless, it looked good and anyway, everyone else was doing the same to varying degrees.

'Well, look at it this way,' Sara said, adjusting thick socks over her Lycra leggings. 'Treat it as a class, then, when they tell you to fuck off, at least you've had a good workout.'

'You say that every time and when you don't go through, you leave with a boat like thunder,' Amanda laughed as she made touching her toes into an art form.

'Yeah, well, you know what I mean. Oh no! Have a look...'

'What?' Amanda asked, straightening and reaching up for a long stretch.

'Guess who just swanned in.'

'Who?' Amanda asked impatiently, now quickly viewing the rehearsal room.

'Miss new shampoo advert.' Sara's voice was saturated with loathing.

'Oh, well, that's one place already gone, and she doesn't even have to lift a foot.'

'Maybe not this afternoon, darling,' Sara hushed her voice, 'but I bet her feet were airborne last night!'

'Oh! Do I detect a showing of teeth and mild snarling from that venomous bitch you'd like to think you keep under wraps?'

Both girls laughed, but Sara silently pondered her friend's words. There had been a hidden message in them. Later she might just ask Amanda what the hell she'd meant. She turned back to Amanda.

'Too right, love, I know she's a good dancer and all that, but let's get real here, we both know it's her other skill that gets her the work.'

'Mmm, they don't call her Martini for nothing,' said Amanda amidst reciprocal sniggering. 'Just need to add "anyone" to the jingle.'

Amanda returned her full attention to limbering up while Sara, unconsciously fiddling with a strand of hair, covertly watched the subject of their malicious gossip, still contemplating what Amanda had been trying to say earlier.

The girl seemed to glide through the room, seeming oblivious to all the other performers and their frantic pre-audition routines. She certainly had 'that thing' you needed to be noticed. The *je ne sais quoi* aura you found present with most of those who made it into the golden one percent.

She was taller than most, maybe five ten, slim but not anorexic, like several of those there, and had a face to melt the coldest heart, well, maybe not Amanda and Sara's. Then there was THAT hair. Straight, silky and a sickening natural creamy blonde that fell to just above perfectly toned buns.

The urge to spit visited Sara briefly and not for the first time.

She had worked with Ms Perfection once, in a pantomime. Sara had found the girl nice enough, if a little aloof. Not really mixing with the others unless absolutely necessary, and spending much of her time talking to the ex-sportsman-turned-television-personality who was playing Buttons. An increasing addition to show business, usually with no real acting or singing talent, and certainly not appreciated by good honest troopers like Sara, only by the money-makers and their producers who delighted in the extra publicity. In fact, as Sara remembered it, Miss Shampoo spent ALL her spare time with him. His Buttons to her Cinderella.

It was always amusing to observe them avoid each other when his wife came backstage. Quite a stunning woman herself, but rather fraught after the birth of their first child, her topless modelling career was on temporary hold, if not permanently altered. She had no idea her doting husband

and their baby's father was poking Cinders. But then, they never did, the wives.

Before Sara could warn Amanda, who was still on the floor, hands clasping her right foot and nose to knee, Cinders approached and stood smiling in front of them. She looked at Sara in particular.

'Hello, haven't we met before?' The voice was classy, matching the rest of the package.

'Yes, panto. The Mayflower, Southampton?'

'That's it, never forget a face. It's names I'm hopeless with,' Cinders said with a sweet smile, showing the whitest teeth. Was there no end to the torture?

'Sara Harmsworth.'

'Oh, Sara, yes, now I remember. Nice to meet you again. Summer. Summer Laine.'

With bile rising, Sara used every ounce of her acting experience to hide what she was truly feeling toward Summer Laine, who stood there, more gorgeous than Sara cared to admit and so bloody polite. 'Hi, Summer,' she said brightly while thinking you couldn't have thought up a stage name like that. Unbelievably, it was the girl's real name. Conjuring up images of meadows and picnics, and somewhere, among the buttercups and daisies, a vision of Summer Laine executing a more horizontal audition. 'Oh, congratulations on the advert, that's a nice little earner for you.' *Sodding great big one*, she thought.

'Thanks.' Summer seemed genuinely flattered. 'It is, but dancing is my first love, really. I'd better start getting ready. Perhaps we can meet up afterwards for a drink?'

'Sure,' replied Sara, who had no such intention. It wasn't that she didn't like Summer. On the face of it, she was no different to many of Sara's peers, but she did have an undesirable name among friends and associates and it was best to keep a distance, in the way everyone else did. Dirt sticks. It also rubs off.

Just as it seemed they would all be there *ad infinitum*, the director and choreographer made their decision on who would be called back for a second audition.

'Okay, listen up, people,' came the booming instruction into a crescendo of chattering. Such a loud projection from the choreographer's tiny frame. It brought an instant hush to the proceedings.

Marcia Raeburn was a delicate little thing, just about retaining her chocolate box prettiness that had embellished many of the dance troupes in her heyday. And boy, could she move. They hadn't nicknamed her 'Olive Oil' for nothing. Now she commanded huge respect from old and new performers as a ground-breaking composer of liquid routines for stage and television.

'Pay attention, please, because I'm only going to read this list out once. If your name is called, stay where you are. If not, thank you very much. You all worked very hard but better luck next time.'

Yeah, and the rest, was the bitter silent retort throughout.

'Ryan Lewis, Peter Moran, Ashley Craven, Sally Trent, Summer Laine -'

'There's a surprise,' Amanda said sarcastically under her breath.

'- Amanda Jacobs -'

'Fuck!'

'Greta Williams, Simon Partridge, Pip Levy...'

And so the list went on. At the end of the prized roll call, Amanda was proved accurate in her assessment. Sara's boat was like thunder.

The calm atmosphere of the small clinically white room was truly blissful. Body and limbs suitably at ease, aromatic oils soaking into the skin and mind, while a heat lamp radiated soothing amber light that caressed every curve of her back. The sensation of floating increased pleasurably as she lay serene under a warm fluffy towel.

Gabrielle Delany lived for these twice-weekly visits to Tania, her masseuse. They were the only times she could really let go. Let herself feel. Outside the sanctuary of this sensory enhancement was life with Doug.

Gabrielle had been a young dancer, fresh from a local stage school when she was lucky enough to audition for and land a place in the top variety show at the Pavilion Theatre in Bournemouth that summer. It was usual for the big residential shows to employ some local talent, if talent was the word sometimes, as an exercise in PR for the local population and tourist trade. Fortuitously for the burdened choreographer and the director's angina, among the gaggle of dubious dancers put forward from various stage schools, a very capable young girl shone through and was gratefully snapped up for the chorus.

Doug Delany happened to be in Bournemouth, securing a flat for the season, and called into the theatre to watch the dreaded auditions. There might be a snippet of material he could work into his cabaret act, though certainly not for airing during this family seaside show. He instantly noticed the young Gabrielle, average in height but with legs that went on forever and a small perky bottom sitting perfectly above. Just how he liked them. This girl was incredibly attractive as well, always a bonus. When he realised she had been chosen for the show, Doug was highly delighted. This new recruit, now talking with the production manager about wardrobe fittings and rehearsals, would ease his summer season boredom, providing the star of the show with some private entertainment.

At the time, Doug was extremely single. There had been a near miss a few years before but he had managed to survive that blip intact. It suited his career crusade, but even a confirmed bachelor has needs and those had been more than catered for in the nubile shape of Gabrielle Weston.

The door gently clicked open and a soft voice asked if Gabrielle was comfortable.

'Mmm,' came a dreamy response. It was all she could manage in her heavenly state.

'I'll give you some extra time today,' the voice still a whisper as the masseuse soundlessly redirected the lamp onto Gabrielle's legs. 'You were particularly stressed when you arrived this morning.' There was a friendly concern in the tone.

A rustling of starched tunic and another soft click of the door and healing peace befell the room once more.

Bournemouth was, and still is, a more upmarket seaside resort in the gently middle England county of Dorset. Its gardens and parks, renowned for exceptional floral displays, and the long, well-groomed sandy beaches, packed to within an inch of their lives during the summer, all help entice copious visitors throughout the year. With three prominent theatres in the town, locals and tourists alike are spoilt for entertainment choices. This summer though, they had the bonus of cheeky, loveable and stratospheric Doug Delany at the Pavilion, a lovely theatre set on the main promenade and held with much regard in the hearts of many who have performed there. The booking office had been deluged before rehearsals had begun and the first two months of the run were already sold out. Such was the draw of Doug, confirming to him, as if he needed it, that he had well and truly arrived. And about bloody time.

His had been a long journey to this coveted place.

Starting quite by accident in his father's social club. A cabaret act had failed to turn up for a stag night booking. Some garbled message had reached the club of an unforeseen personal matter, but though it had caused the club manager a nasty bout of acid reflux, the sudden cancellation had given Doug his chance. Ever the joker and purveyor of witty stories about real life situations, Doug asked if he could fill in. After all, where was the club going to find another act at such short notice?

They didn't let him off the small corner stage until midnight. This then became a regular spot for Doug, his father always at the bar, puffed up with pride when manic laughter and applause peppered his son's routine. Then, one evening, as Doug was standing by the bar chatting to his dad, a man's voice cut through the throng.

'Can I get you a drink, lad?'

Doug turned to face a stout ageing man, with thick sandy hair that could have been an Irish jig but in the dim light, it was difficult for Doug to see clearly. Flabby jowls hung from a big pitted face that sported a slab of ginger moustache.

'Err... thanks, I'll have half a lager.'

'Not a Scotch man then?' The man smiled. Doug noticed a genuine regard in the piggy little eyes looking back at him.

'Well, yes, I am but not during the act.'

'Very sensible, lad. A half it is, then. Harold Hall,' he said, holding out a chubby hand with fingers that resembled a half pack of Walls' sausages.

'Doug Delany.'

'Yes, lad, saw it on the bill outside,' said Harold and then laughed.

Doug suddenly felt like an ant. Very small and crushed. When their drinks arrived, they touched glasses and took a sip.

'Saw you a few weeks ago,' Harold started, 'thought I'd come back and see if you were a one-night wonder or worth me taking you on. I think you're going places and I can help you get to them.'

'I see,' Doug said, bells finally ringing. He now realised who Harold was and his heart had begun to pump hard and fast. A thin layer of sweat beaded on his top lip. Was this one of those defining moments? In everyone's life there are but a few, each remembered as a significant event that changed the course of our personal journey. Doug considered this might be such an occasion.

'I can get you a season at Butlins, maybe even the biggern at Pwllheli in North Wales. I don't need to tell you the names of our most famous comics who started out as Red Coats.'

'No,' replied Doug, trying to conceal his shaking legs. 'No, you don't.'

By the time he had finished for the night, he was as good

as signed up to the Harold Hall Agency. Doug never looked back.

Gabrielle showered and then took a ten-minute dip in the mineral-infused spa pool, letting the jets work their magic before she had to go and face the outside world again. The wonderful world of Doug Delany. The star comedian. A husband. Bastard.

Mrs Delany only had three reasons to stay within the tortuous bubble of her husband's glittering life, Alexander, eight, Sasha, six, and little Phoebe, three. For them, she would linger in the family unit. The required appendage. An afterthought. Wife.

Sometime in the future, when the children had grown and moved on, Gabrielle had plans for herself. Plans that didn't include Mister Me Myself and I. Her thoughts drifted...

Sitting together in the front stalls during rehearsal, the dancers watched the various acts going through the laborious technical checks with lighting and sound engineers. Their hushed chattering and occasional muffled giggling stopped abruptly when Doug walked out on stage. He was different to the others. There was something about him. Star quality.

Gabrielle was only nineteen but could spot it a mile off. He was also quite handsome, in an older experienced kind of way. She knew he watched her rehearse but kept it to herself. In her shaky, and to some, resented existence in the show, she felt it best not to start up unnecessary gossip. God help her career if it reached the man himself. To Gabrielle, her dancing was everything. She had dreamed of being on stage since the age of five.

Doug finished his piece and stood waiting for confirmation from the various technicians.

'That's fine, Doug, thanks,' a voice echoed from the back of the auditorium. He looked down at the girls and caught Gabrielle's eye for a beat, then exited stage left. She watched him go. Was that a slight nod of the head? Had she just been summoned?

Quick, think of something. 'Just popping to the loo,' she finally said and made her way out of the stalls. As she stepped through the connecting door to back stage, Gabrielle was surprised to find Doug waiting for her. 'Oh,' she said with an embarrassed smile.

'Gabrielle, isn't it?" Doug said, eyes twinkling.

'Yes.' Gabrielle realised her mouth was tinder dry and a nervous cough was making its way up her throat.

'Listen, I'm parched. Fancy a coffee?'

Gabrielle hesitated, briefly looking back at the connecting door.

'Oh, don't worry, you won't be missed. The Rubinis will be ages with all that trapeze stuff. Come on, I know a great little place on the seafront.'

Gabrielle wrestled with conflicting thoughts. *Stop dithering*, she told herself. 'Okay, I'd love a coffee, better put something over these,' she said, indicating her leotard, leggings and tap shoes. Doug glanced over them too, but he wasn't looking at her attire, more imagining what was underneath.

'Yes, good idea. That lot might put the pensioners off their cornets, love!'

Gabrielle giggled nervously and vanished into her dressing room. She quickly threw on jeans and a sweat shirt, while frantically contemplating what she was about to do. *Oh, do get a grip, Weston*, she scolded. *It's only a coffee, for God's sake...*

That was twelve years ago. Now, Gabrielle got into her shiny new convertible Porsche with a weary heaviness in her heart. Her life was the envy of millions of women. And why not? Famous husband, beautiful children, huge manor house on the Thames and a villa in the Algarve. She attended top social events dressed only in designer couture. A charmed existence.

Apart from her three offspring, it was all material and

brown-nosing crap. It all meant zip in the broader spectrum of life, her idea of life, anyway. For Alex, Sash and Bee, Gabrielle endured. They deserved the very best she could provide as a mother and if that meant playing the loyal supportive wife, so be it.

During the first lustful, heady months of their clandestine affair, Gabrielle had believed Doug when he told her across the pillows that he would help her career. Oh, how young and naive she had been. As they progressed somewhat unexpectedly into a full-on relationship, going public and setting up home together, much against the wishes of her parents, especially Mother, the plan was for Gabrielle to be a successful wife to complement Doug's good name. A celebrity team. The fans would love it.

How stupid can a girl be? Very stupid indeed when swept away by someone like Doug Delany, promising the Earth and more. The years had rolled on and Doug began to pester for children. They had several heated exchanges about it but in the end, Gabrielle gave in to his odd persistence, and so her own career slid downward, slowly at first, as Doug's rose higher than ever, and then very rapidly came to a full stop. All the childhood dreams faded to a silent place inside her.

She would never forgive Doug Delany, but most of all, Gabrielle would never forgive herself.

CHAPTER THREE

Carlo's wine bar had its usual mix of early evening clientele. Mostly suits, male and female, catching a quick networking session while the rush hour died down, making for an easier journey home. Or for those who simply lived to work, an aperitif prior to business meetings over dinner.

Summer took her place at the end of the large sweeping curve of the bar, her audition kit stuffed into a canvas knapsack, seriously labelled but discreetly so. Summer believed in discretion while still adoring all things classy, expensive and savvy.

Fiona Hayes recognised the vision sitting at her bar and promptly attended to her. Summer smiled as she approached.

'Hello, Fi.'

'Hi, Summer. How'd it go?'

'Oh, I got a recall, so I'm hopeful. Though I'm not so sure about "sir",' Summer said with some seriousness, eyes looking toward the ceiling.

Fiona raised an eyebrow and replied, 'Well, you'll work it out. Drink?'

'White wine and soda. Lots of soda. Is he here?'

'Where else? I think there's been a problem with the new furnishings for the refit, so he's been up there most of the day. You know, making them wish they hadn't been born!'

'Oh, he's sooo picky!' laughed Summer, holding her hands up in mock exasperation.

'You could say that, but then, that's why he's with you,' Fiona replied and gave Summer a look of friendly resignation. There were just some women on the planet it simply wasn't worth competing with.

'Mmm, and my money, Fi,' Summer said cynically. Her face hardened, brow slightly furrowed. She looked down at her misty reflection in the highly polished teak of the bar.

'Don't be so critical, it doesn't suit you.' Fiona's friendly smile went unnoticed and she went about preparing a spritzer.

Summer lazily glanced around the wine bar and found many eyes upon her. It was something she had become used to, though on occasions, and this was one of them, she wished she could fade into the crowd. Fiona returned and placed a frosted long tumbler on a small square of paper napkin. Next to this, she put a bowl of pimento-filled olives, Summer's favourite nibble. One of the very few things she had inherited from her father, Johnny. A sudden wave of resentment threatened to crash over Summer, but she ducked under its curl like an expert surfer and rode the surge until the feeling subsided. His constant dismissal of Summer as anything remotely important in his life stuck fast like an irritating fur ball, sometimes causing her thoughts to choke on it. Summer had her ways though, to get Daddy's attention.

Fiona dipped her head to the side as she tried to get Summer's attention. 'I buzzed him for you. He'll be right down.'

It brought Summer back to the bar. 'Thanks, Fi.'

Almost immediately, a door opened at the other end of the bar from where Summer sat sipping her drink, rummaging in the olives with a cocktail stick. A tall, impeccably dressed man appeared, turning to close and lock the door behind him. As he looked up at Summer, his fine Latino face softened into a stunning smile. His day was never quite complete without at least a glimpse of this woman. Giancarlo Scarlatti was a proud man, but rarely more so than when he was seen with Summer Laine.

'Bella!'

Summer just watched him as he came around the bar and pulled up a stool. He manoeuvred himself into a position where their knees were interlocked and placed a hand on each of Summer's thighs, slowly stroking them, gradually creeping under the hem of her short skirt. Summer picked up an olive and eased it provocatively between her lips, holding it there for a second, and then gently sucking it into her mouth. A moment later, Giancarlo's mouth was on hers. Pulling away, Summer said, 'Carlo, no, people are watching.'

'Let them,' he responded in his usual air of arrogance. He tried to kiss her again, but Summer turned her head, picked up her drink and sipped, her eyes flashing at his. 'Baby, I missed you last night. I hate these auditions. Why can't we be together the evening before? Hmm?'

'I have to prepare myself, Carlo. We've discussed this before.'

Giancarlo reached for her face. 'But you don't need the work. Why must you pursue these things all the time?'

Summer sighed. *Oh God, here we go again*, she thought. *Like we haven't had this conversation a thousand times.* 'I do need the work, Carlo. For this...' she said, prodding a temple with her finger. 'For me.'

Giancarlo smiled at a distant memory. Then he shrugged. 'Whatever you say, but if you get this show, you will be away from me for months.' He returned his hands to her thighs.

'You could visit me,' Summer replied, sarcasm dripping from each word.

'It's difficult for me...'

'Because you make it difficult, Carlo.'

Oh, she IS in a mood this evening, he thought, but he knew what would cure it, and his ample leather-topped desk upstairs would be ideal. It had worked before. Sadly, he still had urgent business to attend to, so he would have to unburden his beautiful woman later. 'Will you have dinner with me tonight?'

Summer popped another olive and chewed a little before responding. 'You know I will. Why do you think I'm here?'

'Of course, I'm irresistible, I know this,' Giancarlo said through a roguish smile. 'Where would you like to eat? Here?'

Summer's answer was quick and succinct. 'Angelo's.'

It was his cousin's restaurant, typically Italian in decor

but with no expense spared. It was also almost impossible to get a table reservation in the evening. On any day, unless you booked several weeks in advance and even then, it was helpful if you were one of the many rich and famous who frequented it. Then again, if you were 'family'... that was quite another matter.

Giancarlo's family were wealthy, powerful and from the spectacular town of Taormina in Sicily, perched on high rocks above the sparkling Mediterranean and under the threatening shadow of Mount Etna. There was a suggestion of danger about the Scarlattis and it was that sweet nectar that drew Summer to Giancarlo. It drove her father into incandescent rages. And so, the longer she remained with the Sicilian.

Giancarlo stroked Summer's hair, gently pulling a gossamer strand away from her face, letting it catch the lights. He placed it carefully on her shoulder and with a feather touch, brushed her left breast while removing his hand. There was an instant response to the brief stimulation which pleased him. 'Now I have business upstairs. I come to you later, say, nine?'

'I'll see you at my place for nine, then. Go on, go and give them hell!'

Giancarlo leaned forward and kissed her. She parted her lips just enough for the tips of their tongues to meet fleetingly. His cock sprang to attention and Giancarlo had to concentrate before leaving the bar stool. Summer watched and giggled quietly to herself. Men. Boys. It took so little. When would it ever dawn on them they were all being had?

Doug pulled his Mercedes to a halt on the paved driveway and slapped both palms against the steering wheel. 'Yes!' He grabbed a small velvet box from the passenger seat and went to find his wife.

'Gabby?' Doug called while closing the huge oak front door and casually throwing his keys into an antique French china bowl. It had sadly never been graced with the fruit it was originally designed to display, only keys, the purpose for which it had been purchased and strategically placed on an elegant walnut table in the entrance hall.

'Gabby?'

'Daddy!' Sasha ran at her father and leapt into his outstretched arms. Doug lifted his daughter in a swinging sweep from the rich parquet flooring and she clung to him like a baby orang-utan.

'Daddy's precious girl.'

Doug hugged Sasha to him, his hand cradling her small head against his neck. His affection was quite genuine. He adored all his children but secretly, Sasha was his favourite. A dainty child with a devastating cherubic face. White blond hair, naturally curling as soft tiny ringlets and huge saucer eyes, grey-green like her mother's. Everyone said she should be a child model, but Gabrielle protected her children from all things show business with a ferocity that even scared Doug at times. He wished he didn't have to leave them so often and sometimes for long periods but needs must. And Doug's needs most of all.

'Daddy, come and watch me making fairy cakes.'

'I will, poppet, but I need to speak to Mummy first. Where is she?'

'Upstairs, I think. Please, Daddy -'

'I will. I promise. Run along and I'll be there in a minute.' Doug gently set his daughter down and patted her on the bottom. She gave him one of her dazzling smiles and ran off in the direction of the kitchen.

'Come on, dear, let's finish these. I have to get home to all my doggies.'

Mrs Green, a rather plump, homely woman who came to help Gabrielle with cleaning and laundry twice a week, handed Sasha the icing bowl and a spoon. She usually stayed on for an hour or two to help with the children. Mrs Delany was often involved with Doug's work, an unpaid secretary, and after several occasions when Gabrielle had pleaded for Mrs Green to stay a bit longer, it had become an unspoken agreement. Doris Green often found a few more pounds in her pay and sometimes a bottle or two for her husband.

Where Mr Delany was concerned, Mrs Green had her own views. How his wife put up with him, she would never understand. But then, these show business types were all the same, weren't they? No doubt this lovely life style had a lot to do with the pretence and Mrs Delany was very good at pretending. It struck Mrs Green that Doug Delany was married to a very gifted actress. Still, they had different standards, didn't they? Different morals to the rest of us mortals. All best left alone really. None of her business.

'Daddy's coming to watch me,' Sasha beamed at Mrs Green.

'That'll be just dandy, dear.' *Heaven preserve us*, thought Doris.

'Got to go, Doug's just arrived. Speak to you later, Val.' Gabrielle replaced the receiver as Doug made one of his entrances into their bedroom. She remained seated on the bed as he bounded over. His face said it all, as it always did. Clear as Waterford crystal.

'Gabs, Hugh's just confirmed it. Opera House for thirteen weeks. I've always wanted to do the Opera House.'

'Blackpool. You always did do well there. Not that that's a problem anywhere these days.'

Except here. At home. With me.

'It's going to be a great show, love. I know it's another long summer season but I'll make it my last, yeah? This'll be the ol' swan song, eh?'

Sure. Right. Whatever you say. 'I'd appreciate it, Doug. So would the kids.'

'I know. I know. Look, I got you this.' Doug handed Gabrielle the navy-blue velvet box.

'What's this?' she said, looking up from the box into Doug's smiling eyes.

'Just something to say I love you.'

'Words do just fine, Doug.' *When said with meaning.*

'I know, Gabs. But I wanted you to have this, you know?'

Gabrielle looked down at the box in her hands. She stroked the soft covering and traced the tiny gilt edging. 'You shouldn't have...'

'Go on then. Open it!'

Doug plonked himself down on the bed next to her, his face close to hers, eyes eagerly watching the box like an excited child at Christmas.

Ever the romantic, thought Gabrielle. She opened the box. It was silk lined in the same navy blue and held a gold and emerald bracelet. It was truly stunning, even Gabrielle had to silently admit. 'Oh Doug, it's beautiful!'

'I know.' His eyes hadn't left the jewels. 'Reminded me of you.' Doug looked into his wife's face. He really did love her. In his way. 'Stylish, elegant and timeless.'

Like a Timex... Gabrielle thought, but hid her mirth and gazed into Doug's brown eyes. She stifled the urge to laugh at her jibe and placed a tender kiss on his cheek. 'Thank you, Doug. It's lovely. Really.'

He leaned in for a more ardent kiss on her mouth, but Gabrielle moved away and stood up. She walked over to an elaborate dressing table. 'Better start getting ready for this dinner tonight.' She sighed quietly but Doug caught it. He went over to where Gabrielle stood in front of a large mirror, putting his hands on her shoulders from behind, and softly rubbing them while he watched them both in the glass.

'It's important tonight, Gabs. Last one until after Blackpool. I think they might want me to host the Variety Club's next pro-am golf tournament. It means a lot.'

'I'll wear this, then.' Gabrielle held up the bracelet and light danced through the pale emeralds.

'I'd like that.' His hands moved to the nape of her neck and his thumbs gently kneaded the curve at the base of her head. Gabrielle eased toward the pressure. Doug still had good hands. 'I'd like that a lot,' he reiterated.

I bet you would, thought Gabrielle and smiled warmly at her husband.

'Mrs Green.' Doug made a perfunctory greeting to the fat busybody standing over his daughter as he entered the kitchen.

'Mr Delany.' A measured response.

Neither spoke again other than to give encouragement and praise to Sasha as she scooped sticky icing from a bowl and dabbed it in a haphazard fashion onto her small uneven sponges.

Giancarlo revved the Ferrari. It was his less than subtle way of letting Summer know he was outside. Why use the horn? The mouth-watering sound of his precious baby was one of the richest he knew. She turned heads and brought people to their windows. Just like his girlfriend. Life was so fucking sweet.

Summer got in the car and leaned across to kiss Giancarlo, who responded rather over-zealously.

'Carlo!' she said, shoving him away. 'For Christ's sake!'

'Don't blaspheme. You know I don't like it.'

'You messed up my lipstick. I hate that.' In truth, she detested sloppy kissing. It turned her stomach. Particularly after last night.

'But how can I resist you, Bella? I want you all the time and you give to me so sparingly. It's not right!' Giancarlo raised his hands in a quintessentially Latin gesture and Summer laughed at the play acting.

'Cut the crap, Carlo, and drive. I'm starving.'

He studied her as she reapplied her precious lipstick. She really did need a good seeing to and Mr Scarlatti would make damn sure she got the best service going in London that night.

In Summer's empty flat, the phone rang and her voice filled the silence. After the beep, a booming baritone spoke.

'Summer, my dear...' Pause for a puff on his cigar. 'Calling to let you know it's all sorted, as promised. I know I was a little vague earlier but felt it would be better to let

you go to the initial bun fight, if you know what I mean...'
Throaty laughter and another drag on his Cuban. 'Last
night was lovely, my dear, quite exquisite. Good luck with
the show. Oh yes, and watch out for Delany...' The message
ended with the sound of a spluttering guffaw, followed by a
phlegmy smoker's cough.

CHAPTER FOUR

The frosty silence was fast becoming another ice age. Giancarlo sat up into enormous pillows covered in special Italian linen, propped against the extravagant headboard of his imported bed, hand carved in a little village near Taormina by a friend of his father. It had been a gift from the craftsman. Pay back.

Giancarlo's left hand flopped casually over the side of the bed with a neglected cigarette dangling downward. A pale grey ribbon meandered through his fingers as it rose twisting toward the ceiling where it would gather and loiter as an invisible blanket.

Summer lay with her back to him. A small tear had pooled in the corner of her eye and when she blinked, it trickled over the bridge of her nose and dripped into the goosedown pillow. Unthinking, Summer sniffed and Giancarlo moved his right hand to touch her head, softly stroking her hair, just as he would to soothe a bambino.

He was still furious, but the sound of Summer weeping dampened his angry thoughts. His father would have let her cry. Good to let the women know who's boss. They respect you more as a man. Giancarlo wasn't entirely sure he agreed with his father and certainly not where the lady lying in his bed at that moment was concerned. He liked her, a lot, perhaps even loved her. She affected him in ways no other woman had.

Summer didn't respond to his touch and he leaned across the bed. 'Summer? What is it? Why do you cry like this?'

'Just leave it, Carlo.'

'How can I? My woman lies in my bed, so unhappy? Talk to me.' He gently touched her arm, skin silky smooth and unblemished. Like the rest of her.

'Carlo, just leave me alone. Okay?' Her voice was a cold monotone and his hand stopped dead on her arm.

'But...'

'Carlo, just stop.' It was a sharp rebuke.

With an exaggerated sigh and incoherent mumbling, Giancarlo moved to his side of the bed and took a long drag on his cigarette. He stubbed it out so harshly in the ashtray on the ebony wood side table that an uncomfortable clattering pierced the tense silence between them. As he hopped about putting underpants on, he spoke angrily. 'You know, I treat you better than anyone before. ANYONE. Understand? I thought maybe you were something special...' He shrugged unseen by Summer who remained still, eyes closed, just listening. Waiting for him to go away. 'Now I don't know anymore. What is it? Time of the month? WHAT?' Giancarlo's voice was now rising, as his English became more heavily coated in an Italian accent. It always happened when he started ranting. His syntax also became dubious. 'I don't see you last night, and tonight I try make love with you and... you pushing me away all the time.'

He stood waiting for a comeback with his arms held out in a dramatic gesture of question. When Summer didn't move or respond, he slapped his hands down onto his thighs, grabbed a silk robe from the bathroom door and slammed the bedroom door behind him.

Summer could hear his rapid Latin expletives as he thumped his way down the stairs to the main floor of his apartment. When the kitchen door also closed with a crash, she rolled onto her back and put an arm across her face. The tears now sprang freely and drizzled onto her reddened cheeks. One travelled down to her ear and dribbled inside. It felt cold. Like her heart. Oh, that it was so simple as to be pre-menstrual tension, but it wasn't. Far from it. In fact, Summer was now beginning to realise the full implications of her complicated and sordid little life. She only had herself to blame and that was the bitterest pill of all.

It had started when Summer was a teenager, vying for position among her three brothers for a place in her father's affections. Born as a last attempt at having a daughter for her mother, Isadora, she was doted on by her until Summer was about six years old, when her mother seemed to lose interest. A series of nannies were brought in but the little girl didn't give up. She made herself a model child. Pretty, well-mannered and intelligent, working at her studies and even helping muck out the stables, for God's sake. But nothing. Not a sniff. All her father cared about was his precious boys and horses, while her mother appeared to have retreated into a world of her own. A private place in her mind that probably accounted for Summer's name.

From the few stolen talks she managed with Isadora's mother, a lady whom Summer aspired to be like but never quite managed, she learned that Isadora had been heavily into the flower power of the late Sixties and early Seventies. When her much-wanted daughter was finally born, perhaps the euphoria had sent Isadora back to those pot-induced carefree times and her baby was so named.

By the age of sixteen, Summer knew she had to get on with her life without the emotional support she needed from her parents, but mostly her father, Johnny. His life was horses and sons. There was apparently no room for perhaps his loveliest filly.

Well, she showed him, didn't she? During a large gathering of Johnny's bloodstock and racing cronies, Summer found her chance to get even. Among the assorted distinguished rabble was Anthony Wiggins, the husband of her mother's dearest friend. He had bred and eventually raced a winner of the coveted Cheltenham Gold Cup. His thoroughbreds had won many of the top trophies, except the one he wanted most. Still missing from his trophy room was silverware from the Prix de l'Arc de Triomphe.

A mild-mannered gentleman in his fifties, but still quite handsome, if you liked that kind of thing, tall, slender and fit. All those early mornings on the gallops at his Irish estate. Anthony had always liked Summer, even as a young girl, often playing hide and seek or garden tennis, when no one else could be bothered with her. He had nicknamed her 'Breezy', and it was a few years before Summer got the joke. Now she would make sure it was all on him.

While everyone chatted and mingled indoors, Summer went outside on the massive stone terrace to get some air, and found Anthony leaning against the balustrade smoking a small cigar. She walked over and stood a little apart from him, looking up to the clear night sky.

'I love the stars,' she said dreamily.

Anthony too looked up and replied, 'Yes, I suppose you can lose yourself in them sometimes.' His soft Dublin lilt sounded relaxed.

Good, thought Summer. 'I'm going to be a star one day,' she said and looked directly at Anthony. She smiled. 'One day I'll be a big star on television or in films. You'll see.'

He regarded her for a moment and nodded silently, then said, 'I think you'd do very well, Summer. Beautiful young lady like yourself.'

She wasn't so sure what Daddy would have to say about it, but Summer had a good idea. Anthony scanned her from head to foot and back again. He could almost smell her pert freshness and his loins stirred. Quickly, he returned his gaze to the stars. *Christ*, he thought. *It's Johnny Laine's daughter, for heaven's sake!*

'Do you really think I'm beautiful?' Summer asked lightly.

Anthony reluctantly looked at her again. Had she moved closer? The urge to taste those plump rosy lips was intense. The jangling in his manhood becoming unbearable. *This is bloody ridiculous*, he silently remonstrated. *She's only sixteen, for God's sake*. 'Oh yes,' he finally replied, turning to face out into the gardens, throwing his panatella into the darkness. 'Any director would be crazy not to have you in his production, Breezy.'

'How about you?' It was swift and targeted. Summer was now up close and personal. Anthony could feel her breath as she spoke. His hands were gripping the railing so tightly, his knuckles were white.

'Me? I don't...'

She wouldn't let him finish. 'Come on, Tony, be honest, you know you want me.' Summer stroked the back of a finger down his arm. 'I know you want me.'

Anthony carefully removed her hand in a deliberate gesture. Summer dropped her hand but continued to stare into his face. She knew, as only a woman does, that she had her man. He grew fidgety under her attention and said, 'Stop it, Summer... this isn't...'

She cut him off. 'Not what? Not exactly what you've wanted since I was fourteen? Don't deny it, Tony. I haven't forgotten, you know.'

'I don't know what you're talking about.' But he did. Of course he did. It was biting into him now like a hungry barracuda. He hadn't wanted it to happen.

Two years before, during some rough and tumble horseplay when they were in dispute over a point of fact and Summer had started it by tipping him off a sun-lounger, Anthony had accidentally fallen on top of her and immediately got a full erection. Summer's eyes had never left his as he lay there and he remembered the suggestion of a smile on her lips. Nothing was said, they had got up and carried on as normal, though Anthony was less tactile with her afterwards.

'Summer, look,' - there was that proper name again - 'if you're talking about that time...'

This was getting boring. 'You know where the pool house is, Tony. Be there. Five minutes.'

'Don't play...' Silly games, he was going to say but she was already down the steps heading for the pool, her long blond hair drifting up behind her, beckoning him like a wicked accomplice.

Anthony wrestled with his wild thoughts. The fuck of his life was minutes away but he knew Johnny too well. If he took this opportunity to discover whether Breezy was everything she seemed to be, could he do it without being found out? Could he really screw that amazing body and get away with it? If Johnny did find out, Anthony had no doubts about how he would end up. Shergar came to mind.

The pool house was in blackness but the door was slightly ajar, and as Anthony stepped through it, a sweet warm mouth met his, an eager tongue searching it out. He was vaguely aware of the door closing and the sound of a lock turning, but it was all he could do to keep up with what was happening to his body. She was voracious. So talented. And so YOUNG! Where in God's name did she learn to do THAT?

Anthony Wiggins had just gone to heaven but it wasn't with any angel.

He had gone on to become one of several, although Anthony was perhaps the most regular. He seemed to relish the secret depravity of it all, but mostly, he craved Breezy's young responsive body and considerable sexual gifts. For two years, Summer picked her way through a variety of her father's friends and associates. The closer to Johnny Laine, the bigger the catch for his daughter. And all, without exception, some even during sex, which Summer found rather a put off, professed undying love for their wives. Almost as if they were trying to convince themselves it wasn't really happening. Though, however lovely some of their lady wives were, not one man turned Summer down.

Her most favourite times were the race meetings, particularly Ascot. The ladies loved Ascot. The hats. It was always the hideous hats. In the presence of Summer, clinging onto their unsuspecting spouses, were the ever-devoted husbands. Clandestine glances flying to and fro. Each man, and her father, completely oblivious. It was such fun.

When Summer decided to attend a London performing arts school instead of the intended university, it caused a huge slanging match between father and daughter. She couldn't have wished for a better confrontation. Their best yet. At least it got her noticed for five minutes. Took Johnny's mind off his precious sons and sodding horses.

Upon graduating from her theatrical studies with some merit, Summer soon realised her now well-honed skills with the opposite sex were perhaps more valuable than ever. Whereas most of her previous conquests had been mere amateurs in her games, producers and the odd agent, some rather odder than others, took it all for granted. While many of her peers vehemently refused to further their non-existent careers with an after-dinner quickie, and yet, when they did make a name for themselves, a nasty little video would surface, Summer was only too happy to oblige. Not that she needed to. She was an honestly talented dancer and actress, often starting in a chorus and ending up with a small feature appearance. But why not use the stupid bastard men? They were all up for it, weren't they? And as long as Summer's carefully chosen career, the one that pissed Daddy off the most, flourished, the longer she could torment him. Then, when, as would surely happen, Johnny tried to stop her mission against him, cutting off the credit cards and rental payments, not to mention the car allowance, Summer would hit him between the eyes with it all. Her bargaining ace was telling all those adoring wives about their diabolically filthy husbands, and she would take enormous pleasure in starting with her mother's dearest friend.

The cherry on top of this delicious cake was Giancarlo. With his dubious connections, it was simply perfection. Yet, in this complex and highly-strung man, Summer found a part of herself, maybe even a mirror image. Sometimes she felt they had been carved from the same rock. He was kind and respectful toward her, though she knew his motives were mostly dick-driven. But for all his tough 'nobody messes with a Scarlatti' talk, Giancarlo was still a little boy inside, just as Summer was really still a petulant child herself. Scared. Wanting so desperately to be loved and yet terrified of letting anyone love her. A sad paradox that, in Summer's case, could only remain so. She was so closed emotionally, their relationship could never work in the long term. Giancarlo needed a real woman. One from his part of the world, maybe. Yes, they were famously fiery and gave as good as they got from their men, but as wives and mothers, they were hard to beat. In the meantime, Summer would stay with her Sicilian. Until she knew it was time to move on.

A time that seemed to be drawing ever closer.

Giancarlo paced the kitchen. Then he paced it some more. There was something very wrong here. He just knew it, had a nose for these things. Was he not his father's son? Summer had been like this a couple of times and he had let it pass. What an idiot. Well, not this time. She seemed to be playing him for a fool. Putting the horns on him. Not an advisable thing to do to a Sicilian. He simply couldn't believe she would do it knowingly. No, of that he was sure. She must be under pressure from someone. Another man. Another man was touching his woman. A manic madness gripped his sensibilities as horrendous visions of hands stroking Summer's skin, caressing places only he had access to, pervaded his disturbed mind.

It was time to seek out the maggot from its putrid burrow.

Teach it a lesson.

Squash it.

CHAPTER FIVE

Gabrielle stood leaning against the counter top, arms folded, while watching Phoebe, her little Bee, create with Lego on the kitchen floor. The warm wheaty aroma of wholemeal bread toasting mingled with the sound of simmering water, into which Gabrielle had just carefully lowered two free range, organic eggs.

'Brmm brmm,' said her daughter as she pushed a scrambled shape of plastic bricks around the terracotta tiles.

She's hanging out too much with her brother, Gabrielle smiled to herself. Though perhaps it was a strategic plan to turn his youngest and therefore more impressionable sister into a tom boy, making up for the fact that he would never have a brother. After all, Gabrielle had seen to it, rightly or wrongly, that there would be no more siblings.

She felt selfish at times. Alexander didn't exactly have the ideal father figure, even when he was at home, and there were precious few male relatives around her son to compensate. Of course, there were droves of Doug's pals, all with their fragile egos and carefully sculptured images. Not really what an eight-year-old needed in his life, or at any age, come to think of it. His uncle, Gabrielle's brother, adored Alexander but detested Doug just as much, which made life difficult at the best of times and resulted in Tom staying away. When he did brave a visit, or the Delany family made a rare family public relations trip to Bournemouth, there was always a brittle tension in the air and sarcastic comments flowing. Such occasions were kept to the minimum to preserve the quality of them for the children. And to give Gabrielle a quiet life when they went home.

It wasn't simply a severe personality clash. If they never set eyes on each other ever again, it wouldn't have been too soon for either of them. At their first meeting, the atmosphere was so viscous with resentment, you could have stuck wallpaper with it. The reservations were mainly from Tom in the beginning. He had never discussed his reasons properly with his sister but as the years had gone on, Gabrielle had a pretty good idea where her brother had been coming from. Then, when Doug realised none of his 'funny-easy-going-guy' act was going to soften Tom's resolve, he too played hard to get. Gabrielle often tried to get them to meet halfway, to no avail. Now, she just didn't care anymore.

One problem she knew got up her brother's nose was Doug's house rule of no family visits on the weekends he came home during a season away, or those dreaded periods between work, when frankly, Doug Delany forgot he was a comedian. In fact, he seemed to have a complete sense of humour failure and was not the best person to be near. The more success Doug enjoyed, the worse this trait had become, and the family knew to keep a low profile when he was in one of his irritable, waiting for the phone to ring, moods. Alexander would withdraw to his room, and Gabrielle wondered whether the boy needed some help but there was no way in hell Doug would agree to any therapy for his son. The golden icon of comedy with a child 'seeing a poxy shrink?' She could hear Doug spitting out the words, so it was never discussed, and Alexander didn't get the assistance he might have benefited from.

Gabrielle had ways of dealing with the problem, and Mrs Green was a handy tool. Since she had started staying behind on a regular basis for when Alexander and Sasha got home from school, her son had opened up more, even to his mother. Mrs Green had that kindergarten no-nonsense attitude around the children but also a warm sense of grandmotherly fun. Something greatly lacking in the house. Whatever it was the woman possessed, Gabrielle would be eternally grateful to Doris Green.

Doug's wife loved her quiet mornings in the house with just Phoebe. Thankfully, her husband was at a follow up meeting to the charity dinner they had attended. What an unmitigated bore that had been. It seemed he had indeed landed the role of host of the next pro-am charity tournament at Wentworth, just as Doug had wanted. *Flies to a web*, thought Gabrielle. At least it kept him busy in the run up to Blackpool. *Thank you, Variety Club.*

For a young aspiring actor or dancer, just starting out in what was one of the most perilous of careers, a contract for a long summer season was manna from heaven. To an old hand, career long since dissolved and married to Mr Show biz himself, a summer season was bitter sweet. Sweet because family life would be calmer without Doug in the house. Gabrielle knew plenty of other celebrities managed a fair balancing act between their family and career but sadly, not for her and their children. Given that Doug had more or less insisted she give up her dancing so he could portray the loving family man, it grated that, with the success of that illusory exercise in public hoodwinking, the man had little or no time for his offspring, let alone the wife who held the whole manufactured package together.

There were sombre moments when Gabrielle was alone, usually at the health club, when she really did wonder if she was any better than a common prostitute. Here she was, living the ultimate lie and yet not willing to give it up. Why? What was it that kept her there? The lifestyle? Could it truly be so shallow a motive? Gabrielle knew using the excuse of her children's welfare sometimes didn't even ring true to herself. After all, Doug would be forced to make a huge divorce settlement, including the house, and they would want for nothing materially. As for the absence of their father, what difference would it make? They hardly saw him now, unless, of course, they turned on the television. He was all over it, like an annoying rash. So just what was the honest reason she stayed? Could it possibly be that even now, after everything, Gabrielle still loved the bastard? The idea wasn't too far-fetched, but maybe his meter had been ticking for a long time and she was running low on change. It was a thought she often wrestled with.

Certainly not sweet about summer seasons were the brief and infrequent weekend visits home. Everyone had to be on their best behaviour during what amounted to an early morning arrival on Sunday, a hot and cold twenty-four hours and then a panicky departure on Monday morning. Gabrielle decided long ago that her stress levels weren't worth it but the children loved to have their father home, so a few Xanax pills every now and then eased the whole sorry process. Then there were the family visits to the venue. Now they were a totally different kettle of fish.

Sometimes they went well, and everyone seemed to enjoy themselves, even Doug. But it all depended on whether he was also 'otherwise involved', as Gabrielle liked to call it. And that was the bitter part.

Increasingly, it appeared he was unable to keep his prick in his pants. Years ago, it devastated Gabrielle. Years ago, she was distraught. Perhaps too much so. Now, many trials and tribulations later, she had given up. As long as he kept it discreet and out of the papers, away from their children and their friends, she let him get on with it, because Gabrielle knew whoever the season's fancy was, it would never be so serious as to wreck the valuable family unit. Through an extensive grapevine that her husband knew nothing about, Gabrielle knew that a couple of naive girls had got hurt on the way. Well, sweethearts, if you will fuck around with very married men, what else can you expect? Doug Delany was extremely married, to the business and in turn, Gabrielle and the kids. A public divorce, for that is what it would amount to, would damage Doug's popularity ratings. God forbid! Especially as a good ratio of his fan base were bored, forty-something ladies, languishing in their own hopeless marriages 'for the sake of the children'. Gabrielle often laughed at the sick irony.

Not informing Doug about her small clinical procedure, the one that prevented his brood mare producing again, gave Gabrielle the perfect excuse to insist her husband wore a condom when they made love. Or was it just sex now? A few well-practised caresses and positioning, some eager kissing and three minutes of unimaginative humping was about her lot these days. Doug certainly didn't want any more babies, he had enough on his plate with planning financially for the three already *in situ*, so Gabrielle told him she could no longer take the pill and didn't suit an IUD. Therefore, when he used the rather awkward contraceptive, she felt protected, to some extent, from the other women. She knew Doug was fastidious in his personal health and still cared enough about her not to knowingly bring anything home. But no one could ever be sure, could they?

The egg timer broke into Gabrielle's increasingly deep thought. By the time she retrieved her 'farm fresh' beauties from the boiling water, they were overdone. *No salmonella there then,* she mused. The organic country bread made by Mrs Green was toasted to perfection. Despite many attempts to get the recipe, Doris steadfastly refused to give it to Gabrielle, saying it was a West Country secret.

After clearing up and before Doug returned home from his meeting, mother would take daughter to her infant swimming class.

Amanda Jacobs limbered up. She had attended classes every day since the first audition, except one day after spending the night with her boyfriend, a burly but scrumptious stage hand, or 'crew' as he preferred. Amanda always had a good aerobic workout whenever she and Jason got it together, which was less often than both would have liked, mainly due to his touring with a well-received production starring a British actress who had recently become a well-known American soap star. There had been a week's break while Beverly James made a trip to Los Angeles for a spot on America's favourite late night chat show to promote a new drama she was filming for their HBO channel.

Jase, as Amanda called him, hadn't hesitated to drive down from Edinburgh, the last venue for the play, to spend a couple of nights with the love of his life, and Amanda simply couldn't drag herself from bed for the strict disciplines of a ballet class.

Now she stretched and flexed, ready for whatever Marcia might throw at them. The diminutive choreographer had a reputation for making those who got through to a second round sometimes wish they hadn't. There was also a rumour, among the millions of others throughout the business, that there was to be a grand Broadway finale to the show. Amanda had even taken a few refresher tap classes. She was as ready as she could be for Miss Olive Oil.

The audition hall was quieter than last time. This was where it got serious. From here would come the contract. Rent and mortgages paid comfortably for several months. No one was prepared to hand that temporary peace of mind to anyone else without a good fight.

The double doors opened and there was a collective private sigh. Summer Laine had arrived. Amanda reached down into her holdall for a bottle of Purdeys to drown her sorrows.

'Hello.' She recognised those plummy tones and straightened to face Summer, who smiled in a genuinely friendly manner. 'We didn't get to talk last time. You were with...'

'Sara Harmsworth, yes. We're good friends,' said Amanda, making sure Summer knew the position.

'Oh sure, I could see that. I'm sorry she didn't make it through. This one's a toughie,' Summer said looking across to Marcia. She shrugged, eyes skyward in a gesture of 'what can you do?'

Yeah, for some, thought Amanda, but smiled sweetly, belying her less than sympathetic considerations as she replied, 'I know what you mean.'

'Well, break a leg!' Summer said and walked over to an empty corner to get ready.

With her now trademark voice projection, Marcia Raeburn called the room to order. The fight was on.

Round two. Ding ding.

Summer had attended this audition for obvious reasons.

Even though Mr Weiss had secured a contract for her, to miss this and then turn up for rehearsals would seem rather obvious. Summer was never obvious, despite what most people thought. She had wondered if the choreographer actually knew anything, as it would be a real boost if she got a place in the show on her own merit. Dancing merit. As she changed into her audition gear, Summer reluctantly thought about George. He was a good friend of Buzz MacIntyre, who was producing the Blackpool show, and it had been a stroke of luck that he had seen her shampoo advert and contacted Summer's agent, Cynthia Hersh. George had liked what he'd seen of the lovely girl with the stunning hair and oodles of sex appeal. He was backing a new but small British film, and she looked perfect for one of the cameo roles. Could he meet with her for dinner one evening to discuss options? True to form, Cynthia called Summer in a state of excited flux. George Weiss for Christ's sake! Summer had of course agreed to meet the famous show business entrepreneur. Even if she hadn't, Cynthia would have made damn sure Summer met him anyway. By chance, he had mentioned Buzz and the rest was pure Summer Laine...

While his considerable bulk heaved back and forth on top of her, his sour cigar breath mixed with the delightful aroma of industrial strength cologne, Summer had to keep herself from gagging during his floppy wet kissing. George had obviously missed out on breast feeding as a baby, judging by the way he pawed, squeezed and sucked at hers.

When at last, and it took some time, he came, George rolled off her with the finesse of a lorry leaving the ramp of a cross-Channel ferry. As he lay there panting, Summer had started to get out of his enormous round bed and make for the cleansing sanctuary of the bathroom, but his hand had grabbed her wrist. Without opening his eyes, he said through wheezing gasps, 'Where do you think you're going, my dear? There's still some life in the old pencil, just needs more, how shall I say? individual encouragement,' a sickening smirk spreading across his sweaty face.

At that point, Summer cut short her recollections. They were just too vile.

Something within her was slowly changing. George Weiss had to be the last. She would have to think of other ways in which to get at her father but hopefully, she was talented enough to keep her career going without the assistance of such revolting creatures. Or so Cynthia seemed to think. Summer wondered if it was the influence of Giancarlo in her life that was making the difference. He had shown her another type of man. One that appeared to want her as her, not the fantasy. Sure, she was under no illusions, she and Carlo made great sex together and the Ferrari was a bonus around town. Nobody's motives were pristine.

Whatever the reason she was beginning to feel this way, Summer knew it was for the best. It was time to take stock and move on. To allow herself to be herself for a change. But who exactly was she now? Who had she ever been? An enigma of her own making. In that case, she would just have to unmake herself and start over.

Although Summer felt it could never be a lasting thing, she decided to hang on to Giancarlo Scarlatti for as long as possible. Even when they did go their separate ways, an event she saw as inevitable, Summer could remember him as someone who had really cared about her. A man who had unwittingly pointed her in the right direction. The least she could do then was go there.

CHAPTER SIX

The honey crooning of Tony Bennett eased from the speakers and into Doug's thoughts as he cruised along the M4 toward home.

He felt like a little boy who had just been voted class prefect. It meant not only had he arrived in terms of being the top-rated comic in the land but also as a highly respected colleague within the hierarchy of the business. He guessed his almost scratch game had helped them along in their decision, but Doug believed in was mainly down to him. And that felt so damn good.

Here he was, driving his Merc, hugely successful and going home to a lovely wife and family. Did life get any better than this? Doug couldn't imagine how.

These last thoughts lingered. Wife and family. He would never find another woman like his Gabs. She had stuck by him where others had fled from his friends, and at the cost of her own bright career. She was an invaluable asset. So why had he treated her so poorly? What possessed a man with everything he could ever want, to screw around? Jeopardise it all for the thrill of what truthfully was a futile chase? Doug knew it was futile because being who he was, the chase always ended as he expected, a quick romp with some adoring girl. In the question lay his answer. Chase and conquest. Powerful motives. Though recently, Doug had to admit he found the resulting physical encounters rather lacklustre.

Perhaps it was his choice of quarry. Maybe they didn't make them like they used to. A few years back the girlies were more challenging, led him a merry dance before surrendering, and when they did, certainly knew what Doug needed.

Now, having decided he needed a younger, firmer version, at the moment of triumph they seemed to be in awe of him, lying there like startled deer, waiting for him to perform.

Sometimes Doug didn't know whether to fuck them or tell them a joke.

What the hell was this stupid arse hole doing? thought Doug as he realised on his left in the inside lane was a Volvo pulling alongside him, two smiling faces looking across. Doug shook his head and eased onto the gas. The Merc pulled away from them like a soft silent dream.

It happened from time to time. What pissed Doug off the most was the dangerous driving. Mainly because, as with those two idiots, they weren't looking at the road. For all his faults, and he had his fair share, Doug prided himself on his careful driving skills. Having to tour the country for many years, unless he drove well, it wouldn't only have been his career that was over. Perhaps he should change his personalised number plate. Since his last television series, these incidents were happening more frequently but no, bugger them, he'd worked for that £10,000 plate. Why should he change it?

Suitably distanced from Neanderthal dick heads, Doug resumed his earlier ruminations.

He really had to try to make Blackpool his last summer season, for the sake of Gabs and the kids. Doug knew he had missed Alex growing up and was fast achieving the same feat with Sasha. Maybe little Phoebe would have the best of him. Or maybe he should save that for his wife.

Doug was in an enviable position, picking and choosing his work. After Blackpool, he could choose London-based television or West End gigs. It wouldn't be easy. Not because of the lack of offers but because of Doug. He simply loved a good seaside show. There was something quite unique about them. From the production itself, usually light, easily watched and zippy, to the camaraderie among the company. Away from home and loved ones for a lengthy period, they became like an adoptive family. Well, most of them did. Perhaps family was the wrong word. Considering. Finally there were the audiences. Always a local contingent throughout the run but mostly holidaymakers, relaxed and ready for a fun night out. Doug never failed with them. That was one of the greatest lures for him. It would also be the hardest to give up.

Gabrielle. Yeah, she was worth the sacrifice. He hadn't been the husband she deserved but she married him knowing who he was and where he intended going.

Doug had never expected to get hitched when he did. In fact, Doug had rather assumed he may well never commit to a full-term relationship at all. Then Gabs came along and he just fell for her in an instant. In Gabrielle, he had someone who was natural, something almost impossible to find in his business, particularly once you had reached the heights he had at the time. No secret agenda, no act, just her funny ways and sharp sense of humour that found their way through all his barriers and straight to his heart. Of course, initially, he had been drawn to her tantalising body, long legs and lovely eyes, but for once in his life, Doug had managed to see deeper. Even after all this time and three pregnancies later, nothing much had changed. Gabrielle kept herself fit and Doug appreciated that. No one wanted some old bag on their arm, and there were a few about. It was like they had given up. Doug didn't want that to happen to his Gabs.

But before he considered what to give up for the sake of his family life, Doug would go to Blackpool for one last party.

Amanda Jacobs jumped around her living room punching the air. Her agent had just called. She was going to Blackpool. Now that hot Barclaycard statement looked less ominous, but the loan from her mother would be first priority.

She had recently bought a small flat in Kilburn, the Queens Park area, mind, as she was always quick to mention. This on the strength of a contract for what promised in the reviews to be a huge success at the Adelphi theatre in the West End. Unfortunately, after the first two weeks, the young male lead only made two or three performances a week and then had a lengthy time off with 'exhaustion'. What could have been a long run, folded. Many of those involved put it down to the increasing use of young television stars to get the audiences in. Unfamiliar with the mental and physical requirements of big theatre productions, they simply weren't up to the task, though occasionally some of the older, more established television actors made valiant efforts and became surprise and very worthy successes. Some even making it all the way to Broadway.

After much soul searching, Amanda had reluctantly called her mother for help. On the promise she not tell her father, Mrs Jacobs sent her daughter a cheque for £1000 from her private savings.

The very best thing about this new show was being able to pay that back by the end of the run. Hopefully then, there would be better prospects in London for Amanda.

I must phone Sara, her thoughts were suddenly back on track. *She's done Blackpool. She'll know of some good digs.* As she picked up the telephone, it rang.

'Hi!' Amanda said with exuberance.

'Hi,' replied Jason.

'Baby! Guess what...'

'You got it.'

'I got it. Wish you were here with me to celebrate.'

'Yep, me too. It's brilliant though. Well done.'

Amanda sensed something down the wire.

'What's up?'

'Oh nothing, just work stuff. It looks as though we've picked up a few more dates, which is great, but not as far as seeing you goes.'

'I know, but now I've got the show, I can afford to come up and see you before rehearsals start.'

'That would be great.'

But Jason knew it would never happen. Amanda would be too wrapped up in preparing for the show and looking for a place to stay. All par for the course when you were going out with a 'twirl', old variety speak for dancer, and he should have been well used to it by now. But he did love Amanda and this situation really sucked...

'Jase, can I call you back in a minute? I just want to get hold of Sara about digs.'

'Of course you can. I'll keep the phone on until six when I go in. Otherwise, leave a message.'

'I'll call you before then, silly!'

He knew she wouldn't. Now Amanda had more important things on her mind.

Giancarlo reached for the bottle to pour more wine but was beaten by the waiter who appeared like magic.

'Sir, allow me.'

The waiter's job depended on the service being perfect for this restaurant's most valuable client.

Summer placed her hand over the rim of her glass.

'Not for me, thank you.'

'Would the lady like more mineral water?'

'Thanks, that would be fine.'

Summer looked at Giancarlo and smiled. He responded in kind but knew it was time to get to the root of their problem. Her whole persona seemed to have changed during that dreadful night in his flat. Although they had parted on good terms, he knew more than ever there was something wrong. He also knew as a man what that something was. Like one of her father's racehorses, chomping at the bit to burst out from the starting stalls, Giancarlo couldn't wait much longer to confront his rival and deal with him. Swiftly.

'Summer...' he reached across the table and placed a hand on hers. 'What is the matter? Please, I don't like to see you this way.'

'What way?' Summer asked, withdrawing her hand and picking up her half glass of red wine.

'Your face. Such a beautiful face, but so sad all the time. This is not you. Tell me. I can help you.'

'No, you can't, Carlo, but thanks for the offer. I'm sorry I haven't been much fun lately. It's just personal issues.'

'I think it is more than this...' He took her other hand and held it quite tightly over the table. 'I think maybe... maybe there is someone else?'

Summer's eyes widened and she became very still. Could he know? How could he know? No, she was being silly. Of course he didn't know.

'Carlo, what a stupid thing to say. There's only you. You know that.'

'I am a man, Summer. I can see the signs. If it is not a man, then what?'

'Oh, Carlo, you just don't give up, do you?'

Summer took her hand away and placed both out of reach on her lap. She looked at him watching her, eyes intensely moving back and forth between them both. His expression was one she hadn't seen before. It chilled her, and Summer didn't understand why.

'Look, Carlo, it's just work. I met with someone who possibly wants me for a film. He saw my advert and called Cynthia. That part's great but it's the knowing we'll be seeing very little of each other for a while, should I get the part.'

She hoped he bought it.

'*Si.* I agree it will be difficult, but I can come and see you in Blackpool.' It would be very difficult but Giancarlo was not about to let Summer get away from him. He had never felt this way, so jealous, about a woman before. It meant something. Something important. He would just have to make the time to be with her.

'You'd hate Blackpool, Carlo,' Summer said with a well-informed smile. 'It's not exactly... you.'

Giancarlo raised his eyebrows and then laughed. Summer laughed too. So far, she seemed to have gotten away with it.

'Perhaps you don't want me there for another reason.' His stony face and flat voice said everything. He hadn't bought it at all.

'Carlo, stop this, or I'll leave the restaurant.' Her last resort.

'Okay, I'm sorry. Forgive me? Let's eat.' He lifted an arm and clicked his fingers, then lifted his wine glass. Summer did the same. He tapped his glass against hers and said, 'To us, Bella.'

The Sicilian watched Summer over the rim of the glass as he sipped his wine, content in the knowledge he had all the information he needed.

Doug put the car in their three-vehicle garage and entered the house through the connecting door into the utility room. A pungent damp chemical smell from towels in the basket told him Gabrielle and Phoebe had been swimming.

It occurred to Doug that one of the first things he would do when Blackpool was over would be to organise the building of their own indoor pool. When they bought this house, Gabrielle had made him promise the children. That was over three years ago, and before Phoebe was born.

'Just a few more months, kids,' Doug said out loud to himself as he made his way upstairs toward the sound of mother and daughter laughing. Slowly opening the door to their en-suite bathroom, Doug listened to Phoebe's infectious giggle. It was a mini version of her mother's and Doug realised how long it had been since he had heard Gabrielle really laugh. A long time.

Before he was fully in the room, Phoebe caught sight of her daddy in the mirrors surrounding the huge corner bath and splashed the water with both hands in her excitement.

'Daddy!'

Doug, now standing in the doorway, looked at Gabrielle. She smiled through rivulets of bath water, and an expression that said 'Great. Thanks, Doug'.

He pulled a face to say 'oops', then said to his daughter, 'Hello, angel.' As he knelt beside the tub, he was immediately soaked by two chubby arms being wrapped around his neck as Phoebe hugged him and placed a wet kiss on his cheek.

'Just got back. It's all set for the week before I go to Blackpool for rehearsals,' he said to Gabrielle.

Not that she needed Doug to tell her the outcome of meeting. He was too up beat.

'Will you need me to attend as well?' Gabrielle kept the enquiry as light as possible. The thought of spending a day with the other showbiz wives raised a feeling of dread. Gabrielle would rather stick pins in her eyes. Apart from the odd one or two, none of her friends were show business-related and in Gabrielle's mind, that made them real people. Strange from a woman who started out with ambitions of a theatrical career.

'I'd like you to, but we can discuss it nearer the time. Think I'll take a shower.' Doug smiled warmly at his wife and stroked her cheek, then kissed the tip of his finger and touched the tip of her nose. 'I'll go in the other bathroom.'

He grabbed a couple of towels from their arty wire and chrome rack and went to the guest shower along the landing. Doug much preferred the roomy, 'enough for a party' walk-in affair in the en-suite but he wasn't one to walk about nude in front of his daughters. Not now. Not since Sasha was sent home from her convent kindergarten with a drawing of her father with three legs and a brief but pointed note from Sister Columba. Gabrielle had been hysterical with laughter for days and Doug now covered up. It didn't help matters when his wife found it necessary to display Sasha's artwork on the fridge door for everyone to see, including his friends. He was still referred to by some of them as 'Doug the Dong.'

While Phoebe took her afternoon nap, Doug took the chance to speak to Gabrielle. They sat across a large antique oak table in the kitchen, a chilled glass of Sauvignon each.

'This sounds a bit serious,' said Gabrielle. Her fingers stroked the stem of her glass, eyes firmly on her husband's. It wasn't often these days that Doug said, 'Can we talk', so Gabrielle waited with bated breath.

'It is serious, love, but good serious.'

Gabrielle took a healthy gulp of wine. 'Well that makes a lot of sense. Come on, Doug, just spit it out.'

'You know I'm crap at this kind of thing, Gabs, so let me say it all in my own way.'

Doug got up from the table and took the bottle from the fridge, now thankfully sans Sasha's masterpiece. He refilled both their glasses and set the bottle between them.

'You really want this to be the last summer away, don't you?' His wife nodded slowly. 'Well... so do I.' Gabrielle didn't react, only to sip more wine. 'I've been thinking...'

'Thought I could smell wood burning...'

'Gabs, please, just listen.'

'Sorry.' And she genuinely was, for some odd reason. Was it the sound of sincerity in her husband's voice for a change? Or was she just wishfully imagining things?

'Okay, Blackpool will be the last one. You have my solemn promise.' He held up a hand in anticipation of a sarcastic rebuke from Gabrielle but she remained silent. 'Before you say anything, I know my promises have dubious provenance but this one you can count on. You mean the world to me. You always have, and I don't want to fuck things up like some of our friends.'

'What's brought all this on, Doug?'

'Nothing in particular. I've just realised how important you and the kids are. The support you've given me through the years. Giving up your own career.' *Like I had a choice*, thought Gabrielle. Doug continued, 'I really do, and always have appreciated that, Gabs. You do believe me, don't you?'

Gabrielle smiled and got up from the table, turning away to fetch a coaster for the bottle of wine that now drizzled condensation onto her just-waxed table top. The smile faded. She sat down again and placed the coaster under the bottle after wiping away a wet ring with a piece of kitchen towel.

'Do you? I mean, REALLY? I've often wondered.'

'Oh, love, that's my fault. Look, I don't want to end up like Leo Davis or even Stevie Todd with their lives splashed all over the press by their ex-wives. Not for my sake but for yours and the children's. I just couldn't bear it.'

Gabrielle laughed softly and shook her head. 'Oh, Doug,

let's get really serious here, shall we? What you don't want is an incident like Scarborough...'

'Scar... oh yes, Scarborough. But you're nothing like that witch,' Doug replied, when he realised with some relief his wife wasn't referring to him, or one of the few things that had happened to him which Doug had chosen never to tell Gabrielle. Instead, she was speaking of a much-celebrated incident during a summer season there.

'That witch' was the wife of Leo Davis. A spectacular magician. He had been the star host of a summer show at the North Yorkshire resort some years back. Leo had a reputation for making his carnal way through most of his assistants, usually chosen from the shows' choruses. But this particular year, the rumours were that Leo was closer to his assistant than usual. In fact, it was whispered he might actually leave his wife of fifteen years. That was before Doreen Davis visited the stage door one night, all the way from their substantial home just outside Swansea.

Leo was on stage at the time doing his compère duties, Doreen perfect with her timing and not by chance. She asked the doorman if he could tannoy a certain Lisa Jones. The doorman didn't recognise the woman standing resolutely just outside the stage door with a large black bin bag.

Lisa Jones made her way toward the stage door, flimsy robe draped inadequately over naked breasts. *Charming*, thought Doreen. *They never change.* She also noticed the direction from which the girl came, it was the corridor housing Leo's dressing room.

'You wanted to see...' *Me*, she was going to say but upon closer inspection, Lisa Jones realised the woman was her lover's wife. Her quite pretty features and startling green eyes changed from an expression of mild irritation to a look of abject horror. 'Doreen,' she said, now pulling the silky robe tightly around herself.

'Yes, Lisa, but it's *Mrs Davis* to you.'

Lisa's eyes momentarily focused on the bin bag and then reluctantly back to Doreen's hard face.

'Mrs Davis, I...'

Before Lisa could say anymore, Doreen opened the bag and tipped it upside down. Out fell a pile of men's underwear. Leo's underwear. The doorman, who was still standing outside his booth, and Lisa both looked aghast at the Marks and Spencer specials and then back to Doreen. Her expression had remained the same.

'You seem to have my husband at the moment,' Doreen said. 'But you don't have the best part.' She shook the upturned bag and the last pair of dirty underpants fell on top of the others. Doreen dropped the bag on top of them and wiped her hands together in a 'finished with' manner. 'So, Lisa, here it is. The best part. His stinky, skid-marked pants. You can wash them now.'

'But Mrs Davis...' stuttered Lisa. 'Please, this isn't...'

'WHAT?' snarled Doreen, her carefully composed dignity slipping just slightly.

The doorman quietly retreated into his booth. The claws were out.

'What I mean to say is...' Lisa stumbled for words. 'I never meant for any of this to happen.'

'Well it has, young lady,' Doreen snapped. 'And if you don't like his shitty knickers, you can get rid of them. Just say abracadabra.'

With that, Doreen Davis turned and walked away from the stage door, into the night and out of Leo's life. Straight into the *Sunday Mirror*.

Gabrielle shrugged and finished her glass of wine.

'No, I suppose I'm not much like Doreen Davis, although I like her style.' A faint grin passed over her face. 'But I could be, Doug. If pushed far enough.' She got up from the table and started to clear it while Doug still sat looking up at his wife.

'Trust me, Gabrielle,' he said, a healthy dollop of gravitas in his voice. 'Blackpool will be the last.'

CHAPTER SEVEN

'And you can stick that bloody elephant's trunk where the sun don't shine!'

'Jaynie!'

'You promised me, Adam. You even promised my father this time. Huh! Get out of that one for a change.'

'Jayne, please, let me get a word in, will you?'

'Why? Why the hell should I? You reneging piece of shit.'

'Now that's ENOUGH! Cut it out...'

'Don't tempt me, Adam. Just don't tempt me.'

A moment's pause as both stared each other out. Jayne saw the flicker of a tick over Adam's left eye. She had never noticed it before. Simultaneously they looked away, Jayne to her Rolex and Adam down at his buck skin loafers.

'Hear me out, at least.' Adam's voice was calm again. He looked back up into his wife's eyes, unfathomable and dark. Her mouth was set firm in a thin line as she crossed her arms and gently tapped her right foot. Realising he might actually have just been granted a silent audience, with a preliminary sigh, Adam continued. 'Why must we always do this? It doesn't get us anywhere, does it?'

Jayne simply watched him. She remained mute.

'This is my life, Jaynie. You married me knowing that. Nothing's changed where my work is concerned. I just got a break and now I'm working more, that's all. You wanted me to make it and now I have. For Christ's sake, I'm doing this for both of us...'

A finger shot up and pointed at his chest.

'Don't even THINK of saying you're doing this for both of us. You do what you do FOR YOURSELF. No one else. As and when you feel like sharing part of your life, I then get a look in. I feel like there's four of us in this sodding marriage. Me, you, and those fucking puppets. I'm not so sure they're not an extension of you.'

The pointed finger slowly lowered and Jayne crossed her arms again. The obvious inference of her words crept across her mind and she inwardly shivered. The thought of telling her father they would not now be going to Australia for his long-planned sixtieth birthday celebrations, was enough to make her want to crawl under a rock. Jayne knew she could go alone but she preferred to remain near her husband. Jayne had her reasons.

'But I thought you loved the boys.' Adam's response prompted a surge of feral instincts from his wife and she exploded.

'NO! You stupid man. I loved you...' She quickly corrected herself. 'Love you. But you see...' Arms flying about as though she were directing an aircraft to a passenger ramp, Jayne struggled to keep up with all the things she wanted to say that were moving through her mind at the speed of light. 'I've always been second, or maybe third or fourth, but never first. Only on our wedding day was I first. I thought I could handle it, Adam. I really did. Now...' She put her hands to her face and tried to calm herself. When Jayne took her hands away, she was crying. 'Please don't do Blackpool. Come to Australia. We haven't had a decent holiday since our honeymoon.'

Adam reached for his wife but she took a step back. He ran his hands through his hair, what was left of it at the sides, and then shoved them into his trouser pockets.

'Jaynie, listen to me. Doug Delany is the hottest thing going and I'm getting to the stage in my career I've been working toward since I was sixteen. If I do this show, I'm certain to secure all sorts of great things in the future and...'

'Not me, Adam. You won't have me.'

'Jaynie!'

But she was already through the door and placing a full stop on the debate by slamming it behind her. Adam just stood looking at bits of paintwork that had shattered off the door frame. Perhaps they were a graphic reference to the state of his marriage, or whole private life, come to that. Little pieces here and there but never a whole. There was Jayne and her family, his family, and somewhere, just occasionally, a home life. None of the pieces ever seemed to join up anymore. Like a jigsaw with several vital components missing, so was his life. A life he had chosen and a life he honestly thought his wife was willing to participate in. A cold sickly feeling he had been terribly mistaken rose up from his stomach and grabbed at his throat.

Looking down into the special case that held Floppy, his elephant and a winner with the children, Adam realised that he had a simple choice. Go to Blackpool for the summer season with Doug Delany and hopefully climb another rung on the show business ladder but lose his wife. On the other hand, not do the show and possibly save his marriage. Possibly. The word loomed large.

Adam smiled ironically and shrugged. He looked down at the elephant's latex baby face that had been watching the whole debacle. One of its over-sized ears was draped over the edge of the case and Adam gently replaced it before closing the lid. Then he opened a second case. Rasher. The puppet that got him known initially in late-night clubs and later, in minor seaside shows, where he moderated the X-rated base humour, for more general audiences and those with children.

Rasher was preceded by Snitch the Snake, but after several speeding tickets and accumulation of points while travelling between venues, culminating in a three-month driving ban, Rasher the Pig seemed to drift from somewhere deep in Adam's psyche and was born, stealing all the glory. Adam wanted to reintroduce Snitch. He'd missed him. Perhaps Blackpool was the place.

Dressed in traffic police uniform, Rasher had stormed the clubs and got Adam noticed by those that mattered. For the sake of censorship and probably his driving licence, the police uniform was removed and Rasher became Adam's annoying sidekick. A sarcastic interfering character that people of all ages adored. From there, as he became better known, Adam created Floppy. Careful to keep all referrals to circus and flying at nil, he managed to get away with having a Dumbo-like puppet which did for his career what Dumbo's ears had done for him. Adam was flying high. His marriage, on the other hand, was fast falling with terminal velocity toward oblivion.

As he closed Rasher in his case again, Adam's thoughts back to the present, he knew what his decision would be and the most likely consequences. Adam Nash would just have to live with them, if he wasn't already.

'Cousin!'

'How you doing, Angelo?'

'Fine. Yourself?'

'Good. And the family?'

'Well, very well. Little Luisa is growing so fast. She'll be walking any day.'

'That's great. Great. Angelo, listen...'

He wasn't listening. 'So when am I going to be formally introduced to this wonderful girl I'm hearing about?'

'I don't think... I don't know. Angelo, just listen.' Giancarlo's voice projected just the right edge for his excitable cousin to become silent. It was strange how certain traits, however insignificant to outsiders, seemed to bridge generations and get passed down from father to son. Whenever Paulo Scarlatti said 'listen', even the pontiff would have shut up. 'I need you to organise something with your people.' Giancarlo paused, a tiny juncture that spoke volumes.

'Understood. Let me take this in my office, there are people around. I'll call you straight back.'

The line went dead.

While Giancarlo waited, patience not being one of his very few virtues, he tapped his fingers on his desk as if it were a bongo drum. Was this nervous tension? Never having experienced such a trivial thing before, Giancarlo stopped his rhythm play and almost comically looked at his hands. Perhaps this WAS serious. It was either cause for much concern or great rejoicing. Why was this 'wonderful girl' affecting him in this way?

Summer was certainly a big part of his life now, like no other woman had ever been previously, and he was allowing her life to mix with a place in his that she had no right to. But he was calling the shots. It was all his own doing. Did he really have a choice? Like fuck he had a choice.

That sobering thought brought Giancarlo crashing back to his office. Feeling centred again, his usual calm controlled self, he watched the telephone. A motionless stare, not unlike that of a praying mantis. When the instrument rang, his hand pounced upon it with the same speed as the insect's own devastating strike.

'What do you want?' Angelo asked. Straight to business.

'I need some information...'

'But you don't need me for...'

'Don't tell me what I do or don't need, cousin.' It was an unusually sharp retort toward a family member. Giancarlo had some serious thinking to do on a personal level. He continued. 'The information is in someone's office,' he said with less impatience.

'Understood.' *Never jump the gun, Angelo. Did your father teach you nothing?* 'Give me the details. It's as good as done.'

As Giancarlo discussed what he required, Angelo listened without writing a single note. Something also learned from his father. And Paulo. Never put anything on paper where 'business' was concerned. Keep it all in your head. If they can't see it, you know nothing about it. But logged in Angelo's memory were names and numbers for all the people who worked for him. His other business. They liked to call themselves 'professionals'. The authorities across the world had another name. Angelo preferred 'friends'.

Cynthia Hersh sat back in her ageing but comfortable chair and lit another cigarette. She took a long thoughtful drag of hot smoke into her lungs, held it for a moment with her head tilted back, then, in a smooth measured stream, blew out the spent product toward the light above her desk. A satisfied smile spread across her face. George Weiss had just called. Summer had an interview with Martin Thurlow, producer and director of some of Britain's premier talent in his small but vital art-house films.

This could be the beginning of something huge. For both of them. Cynthia knew Summer could dance like a dream and had the looks and body of a goddess, but unknown to most was her acting talent. The girl could act her socks off. Even cry on cue. She had just never had a break. Where had she heard that one before? That was, until now, and Cynthia was the agent fielding the deal. George Weiss had even given the agent his home number!

As she was reaching for the phone, it rang. Cynthia rested her Consulate on an ashtray she had taken as a memento from the *Canberra*, when the grand old lady was still in fine fettle and Cynthia had been part of the entertainment troupe on board. A fleeting nostalgic flutter skipped across her heart.

'Cynthia Hersh Agency.'

'Good morning. Is that Ms Hersh?'

'It is. Who's this?'

'Cranshaw Estates, Ms Hersh.'

'Oh right, morning.' A small frown wrinkled Cynthia's brow and she took another puff on her menthol. 'What's up?' Why the hell were the management company that ran her office building calling? For once, she'd paid the rent on time.

'We need access to inspect some damp.'

'Damp?' She asked, looking around her office. No sign of damp as far as her untrained eye could see. Never had been.

'We've noticed a crack in the mortar just outside your office window and we'd like to inspect it from your office. Would that be a problem?'

'I suppose not. When? And how long will it take? I'm very busy.'

'Later today, if possible.'

'Okeydoky, then. But make it before six thirty. I've got an appointment.'

'Great. I'll get someone round right away. Thank you, Ms Hersh.'

As Mr Charming hung up, Cynthia realised she hadn't recognised the voice. Probably a new guy. At least it wasn't the usual stuck up little shite, Toby Cranshaw. What a snotty, patronising public school boy he was. Just because Daddy handed him a career on a plate, it didn't mean he could speak to their hundreds of tenants, commercial or private, in the way he did. Pleasing sadistic thoughts of what she'd like to do to the 'I'm so superior' Toby meandered through her head as Cynthia dialled Summer's number.

Giancarlo snapped at Fiona when she called up for him to assist with a difficult customer. After apologising, he said he would be down immediately. He liked to keep a tight ship and calm ambience in his bar. Before reaching his office door, the phone rang again. It was an outside line.

'Good news.' Giancarlo smiled. He loved good news. 'I'll have your information later tonight. Easy job. Silly cow has no security.'

'Maybe she didn't think she needed it.'

They both laughed.

'Cousin, what's up?'

Giancarlo's smile vanished. 'You know better than to ask that.'

'I know, but this seems to be something very personal...'

'So don't get involved, eh?'

But I AM involved, Angelo thought as he heard the tone in Giancarlo's voice turn to ice. 'I'll call you tonight, then.' Angelo hung up without saying goodbye.

Angelo knew this was not a healthy situation. He didn't like dealing with 'family stuff'. He WAS family. Giancarlo was supposed to use other people for this type of enquiry. But could Angelo refuse? Not if he wanted to retain his status with his cousin. Okay, so maybe there was a good reason for Giancarlo to call on him like this. He just hoped it wouldn't get messy. He hated messy, and personal stuff always got messy. A wry smile broke through his disquiet.

For Giancarlo to be so worked up about something, Summer Laine must be some piece of arse.

After dealing with the drunk, Giancarlo poured himself a large Bloody Mary, splashing a good measure of Tabasco into the mix. He downed it, under the quiet gaze of his bar manager. Fiona had never seen her boss quite like this. Perhaps the recent absence of his girlfriend was the reason. Whatever it was, the usually impeccable and strong demeanour Mr Scarlatti was renowned for, seemed to have temporarily deserted him.

Summer had made an excited call to him just after Angelo. She was going to meet a film producer. And not just any old producer. It was Martin Thurlow. Now pieces started to fit. It was all falling into place. That night in his flat flashed into his thoughts. Giancarlo's blood was just about at boiling point. He knew how these things worked. How desperate some people are to succeed in show business. He was only too aware that in many languages, the word for actress was also the word for prostitute. The stupid bitch. He'd thought better of her. Thought she could make the grade. In good time, he might have taken her home to be introduced to mama and papa. But no, his lovely lady was just another English tramp. So why was it hurting so much?

Burning so badly, he was going to have to make someone pay.

CHAPTER EIGHT

Big George, as he was affectionately known among good friends, made slow progress down the length of his vast indoor pool, housed in the basement of his sprawling Richmond home. His lumbering, chalky white bulk heaved through the barely tepid water, just how he liked it. He detested pools that felt like you were swimming in a Turkish bath. He moved with all the grace of a beached walrus.

No gentle rippling wake behind George. Small waves parted in a giant V-shape, slapping at and over the pool's edges, and returning to meet again in the centre of the pool, exactly where George still rolled along. His stroke floundered slightly as he spat and spluttered, he hated getting his face wet, his facial expression now resembling one of his prized Koi carp in the specially designed marble pond that commanded the centre of his grand oval driveway. As he turned for another length, George's thoughts had drifted onto a toned, silky-skinned body, yielding to his. Long gossamer hair stroking his chest as she sat astride him. His preferred position. Much easier on the old ticker.

Summer. Such a sweet name, he mused. Perhaps she should have been called Santa, for all the wonderful gifts she bestowed upon him. Shame Marty would miss out. Gay as a Toc-H lamp, but still one of George's dearest friends. An excellent investment as it turned out. It was just that George didn't much like Marty's 'persuasion', or anything that didn't have a natural order about it. George preferred to be a raging heterosexual and, however deviant he might be within that genre, no matter. If the whores, of whom there were endless numbers, were game, and most of them gagging for it, where was the harm? They usually achieved a little step up their career ladder, some more than others.

So they got what they wanted as well. But with Summer Laine, he could see the young girl going very far indeed. It was why he had called Marty in the first place.

A watery grin smeared across George's features. *And that, my dears, maketh Georgie boy a very happy individual.*

A bell echoed throughout the mosaic tiled pool room. The phone was ringing but George wasn't concerned about it. His elderly loyal housekeeper, Mrs Bruce, would take the call upstairs. If it were urgent, she would let him know.

George walked up semi-circular steps and out of the pool, draping a large monogrammed towelling robe around the twenty stones that rested precariously on his five foot four inch height. Rotating aching shoulders, he lowered himself onto one of many loungers, next to a table set with champagne on ice and a small mahogany box inlaid with mother-of-pearl. There was nothing George Weiss liked more than an early dip, followed by a glass of chilled champagne and one of his precious Cubans.

Oh, I don't know, he thought. *Miss Laine was a close second.*

Just as he had expertly tipped the cigar and held the flame of his lighter poised, Mrs Bruce entered the room. He could hear her shortness of breath and decided it was time to get that intercom installed. George didn't want to let Winifred go, despite her age. She had worked for him for fifteen years and had been like a second mother to him when his own succumbed to a poor heart. The least he could do was make what was left of her life in his employ, that much easier.

'Sorry to disturb, Mr Weiss,' she said in her gentle Highland accent. However many times he had asked her to call him George, she remained formal to the letter. Probably a strict Scottish upbringing. Still, he rather liked the reverence. 'That was Serena. She might be a bit late. About an hour. I'm to call her back if you want to cancel.'

'That's all right, Mrs Bruce, just call the restaurant, they should be used to it by now!' He laughed. 'Ask for Phillipe and tell him we'll be there for 1.45pm instead. Thank you, Mrs Bruce.'

'Will do. Water nice for you this morning?'

'Excellent.'

'Good, I should think so. The pool maintenance company called twice this week.'

'Twice?' George enquired with a frown.

'Aye. The young man said they'd been having problems with their cleaning equipment. He asked to use the phone quickly to call his office. I hope that was the right thing to do, letting him use the phone.'

'I suppose, but didn't he have his own?'

'He said the battery was down, or something like that.'

'I see. All right then. I trust they sorted the problem?'

'Yes. He seemed quite satisfied when he left.'

The housekeeper made her way back up into the house and left George to finally savour his hand rolled cigar.

Serena Stowe was his long-term girlfriend. An accomplished RSC-trained stage actress, and an absolute lady. Theirs had been a conventional meeting at her first night of a much-acclaimed play at the Old Vic. It took all of George's powers of persuasion even to get Miss Stowe on a lunch date. Thereafter, they quickly, if rather unexpectedly, drifted into a relationship.

Serena knew only too well about George Weiss, hence her initial reluctance. But during their lunch at the Savoy, they both realised they shared the same humour and found each other easy to talk to. A meeting of minds. In Serena, George discovered a natural intelligence and wit, enhanced by an excellent education. Though perhaps the thing that he loved most was her complete refusal to allow George to help her career path. Already established as the first lady of theatre, she held little desire to break into films. The only time she gave in was to make one with Martin Thurlow. It was simply too good an opportunity to work with a maestro, that might otherwise not have come her way.

Because she didn't want anything from George, except him, the person, the human being, he was able to forgive her lack of talent in the bedroom department. Not that she didn't try. Nobody's perfect. George was never sure if Serena was aware of his little dalliances, but if so, being a certain calibre of woman, not a word was ever said.

There was just one small irritation that sometimes drove George to distraction. Except for a performance, Serena Stowe was permanently late.

Giancarlo swivelled and weaved his Montblanc through the fingers of his left hand. Decisions, decisions. The options had been surprisingly numerous, even to one who was used to such dealings. After a few more deliberations, he chose the uncomplicated option. If there was one thing Paulo Scarlatti had taught his son, it was about simplicity. The less margin for error and suspicion, the better the assignment.

Paulo was a small man physically, something that had irritated him through his life. Maybe it had been the driving force behind his rise to the lofty status he held among his peers, even now, at his fragile age. Giancarlo had no such handicap, inheriting from his mother, Fabia, tall good looks. Where she had been a graceful beauty, her son was athletic in build, but held himself as she always had, ramrod straight and proud. Sadly, with the ravages of osteoporosis, Fabia's once five foot ten frame had been cruelly diminished by six inches, and she now stood equal to her husband. In fact, Fabia was probably the only person to whom Paulo acquiesced since his own parents passed.

Giancarlo had hoped to find a woman like his mother. Someone to adore and fuss over him, but at the same time, have plenty of fire and spirit. Be unerringly loyal. Beautiful. A wife to be proud of. He thought perhaps he had found such a lady. How spiteful life could be, but like his mother, Giancarlo would fight back.

Summer pressed the entrance intercom and waited. The family estate sat in the distance as she looked through the traditional five bar gate and up the long farm track road.

After a minute or so, Isadora Laine's velvety tones unflatteringly crackled through the speaker.

'Welcome home, darling,' she said as the gate opened to the accompaniment of a dull buzzing and metal clunk of electronic lock. The wooden barrier, always freshly painted white each spring, slowly eased back and Summer started up towards the house and stables. The car jolted over several pot holes. *No change there then,* Summer thought with a smile, all the while hoping the suspension on her new Peugeot Roland Garros wasn't being damaged. Thankfully, the horses were never brought in via this road, and a good job too. They probably wouldn't have had any legs left to race on.

As the main house loomed large in her windscreen, Summer let out a sigh from somewhere deep within her. She had a love-hate relationship going on inside. It was always great to come home to this peaceful place, close to Chepstow. Summer looked forward to seeing her mother. In recent years, they had become close once again, though Summer harboured the thought that it was probably due to the boys all being grown and involved with the business, which left Isadora feeling like a spare part, that had prompted this renewed interest in her daughter. Whatever. She would take anything she could get in the way of parental attention. And there lay the downside of coming home. Johnny Laine. Father. Daddy. *Huh! Daddy,* she thought dryly. *In your dreams, girl.* Summer then pondered whether a film made by the highly respected Martin Thurlow, might just be a turning point. Sure, and she was the Queen of Sheba.

Another crater jarred the car. An omen perhaps? She smiled. The worst that could happen was the standard row with her father, and Isadora getting upset by it all. After a lifetime of it, Summer knew handling that would be mere child's play. As it always had been.

Pulling to a stop in front of the house, Summer realised with a sinking feeling that her reflections about an omen may have been only too prophetic. Standing on the porch next to her mother was Anthony Wiggins. What the fuck was he doing there? Then the irony of her question pricked her mind with the sting of a syringe, and a heaviness settled onto her chest. She felt cold and isolated. She knew, in her mixed-up heart, that what she was experiencing now came from her own self-serving and scheming little ways. What was it her grandmother had always said, at least once a day? What goes around, comes around? Quite. Past deeds flooded back to haunt her, and Summer took a long calming breath. Tony might just be in for a big surprise.

Isadora walked over to greet her daughter with arms outstretched. 'My darling girl, come here and give Mummy a hug.' She enveloped Summer in a warm embrace and then took her daughter's face in her hands and kissed both cheeks. She stood back, admiring the beautiful woman standing in front of her. Supreme pride swept over Isadora. *I produced this,* she thought. *My life wasn't a waste, after all.* 'You look absolutely gorgeous. No wonder Martin Thurlow wants to audition you. Oh! It's all just too exciting!'

Summer smiled but only for show. The real reason she stood on the frontier of a career wonderland sat in the pit of her stomach like a dollop of leaden suet pudding. In that instant, Summer loathed herself more than ever before.

Without speaking to the man standing smiling at her, eyes twinkling in a sickeningly lurid sort of way, Summer walked straight past him with a slight nod of her head and the briefest of perfunctory smiles, for the sake of her mother who flapped about behind her daughter.

'Oh darling, leave those bags, Daddy will take them up for you. Or perhaps Tony...'

'No!' As she said it, Summer heard the harshness of her retort. 'I mean, no thanks,' she continued, smiling sweetly over her mother's shoulder at him, her voice smoothed. 'I can manage.'

'You run along then and get yourself sorted, darling. I've arranged a little soirée for you tonight. That's why Tony's here with Sonia, and some others are coming over later.'

'That'll be great fun. Thanks, Mummy.'

Summer trotted up the stairs, dread settling over her like suffocating cling film.

Isadora took Tony's hand. 'Come on, let's find your darling wife and have a drink. It's so good of you both to be here at such short notice.'

'I wouldn't have missed it for the world, Issy. Give our little Breezy a good send off on her summer season, and hopefully greater things.'

He smiled, but mostly to himself. It had been a long time and Tony had jumped at the chance. Despite her cool reception, 'not so little' Breezy had looked delicious, a feast of pleasure for him to devour later. Just an ephemeral waft of her personal scent as she had passed him in the doorway was enough to stir dormant tinglings in his loins. After so long, he hoped he could make it last, and not let them both down by exploding his load too soon.

Summer closed her bedroom door on the rest of the world and the stench that was Tony Wiggins. She threw her weekend bags on the bed, closely followed by herself. Lying back, arms above her head, Summer felt the comforting touch of the hand-woven willow head board. As a little girl, she had fiddled with it, picking at the swirls and scrolls during periods of intense thought. Or silent tantrums after a scrap with her father.

God, this was going to be a trial. Maybe she could pretend to get a call from Cynthia and hurry back to London. No, that might appear too obvious and anyway, it might be amusing, even inspired, to find ways of taking Tony to the brink and then, just leave him dangling there. Literally. Such thoughts brought the first true smile to Summer's face since she had arrived.

Suddenly, the weekend looked rather more appealing.

Serena turned up exactly fifty minutes late. She was always sincerely apologetic and looked so damned lovely, that George simply found it impossible to admonish her. Maybe she planned it so. On this occasion though, George was ravenous. His ample gut had been groaning and pleading for over an hour, so it wasn't long before Serena was ushered into his ancient but beloved Bentley.

As they drove out through high security gates and turned right onto the road, heading towards their favourite riverside eatery, another car, strategically parked, eased out onto the road behind them and followed at a moderate distance.

CHAPTER NINE

Johnny Laine quietly observed his daughter through the open French doors and his hidden surveillance spot out on the terrace. There, he watched her talking in animated fashion to her youngest brother, Dermot, who was laughing heartily at something Summer was saying. The sight of this warm and spontaneous interaction filled Johnny with a rare surge of parental love and pride for his only female offspring.

Dermot had always been the closest to his little sister as she grew up. It was good to see some things didn't change, though the difference in his daughter stunned Johnny to the core.

When had it happened? Where had he been when this miraculous transformation took place? An innocent, slightly gawky girl had become a breath-taking, self-assured woman. A large lump formed in Johnny's throat, and he felt the stirrings of an emotion he was unfamiliar with. Deep regret. His thoughts rampaged through the past, then settled on the day he first lifted Summer onto a trusty old dappled grey called Sky, a name reflective of the mare's unusual blue-grey eyes.

The six-year-old sat nervously in the saddle, little legs spread over Sky's wide girth, feet nowhere near the stirrups. Normally, as with his boys, Johnny would have introduced his daughter to riding much earlier, but ironically, she hated the great big beasts that snorted and bucked, were bad tempered and 'quite smelly, Daddy.' It had taken until this moment to persuade his stubborn daughter that not all horses were akin to the temperamental thoroughbred racers he trained. Like gentle, dependable Sky. So there she finally sat, looking daggers at her father.

'Don't let it run off, Daddy,' she said nervously.

Johnny had smiled and replied, 'Of course I won't, Peanut. Now sit up straight. Here, take the reins...like this...that's it, there now. You look like a champion show-jumper already!'

'A what?'

'Something you could be one day, Peanut. And Daddy would be very proud.'

'Don't let it go too fast, Daddy.'

'Her name's Sky, not "it",' Johnny laughed. 'And I won't let her go too fast, I promise.' He gave the horse a pat on the neck and said, 'Walk on, my lovely.'

Oh, how the years had flown by. Just who was the spectacular creature holding centre stage in the sitting room? The question increased the intensity of the lump in his fast-constricting throat.

Remembering his words to Summer on that distant autumn day, Johnny realised he should have been proud of his daughter whatever path she chose in life. Just because she didn't conform to what seemed right to him, it didn't mean she wouldn't make a decent life for herself. The terrible truth was that this father had never really tried to know his little girl, who stood before him now, a grown woman that he didn't know at all. It was a dreadful error of judgement on his part as a father, and as a man, which seemed impossible to correct. At least not to the extent he believed Summer deserved. Would she accept a belated attempt from him to try and be a proper father to her? And was he brave enough to go against his deep-rooted and very personal feelings toward her present lifestyle? Or was he simply wasting his time and energy on what he had assumed, until now, was a lost cause?

Summer had been on course to take a degree in media studies, but as if to spite him, she changed track and enrolled in a dramatic arts academy in London. Now she was living the very life Johnny had most wished his daughter would avoid. He had met many girls working as models and actresses who mingled about at the race meetings. Some were doing promotional work, mostly for booze and fags, but all were scouring the enclosures for a gullible sugar-daddy with valuable connections. The worlds of racing and show business linked inextricably. Summer was now part of 'that set', as he referred coldly to them. For all the family history with horse training, she detested them. Even so, he knew she had chosen to be a dancer and actress to get at him, and the feeling burned in his chest.

For all their arguments, Johnny knew she was a gifted performer and had probably chosen her career wisely. Unlike her taste in men. That was another, maybe more serious, problem. The boyfriend. Carlos, or was it Gianni? Whatever the greasy wop was called, the man was dangerous, a manipulator, and, Johnny sensed, part of a world his daughter should keep well away from. Once in, well, such morbid concerns didn't bear thinking about.

It was time to bridge the raging torrent of emotion between father and daughter. She still needed his gentle guidance, paternal input. And a demonstration of his love, that had always been there. Johnny had just never blessed Summer with its warm glow. As he walked towards the French doors, Johnny realised a reconciliation with his little girl would probably mean more to him than training a Grand National winner. He smiled ruefully as he realised, if he was really honest, it would be a close call.

'Hello, Daddy,' Summer said brightly as he approached. She stood up from Dermot's lap, where she often ended up when they were mucking about. It was born of earlier times when her brother would take the time to read to her, when no one else seemed to care. Now the poor young man seemed swamped by his sister's athletic, leggy form.

'Peanut.' Johnny put his arms around Summer and hugged her to him. Almost choking, she laughed.

'Peanut? You haven't called me that for...'

'Too long,' Johnny broke in. 'How have you been? You look fantastic.'

'I know! It's a shame I'm her brother!' chortled Dermot, winking jokingly at his father. But Johnny Laine didn't like impropriety, even in jest, and especially with family.

'Enough of that kind of talk, Motty.' Dermot looked suitably chastised.

Summer looked at her father. Was this an act, or for real? Perhaps the gods were cutting her a break, after all.

Anthony Wiggins watched his adorable secret as she chatted to her father and brother. He stood out of sight in the adjoining games room, wishing it was he who could command her entire attention. His eyes focused on her forever legs at the hem of the mid-thigh flimsy little skirt she was wearing. Maybe she knew he would be there. Worn it just for him. An hors d'oeuvre for him to savour before she provided the full menu. The material was layered and tantalisingly almost see-through. It left little to the imagination, at least to Tony's. The suggestion of her upper thigh and the curve of her sporty rump caused his blood pressure to rise. It wouldn't be long now, he was sure of it. Her little glances, cheeky private smiles when no one was looking. Even in front of Sonia. Salacious scenarios played out in his head. Debauched thoughts churned like a stormy sea, and the star was, as always, Breezy. The supporting act performed with the strength of an ox and stamina of a top athlete. *If only,* he said to himself. *Anyway, she'll do all the work. Like before, the clever girl.*

The images were so vivid, they made Tony swallow involuntarily and he had to cough. To his horror, three surprised faces turned to look at him. He hadn't realised that he'd unknowingly moved out from his covert observation place. Red-faced, Tony said, 'Just checking out the new snooker table. I'd like to pot a few later.'

'Of course, Tone. Come in and join us. Don't be wandering about on your own while the ladies prepare the food,' Johnny said, beckoning his friend into the sitting room.

Thanks, Dad, thought Summer as she beamed warmly at Tony when he walked into the room.

'She's turned out to be something very special, hasn't she, Tone?' Johnny asked with a broad smile.

'Oh, more than that, my friend. Breezy...'

'"Summer",' she interrupted. 'I prefer "Summer" now.'
All three men frowned briefly and Tony nodded his head.
'Apologies, Summer. Old habits die hard!' he joked.
I know, you revolting pervert, she thought. 'That's okay,
Tony. No harm done.' But lots of harm HAD been done,
and for once in her life, she was going to rectify some of it.
Isadora called from the depths of the house and Johnny
was summoned. The doorbell rang almost simultaneously
and he asked Dermot to let the other guests in and get
them drinks. Left alone together, Summer and Tony stood
looking at each other in silence. Then he spoke.
'You really do look amazing, Summer. There's a change
about you, though. Don't know what it is but it suits you.'
'Thanks. How are you?' Summer paused and before he
could reply, said with emphasis on his wife's name, 'And
how's Sonia?'
'Oh, not so bad, you know. We're both well.'
'I'm glad you're in good health, Tony,' Summer breathed.
Tony's brow shot up, then furrowed as an evil grin broke
across Summer's face. She fiddled provocatively with a
strand of hair, putting it between her lips and pulling it
slowly across them. 'How about we meet at the stables?
Nobody there at the moment. Not till the evening
inspection and that's not for a good hour or so. Wanna fool
around, Tone?' she teased, watching him closely. He
simply had no idea how to handle her. Easy pickings. 'Meet
me in Lancer's box in fifteen minutes. He's out at Gerald's
place having fun with Final Showdown. Daddy hopes
they'll produce another Rummy for him. Anyway, I digress.
Fifteen minutes, okay?'
'Okay,' was all he could say. His mouth was desert dry.
Tony could feel his heart pumping furiously, his breathing
quietly erratic. 'I'll be there.'
Summer turned and walked out of the room, a slow, hip-
rolling stroll that caused her chiffon skirt to swing from
side to side in a further enticement. As if he ever needed
one.
'Holy Mother of God,' Tony said under his breath. 'Jesus,

Mary and Joseph.' He didn't know much to start with, but it seemed where sophisticated women, and this one in particular, were concerned, he knew bugger all.

On the road, under a canopy of tree tops that had merged overhead in a kaleidoscope of greens, lay a dead fox, its body pulverised by a brutal force, entrails spilling from an open belly onto the tarmac, sickening creams, yellows and red against a stark grey palette.

Among the bushes and trees in the wood, through which the road meandered, was an alien sound that didn't fit into the sudden unnatural silence. A loud ominous hissing. Not a snake or even a pissed off hedgehog. It was the death rattle of an engine. An old Bentley engine, turned upside down.

Intermittent within the disturbance was another. An on-off squeak, as one of the rear wheels slowly rotated on a bent axis. One by one, the birds - those that had not taken flight at the thunderous metallic thud that had shaken the ground below their perches - resumed their calling, but cautiously. Petrol and oil trickled precariously, along with the blood that gushed from George Weiss's almost severed head as it hung through the smashed driver's window, his glassy eyes still open, horror etched eternally within them.

Against the enormous roots of a huge oak tree, her body thrown from the car on impact, lay Serena Stowe, cast in her carefully orchestrated final role. Rag doll.

She often failed to wear her seat-belt, although strangely, George always had. He usually made her buckle up, but occasionally, he simply forgot to notice. Though on this day, at this time, and with this man, even a seat-belt wouldn't have altered the outcome for the lovely Serena. She simply wasn't allowed to survive. Like Mr Genus Vulpes, lying on the road, the termination of her life had been predetermined by another.

For a few precious moments, and sadly unaware, she teetered on the edge of oblivion, unable to take a last glance at the world she was about to depart. Serena would have liked the woodland about her, not unlike a set for *A Midsummer Night's Dream*. One of her favourite plays, in which she had performed at Stratford-upon-Avon. As the life ebbed softly from her torn and fractured body, the hissing eased to silence and the wheel stopped rotating in a graceful reverence at the loss of a most distinguished actress as she finally breathed her last.

A pristine classic mark two Jaguar pulled to a stop on the side of the road. A man got out with a mobile phone pressed to his ear as he rushed to the top of the short but steep embankment, leading down into the wood. Geoffrey Lonsdale rambled to the operator, while sinking to his knees. His eyes focused on the overturned car first, then, slowly, they moved to a face, George's face, staring back at him. Geoffrey choked as bitter burning bile rose and he heaved.

'Oh God, oh God.' He struggled to give directions to the woman on the other end of the phone. Each time he took a breath, his stomach churned. The policewoman's calm authoritative voice coaxed the information she needed from him as he quietly wiped away foul strings from his mouth.

'... I saw the fox and thought I'd stop, put it on the side of the road... then... I saw the skid trail and heard a noise in the trees. The car...'

'Stay clear of the vehicle, Mr Lonsdale. Remain where you are. Officers are on their way with the ambulance and fire services. Just keep talking to me.'

'I don't think there'll be any need for an... oh no!'

'What is it?'

'There's another... there's TWO people. Oh dear God...'
Geoffrey had caught sight of Serena.

Two miles up the road, a car pulled into a lay-by and the occupant made a call.

'It's done'. After a moment's pause, he pulled out onto the road again. The faint scraping on the paint work on the passenger side remained unseen by the police car that sped, lights flashing, sirens squealing, towards the direction he'd come from.

Sonia Wiggins looked down at her gold slim-line watch and sighed heavily. Why on earth did her husband HAVE to go and look in on Freddie Boy just before supper? God only knew. It was typical though, and after twenty years of marriage, she shouldn't have been surprised. No sense of timing or occasion.

She heard laughter coming from the games room and wandered through to find Summer and Dermot in dispute over a snooker shot. They smiled at her as she entered the room and both smiled.

'Hi, Sonia,' said Dermot. 'I could do with a referee here! My sister is a consummate cheat!"

'I am not!' Summer turned to Tony's wife. 'Hello, Sonia. Lost Tone, have you?'

'Oh, he's gone to the stables to check on Fred. The man is obsessed with that bloody horse.'

'Well, Sonia,' Dermot said in placating tones, 'THAT bloody horse is on the brink of becoming something very special. Dad and Tony might just have another Desert Orchid, so it's important to treat his hock injury carefully.'

'Oh, of course, I forgot about the injury,' Sonia said, now feeling mean for doubting her husband. 'I'd better go and help Issy.'

As Sonia left the room, Summer watched her go. *Poor cow*, she thought, an expression of sympathy hiding a mild ironic smile. Summer hoped Tony was having fun waiting for her, all excited and likely seeing to it he was 'fully' ready among the hay in Lancer's box. Stupid bastard.

'What you smiling at?' Dermot enquired as he studied the position of the blue ball.

Summer turned and looked at her brother. 'A very sweet, but dreadfully misguided woman,' she said.

Dermot, already poised to take his shot, half across the table with one leg askew, didn't really hear her words. Their truth went unnoticed.

A shout went out and everyone was called to supper. They converged on the dining-room, Johnny's little group laughing and joking still, the wives to-ing and fro-ing from the kitchen with plates piled high with food.

Last to appear was Anthony Wiggins. If looks could have killed, Summer would have dropped dead in an instant. She just smiled affectionately at him with an 'oops, I forgot' hand to mouth, and shrugging her shoulders, sat down directly opposite him at the table.

Sonia, the 'poor sweet cow' completely ignorant of their private messages, sat next to her husband and quietly looked at him. She really must address his drinking and smoking. Flushed and sweaty, he wasn't looking at all well.

'Everything okay with Freddie Boy, darling?' she asked, patting his hand as it reached for his napkin.

'Yes, my love, he's fine,' he responded with a loving smile.

Summer wanted to throw up. 'You nearly missed supper, Tony,' she said pointedly, then smiled at Sonia.

'Oh, Summer dear, Tony is always late. It's one of his worst faults.'

Unfortunately, Sonia DEAR, I know what all the others are.

Anthony looked across at Summer, his gaze deep and icy. She had just made a big mistake. He wasn't going to let her get away with it. Somehow, he would find a way to teach the little trollop a lesson she would never forget.

Suddenly, Isadora rushed into the room. 'Oh, there's just been some awful news on the radio,' she said in an urgent, breathy manner, eyes directed to her daughter.

'What is it, Mummy?' Summer asked.

'A terrible car accident... that producer fellow...'

Summer felt a wave of panic beginning to scrape at the edges of her senses.

'Which producer?'

'Oh, Summer, darling... it's him, the one you...'

'Martin Thurlow?' Summer said, her voice small.

'No, no, the other one. That fat chap who's with that famous actress...'

Summer had begun to tremble. 'How bad was the accident?'

Isadora just shook her head. The silence told Summer just how bad it had been. Then her mother said, 'And his girlfriend died as well. It's all so horrific. So sad.'

Summer got up from the table and as she passed her mother in the doorway, Isadora touched her daughter's cheek with a gentle stroke of a finger. 'Darling, don't worry. I'm sure everything...'

'Is ruined,' replied Summer, before bursting into tears and running for the solace of her bedroom.

Everyone looked at one another, not knowing what to say, but Anthony kept his satisfied smirk under wraps. Perhaps the divine forces that be had just done his job for him. He took a sip of wine and silently toasted them.

Cynthia Hersh sat transfixed by the breaking news on Sky, the sketchy details gradually emerging.

...George Weiss and his actress girlfriend, Serena Stowe, were killed outright in what appeared to be a tragic accident. They were returning from a lengthy lunch at The Quay restaurant near Kingston-upon-Thames, when, as far as the police could gather from the scene and a witness, the entrepreneur was possibly speeding when he tried to avoid a fox and lost control of the car. The restaurant would not confirm whether Mr Weiss had been drinking excessively during the meal and the police were keeping an open mind as to the reason for the accident, while waiting for the pathologist's report...

Cynthia lit another cigarette and drew deeply on it before releasing the smoke in a rapid burst, directly at the television screen.

'Aw... shit...'

CHAPTER TEN

'So young man, you find the one you like best, and we'll talk about it. okay?'

'Okay, Dad,' replied an excited Alex as he scrambled from the car and ran towards the entrance of The Pool Emporium.

Doug watched him go and his heart sagged. His son was on the brink of his second decade of life, and as a father, Doug knew almost nothing about him. The boy's thoughts, loves, hates, hopes and dreams. Dreams. The very entities that had kept Doug from his son. Then again, perhaps he should face up to the fact it was more likely to have been something deep within himself, that kept anything other than his precious career at bay. Never allowing anything that could possibly scupper his mission in life, a chance to impede or even prevent him being who he was at that moment. Sitting there, Doug Delany, top of the heap.

It was a lonely place, up on his precarious pedestal. Today, looking down at Alex from its lofty heights, Doug felt sick. He sighed from a dark empty place inside. The void where his son should have been.

What price fame and fortune? The solemn thought drifted about his troubled mind as Doug walked into the store to find Alex.

'... and we guarantee all our products and workmanship for ten years. We also offer a very competitive maintenance package.'

'I see. Well, there's a lot to think about. Which one did you like, Alex?'

'This one,' he replied, pointing hopefully at a photo in the company brochure. 'Can we, Dad? Can we?' His eyes were wide and pleading, looking up into his father's face as if he had turned into Father Christmas.

'Oh, go on then!' Doug said with an exaggerated smiling sigh. He couldn't keep the boy in suspense any longer. He'd come to The Pool Emporium determined to begin putting things right. Scheduling a meeting with his accountant seemed like a good idea as he said, 'So, Mike, what do we do now?'

Mike Forrest was barely able to contain his own excitement. Bloody hell! Doug Delany was about to order one of their pools. That new BMW seemed a step closer. 'I'll go and get the paperwork, Mr Delany. Would you like a tea or coffee?'

'Thanks, but no. If we could do this as quickly as possible, I've got a meeting.'

'Of course, Mr Delany. Just give me two ticks.'

Alex looked up to his father, the brightness of his eyes and the love emanating from them caused a chill to creep through to the heart of Doug's soul. He had reduced himself to buying his son's affections. How pathetic. He was gripped by an overwhelming sense of lost time, missed moments, an irretrievable eight years. Where the hell had he been? Whatever had he been thinking? Doug put a hand on his son's head and ruffled his hair, Alex responded by playfully punching his father in the stomach. Then Doug hugged the boy to him.

'By the way, that meeting I mentioned just now is lunch with you, matey. Fancy a trip to your dad's favourite pub?'

'Cor!... Yes please, Dad!'

Gabrielle and her best friend, Valerie, walked into their most loved West End restaurant. They were immediately greeted with much flap and fluster from various waiters.

As the two women were shown to the very best table, Gabrielle flushed with some embarrassment. She did enjoy the privileged service and recognition she received as the wife of Doug Delany, but sometimes, like today, she just wished she could be incognito, and treated like everyone else, as she used to be, in a distant life, without the Delany factor.

Of course, Valerie lapped it up. Their friendship was far greater than the sum of Gabrielle's secondary celebrity and the otherwise-closed doors that seemed to open because of it, but hell, it was fun. Even Valerie's own brief flirtation with public recognition, as a member of a highly successful British synchronised swimming team, never quite delivered the seductive buzz she got from being with her friend.

They had met through their daughters attending the same kindergarten. While chatting during a parent-teacher, or should that be parent-nun? evening, Gabrielle and Valerie realised they held similar backgrounds and interests. Two lives that had taken comparable paths, both giving up promising careers to bring up a family and support successful husbands, in Valerie's case, an Olympic high-diver. The only difference was that while Gabrielle had performed on a stage, Valerie's backdrop had been vast swimming pools. And it had to be said, Valerie's husband, though well known in sporting circles and as a sometime commentator on television, would never come close to Doug Delany.

From across the floor, came a distinctive booming voice.

'Gabriella! What a pleasure.'

'Angelo, how are you?' enquired Gabrielle as he approached the table.

With outstretched arms and his typically beaming face, he replied, 'Wonderful for seeing you here again. It has been far too long.'

'Ah, well, that's kids for you!' Gabrielle laughed.

'I know, I know,' Angelo said, putting a hand to his brow in mock despair. 'You don't have to tell me this, my baby daughter is so demanding. God knows what she will be like when she's a grown woman. Heaven help me!'

'Probably just like her mother,' Valerie retorted with a teasing smile.

'I think maybe then, I move out of the house!' They all laughed. 'So what are you drinking today? The usual?' Both women nodded. 'Two of my special margaritas it is, then.'

He handed them a menu each and went to make one of his most celebrated cocktails.

'I think Mr Maldini rather likes you,' said Valerie as she perused the delights on offer.

'Oh please! He's like this even when Doug's here.'

'Mmm... maybe. But I sense something rather more. It's in his eyes when he looks at you. Bit of a twinkle!'

'Valerie, you're dreadful!' laughed Gabrielle, but secretly, she too had noticed it, several times, and had summarily dismissed her thoughts on each occasion. Funny Val should voice her private suspicions. A tiny flutter of anticipation surprised Gabrielle as she studied the menu. Angelo was indeed quite a handsome man, though rather too rotund for her liking. Too much of his own food, no doubt. He did possess inviting dark pools for eyes, that did, she had to admit, sometimes look at her with a message. Whatever it was, she wasn't going to go there. Angelo Maldini certainly was an unknown quantity but Gabrielle preferred to put it all down to being Doug's wife, and one of many celebrity wives and girlfriends who ate at the restaurant. Her mind was too full of other life considerations, not least Blackpool, to deliberate about the man bringing two margaritas to the table. 'So what are you having, Val?'

'I simply have to have the spaghetti vongole,' replied Valerie. 'And I'll start with Parma ham and melon, I think. Yes... scrummy!'

'Grilled sardines and penne Angelo for me.'

Angelo placed their aperitifs on the table, smiled and departed without interrupting them. Valerie took a long sip of her drink and sighed.

'Perhaps we should deviate from what we always seem to have. Try something a bit different, for once.'

'True. But not today, eh?' responded Gabrielle.

'Nah... you're right. Stick to what we know and love.'

It had been a throw away statement, but Valerie's words seem to slap Gabrielle in the face. *What we know and love,* she repeated to herself. The sentence jangled about in her head. Apart from her children, just who else did she KNOW and love? And did anyone ever KNOW anyone? Had she ever known Doug Delany? Unlikely. It seemed to Gabrielle she didn't even know herself anymore.

A waiter appeared and Gabrielle asked him to let Angelo choose their wine for the meal. Saved making another decision, and he had never failed her. Not like her husband.

'Guess what I've been doing since we last met up?' Valerie said, thankfully halting Gabrielle's unwelcome meanderings.

'I dare not. So tell me.'

'Learning about Tarot.'

'Tarot? Oh Val! Whatever next?' Gabrielle spluttered.

'It's really interesting, actually,' said Valerie, taking a fair gulp of her margarita and looking mildly offended. 'I was going to ask you if you wanted me to read the cards for you.'

'No thanks, Val. I'd rather not know what's going to happen. It's bad enough THINKING I know what's going to happen!'

'Oh, go on. Please?'

'I don't know, I've never gone in for all that malarkey. Ask me again later. But I'm not promising anything!' Gabrielle smiled at her silly friend.

Doug pulled into the car park of The Wayfarer's Rest. It was the one place he knew no one would make a sing and dance about him being there. Over the years, he had made some decent drinking buddies and they often asked about his children. So, today, he would introduce them to his son.

Alex was made up at the prospect of going to the pub with his dad. It was such an ordinary thing to be doing, like his friends did at school all the time, but to Alexander Delany, this was a big deal, indeed.

Doug pointed to the fenced-off beer gardens and said, 'You go and find a decent table, and I'll get some drinks in. What would you like?'

'Coke, please.'

'Are you allowed Coke, Alex?' Doug asked, remembering a conversation with Gabrielle about cutting down on sugary drinks.

'Please, Dad?'

Oh, sod it. How could he refuse? One wasn't going to hurt. 'All right then, but don't go telling your mother!' Doug laughed.

'I won't, Dad,' Alex replied, his little face full of excitement at having a secret with his father. Then he caught sight of the resident wildlife in the gardens. 'Oh look! They've got ducks!'

'Do you like ducks, then?' Doug seemed surprised. Should he have been? No. How could you not know your only son liked ducks? *You're a prat,* he silently retorted.

'Oh yes,' Alex piped up enthusiastically. 'I like all birds, actually. Mum got me a book about British birds, so I would know what they were when I saw them.'

News to Doug. 'Oh? When did she get you that?'

Still watching several of his feathered interests, Alex said, 'Last Christmas, Dad.'

And Doug hadn't even noticed. He had been there, for twenty-four hours, then it was back to panto in Manchester. Alex saw his father's pensive expression.

'Oh, but I loved my mountain bike, Dad,' he said quickly. 'It was the best present.'

Doug smiled at his wise son. So young, and yet... and yet...

'Go and get us a nice table, and don't go near the river bank. Promise?'

'Promise,' said Alex as he ran into the gardens, sending three ducks quacking and flapping from the grass onto the water.

Promises. How many had he broken over the years? He'd lost count. Doug wasn't even sure he knew what a promise was any more. But he was learning. He had been a bloody fool. Immediately, the words to *What Kind of Fool Am I?* bullied their way into his mind. Doug laughed softly to himself. *A sodding great big one,* he thought. *A funny one, though.*

While waiting for their drinks at the bar, Doug realised he had just learned something about his son, as well. The boy liked birds. The feathered variety, unlike his father. Alex had seemed so pleased to see the wild fowl that lived on a natural island in the river running next to the pub. Doug couldn't remember a time in his life when he had ever appreciated anything in nature, only the females of his species. Oh, and footy, of course.

You're a shallow bastard, Doug, he said to himself.

Alex had chosen a table closest to the river bank. He was sat quietly observing the ducks, his legs swinging to and fro, deep concentration on his face.

'What did I say about going too near the river, Alex?' Doug asked as he sat down opposite his son.

Alex pulled a face and said, 'I know, but... there wouldn't be a table here if it was dangerous, Dad.'

Doug couldn't think of an intelligent response. Caught out by an eight-year-old. There was something of Gabrielle in Alex's defiant justification. He looked a lot like his mother as well. Doug wondered what little piece of him was buried somewhere within his child. If anything at all.

'There's your Coke and I got you a straw. So, what kind of ducks are they, then?'

'Mallard. You can tell which one is the male because of his bright colours and green head. The females are brown because they have to sit on the nest. It's camouflage.'

Doug sipped on his whisky and soda. Blimey! His son sounded like he had an O level in the subject. A delicate wave of pride washed over him, goose bumps tingling on his arms. Alex continued, 'They usually have about ten chicks, they're called ducklings, actually, but the mother duck can have more sometimes.' He paused to take several gulps of his Coke, straw neglected on the table and when finished, Alex had a thin line of Coke on his top lip. Doug just watched in silent admiration enjoying this rare, but hopefully more frequent, interaction with his boy. He swirled the ice around the dregs of his Scotch. The sound made Alex put his own drink down and sit forward, elbows on the table, chin resting in his hands.

'You shouldn't drink and drive, Dad.'

The lecturing tone caused Doug to sit up straight and regard his son with mild annoyance. But the truth of the words soon softened his indignation. 'You're quite right, son. Sorry. I'll get a mineral water next time. What do you want to eat?'

'Do they do burger and chips?'

'You're not supposed to have that either, are you?' Doug smiled in a conspiratorial manner. 'But yes, they do. Is that what you want, then?'

'Yes, please, Dad.'

Doug knew Alex was trying to get away with whatever he could in this time with his father, and no nagging Mummy to spoil the fun. Doug smiled and said, 'Just don't tell your mother!'

Alex gave Doug an impish grin. 'I won't, Dad!'

While tucking into their lunch, Alex trying to stuff too much burger into his mouth with ketchup dribbling down his front, Doug asked him if he would be spending time with him in Blackpool during the summer holidays. It was usual for Alex to take a two-week break with his father during a summer season.

'Maybe,' came the reply, through masticated beef.

'Don't talk with your mouth full, Alex,' instructed Doug.

After a theatrical swallow, perhaps there WAS some of his father in him, Alex replied, 'Then don't ask me a question with my mouth full!'

'Hey! Don't wise crack your father. That's my job!' Doug couldn't help but laugh.

'Does it have to be your job, Dad?' Doug's heart lurched. Alex continued, mouth free of food. 'Like Blackpool, I mean. Do you have to go away again?'

Father looked at son. Father loved son. Father hated himself. Out of the mouth of babes. Doug's heart seemed to have slipped down somewhere near his churning gut. 'But I thought you looked forward to your time with me at the theatre. Meeting all those famous people back stage. Going to the fêtes and helping me pick the raffle tickets. Eh, son?'

'I do... but... oh, it doesn't matter,' Alex said, eyes downward while playing with his chips.

'Yes, it does, Alex. Talk to me. What's the matter?'

'It's just sometimes, Dad, I wish you were like the other dads. You know, like my friends' dads?' Alex was thoughtful for a moment, then looked deep into his father's questioning eyes. 'I do love you, Dad, but... I wish sometimes you could be a different dad.'

Doug had to swallow back a choke of emotion and it came out as a strangled cough. He punched his chest, laughing, 'That water's strong stuff!' It was the only way he knew how. Make a joke to block the pain. Take the piss. Distractions. Anything that wouldn't let the world, and in this case, his son, see his anguish. Truth, a painful truth, particularly an innocent and genuine truth, said with love from your child, hurts like nothing else in life.

He had always assumed Alex had loved his unusual time with him each year. Being part of an extended 'family', often playing cards with famous ventriloquists or being taken for a bag of chips by the girls in between shows on matinée days. For them, the girls, it was a chance to get noticed by Doug. Perhaps if they were nice to the boy...

On occasion it worked like a dream, but invariably, the fantasy was only for a short duration.

Until the end of the run.

When they had finished eating, Doug said, 'Better get you home, Alex. Just remember not to mention the burger and Coke, okay?' Alex nodded happily. 'Wonder what she'll think about the pool?'

'Can't wait to see her face!' giggled Alex.

Nor can I, thought Doug. Still, perhaps she might see it for what it was. A beginning. Like this day with his son. A belated attempt at putting things right. Being the family man his adoring public believed him to be.

Oh, how naive and gullible his audience was.

Giancarlo opened the front door and found Summer standing in front of him with a desperately troubled face.

'Come here,' he said softly, as he reached for and pulled Summer to him, wrapping his arms about her and nuzzling his face into her neck and hair. God, she smelled so good. 'It's going to be all right, my darling. I'm sure his death will have nothing to do with the film producer wanting to see you.'

He sounded so sincere. Like father, like son.

'I do hope so, Carlo. I really do hope so.'

She was trembling against him. Suddenly, Summer felt like a frightened little girl in his embrace. More than anything, it gave Giancarlo the sense of finally being in control of her.

'You are with me now,' he whispered. 'Giancarlo will look after you. No one will ever hurt you. Understand?' He kissed her with a genuine tenderness.

Summer nodded and smiled weakly, looking at him with tears pooling in Bambi eyes. 'I love you, Carlo.'

At last. Finally. The words he wanted, needed, had silently demanded. 'And I love you too, Bella. Come, you must be tired from the drive. Go run yourself a bath and maybe I'll join you.'

Summer mutely climbed the stairs with a heaviness in her step, slender shoulders drooping. Not the energetic nymph-like goddess Giancarlo was used to seeing. No matter. It would do her good. Giancarlo heard his father and smiled.

He opened a bottle of Prosecco and took it upstairs on a tray with two chilled crystal flutes. Thinking all the while, she was his alone again. But he had few illusions. Giancarlo knew how these things worked. He would have to keep an eye on her. The 'love' thing was good. Very good. It was progress. He intended for that to continue.

He set the tray on an ample marble bath surround. Italian marble. He watched Summer for a moment, her eyes closed, foamy water lapping at pale pink nipples, silky blonde hair cascading over the end of the tub. She was truly the most beautiful woman he had ever known. And now she had said that she loved him. He wanted to believe her. Giancarlo willed it to be a lasting truth, but a deep-rooted caution prevailed as he dropped his robe and stepped into the aromatic bubbles.

He poured Prosecco and, with froth spilling from the glasses over his fingers and into the water, handed Summer a glass. They clinked crystal in silence and drank, eyes on each other. Giancarlo decided to forgive her for all past indiscretions.

It was a hand of amnesty he had never granted before. A reprieve the Sicilian would extend to this woman only once.

CHAPTER ELEVEN

Valerie set the atmosphere for her first 'guidance' reading. In other words, an interpretation of the cards for someone else. She was mildly nervous but equally confident in her abilities. Valerie found that she might have a flair for the cards. She felt at home with them, like she should have done this years ago. A natural intuition previously untapped, never listened to.

But having Gabrielle Delany as her first querent or client was making her uneasy. On the one hand, it was only between two good friends, having a bit of a laugh. On the other, if Valerie really did see something ominous in the cards, should she counsel Gabrielle accordingly? Or should she say nothing at all... controversial? Tricky.

Dismissing these unsettling thoughts and clearing her mind, Valerie called Gabrielle into the dining-room, where she had made the table her reading station. Two candles burned gently with the Tarot placed between them and the opposing chairs. Almost creating a cross, with the cards at the centre.

As Gabrielle entered the room and looked at the setting, she stifled the urge to giggle. Was Valerie also going to don a brightly coloured scarf and brass hoop earrings to complete the scenario?

'I thought this was just a bit of fun, Val?'

Valerie smiled and shrugged. 'It is, but I also thought I'd try and make it as authentic for you as possible. Come on, sit down.'

Gabrielle sat like an obedient child and was very pleased to see her friend remaining in normal attire, and more to the point, producing a bottle of wine.

'Not sure this is allowed on these occasions, but... what the hell, eh?'

While pouring the chilled Chardonnay, Valerie led

Gabrielle through the 'spread' she was going to use for the reading, the way in which she would lay the cards out. Then Valerie handed the pack to Gabrielle and asked her to shuffle them carefully. 'Take your time. Place them back on the table when you feel ready.'

'Can I have a drink first?' Gabrielle enquired, feeling a trifle silly for asking, but there was something... anyway, whatever it was, she needed a drink.

'Of course! Here...' Valerie lifted her glass. 'Here's to friends and the stupid things they get up to!'

'I'll drink to that!'

'Trevor!' *Oh shit...* 'What a surprise!' *Why did I pick it up?* thought Adam ruefully.

'Good day, Adam. So, tell me, mate, what's this about you's not flying over for my birthday bash?'

Adam was momentarily silent, desperately trying to figure out how to handle this call. Obviously, Jayne had dropped the bomb, and he was about to deal with the first fallout. She could have warned him, but as they still weren't talking to each other... *Tread carefully,* he said to himself. *Trevor might sound light and airy, but you know him too well to let it fool you.*

He was only too aware that his ex-pat father-in-law held no great affection for him. At times, he was thankful the overbearing man lived many thousands of miles, and at least a twenty-four-hour journey, away. Unfortunately, Alexander Graham Bell, in wicked spiritual cahoots with satellite technology, had seen to it that Trevor could get to Adam within seconds. Adam wondered sometimes how Jayne managed to grow up to be the normal lovely girl he met at the BBC while filming a programme.

She had left Perth in Western Australia, where her parents had emigrated when Jayne was seven, to study stage production and design in London. Luckily for Adam, she never went back, much to the discontent of her possessive father. She had been an assistant producer on the children's show that Adam was guest appearing on, and it wasn't long before they were dating. In under a year, they were married. It did little to help strained relations with the Australian contingency, and not much had changed in the years since.

'Adam?' The voice sounded impatient.

'Yes, Trevor, I'm here.' *Unfortunately.*

'Well, put me out of my misery, son. Tell us you're coming over as arranged?'

'Look, Trevor, it's like this...' *And don't call me 'son'.*

'Strewth, mate, Jayne wasn't winding her ol' pa up, then?'

Rasher would probably have had the perfect retort for this brash overbearing man, but Adam decided perhaps he was in enough trouble as it was. 'Well actually, Trevor, it's work. A contract I simply can't get out of, and you know I'd let Jaynie come over anyway. There's no problem with that.' Adam tried to sound positive. His insides suggested otherwise.

'Nah... come on, Adam, this is a piss-take. Jayne's always doing things like this,' Trevor laughed down the line.

'Sorry, Trevor, not a piss-take.' Adam's voice was now serious and business-like.

'So you're doing the big "I am" on me?'

Something in Adam finally snapped. Fuck him.

'ME do the big "I am"?'

'Don't raise your voice to me, Adam.'

'What difference does it make if I'm not there? Especially if Jayne comes over anyway? For Christ's sake, Trevor!' *It's not like you really want me there, you old fart.*

'Yeah, well... we both know why she WON'T come over without you.'

Adam caught the cold, dripping derision. 'What the hell does that mean?'

'You want me to spell it out, mate?' Adam's blood was fast reaching boiling point as Trevor continued. 'I mean... between you and me, Adam, my kid doesn't deserve it.' His tone was sharp and hateful, bouncing from the satellite all the way into Adam's burning ear.

'I think this conversation is well and truly over. Oh, and

by the way, Trevor?' Silence at the other end. 'I'm not your fucking "mate".'

Dead line.

Adam rocked back and forth on his sprung leather desk chair, quick jerky movements as he stared furiously out of the study window. The chair squeaked gently into the seething silence. How dare Jayne's father insinuate anything. He had no bloody right to take that sanctimonious tone with him. Fucking kangaroo jockey.

The fact was, though, that Trevor spoke the truth.

It stabbed at Adam like a homicidal wasp.

Gabrielle placed the Tarot cards in the centre of the table as instructed and watched as Valerie carefully took them, keeping the pack face down, and made a misshapen H on the cloth.

'This is called the Celtic Cross,' she said, anticipating a question from her friend. 'Always a good spread to use when reading for a querent.'

'A what? *Querent?*' Gabrielle asked with a frown.

'Oh sorry, you are the querent, client, person I'm reading the cards for.'

Gabrielle nodded.

'Why are those two crossed and touching each other?' Gabrielle asked with real interest as she saw two cards at the centre of the H that were set differently to the others.

'That's because we'll look at those ones first, you see. They represent your present circumstances in general, and also, specific terms.' Pause for a girlie smile. Valerie liked the way she sounded. Quite an authority on the subject. Not! Actually, she'd only just finished reading up on it for the umpteenth time. 'Think so, anyway!' She saw a tolerant scepticism on Gabrielle's face, but continued regardless. She was truly into this now and enjoying every moment immensely. With great anticipation, Valerie turned over the two central cards.

The Tower and The Hanged Man. *Hmm...* 'Okay,' Valerie said in a calm, soft voice. 'Let's take a peek at this...' She flicked through a small book that had been on a chair beside her.

'I thought you knew all this stuff?' Gabrielle gently mocked, taking a deep swig of her wine. She couldn't seem to rid herself of the creepy feeling that had taken a hold. Why was she suddenly so apprehensive? A tower and a hanged man... typical! She might have expected something like that, at the very least. Perhaps they were the Blackpool tower and Doug suspended from it. *Oh, Gabby, that's a bit evil, even for you!*

Valerie read quickly and then said, 'Well, as I thought, but wanted to check, The Tower means the foundation of your life as it is now. You know, is what your life is built on secure? Can it easily be destroyed?' The words cut into Gabrielle with the precision of a scalpel. 'You might have to face a few uncomfortable facts and take action to change things,' Valerie carried on. 'Does that make any sense to you?' She reached for her glass. 'The Hanged Man means "going with the flow", never "rocking the boat"...' Both emphasised by fingered dittos in the air, '... so to speak. If you get my meaning. You need to let go and move on.'

Good grief! Of all the cards to come up! But, Valerie told herself, these two cards together weren't necessarily bad. But they did indicate a need for inner change, a warning of uncertainty if the querent allowed their situation to remain the same. The Tarot was telling Gabrielle her life was on precarious ground and that she had been complacent for far too long.

The fledgling Tarot reader gulped down her wine and refilled both glasses. The very dilemma she had hoped to avoid was right there in front of her.

Whose stupid idea was this anyway?

Doug was mentally exhausted. He had never been the greatest mathematician, but two hours with his accountant bluntly proved the point.

His tax bill was higher than he'd hoped. In recent times and with more success, such hopes had been dashed every year. Ah, well, at least he could pay the bastards. Not everyone was content in that luxury. Doug had often worked on a script about the Inland Revenue, and he always came to the same conclusion. Just don't. Probably best to stay on the right side of them.

As he wandered through to the kitchen, he noticed how quiet the house was with just him in it. A cold feeling passed through him. For a split second he felt terribly lonely, then it was gone.

With Alex and Sasha at school, and Phoebe at nursery, Doug had hoped to find Gabrielle alone. Have a quiet couple of hours together. A rare event these days. He had even considered a rampant interlude with his wife. That would have been nice. It also made him happy that they were still attracted to each other, unlike some of his friends. He was lucky in that department, Gabs had kept herself trim and fit, and was still stunning without any cosmetic help. There remained a good level of enthusiasm in their love making, although, Doug had to admit if he was honest, it was all a bit familiar now.

All of a sudden, his best mate, Andy, popped into his head. Andrew Edwards, impersonator extraordinaire and one of the finest blokes you could wish to meet. Married for twenty years to Linda, herself a decent sort. Always made you more than welcome, and the life and soul of any party. Embarrassingly so sometimes. She had been a looker when they first got together, but time hadn't been kind to Linda. She had not aged well. Now her puffy face looked like a slapped arse. God knew what the rest of her was like.

Shuddering, Doug quickly banished explicit thoughts of having to perform with it from his mind. Instead, he would get a Scotch while he was waiting and take a shower for Gabrielle. Just in case. But where the hell was she?

'Now the sixth card,' Valerie said. 'This will show you what situations you might expect over the coming twelve months and what you could do about them.' She slowly turned over the Queen of Swords.

'Ah... this is interesting.' Gabrielle watched her friend expose the face of the card and almost expected the Gothic woman sitting on a throne to speak for herself. Valerie continued. 'The Queen of Swords shows us a strong woman. One with many façades against the world. The real person hidden. But this woman knows what she wants and stops at nothing to get it.'

Gabrielle gave out a burst of ironic laughter. 'I know who that is!'

'Who?'

'Well... ME, of course!'

Valerie knew her friend had taken the obvious meaning of the card. Exactly what most people would do. But the Tarot were anything but obvious. She felt chilled. Something didn't feel right. Perhaps it was her lack of experience, or maybe she was letting her imagination run riot. Gabrielle might have been right, they shouldn't go in for all this malarkey. 'Let's look at the seventh card. It will give meaning to why the Queen of Swords appeared for you.'

Gabrielle picked up the nearly empty bottle of wine and then set it back down again, thinking better of it. After all, she had to drive home. Valerie turned over the seventh card, her hand trembling slightly.

Death.

A gasp sounded from across the table but Valerie smiled comfortingly at Gabrielle, hiding her own true feelings.

'Don't panic!' she laughed gently. 'It's not what it seems.'

'What does it mean, then?' Gabrielle's voice had an urgency about it. Suddenly, this just wasn't fun anymore.

Valerie had returned to her book. It was easier than having eye contact at this moment. She needed to steady herself. Valerie considered she might make this her one and only reading. Then she spoke, still reading from the text. 'Renewal. Starting afresh. The spring after winter. We shouldn't live in the past, allow it to shape our present and future.' She now looked up into Gabrielle's troubled face. 'We mustn't be afraid of change.'

Gabrielle thought about the explanation. It was all very well, but on the table lay a card bearing a full skeleton, holding a huge scythe. Upon its bony effigy for a face, a sinister smile. The number of the card, written in Roman numerals beneath cadaverous feet, was thirteen.

CHAPTER TWELVE

A myriad of light bulbs and neon, night and day. Perpetual sound from man and machine. An indelible aroma of chip fat and donkey distinct on the air. For those that demand non-stop fun, twenty-four seven, this was the place. Their Mecca. Still the most frequented seaside resort in Britain and a quintessentially English attempt at Atlantic City.

Blackpool.

Once experienced, never forgotten. Its goodness and badness. The way it was, the way it is and the way, probably, it will remain forever. To some, their arrival heralds the beginning of their annual summer break, two weeks, often taken at the same time each year. For many, it comes down to the curse of the school holidays, but for others, the structure of their employment demands they book their fun on a strict rota. It is not unknown for comrades in work to holiday *en masse*. They toil together and see no reason not to play together. Then there are those who spend a weekend here and there, dipping in and out of the frantic madness that abounds all hours of the day.

But there are a select few who will be the entertainers, bringing numerous theatres alive with various spectacles. Serious plays at the Grand. Madcap 'not in front of the vicar' type comedies on the North Pier, and, the all singing, all dancing extravaganzas at the Opera House.

Many years previously, famous American stars, singers and comedians alike, would 'try out' their Limey audiences there, before venturing into the melting pot of the West End, with its highly critical expectation. In some cases, those Blackpudlian guinea pigs had a lot to answer for. Or so thought Doug, as he drove along the long sprawling waterfront, his mind drifting on the plethora of new and familiar sights, re-establishing themselves in his memory.

Miles of, on this particular day, muddy-looking sands on his left. Vast flat plains when the tide was out, stretching far from the promenade until meeting the edges of an equally murky Irish Sea. Trams trundled back and forth and on Doug's right, the fun fairs, games palaces, for palatial they were, gift shops and of course, the famous Blackpool Rock shops, selling a mind-boggling array of the sickly-sweet pink and white candy.

All these units were never more than a few metres away from a fish and chip or burger bar. Whatever your preference, Blackpool provided, and then some. But usually with chips, and that truly Northern fare of mushy peas. Actually, Doug quite liked the green globular slop with a sprinkle of malt vinegar on it. He didn't telegraph the fact, though. Image...

Covering every inch of brick, cement and ironwork were the millions of lights. All sizes, type and colour. Flashing, rolling or constant. Even suspended in the air above roads and between buildings, as if it would offend some mythical God of Light should they not cover every possible space with illumination. At night it would be impossible not to find Blackpool. Just look for a nuclear glow in an otherwise darkened sky.

It never changes, thought Doug affectionately. And there was a certain comfort in that fact. In his ever-altering life and career, any constant was a bonus. Like his wife and kids. *Enjoy this season,* he told himself. *You made a promise to Gabs, and this time, Delany, you're going to keep it.* Doug's eyes settled in the distance on the famous replica of the Eiffel Tower. White lights crawling all over its structure like a rampant electric caterpillar.

After a careful perusal of the billboards outside the Opera House, Doug was very pleased indeed. They were great. Lively. Enticing. Bums on seats, and that was just what he needed. Doug, apart from his enormous fee, was also to receive a share of the box office receipts. Good job, he now had a new swimming pool to pay for. Recalling Gabrielle's gaping mouth when Alex had rushed into the house, shouting at the top of his voice about it, Doug smiled. After her usual 'Well, didn't I get a say in the choice?' chiding, she seemed almost as excited as their son. So, bums on seats, please. He didn't care what size or shape they were, just as long as there were copious amounts of them.

Satisfied with the substantial advertising of his pending presence in the resort, Doug turned south and headed towards Lytham St Annes, where his prospective house rental awaited his inspection. Lytham was the 'posh' end of the bulge of land upon which Blackpool took centre stage. To Doug's delight, the house was only minutes from the celebrated golf course at Lytham.

There was only one minor irritation among all this contentment, the agent. Whether it was because Doug was Doug, or whether he was naturally a snotty little shit, Doug wasn't sure. If the house suited, and Doug couldn't see why it wouldn't after having received photographs from Rory, and if the property really was almost overlooking the club, he might cut the guy some slack.

Occasionally, certain people forgot Doug Delany was also just a bloke, somewhere inside, still a normal person. Not always the happy smiley comedian but a man who deserved the same general level of respect as everyone. Most seemed unfazed by being in his company, but he knew it was difficult for some to treat him normally. It came with the territory of being a household name, and probably from their own sense of unworthiness turning into a warped inverted snobbery. And sometimes, it really got on Doug's tits. Big time. Like now.

It didn't take long. The house was perfect and Doug signed the contract. On this occasion then, fortunate snotty little shit.

Gabrielle sighed. She counted slowly to ten. Took a long breath in, one two three, out, one two three.

How many times? Until she was blue in the face. Okay, they were working like Trojans and she really did appreciate their effort. They had promised it would be completed on time and it seemed everything was on course. The final result would be splendid indeed, a welcome addition to her home. But until her new little extra was built, Doug's consolation prize for buggering off on yet another summer season, until Gabrielle was resting on a floating lounger with wine to hand, she simply wouldn't stand for any more dusty cement footprints on her kitchen floor. Her new, real terracotta, kitchen floor.

Leaning out of the utility room window, she called to Jim.

'Yes, Mrs Delany?'

'A word, Jim?'

Jim looked from his client to his men, who were digging, clearing and reinforcing the deep rectangular pit that would become a state-of-the-art swimming pool.

A word, he repeated. He knew what that usually meant. As he made his way to the house, he stopped to speak to his new apprentice, Simon. 'I think Mike'll need a wetter mix than that, son. Wait till I get back and I'll show you again.' He patted the nineteen-year-old on the shoulder.

Simon felt crushed. He'd been trying so hard. His dad was a builder and the cement he'd made up seemed fine to Simon. It was the same as Dad made. But it seemed nothing he did was right for Jim Sargeant.

Jim approached Gabrielle with a broad smile. 'Mrs Delany, what can I do for you?'

'Jim, look, I don't want to sound like a moaning old bat...'

'Impossible, Mrs Delany,' chuckled Jim as he gave her some of his special flannel.

Gabrielle smiled demurely. Sweet. But it wasn't going to help him. 'I've got builders' footprints all over my kitchen, Jim. They really should take their shoes off before coming through to the loo. Can you have a word?'

'Mrs Delany, I'm very sorry. I'll send Simon in to clear up the...'

'Oh no, that's not necessary, he's got enough work to do, just let them know it's a very expensive floor.'

'It won't happen again.' Jim turned to rejoin and admonish his workmen when Gabrielle called after him.

'Tea and biscuits all round?'

Jim looked back and smiled, 'That would be great, Mrs Delany. Thanks.'

Gabrielle set about making elevenses and then took it all out on a tray, that was gratefully and somewhat guiltily received. If they'd had them, they would all have probably doffed their caps.

Back inside, she started cleaning her precious tiling, knowing she could have let them put sheets down but frankly, she didn't even want them traipsing through with those heavy builders' boots all day. She also wondered if all their clients got such polite and co-operative behaviour. Gabrielle giggled to herself. *Don't be stupid!*

They no doubt got the dusty cement footprints, though.

Terracotta lovingly restored, Gabrielle called Doug to see how he was getting on. A dull hissing in the background told her he was in the car.

'Gabs, hi,' he said, sounding upbeat.

'On your way back?'

'Yep. Just turned off the M55, should be home about eightish, love. How's it going there?'

'Oh, fine.' She kept the footprints to herself. 'You take care on that M6, Doug.'

'Oh, Gabs! I've driven it loads of times. Know it like the back of my hand. Don't worry.' A welcome warmth rippled through him at the sound of her concerned tones.

'How was the house?' Not that Gabrielle really cared.

'Brilliant, love. You'll like it. Honestly.'

No, I won't, Doug. I never do. Never have. 'That's great. One less thing to worry about, eh?' Because Doug Delany, just before a new show, was a nightmare on legs. 'Better let you get off the phone. I'll see you later.'

'Bye, love. Give the kids a kiss for me.'

After a moment's reflection, Gabrielle found herself calling Valerie. They needed to talk.

The digs Amanda had chosen, subject to meeting the landlady, a female icon for which Blackpool is famed, was in Fleetwood. A small town and still an important fishing port, sitting on the northern edge of the same Lancashire hump that supports Blackpool and Lytham St Annes. Almost the polar opposite to its richer southern sister.

Fleetwood overlooks the massive sweep of coastline that's Morecambe Bay. The sea comes in and goes out on a wave, much like its French counterpart, the Baie du Mont St Michel. There, watching over the inlet on the Normandy coast, sits a huge crag, upon which is an ancient abbey. In Morecambe, the locals know the treachery of the massive fields of sand. Hidden and waiting, along with the odd beached Portuguese man-of-war jelly fish, are savage quick sands and thick sucking mud pits that, once they have you, are merciless. Warnings abound for the reckless but still they wander out away from designated safe areas, 'It won't happen to me', then it does, and no one can hear their screams for help, struggling to free themselves while watching in terror as the incoming tide approaches. Dark and deathly cold. Most times, the dedicated and tireless search and rescue of the coast guard will save the stupid from themselves. In more recent times, a mobile phone has come to the rescue. Other times, there simply isn't enough time.

Amanda looked at Jason with a question in her eyes, then looked up at the small red brick terraced house. Without saying a word, they simultaneously began to hum the theme tune to *Coronation Street*.

'Well, it's not Notting Hill, is it?' he said through a sarcastic grin.

'Or Kilburn, for that matter!' Amanda laughed. 'But hey, it's in the right place, it's at the right price, and beggars can't be choosers!'

'Oh, babe! You poor old cow!' Jason replied with a cheeky stroke of her face. 'Come on then, Stony, better go and meet "the landlady",' he said, holding up his hands and shaking them in mock terror.

Getting out of the car, Amanda frowned. "Stony?' she enquired.

'Broke?'

'Oh...' she replied, feeling like a right div. He was sometimes a bit quick for our Amanda, was Jase.

They were greeted by a short, well-rounded woman, who had a pleasant rosy-cheeked face and a big smile. Wafting from her floral cotton housecoat were mild tones of Pledge.

'Hello there, I'm Amanda Jacobs.'

'Oh, aye,' the woman replied, holding out a hand. The skin looked over-scrubbed and slightly red but was soft and warm as it took Amanda's. 'Mrs Hargreaves but call me May. Come in.'

They stepped into a long narrow hallway, walls heavily decorated in florals and stripes. May, in her housecoat, almost vanished as she stood against them. The carpet was a deep ruby red and a thin runner mat covered most of it from the door to the distant kitchen at the back. The house looked and smelled clean and homely, much like its owner.

'It is only for you though, in't it?' May asked while casting a passing glance over Jason.

'Oh yes, Mrs Hargreaves... May... Jason just drove up with me for the day. He works in the theatre too, but touring. We don't actually see much of each other.'

More's the pity, thought Jason.

'Aye, well, let's take you upstairs to see the room.'

They followed her in silence, looking at the many framed head shots of previous guests. Most signed, 'with love', 'the best breakfasts in town!' 'best wishes', and so on. A wall of questionable fame. Amanda pondered whether she would add herself to the gushing black and whites.

The bedroom was surprisingly spacious and sported a double bed. A quick look between Amanda and Jason was caught by May. She was sharp, had to be, a prerequisite for all successful landladies.

'I don't mind your gentleman friend staying occasionally, but I'll mind you to be discreet about it,' she said with a firm nod of her head.

The statement was motherly but commanding. Amanda felt like a schoolgirl getting a warning from her headmistress. Or her own mother. She smiled inwardly at the comparison. 'Of course, May.'

'How do you like the room, then?' Back to business.

'It's fine. Lovely.'

'Right, well, it's at the back of the house, so it's nice and quiet for you. I know you dancing girls like your sleep! Let me show you the bathroom. I keep it clean, so will expect the same from you.'

Amanda and Jason followed her to the bathroom, quietly sneaking a glance at each other, a suppressed grin on both their faces. The bathroom was indeed clean, and Amanda said she was happy with the arrangement.

'Good,' said May, 'let's go downstairs. I've got tea on.'

The landlady liked this girl. She seemed respectful. They weren't always. Like that other one... what was her name? Oh yes, Sara something. Now, there was another kind of girl. May indicated for them to sit at the kitchen table and produced a huge dull silver catering pot of tea. The sweet doughy scent of toasting tea cakes made Amanda and Jason drool.

'Ninety-five pounds a week? That'll include a good breakfast and sheets changed once a week.' She poured deep caramel tea into ample white cups.

'That's fine. Do you want a deposit?'

'No, that's all right. I trust you. Anyway, I know where to find you in a few weeks' time.' It was said with a sense of jest but Amanda heard the underlying warning.

She couldn't imagine anyone wanting to get on the wrong side of May Hargreaves.

'Now, I'll clear a cupboard for your own bits and pieces of food. George and I always try and keep the kitchen free for our guests after the show. Though it seems to me you girls don't eat. Far too skinny. Where do you get your energy from?' May asked while fetching tea cakes from the grill.

Slightly taken aback, Amanda raised her brow at Jason who shrugged, also at a loss for words. 'Well,' she said, 'comes with the training. I do eat though, and those tea cakes look delicious.'

'You tuck in,' May said, pushing the plate of hot buns and butter towards Amanda. 'You look like you need all of them inside you!'

They drove away, leaving the landlady smiling and waving from her doorstep. Both Jason and Amanda were quiet on the homeward journey, each privately wrestling with the fact they would be seeing little of each other over what would be a very long summer. They should have been used to it by now, but the longer their relationship survived, the more difficult it was becoming to be separated, especially for Jason, though he said nothing, steadfastly hoping they would make it together. So many of these show business couplings didn't.

He now knew he really did love the slightly dim, but gorgeous and talented Amanda Jacobs. Maybe at the end of this season, it would be the right time to tell her. The second anniversary of their first date was in October and Jason wondered if Amanda might then be ready for a certain question. He had much to think about between now and then, not least where he might get some petrol.

His faithful jalopy was running valiantly on fumes.

CHAPTER THIRTEEN

From her vantage point at the end of the bar, what Giancarlo referred to as his 'Summer place' and thought he was just SO funny, she watched as Fiona became ever more frustrated with a new bar assistant. She would probably have preferred to have coped with just trusty Philip on this exceptionally chaotic Saturday lunchtime at Carlo's, but that's not quite how it was for her.

After a few minutes, Fiona stood before Summer, a slightly wild expression on her attractive face. 'Oh, Summer, I'm sorry to keep you waiting...'

'Nonsense, Fi,' replied Summer. The poor girl looked ready to commit hara-kiri. 'You take your time. I'm in no hurry.'

'What'll it be?'

'Tell you what, a tea towel. I'm coming round.'

'That's really kind, but I don't think I'll have a job if "sir" finds you behind here!'

'Leave him to me,' Summer said as she made her way behind the bar.

Fiona walked up to meet her as she approached. She hadn't really been joking when she mentioned the job. Fiona had been working for Giancarlo since he opened the place, helped in part to get it off the ground. He had been generous in his appreciation, but, and it was a huge but, although he had given Fiona a good deal of rope to run with, she was in no doubt he would also happily throttle her with it if he found Summer working the bar.

As she took up station by the glass-washing gizmo, Summer saw the apprehensive look on the bar manager's face. 'Don't worry, Fi. I'll deal with Carlo. Get those two to bring me the empties and let's get this show on the road.'

Beaten, and secretly glad, Fiona gave a shrug of resignation. She hoped it wouldn't turn out to be in the literal sense. Summer got to work. It felt better than being an eye-pleasing bar prop and took her mind off other things. A glass of ice-cold Frascati appeared to her side under the counter. She looked up. Fiona whispered, 'Thanks.'

'Oh, you silly thing, this isn't necessary.'

'No, but I bet you want it!'

'That's a different matter! Thanks, Fi.'

Behind them came a slightly timid voice. 'We're out of Becks.' They both turned to face Imelda, twenty, working to help pay for Uni, and completely useless.

'Well, go and fetch another crate, then,' Fiona said with some degree of impatience. She'd just about had enough.

'I can't really manage a crate,' came a nervous reply.

'So, use your initiative. Go and ask Philip,' Fiona almost spat at the girl. 'Then, perhaps you could "manage" to serve that gentleman at the end of the bar.'

The student gave Fiona an indignant look. *Don't get your knickers in a twist,* she said to herself. *It IS my first day, and nobody said I'd have to lug bloody great crates.* 'Of course I can,' she said as she turned on her heel with a defiant flick of long wavy dark hair, and a nose held ever so slightly in the air.

'Honestly!' sighed Fiona. 'What was he thinking of, employing that one?'

Watching Imelda saunter suggestively to the tall handsome chap at the bar, Summer said simply, 'His dick, probably.'

They both laughed quietly between themselves.

Giancarlo finished a call to his mother and sat back in his chair. He sighed. Picking a piece of fluff from his trouser leg, he rolled it about for a while, then flicked it at the wastepaper basket. The feather lightness of the projectile meant it fell far short, floating down to the Persian rug underneath it.

Every Saturday, without fail, Giancarlo spke with his mother in Sicily. It was a day his father was guaranteed to be elsewhere and they could talk more freely. His father, Paulo, was getting frail now, but, as always, he had refused to give in to age, going out and about, keeping in touch with the business of the day. Now though, it was along the lines of sitting with equally old friends and talking about it. Active involvement had long been passed on. Even so, frail or not, Paulo still ruled the family with a rod of iron, although his wife could turn it on him when necessary.

Giancarlo's mother loved to talk with her eldest son. She just wished and prayed he would come home more often, even stay where he belonged, but she had understood the need for him to leave their beloved island. The poor economic structure of Sicily at the time demanded Paulo find elsewhere to protect the money. Giancarlo was a good boy and had become very successful in England. He looked after them, and Fabia was extremely proud of him. So was his father, though such things were never aired by father to son. A son should know when his father is proud of him.

Fabia would unburden herself to Giancarlo each week, more than she ever dared at confession. She was never truly sure if what she told the monsignors, in the tiny claustrophobic booths, wouldn't reach her husband. Devout to their sacred oaths they may have been, but they were also men. And most men of weak will and timid nature were terrified of Paulo. The holiest would squeal for him, even if it did mean eternal hell and damnation.

Paulo's wife was under no illusions where her husband was concerned. Not now, anyway. It had been a fact of life since she married him. For years, she'd been in denial of the ideas which came to her about the man she loved. Now, her secret thoughts ebbed and flowed with the truths she knew to be so, that had always been. Where blind love and loyalty in the beginning had kept her safe, reality had slowly eaten its way out from her subconscious to open her eyes very wide indeed. Her love for Paulo had changed in many ways over the years, but it had never died.

When they were in the later stages of their courtship, Fabia had overheard a desperate conversation between her parents. They were panic-stricken at the prospect of their little girl marrying into the Scarlatti family. What it would mean for her. What it might mean for them. She had kept it to herself and went ahead with the marriage. She still recalled it as one of the most beautiful days of her life. Her happiness knew no bounds. But now she often wondered if her parents had succumbed under delicate but sophisticated pressure and spent the rest of their lives praying for forgiveness.

The same way in which Fabia had, since Giancarlo's birth.

In a moment of clarity during his arrival, when the stark focus of labour tore away all her defence shrouds, and only a brutal verity prevailed, both physical and mental, did the dreadful truth of her husband's life hold court in her mind. At the moment of her final desperate, torturous push, expelling her son from the sanctuary of her womb, his destiny was branded onto her soul, a lasting reminder of what she had done in bringing the innocent child into her world. Paulo's world.

Giancarlo looked at the telephone on his desk and reached out to gently touch it, as if it were his mother.

'Mama,' he said softly.

How she had coped through the years, he didn't know. His father had been, and still was, a reserved and complex man, at times a tyrant, even to his family. Giancarlo could still feel the vicious bite of his father's belt like it were a moment ago. But his mother had kept her good grace and Giancarlo admired her for that. She alone seemed to have the measure of his father and Giancarlo hoped one day he might understand the enigma that was Paulo Scarlatti. For now, he worried about his mother. There had been a tiredness in her voice, something spiritual, like an old fatigued soul. One that needed to live a few years with the freedom to be who it really was. In tune with itself. The true self.

His respect for Fabia was total. For Paulo, it had been destined. By birth, the first son would respect the father, no need for Paulo to earn such reverence from his child. Or for Giancarlo to deliberate whether the man deserved it. Somewhere deep within him, Giancarlo knew respect was natural for his father. They were connected. One came from the other. They were each other.

There was one thing about his father's life Giancarlo couldn't seem to achieve. A good woman, like his mother. Yes, he had 'a woman', but was she worthy of his name? The family name. Could Summer Isadora carry the mantle as Fabia Luisa's apprentice with the same dignity and refinement, despite her chequered past?

Until The Maggot had been eliminated, Giancarlo had doubted Summer, even begun to dismiss the possibility. But now, since he had freed her to be solely his once more, she had shown great loyalty. There was a new softness about her when they were together, a pliability he could work with. But could any woman, even the improved Summer, reach the exalted place in him now occupied by his mother? Maybe.

In matters of the heart, use your head. His father's words drifted out from a distant past. *Like I did with your mother. A more beautiful girl I had never seen. She was perfection. The angels had surpassed themselves. She was from a good family with hardworking, honest parents. Easy people. No questions. That their daughter was the sweetest of fruit was a bonus for your papa. The head, my son, always use the head. Your heart will lead you into trouble. Leave trouble to business.*

The words faded and Giancarlo was left with images of his father tapping a finger to his temple to emphasise his point, as they sat in his grandfather's old fishing boat. It rocked gently on the impossibly blue waters that caressed the shores of Taormina. In more recent years, the world's greatest free-divers gathered there to compete for supremacy, diving deeper each year on a single measured gulp of air. It was also a place Paulo Scarlatti often took himself. A little fishing always helped to elucidate his thoughts. Many a 'business' decision was made in that small hand-built vessel. Later, it was a place of fatherly counselling with his eldest son.

Giancarlo glanced at his watch. Time to collect Summer from the bar and go to lunch with his cousin and his wife, Donatella. It was a gamble at this stage in their relationship, but Giancarlo felt he must test this change in Summer. Perhaps it was also time for him to chance another level of trust with her.

The head, my son, the head.

He entered the welcome hubbub of his thriving wine bar to find Summer washing coffee cups and wine glasses. And worse, taking an unladylike swig of wine. In front of all the customers! What was she thinking?

'Summer.' His voice was brusque and icy.

She waited a while. A dramatic licence learned at drama school during some tutorials in television and film acting. Quite different to the technique required for theatre. Finally, she turned her head and looked at Giancarlo, meeting his furious expression with one of playful confrontation.

'What... are you doing?' he asked as Summer turned back to the sink.

'Hazard a guess, Carlo,' she responded, knowing it would provoke, ready for his reaction. Something stirred inside her. This was familiar territory, a place she was comfortable with, had much experience of. There would be no contest.

She could feel the intensity of Giancarlo's outrage wafting across from where he stood, rooted to the spot. Her disobedience fanned his fury and Summer could feel him smouldering.

Giancarlo finally walked over to her, suddenly remembering where he was and smiling at various regulars standing at the bar. A few pleasantries were exchanged. He firmly took the tea towel she held and dropped it beside the sink. She held her breath and waited. God, he was pissed. A tingle she recognised rippled through her, a reaction usually confined to bouts with her father. But this time, it had a special and more inviting quality. A wave of arousal surged across her pelvis as his arms encircled her waist, hands stopping to rest on her tummy. Another pulse of sexual anticipation sent shivers up her spine. Giancarlo pulled her to him, his mouth finding her ear and she shuddered as he breathed, 'You dare to embarrass me in front of my staff and customers?' It was low and feral.

'I was just helping Fi...'

'Shush, don't talk, just smile and follow me.'

He broke off the embrace and walked back to the door to his offices. He stepped through without looking back and Summer followed, smiling as sweetly as she could. Perhaps she had gone too far. Daddy never sounded like that.

As she walked through the door, she said quickly, 'Carlo, I'm sorry, I...'

The apology was cut short by Giancarlo closing the door and kissing her roughly. She couldn't help but respond. Then he took her hand and pressed it against a solid erection. Summer automatically started to caress him while closing her hips to his.

'Here... now,' he commanded into her mouth, his voice strangled almost to a whimper by urgent desire.

'No,' Summer replied in a cool, matter-of-fact manner as she pulled away. 'After lunch, maybe. We'll be late.'

She opened the door and walked out into the bar again, as though just finished with a business meeting. Leaving Giancarlo to watch in silence and with a need to compose himself. Calm his straining cock.

A wicked smile crept across his lips.

She was magnificent.

Valerie's face was a picture when Gabrielle opened the door. A wry smile greeted her friend who looked relieved to see Valerie standing there, and yet, wearing a mild frown of worry. Gabrielle grinned like a silly child. She did feel a bit daft, but all the same...

'Thanks for coming over, Val.'

'Well, I couldn't possibly keep you... what was it you

said?... dangling?' Valerie teased as she placed a kiss on Gabrielle's cheek.

'I just need to go over those cards again. You know the ones,' said Gabrielle, leading Valerie through to the kitchen.

'I'm no expert, Gabby, by any means. And quite frankly, I really don't think you should take it too seriously!' But Valerie recalled with a chill the unexplained atmosphere during the reading. Even when Gabrielle had left, it seemed to pervade her home for several hours afterwards. Or maybe it was just Valerie being stupid and getting carried away with the occasion. When Gabrielle had called her that afternoon, the thought had occurred that perhaps talking about it again with her friend might dispel her own feelings of unease.

'Please excuse the excavation site outside the windows.'

'Oh! How's it coming along? I bet you can't wait.' Valerie took a quick peek out the back and saw a variety of bare chests and muscular backs. 'Oh, the excavation site looks fine to me!' she smiled.

'Val! You're terrible! Gary's still in bloody good form.' Gabrielle was mildly jealous of her friend's still very athletic husband. Passing thoughts of Doug skimmed unsatisfactorily across her mind. 'You don't need to ogle.'

'Yeah, but it's the same old Gaz, isn't it? Every day. A girl's got to have some spice in her life! Did you insist they strip to the waist, darling?' Valerie laughed, taking another look.

'Oh please! They're a decent bunch of lads. Stop it!' Gabrielle replied. 'Come away from the window, you're making a spectacle of yourself, woman! Tea or coffee?'

'Coffee. Strong. Had a bastard morning trying to track down a package my mum has sent for Joe's birthday. She sent it two weeks ago and no sign as yet. Probably never see it again. Anyway, let's get down to business.' Valerie produced her well-thumbed little book from a rather oversized handbag, just as Gabrielle exclaimed, 'I don't fucking believe it!'

'Whatever's wrong?' Valerie asked, a little taken aback by her friend's sudden expletive, then she looked over to where Gabrielle stood and followed her gaze to the floor. 'Ah...' she said with understanding.

'*Ah*, is right. Excuse me a moment, Val.'

Gabrielle trounced out through the utility room, swearing like a fish wife under her breath.

No more 'impossible to be a moaning old bat'. No more nice Mrs Doug Delany. This time, boys, you're gonna get Gabrielle Weston in full fucking flight.

'You were wonderful.'

'Thanks, Carlo. I just tried to be myself.'

'My cousin adores you.'

Summer smiled coyly. She'd noted the straying eyes, mostly to her chest when Donatella was otherwise occupied. She sighed inwardly.

'Even Donatella warmed to you... eventually!' laughed Giancarlo, casting an affectionate smile in Summer's direction. They both giggled.

'She is a fabulous cook, though. But then, I suppose all Italian wives are.'

'Why do you think Angelo looks the way he does? He eats at home, then eats at the restaurant. He's always eating!'

'Sometimes I wish I could eat all the time. Just stuff my face whenever I wanted to. Wouldn't that be great?' Summer said, smiling like an excited child at the prospect.

'Maybe, when you give up dancing and become a wife and mother, then you can cook, eat, cook some more...'

'Oh, sure! I can really see myself doing that, Carlo,' Summer chuckled at ridiculous images of herself with a large brood and slaving over a hot stove. 'That's about as likely as you driving a Skoda!'

Giancarlo smiled and raised his brow in agreement. She was right. He'd rather walk. Her other words troubled him slightly.

Summer leaned back into the seat and closed her eyes. She was tired. Meeting 'family' and having to be effervescent was not what her psyche needed just then. She still hadn't got over George's death. It hung over her like a bucket of ice water, ready to tip at any moment. Summer couldn't be sure there wouldn't be any sudden revelations. Did anyone else know? Might their sordid little 'business' tryst be exposed at some point in the future? Likely when she became well known, which Summer had no doubts about, nor did Cynthia. It would make excellent copy for some tabloid needing to boost its sales figures. But she'd known that at the time, hadn't she? It was always a considered risk. Wasn't it? Summer felt as though a few tiny droplets of that freezing water had just dripped menacingly from the teetering bucket.

'I have a little surprise for you, Bella.' Giancarlo's words rid Summer of her unpleasant thoughts in an instant. She opened her eyes.

'Surprise?'

'Mmm. We leave tomorrow.'

Summer sat up straight, straining against the seat-belt. 'Leave tomorrow? What's going on, Carlo?' Her tone was bordering on extremely unamused.

'But it's a surprise. You'll love it, I promise.' Giancarlo briefly touched her thigh, patting it gently in reassurance.

A darkness had descended over Summer's face now. 'Well, I can't GO anywhere, Carlo,' she said rather stuffily. 'I have meetings next week with Cynthia and it's our first rehearsal. Sorry. But you really should have asked.' She slumped back into the seat, eyes closed again. Waiting. She felt the car slowing, turning gently, and eventually stopping and she sensed Giancarlo shifting in his seat to face her. Summer opened her eyes and turned her head to look into an unimpressed expression.

'Why do you treat me like this?' he snapped, his cultured Sicilian accent strong. It always happened when he was angry. 'Why do you speak to me like that? It's not necessary.'

'Sorry,' Summer retorted haughtily, a slight tilt of her head, mouth turned down. But she didn't look at him.

'I have made arrangements for tomorrow and you WILL be coming.'

'Carlo, as I said, I have a meeting...' she continued nonchalantly.

'With your agent and a rehearsal,' he finished for her. 'I know this.' Stupid girl. He knew everything. Didn't she get it? 'This won't interfere with your precious career.' The words came out heavily coated in dark sarcasm.

Summer shot up in her seat again, pointed a finger at Giancarlo and spat, 'DON'T deride my career, Carlo. Just DON'T. You took me on knowing what I did...' *Well, not everything, perhaps.* 'Don't pretend you didn't like the fact you were dating a showgirl, as you so delightfully referred to me once.' And never again. 'So don't sit there and...'

'Okay. Okay. I'm sorry. I shouldn't have said that. But please... come with me tomorrow. I promise you will be back by Monday evening. Plenty of time for the rest of your week.' Giancarlo reached across to stroke her face with a feather caress of his knuckles. The same faint nuzzling he had bestowed on someone else once. Before sharply thrusting thin cold steel up under their ribs and piercing their heart.

Summer felt the frigid hardness of the solid gold and black opal ring he wore on his little finger. Its touch sent a shiver through her. He gently traced a southerly course down over her jaw line and towards her breast. Summer stopped his hand with a soft touch of her own. She turned to look at him. 'Okay. I'll come. Just this time! DON'T make arrangements for me again without asking!'

Giancarlo held up his hands in mock surrender. It was the only surrender he ever allowed. In this case, it got him what he wanted. Which had always been the plan. He admired her fight, though. The fire in her angry eyes and twist of that beautiful mouth as she ranted. It reminded him of someone.

Giancarlo took in a deep breath of satisfaction. He would plan Summer's life with careful precision. Eventually, she would WANT the future he made for her. She had said that she loved him. He must believe that, believe he had finally found a wife. That one day, soon, she would be his forever.

Then he smiled to himself.

Maybe it was time to find out if Summer could cook.

CHAPTER FOURTEEN

The restaurant door swung open as they approached. Stepping into the ornate galleried entrance, Gabrielle and Valerie were startled to find the man himself holding the door, giving his usual smile as he closed it behind them.

'I was passing and saw you arriving. What a lovely surprise!' he beamed at Gabrielle.

'We haven't booked, Angelo. Last minute decision.'

'A good decision,' he responded softly. 'And for you and your delightful companion,' Valerie flushed at his flattery, 'there will always be a table. Come, I have the perfect one.'

Gabrielle shot a glance at Valerie as he walked ahead of them, down the rather spectacular staircase for which the establishment was famed, to the main floor of the restaurant. Valerie raised a meaningful eyebrow and whispered, 'I just KNOW he has a thing for you!'

Gabrielle raised her own curious brow and breathed back, 'In the cards, was it, ducky?'

Both giggled silently as they were seated, with oversized napkins placed 'just so' on their laps by a young, but very efficient waiter. No sloppiness in this place. Everything was impeccable, down to the fresh orchid on each table, on this occasion, Gabrielle's favourite, a slipper orchid. So delicate with its shoe-like bloom. Doug used to regularly bring one home for her in years gone by. She smiled at the irony, taking a menu from the waiter. Now her husband could afford a field of them, Gabrielle couldn't remember the last time he had presented her with ANY flowers. Okay, so she got a bracelet. Yes, it was lovely. The stupid thing was, Gabrielle would have preferred the natural simplicity of another slipper orchid.

'May I offer you ladies an aperitif?' the waiter enquired in a heavy Italian accent. Obviously newly arrived. Angelo seemed to have an endless supply.

'Just ask Mr Maldini to prepare our usual. Thank you.'

'Of course, right away,' he replied with a gracious bow and left them alone.

Gabrielle had soundly admonished Jim and his 'bunch of useless items', as she had succinctly called them to their downcast, shifty faces. After a begging call to Doris for a spot of impromptu baby-sitting, she decided to eat out. Get away from the house, and the mud pit that was her once pristine garden. The choice? What else! An afternoon of complete pampering and irresistibly delicious food was exactly what the doctor ordered. Especially as apart from the builders, Gabrielle had Doug to contend with that evening, full of Blackpool. She would lend an ear, make the right wifely noises for as long as she could stand it, then an early night and Xanax.

Gabrielle sipped her margarita, relishing the feel of the grainy salt from the rim of the glass as it blended magically with the tequila. It soothed frayed nerves and appeased her mind. Then Valerie's quip on the stairs seemed to barge its way through and Gabrielle began to seriously contemplate the possibility. An admirer.

She was quite sure that Angelo Maldini was not her type. But then, nor had Doug been, and look at her now. Maybe in those heady days in Bournemouth, even a good while afterwards, but not longer. Yet, conversely - or was that perversely? - she still felt the occasional pang of concern for his welfare. Such as his driving home. Was it an indication of a love still intact, albeit scarred? Or just a selfish worry about what her life, and that of the children, would be like if he were to suddenly be gone? The media and his public would descend into one of their mad frenzies, Gabrielle and the kids at the centre of it all.

Valerie watched her friend gazing into the cocktail glass held delicately in both hands. Gabrielle had been a lot like this lately but her reaction to the reading was a surprise. She was normally so level. That nasty feeling started to creep over Valerie again.

'So! What'll it be today?' she said rather more loudly than

she'd meant to. Several people turned to look at her. At least the feeling had gone away again. 'I'm going to have something completely different.'

Setting her glass down and looking at the menu again, Gabrielle nodded. 'I agree. Let's be bold!'

She used to be bold. In fact, Gabrielle Weston had been in fine form earlier. It was good to know she was still around, that stubborn child with the same fire in her bones. The workmen had positively cowered. Perhaps she should bring Miss Weston out to deal with her errant husband from time to time. That would be a show.

Gabrielle tended to bottle things up now, stash them away deep inside, until her vessel was full to the brim. Like her mother, Rose, who could bottle up tension for ages, then, and usually without warning, though maybe, if you were lucky, you would catch the preliminary cold stare, all hell would break loose. Gabrielle and her siblings had scattered in different directions on many occasions. All now much older and sadly, quite apart, with differing experiences of life behind them and still ahead. None more so than Gabrielle, who suddenly felt terribly old and resentful.

Age and experience, she mused, remembering a particularly spiteful scene from Noel Coward's *Private Lives.* One set between the young and silly Sybil and the sophisticated bitch Amanda, who is rendered almost speechless by the sudden vitriol from her previously mouse-like rival.

'Age and experience,' Gabrielle said aloud to herself.

'Pardon?' Valerie replied.

'Age and experience,' Gabrielle repeated. 'The baked aubergines sound heavenly.'

'What about age and experience?' Valerie insisted.

'It has its benefits,' Gabrielle said simply.

'Could do without the wrinkles and submission to gravity, darling!' Valerie chortled.

'Speak for yourself,' Gabrielle retorted with a wicked smile in her eyes.

Valerie's own eyes widened in mock anger and they both collapsed into laughter. Heads once again turned to watch them.

'Ladies!' A booming voice cut through the restaurant, heads returned to their own groups again. Angelo stood close to Gabrielle and casually put a hand on her shoulder, duly noted by Valerie. *Thought so...*

'Before you make a decision, I have the most wonderful special for today. Fresh succulent sea bass, gently cooked with garlic, olive oil and peppers, served with...'

'Oh, stop there... I'll have it, Angelo. Perfect,' Gabrielle beamed.

Angelo patted her shoulder, but the hand remained resting there as he spoke to Valerie. Her face was a picture of discreet ignorance. Beneath the carefully posed expression was a woman straining at the bit to say, 'I told you so'.

'And for the lovely Valerie?' the scoundrel asked her.

'Oh, baked aubergines for me, thank you,' she replied smiling sweetly.

Angelo nodded and left the two women alone. Valerie drained her aperitif.

'Well, darling,' she whispered. 'He's finally moved onto covert physical contact!'

Gabrielle frowned. 'What ARE you talking about?' She truly had no idea.

'Oh, Gabby, honestly! His hand was on your shoulder for ages. You MUST know he likes you.'

Gabrielle had been so engrossed in her private little world of happy days at home with her mum, despite her foul temper, that she genuinely hadn't realised. She shrugged. 'Well, there we are, then,' she responded dismissively. But her thoughts had now been prompted into running with unsettling ideas.

Mr Maldini was certainly a master of charm. The best restaurateurs always were. They had to be. And she had once fallen for such a maestro within another profession. It was a mistake Gabrielle would prefer remained in the singular. However, she knew Valerie was probably right. A woman can spot a man's attraction to a rival, a mile off. She'd done it herself, many times. Funny then, when you were admirer's subject, that perception seemed to go awol.

Angelo returned to the table and fussed about the settings, unusual for him. Valerie watched in droll fascination, while Gabrielle became aware she didn't want to meet his eyes, instead fiddling with her napkin, picking at non-existent specks. Angelo noticed her awkward demeanour and it pleased him. Greatly. A wry inward smile warmed him.

She was cracking, slowly but surely, and he was certain that very soon, he would have a long-awaited pleasure of tasting what he believed would be considerable delights.

Jayne Nash perused details of an idea for a new programme she had been invited to help produce. It was a deviation from her normal theme of children's television. Or maybe not, judging by the way in which MPs behaved in the Commons from time to time. Perhaps there was another meaning to political 'party' in Parliament that was lost on the rest of us. The prospect of working on a documentary about the life of a minor MP at a forthcoming party conference, code for 'big rave up' judging by what a friend had witnessed during one such gathering in a Brighton hotel, gave Jayne a real buzz. It would certainly be a hectic schedule. All-consuming, but best of all, it would take her away from her current situation with Adam.

Her work sometimes was indeed a welcome release from her marriage these days. It seemed there was yet another 'episode' brewing and Jayne didn't know if she could take much more. Sadly, and just mildly irritating, her father was probably right. And had been all along. The reluctant acceptance of this sat like a grumpy old man in her mind, mumbling hurtful things to her through his miserable scrunched-up face. Then she smiled at the image. Perhaps she should make a puppet of the old codger, her rival to Adam's alter egos.

Jayne knew Adam loved her, that was what made everything so stupid and tragic. He was a man able to share himself about and yet still feel deeply and honestly for one woman. Was it really all going to start again? Would Blackpool end up yet another place Jayne would remember with that sick nausea? Jayne already knew the answer. It was an unavoidable reality set deep in her bones.

She tried to concentrate on the papers strewn over the bed. Adam had stolen enough of her mental capacity, but she couldn't seem to release herself from her thought process. She put her hands to her face and massaged it in slow, outward circular movements, stopping with them held at her temples, face stretched. Jayne looked across the bedroom to a full length antique dressing mirror, a wedding present from her grandmother. She saw her distorted features and wondered if this mildly grotesque effigy was a true physical representation of what she felt inside.

She heard Adam coming out of the bathroom and dropped her hands, picking up some papers and pretending to read them. He walked across the bedroom naked, still rubbing his thinning fair hair with a towel. He had retained a decent physique, looking after it with a moderate diet and copious squash at the club. Jayne couldn't shift the horrible thought that it wasn't only for her.

Before his first fling, she would have believed so. Even after the event, after many tears while pleading for forgiveness on bended knees, arms wrapped around her legs, a desperate face looking up into her own red and watery eyes. Jayne had relented when Adam promised on his mother's life, it would never happen again. Luckily, the poor woman was still alive and well, totally unaware of her dubious sentence.

The second time, Jayne had waited for the next recipient of false oath from her husband, but this time, he spared the unsuspecting soul. This time, Adam was reticent in his guilt, playing an excellent 'quietly ashamed'. She also got a huge diamond ring out of it. A pay off. Charming. And so, in her weakened state, Jayne forgave the mangy bastard once more. Her stupid sick love for him demanded it, whilst Daddy had one foot on Qantas, ready to come over and show what a 'real bloke' does to conniving little cheats like Adam. Somehow, Jayne had managed to prevent a certain blood bath and since then, her husband seemed to have reformed himself. Until the call came. That fucking call from his agent with the contract to work with Doug Delany.

Now all the little signs were back. The excitement that came with such a break. Letting himself get caught up in some manic purpose, which usually escalated into Adam becoming that other person who lived inside the one Jayne was married to. The other man was weak-willed, paranoid about his act, changing the script several times, chanting it like a mantra at all times of day and night. Fussing with his 'boys', fiddling with his own appearance. All a precursor to Jayne's nightmare. The inevitable affair.

But he was no different to many of his peers. There was a childlike quality about them all. In the theatre they were strong, all-powerful beings. Real life, with its responsibilities and restrictions, was the problem because for them, 'real life' WAS the theatre. It took a strong-willed husband to avoid the obvious temptations while away from home for several months, especially if the wife had her own vital life to lead. Temptations in the form of very pretty, very willing, young girls. To Jayne, now several painful years down the line, it seemed they were all part of the package called Summer Season.

The previous evening, they had managed to discuss Adam's altercation with Trevor. As usual, Jayne had mediated but this time, her heart wasn't in it. She was tired of it all. Was there any point? Maybe she should go to her dad's party and leave Adam to it, whatever 'it' turned out to be. Normally a petite blond if his track record was anything to go by. And whether Jayne was here or in Perth, if Adam was intent on dipping his adulterous wick again, it wouldn't make a blind bit of difference where his wife was in the world. At least she wouldn't be there to receive the anonymous phone calls.

Brief, one-sided conversations that came late into the night as she slept alone. It was how Jayne had found out about each of Adam's infidelities. Not that she had believed a single word from the first sinister whisperings, but that misplaced loyalty was soon cast mercilessly out into a wilderness where only mistrust and jealousy thrived.

She watched Adam putting on a pair of his preferred underpants, briefs as opposed to boxers, standing in front of Granny's mirror adjusting his tackle into them. Always dressing to the left. *If only you could see, Gran!* Jayne giggled to herself, imagining a rather shocked face. As he continued to admire himself, Jayne considered that Adam didn't have spectacular 'equipment' but he knew what do with it. And not just with her.

An unwanted lightning flash of Emma Smith's piggy little face flashed across her mind. She was a very attractive pig, though. The original little tramp. The first, and therefore imprinted on Jayne's thoughts forever. Emma faded out and a more pleasing image of frying bacon came to mind.

Adam was dressed now, blow-drying his hair and obsessively styling the wispy strands with a brush. Jayne quietly observed him and smiled to himself, she did still love the stupid vain fool. After everything. So who was more the fool? The fool, or the fool that follows him?

'You know,' Adam suddenly said, looking at Jayne through the mirror. 'I've been thinking of having one of those implant jobs. The one where they take plugs...'

'Plugs of exactly what, Adam?'

He turned to face his wife, her incredulous expression burning a track to where he stood, poised with brush and dryer. 'Plugs of skin and hair from the back of the head.'

'Skin, yes,' she replied, hardly managing to suppress her mirth. 'But hair? What hair, Adam? Bum fluff, more like! Oh, Adam, do stop. You'd look hideous! People wouldn't know which one was the ventriloquist or the puppet!'

'They're my boys, Jayne. You know I don't like you calling them puppets,' Adam retorted indignantly and turned back to the mirror.

Jayne stopped laughing. On occasion she had deliberately referred to his boys as puppets, but strangely not this time. It was an honest slip. *Australia, or stay home and be a good little wife and make a documentary?* She pondered. *Sunshine, surfing and beer, or traipsing after some boring old political fart?*

'Do you think you will go to Perth, Jaynie?' Adam suddenly asked, as though reading her mind.

'What if I did?' she responded cautiously, eyes firmly on a sheet of A4.

Adam shrugged, 'I won't stop you.'

'But what?' asked Jayne, sensing a 'but' in Adam's tone.

'You know what I'm saying,' he said.

And she did know.

'I might not, then,' Jayne replied.

Adam walked over to her, bent down and kissed her gently on the lips. 'I do love you, Jaynie. You know that, don't you?' Then he turned before she could answer and left the room.

She decided not to go to Perth. Sod it. Jayne knew another affair would destroy them, even if she was on the other side of the world. Jayne suspected those night-time voices would somehow seek her out and still send their vile messages in the dark. She may as well take the calls at home. So Jayne would stay put and make the documentary. It would almost be a perverse light relief from what might lay ahead. She would spend as much quality time with Adam as she could before he went to Blackpool.

It was just possible, they might be the last good times Jayne and Adam Nash would ever share together.

CHAPTER FIFTEEN

Angelo hadn't been lying. Not that Gabrielle suspected for a moment that he would. The sea bass was sublime, while Valerie enthused about the aubergines and how she simply HAD to have the recipe.

Then he brought their coffees to the table and promptly sat down with them. There was a second or two of slightly stunned silence between Gabrielle and Valerie, then Angelo sighed. His brow had a fresh glow of perspiration as he seemed to confine his gaze to Gabrielle. The two women exchanged amused looks. Oblivious, Angelo spoke. 'I have a few moments and thought I should take the time to be with you lovely ladies.'

'Honoured... I'm sure!' Valerie said with playful sarcasm.

'The sea bass was truly delicious, Angelo. I think you surpassed even your previous best efforts,' Gabrielle said with a genuine smile.

'My pleasure,' he graciously responded. Then, after a brief pause, 'How is Mr Delany? I haven't seen him here for a while.'

'Oh, Doug...' *God, I just can't get away from him, can I?* 'He's got a big summer production coming up,' Gabrielle said with mild uninterest, hoping her tone would stop this line of conversation. *Just ONE afternoon without him cropping up... please!*

'The West End?' Angelo asked quickly, perhaps a little too quickly. Suddenly his little plans for Mrs Delany might have to be altered.

'No, Blackpool. For several months, in fact. He leaves quite soon to start rehearsals up there.'

Angelo could feel his collar getting tight. 'And you will be going with him, then?'

'Oh no!' Gabrielle's small accompanying laugh was double-edged. *Wives not allowed, Angelo. Not this wife, anyway.* Then she thought again. Actually, she was the one who insisted on staying away. Well... for the last few years, anyway. 'The children have their school. He comes home from time to time throughout the run, to see the children.'

'And to see his beautiful wife,' Angelo beamed, discreetly wiping his brow with a white handkerchief. Valerie's brow shot up and she had to work hard at keeping the giggles from exploding across the table. She kept her eyes on her coffee, added a rough cane sugar cube and stirred for England.

'I suppose...'. Angelo sensed her disquiet. Excellent. Her husband was obviously playing right into his hands. The same hands that hopefully soon would be exploring the careless man's wife.

Angelo Maldini knew a neglected married woman when he saw one. They carried a particular scent. Sexual need. Until now, he had enjoyed flirting, at times outrageously, with such women. His love for his own wife never diminished, and his deep belief in their marriage kept a rein on his fantasies from becoming reality. But Gabrielle Delany was different to the rest. She was so ripe for the picking, he couldn't resist the succulent harvest and luxuriating in her hidden flavours.

'You must get lonely when your husband is away.'

Valerie sipped her coffee, eyes roaming anywhere except to Angelo and Gabrielle.

'Oh, I'm used to it, Angelo. After so many years of his touring, a show business wife finds a life of her own when their husbands are away. It makes for a better marriage in some respects.' She sounded so sincere, so loyal and understanding. Perhaps she should have become a professional actress, as was her original game plan before the black hole of Doug's life sucked her in.

'That's why she's got me!' Valerie finally found a voice again. She couldn't stay out of this for any longer. Gabrielle looked at her friend and smiled affectionately, reaching across the table to touch Valerie's hand.

'Val's a wonderful friend, Angelo.'

'This I can see,' he replied, looking at the woman with a kind expression. She might prove an obstacle on his course towards the lovely Gabrielle. If Valerie presented a problem, he would find ways to deal with her. Discretion was everything in such matters, and this woman didn't seem like she would be very proficient in the art of it.

'So, what do you do, Valerie?' he asked her, leaning forward on the table, face full of interest. Of course, any information would be beneficial to his 'project'. He may only be Giancarlo's cousin and Paulo's nephew, but he too had learned much from the don.

'Oh, you know,' Valerie responded demurely, suddenly finding herself rather shy under the restaurateur's attention. 'Just a housewife, mother, chief cook and bottle washer!' She laughed, then felt very small and inadequate compared to Gabrielle. Although she too was all of those things, being married to Doug Delany made Gabrielle THE BEST of all those things.

'My dear lady,' Angelo said gently. 'There is nothing wrong with making a home for your family. Having children is the most important job of all...'

Tell that to Doug... thought Gabrielle.

'Without our children, what future would there be?' Angelo continued to ooze across the table to Valerie, who was now completely under his spell. Were those eye lashes fluttering just a little teensy-weensy bit? Gabrielle stifled a knowing smile. The guy was good. She was impressed. It wasn't easy to get Valerie so worked up. Took a man with know-how. Angelo knew how.

'Well, it wasn't exactly how I had set out in life, actually,' Valerie said, leaving her meaning suspended, hoping he might ask...

This might be just what he needed, Angelo mused, then said, 'No? So what was it you had meant to do?' Play along, she obviously wanted to tell him. He glanced at Gabrielle, sending her a fleeting smile, and something else... she couldn't quite decide what. Valerie drew in a deep breath, getting ready to blow her own trumpet for once.

'I used to be with the British synchronised swimming team,' she said with an air of pride. 'I would have tried for the Olympics, but, well... I met my husband and he was a successful high diver. I'm afraid there was only room for one competitor in the family.' As Valerie spoke, she knew there had been plenty of scope for them both to continue in their sport. What she should have said was, there had been only room for one enormous ego. Her husband's. Like a fool, she had acquiesced. 'What could I do?' She finished with a smile and shrug, covering a deep-rooted disappointment in herself.

Angelo caught a whiff of lost dreams and said, 'But you must have been very good to be in the British team.'

'I was,' she replied, sitting slightly taller in her chair.

'Oh, do tell him your funny story, Val,' Gabrielle said.

'Funny story?... Oh, yes, I know. Oh, Angelo doesn't want to hear about some silly teenagers...'

'I would love to hear about them,' Angelo said. 'What about these silly teenagers?' he asked encouragingly, a hint of the mischievous in his eyes and voice.

'Well,' Valerie began. 'I was part of a swimming troupe called The Mermaids. It was considered more a water ballet in those days. There were about twenty of us, all in our late teens, all being coached by a retired policeman of all people! Anyway,' she took a sip of water, 'on this occasion, we were performing a version of *The Pirates of Penzance* at a holiday camp... all the best venues! And it was absolutely freezing.' She looked at Gabrielle who was already in fits of silent giggles. 'The water in the pool was just as cold. My nose was so frozen that the clip we usually wore kept falling off. I don't know how I didn't drown. So, then, as we were doing our standard line dive into the pool...' Valerie saw a brief frown from Angelo. 'That's when we stood in a line next to the pool and one by one dived in sideways?' He seemed to understand. 'Well, we held our fins for diving in and were supposed to put them on once in the water, but I dropped one of mine. So there I was, with one fin and the routine had started. I pretty much went round in a circle for most of it!' Gabrielle was laughing out loud now, she always found the image hysterical. 'It wasn't funny at the time, I can tell you,' Valerie said pointedly at her friend with a wry smile. 'Anyway, none of the campers noticed and we got a very good reception afterwards. That's about it.'

'What a wonderful story,' Angelo chuckled, seemingly genuine. 'But now, I must leave you both,' he said in more business-like tones, looking straight at Gabrielle.

There it was again. That look. Something...

'It has been a pleasure sitting with you, ladies. And, Gabriella, when your husband is away and perhaps you are in town for shopping, please, don't be worried if you are alone, come in for coffee. Any time.'

'I will, thank you,' Gabrielle said. 'Maybe when I'm without the children.'

'Are they good children?' Angelo grinned. 'But of course they are!' he gushed.

'Sometimes!'

'Then come WITH the children for coffee. They can have ice-cream.'

'You are very kind, Mr Maldini...'

'Oh, *Angelo*. Never *Mr Maldini*, Gabriella.'

He smiled at them both before taking his leave.

Good. The seed was firmly planted. He trusted it would take root, become strong and grow well inside her mind. Then Gabrielle Delany would soon be his.

'I'm home,' called Doug as he kicked off his shoes in the utility room. Gabs was just a tad obsessive compulsive about her terracotta kitchen floor tiles. He'd already taken an ear-bashing when he recently forgot to take off wet loafers after coming in from the rain.

Something smelled gorgeous and he lifted the lid of a large earthenware pot on the range. Gabrielle's famous egg curry. It was celebrated among his friends. 'Mmm... wonderful,' he said to an empty kitchen. 'Where is everybody?' He often talked out loud to himself. An affliction common among his kind. Never switched off. Always looking for an angle or subject to add to his numerous scripts. Mostly, though, Doug just liked the sound of his own voice. In a way, it was a comfort. Especially when he was alone on tour.

He walked through to the connecting family room and found Alex and Sasha watching television. The little he did know about his son, poor Sash was probably having to endure yet another sci-fi programme. Alex was addicted to them. Doug had tried to watch an episode with him once, but frankly, didn't understand it, the costumes and make-up were ridiculous and the acting was... well... crap. Still, at least he'd tried, eh?

Sasha caught sight of her daddy and ran over to greet him in her usual excited way. Alex just smiled, lifted a hand and remained at one with the television. Doug set Sasha back down and sent her to sit with her brother while he went in search of his wife. He met her on the landing, on her way down.

'Shush,' she said with a finger to her lips, then whispered, 'just got Bee down. She's been a little bugger this evening.'

Phoebe had indeed been difficult for Gabrielle. Given her mother two hours of hell trying to get her bathed and into bed. More than likely because Gabrielle had broken their routine that day by going to lunch with Valerie. Her youngest was letting her know she wasn't amused. Big time. The terrible twos seemed to have merged with the threes. Roll on five when she would have several hours at school to wear her out. *Yeah, some hope!* Gabrielle thought and at that moment, decided to book an extra massage for the following day. Her neck and shoulder muscles were already in spasm with spiteful knots of tension, and now she had Doug to contend with. Oh, happy day.

'Is she all right?' Doug asked, also in whisper.

'Bee's fine, it's the mother who's run ragged. Come on, I'll open some wine and get dinner on.'

'Okay. I'll just go up and have a quick shower, love. Then I'll be down for some of that fabulous curry.'

As Gabrielle passed him on the stairs, Doug grabbed a hand and pulled her back to him. He planted a kiss on her lips. 'I missed you today,' he said warmly. He seemed to mean it, as well.

'I missed you too,' Gabrielle smiled sweetly and tried like hell to sound honest. 'Don't be long. I'm starving!'

Doug inspected himself in the numerous bathroom mirrors. Not bad. Not great. 'But better than the average bear, Boo Boo...' he said, imitating one of his favourite cartoon characters. Then he laughed at his silliness, finished drying himself, and donned his normal house attire of cotton jogging sweats. Before going downstairs, he took a peek at his youngest as she slept soundly, with thumb in mouth, jaw automatically working on it. A tiny trickle of saliva drizzled down her cheek and Doug gently wiped it away with his finger. His little angel.

She deserved a stable family life, didn't she? All his kids did. A happy, secure family unit. But weren't they already? Doug sighed. Not really, if the truth be known. He bent down, taking a kiss from his lips with a finger, and placed it gingerly on Phoebe's button nose. Bananas and custard. Her baby scent always reminded him of them.

'Sweet dreams,' he said under his breath.

Doug knew it was entirely up to him whether his daughter's dreams remained so.

As Summer closed the front door to her flat, her mind frantically trying to decide what and what not to take on Giancarlo's 'surprise' trip, she heard the intermittent beep of the answering machine.

Dropping into the plump cushions of her sofa, she reached across the back to the occasional table and pressed the play button. Summer waited for the message to rewind, still making a fashion decision and then changing it instantly for something else. Like she really needed this right now... Her mother's soft tones filled the room.

'Summer?... Oh I do hate these confounded things... erm,

Summer, darling, can you call Mummy? Got some gossip for you... well, speak to you then...' There was static pause as Summer could imagine her mother hesitating before hanging up. Worrying she hadn't left a message at all. She had given up trying to get Isadora to call her mobile number. Too much technology. Summer smiled and shook her head, then dialled home.

'Oh, hello, Dermot. Is Mummy there?'

'I'm fine, thanks. How are you?' her brother said with gentle sarcasm.

'Sorry! How ARE you, Dermot?'

'Fine,' he laughed, 'I'll get Mum. I guess you've heard then?'

Summer frowned. 'Heard what?'

'Oh, better let Mum tell you. Don't want to spoil her fun!'

What the hell was he going on about? For some strange reason, Summer felt a few more of those icy drips from her imaginary bucket. Why? Tired. That's what it was, and now she had go away for the weekend...

'Summer? Oh good! Hang on, darling.' Isadora settled herself into her favourite armchair for telephone gossiping. 'Are you ready for this?' she breathed conspiratorially.

Summer took in a long cold breath. Why was she shivering? Bath. She needed a nice hot bath. 'What's happened?'

When her mother replied, it was slow and deliberate. 'Tony Wiggins has been having an affair.'

Summer froze. 'Affair?' she made herself say without letting the horror seep into her voice.

'Oh yes! Told Sonia on the way to hospital, darling.'

'Hospital?' Summer almost swallowed the word back down as she said it.

'Oh, of course, you wouldn't know, would you?'

I might... things you couldn't imagine, Mum.

'What?' Summer tried to stay calm, but she was finding it hard to breathe. Something horrible was pressing down on her chest like stone. A ton of it. She realised she was rocking back and forth, nibbling her thumb nail.

'On the way home from our little party, he was taken ill in the car and Sonia drove him straight to the hospital. He had a heart attack...' Summer was deathly still. She didn't breathe, suddenly transported to a silent place of fear, while somewhere, in another dimension, her mother continued... 'During the drive, he told her.'

'Told her what?' Summer responded in a distant voice. *What had she done? It was never meant to go this far. What had she done?*

'Sonia wasn't exactly very calm when she rang me, darling. She'd been at the hospital all night. Anyway, it seems it's a young girl. Been going on for a while.'

Time in her surreal plane seemed to draw to a sickening halt. Summer felt her lip going in conjunction with tears forming. As she spoke again, her tongue felt oversized and awkward, it was difficult to form the words. 'Does she know who?'

'Well, that's the worst part, isn't it? He tells the poor woman he's been unfaithful and then won't say who she is. Said he had to talk to her first. I mean! Don't mind the poor cow he's married to.'

'So he won't say?' Summer could feel the stone easing slightly. *There might be time.*

'Not as yet. Still, I reckon it'll be some blonde bimbo. It usually is. Some mindless slut. So typical. Men! Honestly. Can't imagine what he has to TALK about with her.'

Summer had a funny feeling she did, and her mother's description of the 'girl' slammed about her head like a pinball. Blonde bimbo. Mindless slut. Yes, well, that's precisely what she'd been, wasn't it? But not anymore. If she hadn't already made that decision about her life, her mother's scathing tone would have been enough to put a stop to Summer's silly games. And that is all they were, silly childish games that had gone on for far too long. The game was over now. Forever. There was one problem, though. The other player didn't know the game was over. He was still on the pitch, running with the ball, about to take a strike at goal. Summer had to get to Tony before he got to Sonia. He could destroy everything. Giancarlo; respect from her family, and worst of all, ruin the fledgling relationship with her father.

But would it? And anyway, WAS it her? Before the party, they hadn't seen each other for a long time. The 'girl' could be someone else. Summer's thoughts were a frenzy of possibilities, but in the end, it was the vicious truth piranha gnawing at her insides that brought her back to reality. As soon as she got back from wherever Giancarlo was taking her, Summer would tackle Tony for the last time.

She had to make the save of her life.

CHAPTER SIXTEEN

She had never felt so scared or vulnerable, and at the total mercy of another human being.

After what seemed like an eternity, standing alone on the terrace, a place where many of their liaisons had started, he finally appeared out of the darkness. Slowly, he walked up the steps from the lawn and stopped, just staring at her. Summer smiled. An uncertain, nervous little smile. He seemed to be studying her, searching her face, looking deep into her eyes. It was an uncomfortable experience that increased in intensity as he moved toward her.

Tony's face was gaunt and pallid, bearing all the hallmarks of the recent heart attack. As he approached, Summer caught his scent, not the usual Aramis and musty accompaniment of stale panatella. This was quite different. Faintly putrid. The smell of death. She became quite queasy and had to steady herself, wanting to run away and yet stay and face him at the same time.

Tony started to speak, his mouth moved but nothing seemed to come out. Confusion swept over Summer like a bracing easterly wind, threatening to overwhelm, just as she felt the comforting touch of a firm hand on her shoulder, and sensed someone strong standing nearby. Imbued with a warm feeling of safekeeping, Summer watched Tony's face slowly contort and then freeze into a twisted portrait of terror as Giancarlo lifted the gun to his forehead... 'Summer?' he said, his voice a soft echo.

'Summer?' Giancarlo whispered, stroking her slumbering face with a feather touch of the back of his hand. Her skin was silky, cheeks glowing slightly pink. Summer opened her eyes, looking vacantly straight ahead. 'We're here,' Giancarlo spoke softly as she gradually came to. He smiled to himself. Whenever he had to wake her from a deep sleep, Summer always looked like a child, full of innocence and oblivious to what life might hold for her. Despite what he knew of this woman, to Giancarlo, she was just that, a little girl for him to take care of. Under his tutelage and creative influence, Summer would become a woman for him to be proud of.

Summer was disorientated upon waking, then took in her surroundings and breathed again. She hadn't slept the night before, the conversation with her mother and its possible consequences holding her mind to ransom throughout the long early hours. She had tossed and turned, praying for the blackness of sleep, until eventually giving up and just lying on her back staring at the ceiling, watching it change from the dark grey of night to a bright morning magnolia, the lightness of the daybreak starkly at odds with her heavy conscience.

Summer had taken a long, hot shower, standing with her face lifted to the stinging stream of spiteful water. A mild penance while she tried to banish Tony from her head and life, at least for the next two days. After that, she would be working on it forever.

Giancarlo arrived at nine and immediately commented on how tired and drawn she looked. So much for the shower and professionally applied make-up. He had started to fuss over her which irritated her already jumpy disposition, and Summer had snapped at him a couple of times. She cooled the situation with quick excuses of pre-show nerves. After some gentle counselling and a long affectionate embrace, which on some other occasion would most likely have led them to bed, nothing more was said.

As the Ferrari pulled away on the start of their journey, Giancarlo told her they were heading for somewhere near Blackpool, but that was all he would allow through an inimitably dangerous Sicilian grin. Eyes flashing with playful mystery. He loved to tease her. *But not today, eh?* Summer had said to herself.

Somewhere near Blackpool, she repeated silently as she looked out of the car. It was the last place on earth she wanted, needed, to be.

Sonia Wiggins watched her ravaged husband taking a slow thoughtful walk around their acre of perfectly, but sympathetically, landscaped gardens, set within their surrounding land, consisting of arable fields they rented to a neighbouring farmer. She wished they were in Ireland. That was truly home for her. Where she might recover.

Tony occasionally stopped to look up into the sky, probably admiring the passing heron from a private trout lake nearby. Sonia didn't much like herons. Not since one brazenly ate a pondful of prized golden orfes, then took a leisurely stroll around their lawn afterwards. Sonia had run out ready to murder the bastard bird, only managing to prompt it into flapping its enormous wings and lifting above the trees from a running take off. She was sure the bird had laughed at her as it flew away.

Now Sonia had been robbed again, but this time, her own husband, the man she had loved without question since they had met, was an accomplice.

Tony sat on one of the ornamental stone seats dotted around the gardens. He faced the house but was far enough away that he wouldn't have seen his wife observing from their bedroom. Not that Sonia thought he would have seen her anyway. Whether he was looking up at the house, admiring the flowers or a feathered thief, she considered he wouldn't have seen anything at all.

She had brought him home from hospital that morning. The silence in the car had been deafening. An alien atmosphere prevailed during the drive, something Sonia had never experienced before. Ever. A profuse feeling of dread. Of things to come neither of them was ready for. Had never expected to face. It seemed to seep out from each of them, forming a choking cloud of wasted emotions, violating her senses, until it escaped through Tony's half open window. Sonia had imagined it, trailing behind the car, an ever-increasing chiffon veil, threatening to throttle her like the hapless Isadora Duncan. The image so real, Sonia stole a look in the rear-view mirror.

Now she secretly regarded Tony from behind the net curtains and recalled the events of the last few days. It was startling how clear her memories were, replaying before her with the same intense colour and energy as though they were happening there and then. Every moment, each emotion, all the little fragments, painfully vibrant. It was as close to hell as Sonia wished to be, but it was essential to revisit her recent past if she were to try to make some sense of it all. To find a reason. To do so, she must pull it apart, dissect the pieces, seek out the fettered flesh that had caused her husband to stray. Gouge out the putrescent tissue and suture the gaping wound. Let it heal. If that were possible.

Sonia knew it was the anxiety of his affair that had brought on the cardiac trauma. And somewhere out there, was a nameless, faceless woman, who had in the most callous way, ripped part of her husband from her, and in turn, destroyed a part of her. In one fell swoop, almost annihilated the life they had shared together. But while stumbling through this quagmire of thoughts and sensations, Sonia remained pragmatic. Just. She was only too aware that Tony must bear a lot of the blame, if not all of it. After all, he had been the one in a marriage, the one with a wife, someone innocent to decimate. He would have to accept and live with that responsibility. She would make sure of it.

As for 'the girl', as Tony so quaintly put it, Sonia could only imagine, and she was blessed with a vivid invention. A gift she would have gladly traded for a blank canvas at that moment.

Still watching him, now bent forward on his seat, leaning forearms on his legs, head bowed, Sonia noticed a telling movement of Tony's shoulders.

'You go on and have a good cry, Tone,' she said on quietly sarcastic breath. 'You just do that.'

Apart from the terrifying ordeal in the car and hospital, apart from the sickening shock of her husband's sudden confession, apart from all that, there was something else that still ate away at her, scraping the walls of her mind with needle teeth and relentless jaws, gradually stripping away all that she had been.

The bastard wouldn't give Sonia a name, wouldn't give her a face to psychologically put a fist into.

'I have to speak to her, Sonia,' he had spluttered through the oxygen mask in A&E. 'She's just a girl. I must warn her first.'

Oh fine! She'd thought at the time. *Of course, my dear, you must 'warn' the poor young thing. Just how young is she? Bless her little cotton socks. Don't mind me, will you, dear? I'm just the wife. I can cope while you try and make the other woman's life a bit easier. Give her a chance to run and take cover. So considerate of you...*

A solitary tear eased onto Sonia's cheek, teetered for a moment, then trickled thin and cold, finally free-falling and vanishing into the Axminster.

'I'll get the truth out of you somehow,' she whispered to Tony through the diamond-shaped leaded glass. 'And I really don't care anymore if it finishes you off.'

If her life was about to be washed down the proverbial drain, Sonia Wiggins was determined to take the fucking little bitch with her.

So where exactly are we, Carlo?' asked Summer as they got out of the car. An imposing mansion house stood before them, surrounded by huge chestnut trees, and along the quiet road, there were more of the same.

Giancarlo found her hand and said, 'I've rented a flat for you. A place where I know you will be safe. Can park your car late at night and to be honest, Bella, somewhere I will not mind coming to when I visit.'

Summer looked at him. He couldn't read her expression. Then she spoke in a measured fashion, simmering fury just beneath the surface. 'Carlo, now listen to me for once. I really do appreciate all that you do for me. You are very kind...' He smiled. 'But,' she continued, and the smile quickly faded. 'I am an independent person. It's an important part of my being. This is lovely...'she indicated the house and grounds. 'But I didn't choose it, did I? Because I wasn't given the option. I know you are trying to protect me, Carlo, but you have to see it from my point of view.'

Giancarlo stood silently listening, watching her face, the fire in her eyes, the way in which her defiant mouth formed her firm words, the way she held herself, shoulders set. It was a valiant speech. He swam in waves of satisfaction because he knew he was beginning to really understand Summer, provoke her, anticipate her reactions. But he also knew she would indeed take the flat he had so carefully provided.

'Just see inside,' he soothed. Summer regarded him like she might a lecturer who had just shed new light on a difficult subject. 'Then you can make your decision.'

She shot a look at Giancarlo. *Make a decision? Screw you! I've already made it. And where the hell are we anyway?* 'Where are we, Carlo?' she asked once again, realising he had never quite answered her first enquiry, which was very Giancarlo. She found herself talking to his back as he walked towards the front door of the house. Summer noticed him produce keys from the inside pocket of his Armani jacket.

'It is called... how do you say... Lytham St Annes... yes, that's where we are.'

'Blimey, Carlo! That's a fair old drive from the theatre. I'll be tired and...'

Giancarlo turned to face her as he started up the porch steps. 'It is not that far, and anyway, you cannot stay in Blackpool,' he said with a wrinkle to his nose, some distasteful vision in his eyes. 'It's not... it's not so nice for you.'

Summer had to smile to herself. God, he was such a snob. Though in truth, she didn't entirely disagree. Summer sighed. She knew she couldn't win, but hell, she was going to have fun by putting up a damned good fight in the meantime.

The door opened into a lofty hallway, huge chandelier hanging from a long chain and authentic Victorian floor tiles in misty tones of ochre and black. Summer suspected they had been vibrant in years gone by, now paled by thousands of footsteps. Giancarlo was already on his way up the stairs.

'What floor is it on?' she asked to his back again.

'The first floor. Come on, I'm excited for you to see it. I chose it specially for you.' He held out a hand and waited for Summer to join him on the stairs. He took her hand and kissed it.

Perhaps she wouldn't put up much of a fight.

Isadora kept calling and getting no reply. Eventually, she left a message, trying to keep a lid on herself, not wanting to give Summer the horrendous news on the machine.

It was just so dreadful, Isadora felt she might burst with the burden of it.

In the middle of dinner, Summer couldn't stand it any longer. She simply had to dip her toe into the dark and murky waters. She just had to know. Tony Wiggins sat in her mind like a particularly stubborn sloth, just hanging there, with the remnants of her disturbing dream earlier in the day.

Summer excused herself from the table and made her way to the Ladies. Quite relieved to find a signal on her phone, she called her mother.

'Summer!' Isadora exclaimed at the sound of her daughter's voice. 'Where are you? I've been trying to get hold of you.' There was a suggestion of agitation and urgency in her mother's tone. Summer felt the room starting to spin. She put a hand out and grabbed a basin.

'Why? What's happened?' *What's he said? What has the scheming little shit said?*

'Well, darling, it's Tony.'

Summer trembled now, she could feel beads of cold sweat erupting on her forehead, and a shrill ringing in her head preceded a sudden urge to vomit. 'Tony?' She forced out of her mouth. Voice small and weak.

There was a pause as Isadora drew in a long breath and sighed it out before speaking. Summer stiffened. This was it. *Here it comes...*

'He's dead.'

Summer's eyes were now blindly wandering over the Ladies room and focusing on nothing.

'Summer, darling? Are you all right?' Isadora sounded concerned. 'I know he was like another uncle to you, wasn't he? I'm so sorry.'

A wretched laugh broke free from the deepest part of Summer, followed by a childlike sob. 'When?'

'This morning, darling. Sonia found him slumped over his desk. She's completely distraught, of course. Daddy went straight over, and I'll be going there this evening, to keep an eye on her. Isn't it dreadful?'

'Yes, Mummy, it's horrible. I have to go now, I'll speak to you when I get home.' Summer had to get off the phone before her façade collapsed.

'All right, then. Are you okay?'

'Fine.'

With the phone switched off again, Summer looked at herself in the mirror above the basin. She still visibly shook, her face sheet white. She had to gather herself together before re-joining Giancarlo. If he saw her like this, it would prompt too many questions.

Had Tony told Sonia before he died? And had she told her mother and father? Wouldn't her mother have said? Or was she keeping it for when they were face to face? Isadora Laine was good at that one. Hitting you with it when least expected.

Perhaps Sonia was waiting to confront Summer personally, before vindictively telling the world. Though unlikely from such a meek woman, the most timid cat, once roused by a rival, will fight to the death with no thought of its own welfare. A basic instinct impossible to control. And with her husband now dead, there was nothing for Sonia Wiggins to preserve. Except maybe her dignity. But what woman cared about that when faced with a similar situation? Revenge. That would be the fire in her veins now.

Oh God, oh God, Summer repeated several times. Then she lifted her head and looked at her reflection once more. Slowly she pulled up to her full height, centred herself, checked her hair, and practised a dazzling smile before returning to the restaurant.

Back in London, the Ferrari drew to a stop outside Summer's flat.

'I'll be really busy this week, Carlo,' she said. 'But I'll call you if I have a free evening.'

Giancarlo leaned across and kissed her gently. 'Be a good girl,' he said with a joking, warning smile, and kissed her again.

'I will, I promise,' Summer replied. If only he knew how much. 'Thank you for everything.' Giancarlo just shrugged and tried to look bashful. He never could quite carry it off and Summer laughed softly. 'Ciao,' she said affectionately and got out of the car.

Gratefully slamming the door of her flat, Summer felt she could now begin to contemplate what lay ahead in terms of Sonia Wiggins, or her own mother for that matter. In the meantime, she was safe within the walls of her own abode. Protected from the outside world. From life and her numerous cruelties. Then came an intermittent beep. The battlements had been breached.

Summer dropped her weekend bag and reluctantly walked over to the answering machine, where it sat on the table like a huge cockroach, its beady red eye winking at her. In that moment, machine and insect seemed one and the same, and she hated both equally. Summer pressed the button and waited. A slimy film of fear seemed to vacuum-pack itself around her, then a man's voice filled the air.

'Breezy,' pause, 'it's Tony, if you're there, please pick up the phone.' Another brief interval and a faint sigh. 'Look, we need to talk. Something's happened that shouldn't, but I thought I was going to die at the time.' There was a suggestion of a nervous laugh before he continued. 'I didn't really know what I was saying. I'll call again... Bye, Breezy...'

CHAPTER SEVENTEEN

Cynthia Hersh reorganised the chaos on her desk. To a fashion. Mindful of an old expression she had used herself as a defence from time to time. A tidy desk isn't a busy one. *Hmm, that may be true of some,* she thought, *but not in her case.* She detested this disarray before her, it made life tricky when trying to find information quickly during phone calls, not least, the 'hang on a sec...' or 'just dig it out...' simply made her sound inefficient.

Of course, if Cynthia bothered to use her computer more, a lot of the paper work, notes and correspondence strewn across her ageing desk wouldn't exist. But hey, someone has to put up a fight against total automation and Cynthia Hersh was pleased to do her bit for the cause. She'd never truly got the hang of the confounded thing in the first place, and she much preferred speaking to someone, rather than have remote conversations through emails.

Being an agent, it was important to have actual contact. She could relate to people better. Make good judgements. Cynthia was adept at gauging the possibilities, or not, of prospective signings before meeting them. She rarely failed. It saved a lot of time, of which Cynthia didn't seem to have enough. Today, she'd just have to make time. It was important to make the meeting she had arranged with Summer Laine, her greatest hope for the future at that moment. There weren't many on Cynthia's substantial list of talent that had compelled the agent to sign them in an instant. Summer had.

No agent was tougher than Cynthia Hersh to impress. She was known for being one of the most difficult agencies to get in with. It didn't take any old up-and-coming, they had to have blinding talent. Kick off a certain feeling inside the agent upon first meeting or performance prior to a face to face at her office. Cynthia would wait for that shiver down her spine, a ripple over her skin, the illusory punch that would almost wind her. Summer Laine had produced all those feelings within her, and then some.

She had discovered the girl in a pantomime two years earlier, while on one of her famous talent-spotting jaunts. They didn't always provide the goods but sometimes she got lucky. It had been a small panto in some godforsaken local theatre. Cynthia had initially dismissed the tall blond goddess that stepped onto the stage as Cinderella. A typical casting she had thought. How wrong Cynthia was. When Summer opened her perfect mouth and more perfection came out into the auditorium, the agent literally sat up and took more notice. The girl delivered her meagre lines beautifully, with genuine feeling, and her singing was quite lovely. It needed some training but even the very best are coached constantly. No, there was something about this one. A presence. She had Cynthia's precious X factor, and this Cinders wouldn't be needing her fairy godmother, more a decent agent.

Now her prodigy was on the brink.

It had been a damn shame about George, drink driving will get the best of us, stupid sod, but although the film had been shelved for the moment, it wasn't off the agenda completely. Martin Thurlow had made contact to that effect. He needed to re-negotiate funding and would be in touch, which was great news, but Cynthia was never one to sit around waiting, not where Summer Laine was concerned. It was why she needed to see the girl before she went off to Blackpool. Though it wasn't the primary reason Cynthia wanted to speak to Summer. There was something else which might just be more important. A heartfelt warning.

The agent felt she knew Summer on a much deeper level than in her capacity as the purveyor of auditions and mutually beneficial contracts. With Summer, Cynthia was connected. She saw herself in the young girl, trying to break into acting from a successful dancing career. It was almost like personal history being repeated. But Cynthia didn't want it to be repeated. One spent journey down that road was quite enough.

Cynthia lit another fag. How many was that today? Too many, always too many. She settled back in her chair and looked across to the sash window that provided Cynthia with unrelenting Arctic draughts during winter. It looked like it was going to be a pleasant early summer's day. It also did nothing to dispel the chill that had wrapped itself around her as she recalled events during her own last few months as a dancer-come-actress.

That vile summer season had changed her life course, and probably her whole character along with it. For here sat an unfeminine woman, maybe bordering on dyke, though not a path Cynthia had travelled down. As yet. The offers were in abundance but she still couldn't seem to make the leap. Her face was aged beyond her years and she was quite alone. Not lonely, that was different, just alone. She preferred it that way.

Back in those early years, she had been more than attractive, a less perfect version of Summer, full of life, laughter, ambition. *Huh! Ambition...* she thought ruefully as she sucked on the cigarette. And of course, it was a time when Cynthia Hersh had still believed in love. Until Scarborough.

Until Doug-dazzle-n-ditch-em Delany.

Her first impression upon arrival in the North Yorkshire seaside resort, was the incessant screeching of the gulls. There seemed to be every type. Ones she knew, herring and black-headed, and a multitude of variations in between. All vying for airspace and perches among the roofs of houses, hotels and entertainment venues that sat crammed on the hills above Scarborough's two sweeping flat beaches. North and South bays. Sands not quite golden in summer and an uninviting taupe in winter.

Jutting out from the promenade, almost opposite the Futurist Theatre, where Cynthia would spend most of her time during the season, was a huge sea wall with a small lighthouse at the furthest point. It struck Cynthia as odd because even to her, it would seem obvious from out in the bay that there was land ahead with a bloody great big town on it. But then, what did she know? Her only experience at sea was a single trip on the river Cam, and that was in a punt.

Standing proud and sprawling above all of this, though just a shell of its former glorious structure, was Scarborough Castle. Or 'cassell', if you were to believe the locals. A pleasant enough group of people, typically tough, no-nonsense Yorkshire folk. Cynthia rather warmed to them. They made a welcome change from the social crap that went on in London.

She was to share a fair-sized attic flat with two other dancers, Lorna and Ben, but was fortuitously the first to arrive at the digs, so quite rightly, she stole the small single box room for herself. Lorna and Ben would have to share the large double, but the landlord had provided twin beds, theatre-list landlords always out to get maximum income. However, Cynthia suspected, as usual the sitting-room would probably end up another bedroom. This was your archetypal summer season accommodation, only ever used by performers or stage crew from the various theatres in town. Landlords wanted top dollar and tenants needed to pay as little as possible, hence the overcrowding that sometimes occurred. But it made for fun times. Excellent parties and more importantly, shared expenses.

The flat was basic but very clean and after some of the horrific places she had stayed in when everything else had been taken, it was really quite comfortable, though after two shows on Wednesdays and Saturdays, they might regret snapping up this little gem. Perhaps a drink or two at the artists' bar in the theatre and bag of chips-n-scraps would ease the slog on tired legs. Obviously, a car would have helped but then, so would a decent rate of pay. Far too expensive a luxury to own for a dancer and sometimes actress, not only the running costs but the inevitable parking restrictions. During a summer season in a popular resort, it was a nightmare. If the theatre did provide a car park, it was either solely for the stars of the show or at a price. So Cynthia and most of her peers simply didn't bother.

Rehearsals started at ten the following morning, everyone arriving promptly, except Leo Davis but of course, he topped the bill, so nobody was really surprised. Most of his time on stage was exclusive, apart from his assistant, only joining in with the rest of the cast during the grand finale, where he would have to learn a few perfunctory steps for the line-up.

Also in the show was an up and coming comedian. Doug somebody or other, Cynthia had to look him up in the brochure. Oh yes, Doug Delany. Catchy name, she'd thought. He had arrived in a bit of a fluster, saying something about forgetting his pass for the car park and cracking a couple of jokes in the process. Everyone had laughed. He seemed a good bloke. Nice arse, too, Cynthia had decided upon a covert close inspection. She liked his easy-going style. A few people had also been raving about his cabaret act, so she looked forward to seeing him rehearse the PG version.

Finally, Leo made his appearance. *Another moody Welshman,* Cynthia had first thought, then chided herself for being uncharitable. The poor man was married to the formidable Doreen. Enough to make any man a bit sulky.

A shout went out from Allan, the producer, and Mike, the choreographer, one of the best creative double-acts around at the time. A hush befell the stage and auditorium. Time for work.

The show had opened to excellent revues and Leo's magic was truly awesome. The revelation was Doug Delany. People fell about during his two spots in the show, behind and in front of the stage. Audiences talked animatedly about him while leaving the theatre, some already practising his patter for the pub. Not only that, he had been a real trooper during the exhaustive rehearsals. Hanging around when not required, keeping spirits up when things, as usual, didn't go exactly to plan. Or when Mike got himself all worked up, insisting the dancers do the moves of a routine 'like this, now watch me again', and then failing to get it to the perfect levels he required. Even Allan at times had to have a quiet word. That was light entertainment.

Doug greatly impressed the company, especially Cynthia. But that was as far as she would allow it to go. Yes, she'd noticed the occasional glance her way, and she would have been a liar if she had said it hadn't made her feel good. She just didn't want anything of a romantic nature to interfere with her career at the time. It was bobbing along nicely, if not quite as she would have hoped, so a messy private life was certainly not on the cards.

There was one small disappointment. Cynthia was slightly miffed at not being chosen by Leo for his assistant during the run. Instead, he opted for the rather obvious Miss Prim and Proper herself, Lisa Smith. Yeah, right! More like the company's official welcoming party. Although it had to be said, she proved very efficient at her extra duties as a magician's assistant. Unfortunately, she hadn't stopped there. Apparently, her talents knew no bounds where Mr Davis was concerned.

After the evening performance on their second Saturday, everyone looking forward to their one day off, Cynthia and her flatmates were having a few welcome wind-down bevvies in the artists' bar. So called because it was the private drinking place allocated by most large theatres to the cast and their friends and family. And of course, their agents. The three colleagues were deep in debate over whether to have fish and chips or a Chinese, when Doug Delany entered the room with a quick acknowledgement to everyone there as he approached the bar. Then, to their surprise, he walked over to the table where Cynthia, Lorna and Ben were and sat down. 'Don't mind if I join you, do you?' he'd said with a tired smile. The three had looked at each other and almost said in unison, 'No, not at all.' Ben had got all enthusiastic and said, 'You were firing on all cylinders tonight, Doug. It was brilliant. You dealt with that heckler like a dream.'

Doug had smiled and taken a deep gulp of his lager. 'Thanks, Ben, but don't forget, I did start out in working men's clubs. That gnat's tit tonight was nothing.'

'The clubs must have been hard,' Ben said.

Doug thought for a moment, a memory or two passing across his face, then he replied, 'Sometimes.' He laughed privately at something. 'But you know, Ben? Those buggers got me where I am now. So here's to them,' he said, holding up his lager and taking another sip.

The three dancers nodded mutely. He seemed distant for a second, then came back with a filthy story that was totally gross but extremely funny. Cynthia couldn't help but really like the guy.

'This your first major summer season, then?' asked Lorna, a tall willowy dark-haired Scot with a thick Glaswegian accent that cut through the mellow atmosphere of the bar.

'It is and I'm really enjoying it, Lorna,' Doug replied, but his eyes were wandering over Cynthia. 'I was a bit surprised who Leo chose as his assistant,' he said, looking right at Cynthia. 'He could have done a lot better.'

Lorna sighed into her vodka and orange. The blue-eyed blond had won again. Cynthia felt mildly uncomfortable under Doug's continued and barely disguised gaze. *Come on, Hersh,* she said to herself. *Keep it together.*

'Can I get you all another drink?' Doug asked.

'Not for me, thanks,' smiled Lorna. 'I'm knackered.' *And pissed off.* 'Going to get home, bathed and bed. Ben?' She said looking pointedly at him. He'd also noticed Doug's attention to Cynthia.

'Me too,' he replied and looked at Cynthia.

Bastards, she thought. 'I'll have another, then, thanks.' She smiled at Lorna and Ben as if to say, 'See you later and don't ask questions.'

They got the message and left the bar, both with a knowing expression plastered on their faces. Cynthia didn't really know why she had accepted another drink. But that's all it was, wasn't it? Some friendly after-show chat before going their separate ways? And hell, she liked him. So what?

'What'll it be, Cynthia?' Doug asked getting up and collecting her glass from the table.

'Rum and Coke, please.'

'Rum and Coke it is, then. Listen, thanks for staying. I hate drinking alone and I didn't want to go back to the flat just yet.'

Cynthia just smiled and gave a small 'That's okay' shrug.

Both about to pass out with sheer exhaustion and perhaps one too many, they left the bar and strolled to the car park at the back of the theatre, chatting happily and very easily. When they reached Doug's car, Cynthia suddenly felt a little awkward.

'Well, thanks for the drinks. I'll see you on Monday.'

'Cynthia, don't be a prat, I'm not letting you walk back to your flat alone. Come on, get in. It's on my way, anyway.'

During the short drive, Doug asked if she was free the following day. Her rest day. That precious Sunday when they could be themselves for a few hours. Not always so for the show's stars, many opening fêtes or taking part in charity golf tournaments. Not for Doug Delany yet, so it seemed. He wanted to take her for lunch. Well, that wasn't so bad, was it? Nothing serious about that. Perhaps he was a bit lonely in his first big production. Cynthia was feeling somewhat jaded as well, having just learned she'd lost out on another cameo television role. Quickly considering the pros and cons of meeting Doug on Sunday, she realised she didn't really give a stuff about any downside.

'I'd love Sunday lunch.'

'Oh, that's great. Listen, I know a lovely place. It's a bit of a hike but you'll love it.' There was a thoughtful pause before he said, 'Better not tell anyone, you know, start some stupid gossip and all that.'

Cynthia smiled to herself. 'I think that might have started already, Doug. Bad luck!' He looked surprised. 'Lorna and Ben?' she prompted.

'Oh, I see!' he laughed.

Cynthia suddenly felt uneasy about the whole idea. A strange coldness had descended over her. It felt like a warning. One of those weird occasions you just KNOW you're doing the wrong thing. But then you go ahead and do it anyway...

'I'll pick you up outside Woolworths, say, eleven?' Doug said. It sounded like he'd planned all this. Or done it before.

'All right,' Cynthia answered cautiously. 'Tomorrow outside Woollies. See you then.'

There was a silent moment when both looked at each other, the obvious kiss goodnight hanging over them both, but Cynthia got out of the car before Doug could take advantage of it. Cynthia made her way up the three flights of stairs and turned the key in the lock of the flat door as quietly as possible. She didn't want to wake her friends.

'Cynth!' came a shout from the sitting-room, now Ben's bedroom. *Oh bollocks!* thought Cynthia. She opened the door and found both Ben and Lorna, pissed as farts, amid a variety of Chinese takeaway cartons. Eagerly waiting for a full account of her evening.

CHAPTER EIGHTEEN

Jo Jo's was a little-known bistro, but as it was just down the road from the BBC building in central London, it was frequented by many of those who worked there.

So it served Cynthia well on this particular afternoon. She could meet with Summer, then mosey on down to see the casting director for a forthcoming drama. A period piece, a broadcasting genre where Cynthia felt the BBC was in a league of its own. Creating wonderful historical television plays and casting only la *crème de la crème* of acting talent to anchor the production. Cynthia was confident that Summer could handle one of the minor roles with just a couple of brief scenes as a feisty kitchen maid and was determined to pull out all the stops to get this very selective casting director to consider Summer for the part. At least get her an audition. A casual passing mention of Martin Thurlow might come in useful. Whatever it took.

Cynthia perused the extensive lunch menu, far too many dishes to make up her already occupied mind. Then a bright voice said, 'Hello, Cy,' as Summer sat down at the table. Cynthia peered at the girl over her Dior glasses.

'You know I don't like "Cy", young lady.' Then she smiled, pushing the glasses back up her nose. 'So, how are you? You're looking lovely, as always.' Cynthia cast her eyes back to the menu. 'Cow,' she laughed under her breath.

'Nice to see you too!' retorted Summer. She knew her agent well. 'Sorry I'm a bit late. A close friend of the family has just died. I've had my mother on the phone...'

'Oh, poor love. I'm sorry. Was it sudden?'

'Mmm,' replied Summer. It had certainly been that. At least she now knew Tony Wiggins had gone to his grave without revealing anything about their extracurricular activities. 'Heart attack. Quite sudden. Anyway, let's not dwell on it. We've got more important things to talk about!'

Cynthia regarded Summer. That was a bit cold-hearted. Perhaps she was trying not to think about it. Shutting out the event. Show business people were the best in the world at doing that. Nothing, absolutely nothing, is allowed to interfere with their performance. Strange though, Summer wasn't about to go on stage or deliver lines in front of camera. *Mind you,* thought Cynthia, *being a tough cow will help her in the long run.*

'Let's get a drink, eh?' Cynthia said. 'Only one, mind, got a meeting with Moira Myers after this.'

Summer lifted an eyebrow. 'Isn't that...'

'It certainly is,' Cynthia finished for her.

'Who's the lucky client?' Summer asked.

'Don't like to put a bock on things. I'll let you know, love.'

Cynthia didn't want to get Summer's hopes up, only to be dropped and broken. There would be enough of those times ahead. She felt rather protective of this girl, sensing maybe she hadn't had the warmest of upbringings, although Cynthia certainly knew she had a wealthy family. It was just a look in Summer's eyes sometimes. A look Cynthia understood because she too had left an unsatisfactory home life to seek her love and affection quotas from applause in the darkness.

Summer couldn't decide what to eat, her mind on the conversation she'd had with Isadora before she'd left to meet Cynthia.

Mother had insisted her daughter attend, with the rest of the family, the funeral of her father's dearest client and friend. Make a show of full support for the widow. But as Summer had gently explained why she couldn't be there, making the excuse that rehearsals were about to start, she knew the Four Horsemen of the Apocalypse couldn't have dragged her to the church. Even if Tony was dead and rotting in his coffin. The conniving bastard had nearly ruined everything with his own 'revelation'. So Summer was quite happy to leave the weeping wife to mourn his skinny little body. Let all the usual tributes be aired during the service by those who truly gave a damn. What a great bloke he was. Wonderful husband and father. General all-round good egg.

Summer had cringed at a vision of herself, having to sit there, listening to it all with a suitable expression of mourning on her face. She knew the real deal. Had the full measure and truth of the man. He had been nothing more than a steaming pile of filthy dog shit.

Not a pleasant thought as she tried to choose what to eat.

Cynthia scrambled about in her own thoughts as if she were rummaging around an untidy attic, searching for something, which in this case was the right approach. How to counsel Summer Laine about the dangers of Doug Delany, without offending this obviously capable young woman's own sensibilities, and sounding like some bitter old prune. No doubt Summer could handle men like Doug, blindfolded with her arms tied behind her back. Cynthia silently smiled at the image, but it was not a happy smile. More a grimace. A memory suddenly rushed in, uncovered by her mental foraging.

With their surroundings becoming ever more remote, bleak sprawling hills of bracken, coarse grasses and heather in all its colours, Cynthia asked, 'Where exactly ARE we going, Doug?'

'A place called Ravenscar. Don't you find this scenery awesome?'

'Sort of. What's at this... Ravenscar?'

'You'll see,' he replied with a cheeky smile. He was being annoyingly evasive but Cynthia knew it was all game play, so she went along with it.

'What if I hate it on sight? Ever thought of that? Long way to have come,' Cynthia laughed.

'Oh, I don't think you'll hate it. You're an artist. It will appeal to the dramatic in you. You've got dramatic in you, haven't you, Cy?' Doug said with a knowing curl of his mouth and brief sideways glance at her, then patted her knee.

It was a casual gesture, nothing meaningful involved,

almost absent-minded, but the shock of electricity that shot through Cynthia caused hairs on her arms to stand to attention like a follicular army on parade. She could feel a mischievous smile breaking free and turned her head to look out of the side window as it took hold. *Come on, Cynth. This ain't the time or place and you do NOT get involved with people at work. Just keep it to 'lunch'.*

'I hope there's more than a snack bar at this place. I'm starving!' she said, having skipped breakfast in order to get out the flat before Ben and Lorna stirred and asked questions.

'Oh, love, I should have said, there's a small hotel there, I've booked a table for lunch.'

Hopefully that was all he'd 'booked'.

Finally, they pulled onto a long driveway that led them to an old manor house with open-air pool and golf course. Doug said, 'Follow me,' as they got out of the car and walked Cynthia through the grounds until they reached the cliff edge.

'There,' Doug said, holding out an arm indicating a magnificent view out across the North Sea. 'What did I tell you? Dramatic enough? And see here,' he pointed, 'this is an old Roman fortress wall. Amazing, eh?'

Cynthia looked out to an unusually pristine sea, calm and green under a clear blue sky. *Doug had been right. I love it. How did he know I would? Oh, stop it!* 'It's fantastic.'

'Come on, Cy, let's go and see if they'll seat us early. Seeing as you're "starving",' he said mimicking Cynthia and taking her hand. 'I'm glad you like it here.'

Over lunch, they talked constantly. No embarrassing pauses, no deep delving into each other's lives. Just easy conversation and lots of laughter. Cynthia felt very relaxed in Doug's excellent company. It was a welcome release from the stresses of the show.

On the drive back to Scarborough, a wispy mist began to appear from over the cliffs.

'Oh! And you even get to experience a moors sea fret,' Doug said with some enthusiasm.

'A what?' Cynthia laughed. 'Sea "fret"?'

'Aye, it's what the locals call a sea mist. It's famous over these moors. Tell you what, you watch it roll in and let me know if you see anything unusual about it.'

So, like a good little pupil, Cynthia sat and watched as the 'fret' came in, gathering pace. She wasn't sure what she was supposed to be looking for but something was certainly happening to the mist. Shapes were appearing.

Phantoms.

As the grey-white puffs of moisture took on their own forms, it struck Cynthia that they looked like people. Individual transparent ghosts, roaming free across the moors. Drifting *en masse* over the road in front of the car as though hurrying to some ethereal meeting place, somewhere in the distant hills, and eventual demise as they were drawn upward on to them by the sea breeze.

'Creepy,' she said.

'You can see them, then?' Doug asked mysteriously.

'What... like people?'

'Strange, isn't it. Only seems to happen on the moors. Scared the hell out of me the first time I got caught in it!' Doug laughed.

Then quite suddenly, the mist thickened and they were soon engulfed in a blanket of heavy fog. The road in front of the car had almost disappeared. 'Ah,' said Doug as he pulled the car over to the side of the road. 'Better wait a bit. It'll clear soon enough. We'll just have to talk to each other!' he said, taking off his seat-belt and shifting in his seat to face Cynthia. He looked at her and smiled.

'How long will it take?' Cynthia asked, returning an uncertain smile, while wishing her imagination would be more co-operative and stop bombarding her with notions of some murderous creature, suddenly appearing at her window, eyes savage and hungry. Then she felt a hand reaching to the back of her head, gently holding it and guiding her towards Doug, who then kissed her. Cynthia immediately pulled away.

'What are you doing, Doug?' she asked with an

embarrassed giggle, feeling the colour rising in her cheeks. Yes, it was a stupid question but Cynthia felt it important at this stage to show a modicum of restraint. Well... just a bit. Doug looked like a little boy who had just chanced his first snog and been berated for it. Then a more salacious expression descended over his face and settled in his eyes as they roamed her body.

'We're enjoying ourselves, aren't we?' he asked. 'Like each other a lot?' His gaze seemed to have difficulty extracting itself from her chest.

'Well... yes... I suppose...'

Doug didn't wait for the rest. He closed his mouth over hers and an eager tongue savoured the soft warm sensations of it. One hand still caressing her head, the other now exploring her breasts with rough squeezes through her top.

Cynthia gave up her half-hearted protests. Doug was good. Very good in fact, and it had been a long time since she had broken up with Oliver, a barman on the *Canberra*. Here she was with Doug Delany, both very single, away from home and friends, thrown together for several lonely months. What would be the harm? There was a fleeting consideration that this particular scenario was just a little bit tacky; in a car, on the moors, in the fog... But what Doug's hands were doing at that moment nullified all such thoughts. She moaned through a long, contented sigh.

Doug had managed to manoeuvre himself onto his knees in front of her. Cynthia had a vague passing thought he must have done this before as he deftly shifted her hips further forward to the edge of the seat, and without so much as a 'May I?', thrust himself inside her. They both gasped in unison.

'Is that good?' Doug breathed, hot and wet into her neck.

'Oh... yes...' she replied, voice quivering with arousal gone out of control. Cynthia wrapped her legs around Doug and let herself explore their unique turbulent rhythm, moving together in an unrefined, unrestrained harmony.

The agent regarded Summer as she picked at a piece of bread roll, putting tiny pieces into her mouth. It amazed Cynthia how the girls, and some of the boys, managed to keep their energy levels up on the paltry rations they allowed themselves these days. She knew much of it was financial, work was hard to get even for the best, but that wasn't the case for Summer. The pressure within the industry for them all to take on the characteristics of a stick insect, to look like emaciated catwalk models, was enormous and made Cynthia very angry. It just wasn't necessary or healthy. It certainly hadn't been required in her day.

Her day. Did she ever really HAVE a day? Cynthia pondered for a moment. Oh, there had been 'A' day. One that changed everything.

Back to her task. Gentle advice about Doug Delany. It was no use. However the friendly guidance was given, there was no guarantee the recipient would take it in good faith. Or even take heed. What was it Benjamin Franklin once said so famously? Only two things were guaranteed in life, death and taxes. Well, Cynthia certainly agreed with him on that.

Finishing her one glass of red wine, she cleared her throat in a theatrical manner and smiled warmly as Summer looked at her.

'Can I give you a little bit of woman to woman advice, love?'

With a small frown, Summer said, 'About what?'

Cynthia dropped her voice to a whisper. Just enough for Summer to hear. The bistro was quite full now and the people on the table next to them seemed to have nothing to say to each other. Big waggy ears waiting to hear some show business gossip. They knew who ate there on a daily basis. They were also probably reporters.

'Doug Delany,' she said simply. Summer's eyes widened a little and she smiled thoughtfully.

'Oh?'

'Just steer well clear, love.'

'Oh, I will, don't worry. I'm spoken for, anyway. But isn't Doug Delany married with kids?'

'He is, yes, but just remember what I said.' Then as an afterthought, 'And you didn't hear it from me!'

Summer laughed softly and nodded. Her agent needn't have worried. She had Giancarlo now. Completely. He had given her a reason to change. Perhaps he was 'the one', if there were such a person in the world. He seemed to come very close. When she had said she loved him, Summer hadn't been entirely sure of it. That had changed as well. Now she knew she loved him. The thought of being intimate with anyone else made her feel quite ill.

'Well, I'd better get going, Moira isn't one for being kept waiting! Lunch is on me. Keep in touch from Blackpool, won't you? I'll get up there at some point to see the show, maybe one of the pre-opening reviews.'

Cynthia left the bistro and hailed a cab, her thoughts once again returning to Doug. Perhaps she was being uncharitable. The man may well have changed. Let's face it, she had. Beyond recognition. But she knew somewhere safe and intact inside her was the Cynthia she used to be, and perhaps still was. If she knew this of herself, what of Doug Delany?

It had been a very long time. For both of them. But somewhere in a remote chasm within her, one she rarely peered into, a dusty little bird of truth had been disturbed and fluttered about in clouds of honest doubt.

Comedian and dancer met frequently after their rather impulsive but earthy session out on the North York moors. Doug had a sexual savvy that Cynthia hadn't experienced before. He was older than all her previous partners, perhaps that was it. The thought of how many women he might have had in order to have perfected his technique was summarily dismissed. So what? Cynthia was now getting the full benefit of her predecessors' efforts.

On their eventual drive back to Scarborough, both Cynthia and Doug had been glowing and silent in their respective post-coital calm. Cynthia found herself thinking, rather absurdly she mused, that if Emily Brontë had let Cathy and Heathcliff ravage each other up on their secret crag, would *Wuthering Heights* have been a modern success? Then Cynthia pondered that thousands of school children would have missed out on a wonderful story, such as herself, aged fourteen. Although, she recalled, they could have done without the excessive use of an old Yorkshire dialect throughout, especially when having to stand up and read it aloud in class. It never sounded quite right in her posh all-girls school near Haslemere in Surrey.

Somehow, Doug and Cynthia managed to keep their affair under wraps from the rest of the show, though Cynthia was regularly teased by Lorna and Ben. She was becoming quite fond of the funny man, pitting Cynthia against her own inner self and its well-founded reservations. Doug wasn't just funny and an excellent lover, he was caring, sensitive and kind. They really did have great times together. She also knew that at some point, she was going to get hurt. Perhaps more than Cynthia wished to acknowledge. Then again, they might stay together after the run. It wasn't impossible. Just unlikely. She had tried to test him a couple of times but Doug had simply laughed gently and evaded her carefully prepared questions with some joke or other.

So she would take what she could, enjoy every moment they had, and hope when it ended, she could be gracious.

Then, without warning, a dark molten pit threatened to swallow her whole. Cynthia was pregnant. After a week of no sleep, permanent despair at her own foolishness, feeling utterly isolated and terribly frightened, she told Doug.

'How far gone are you?' was his almost matter-of-fact response to the news.

'About six weeks,' she replied.

'That's okay, then,' he had continued without a drop of emotion.

'Okay?' Cynthia had said with increasing anger and incredulity.

'To make arrangements. Don't worry, Cy, love, I'll find the best place. It'll be discreet. No one will know.'

But I will! she screamed in her head. 'You want me to have an abortion?' Her voice was cold and remote. Cynthia wanted to lunge at him. Beat his chest with her fists. Until he understood what it was like, standing there carrying his child. A child he didn't want. A baby she shouldn't really have, but she would, if he stuck by her, even just financially.

Doug took both her hands in his, bowed his head for a moment, then looked up into her hard, watery eyes. 'You and I both know this baby can't happen.'

'It already has,' Cynthia replied in a low monotone.

'Come on, Cy, you know it would ruin your career...'

Cynthia snapped. 'MY career? Don't you mean YOUR career?' She ripped her hands away from his and flung her arms around herself in defence and small comfort.

Doug's voice remained calm and almost concerned.

'Oh, Cy, please, love, try and see sense. It's just the wrong time. For BOTH of us. You must see that. I'm so very sorry. I really am. You must believe me. I'll organise everything, okay? I'll take you, be there for you.'

He put a soft kiss on her cheek, turned and walked away up the beach. That was it. End of conversation. Doug had made the decision. He hadn't asked for her views at all.

Cynthia watched him go, leaving soggy imprints in the flat sea-logged sands. Slowly, his footprints dissolved back to nothing. As though he had never been there.

As he trudged up to the promenade at the furthest end of South beach from the town, Doug put his hands in his pockets and wept silently. He had never got a girl pregnant before. Not that he knew of, anyway. It was something he had never had to face. Thank God. This was just the worst. He was shocked at his conflicting feelings. Doug had wanted so badly to tell Cynthia it would be all right. They would cope. Find a way. But they wouldn't have, would they? Not in their profession. Not with his career prospects. Bad timing. Such bad timing.

She'd be all right, young healthy thing like Cy. One day she would thank him for making the decision to get rid of it. She was a talented dancer and he knew her acting career was just taking off. So much at stake to throw it all away. Too much to sacrifice, for either of them.

She'll get over it in time, he reasoned.

So would he.

Eventually.

Part Two

Five Minutes before curtain up:

'... OVERTURE AND BEGINNERS TO THE STAGE PLEASE...'

CHAPTER NINETEEN

The muted sensitive scene before him could so easily have been the subject for any one of the most revered master artists, to capture with the eloquent soft strokes of their brushes. Transposing a beautiful reality onto canvas and rendering it an exquisite dream forever. Of course, the Italian Tintoretto immediately came to mind, though he suspected this living picture would have been ideal for the French impressionist, Renoir.

Subdued evening light through the partially open balcony windows settled on her still form like a gossamer mantle. A perfect gentle contrast to the stark blackness of a hand-woven lace veil that caressed the back of her head and fell delicately onto tiny shoulders, also shrouded in the same sombre shade. The graceful touch of the poignant sunset upon her grieving but stoically serene features appeared to erase the lines from her elderly face, perhaps a thoughtful kiss of condolence from God.

His mother was momentarily the striking beauty she once had been, sitting straight and formal in the chair, looking out to where the horizon on the hazy Mediterranean met with a velvet lilac sky. A gift from the angels, a last glimpse of this new widow as her young lovely self for the spirit of her departing husband as he made his way with them to his final resting place.

It was a comforting thought for his mother, but not for Giancarlo. He doubted Paulo would have been escorted from this world by his mother's angels. The complete silence in the room and emptiness in his heart seemed to act as a taciturn rebuke from the heavens, and a firm message, that indeed, his father would not be joining them.

Fabia sat in Paulo's favourite chair. He would spend many hours there of an evening, pondering, remembering times long ago, or simply doing what she was at that moment, taking in the wonderful views across to the lower dark slopes of Mount Etna, and letting their uncomplicated charm imbue a much-needed calmness upon frayed emotions. His time had come very suddenly, in the end. Whisked away from her without notice. Fabia wished He had sent her a small warning at least, then she might have been there with Paulo when he dropped to the ground in the market, quite dead before crumpling onto harsh cobbles. Instead, a frantic wailing from her neighbour brought Fabia to the kitchen door, where the incoherent, gesticulating woman grabbed and dragged her from the house.

Before Fabia managed to decipher the hysterical ramblings from Maria, she knew instinctively Paulo had breathed his last. For many years, the boiler that fired her heart had ticked over on a flickering pilot flame, but even the meagre warmth from that had suddenly disappeared as a chill numbness descended into its place while the two women ran through the streets to the market.

The early evening light had turned to a cool grey dusk, the distant scenery slowly fading into the shadows of the approaching night. Fabia finally allowed her tears to quietly fall.

Giancarlo carefully moved towards his mother and placed a gentle hand onto her shoulder. 'Mama?' There was no response. He now crouched down beside her and took his mother's thin frail hand in both of his. It felt like that of a child. 'Mama? Can I get you anything?' he asked in a soft whisper, frightened his voice might break too harshly into her fragile countenance.

There was a brief pause, then she turned and looked deeply into her son's eyes. She smiled lovingly and stroked his face with her other hand. Her touch felt cold, almost unreal.

'My son, my precious first son. You are a good boy to your mother, but I am fine, I just need this time alone. Go and see to the others, make sure they have everything they need, your father wanted it that way. Go and show them you are ready to be head of this family. I know you are. Your father knew you were. They also need to see it. I am very proud of you, Giancarlo...' There was the briefest pause, as though she had meant to say something but for whatever reason, decided against it. 'Now leave me. I will join you all soon.' Fabia patted his cheek and withdrew both her hands, folding them neatly on her lap and turning her face to look out of the windows once again. Her eyes were no longer tearful but seemed to possess a defiant strength, and were almost bright, her own stubborn spirit very much still intact.

Giancarlo knew this firm tone wrapped around his mother's words. She had willingly given comfort and assurance where required, one of her many gifts, but now mother had summarily dismissed her son. She wanted to be alone. He could at least grant her that wish. As Giancarlo left the fast-darkening room, he took a deep breath, steadying himself to face the many family and friends who filled their house; eating, drinking, crying, laughing, just as Paulo had instructed. But while Giancarlo made his way back to the gathering, he knew in his heart there was something quite wrong with this new family order. He instinctively knew what his mother chose not to say. And only he could put it right.

The thought seared through him like molten lead and left a gaping void where it had travelled like a malevolent river. He could deliberate no longer. His father's death had seen to that. As soon as he felt able to leave his grieving mother, Giancarlo would return to London and make sure he became the man, a son, worthy of carrying the status now bestowed upon him.

CHAPTER TWENTY

Gabrielle watched fondly as Phoebe slept peacefully beside her. With Doug now in Blackpool for rehearsals, she had reverted to bringing their little girl into their bed for her morning ritual of a cuddle and small bottle of warm milk. A habit Gabrielle knew must be broken at some point in the not too distant future, but it always made Phoebe happy and content for the rest of the day, not to say it gave her mother the purest of joys to snuggle down with her youngest and final child in the knowledge Doug would not be able to moan about it.

She could hear him now. 'I love the kids, Gabs, but they shouldn't be allowed in our bed on a regular basis. We must keep certain things to ourselves. The kids need to learn that... blah blah blah...' He spoke such crap, sometimes. As if HE knew ANYTHING about bringing up their children. He wouldn't even let the kids have a dog. There he went again. 'Not healthy things around the house, carry lots of germs and their bloody hair drops all over the place...' More crap, when what Doug had really meant to say was, there were already three life-forms in the house taking attention away from him, a dog would take THEIR attention away from him as well. For let's not forget the most important thing here. Not the children. Not the wife. But Doug.

Gabrielle dismissed these tetchy thoughts, out of place and irritating in this wonderfully calm and delightful interlude with her baby girl. As Phoebe continued to slumber, her mother reflected on the months ahead.

She had plenty to be getting on with, not least the children. Then there were the minor but substantial charity duties on behalf of her husband in his absence during the long summer. And, of course, overseeing the continuing installation of the new pool. Somewhere within all of this,

Gabrielle would try and find more time for herself. Valerie would be full of ingenious ideas, but, somehow, that wasn't really what Gabrielle wanted. Needed. She sensed she required a mad adventure. Alone. Something else to take her out of herself.

She felt trapped, as if squashed into a vacuum-packed bag, trying desperately to break free and not even able to wriggle... but why? Why now? What was so different about her life today as compared to the same situation before? She felt unsettled, agitated, and suffocated. Of course, over time, Gabrielle had felt all these things occasionally, sometimes strongly, others not, but today... they were coming at her *en masse* and with an intensity that she wasn't prepared for.

Wild and dangerous, that's what she needed. Something outrageous. To break out of character, or was that break back IN to character? Reunite with the Gabrielle locked away somewhere inside this fast-diminishing version of herself. But could she get away with it? After all, she was the wife of Doug Delany. Man of the moment. The perpetual Doug moment. She had huge responsibilities, three of them, oh, go on, then... make it four, Doug deserved her recognition, occasionally. When she felt so inclined.

Perhaps a more mature and selective Gabrielle was needed here. Look how the young risk-taker had ended up.

Phoebe had begun to murmur in her sleep and Gabrielle smiled at the little one, gently stroking her baby-fine curls. 'Don't grow up too fast, Bee,' she whispered. 'It's never quite what you expect. Take your time, live every single day to the full. Don't hurry to spread your wings and fly.' Gabrielle could feel tears coming and took a deep breath. 'Whatever you do, my darling, Mummy will always be there for you.' The last came out on a silent, choked-back sob.

Gabrielle thought her own mother would have always been there for her, and she had been, until Doug came along. When Mrs Weston realised she had lost the battle for her daughter and the life she was supposed to live, a truce was made, but afterwards, a space opened up between mother and daughter. It had slowly but surely increased over the years, and although both still loved each other dearly, there was now a gulf of emotion separating the two women that neither seemed willing to cross to reach the other. So they both stood alone on their opposing beaches, stubborn, but not entirely resolute.

One day, either might just chance a voyage across the swirling emptiness and pick up the bloody phone.

Gabrielle's father kept the peace, as was the role of many a husband-come-father in a family with two Alpha females. Kept the family talking in spite of everything that had gone on. Arranged the get-togethers. Never gave up hope that there might be a surrender during his lifetime, only when he'd had a few, mind. He was their faithful go-between. Whatever Daddy really thought about Gabrielle's life decisions, he never made an issue of them with her. He left that to his wife. She said plenty enough for both of them. He wisely counselled his daughter when she needed it, and loved her with every ounce of his being, but he would not allow himself to get involved in the minutiae of it all. Bernard Weston was simply a husband and father doing his best in a difficult situation.

The phone suddenly rang beside the bed and Gabrielle lunged for it to prevent Phoebe being woken. She failed in her effort as the sleepyhead opened her eyes, stuffed a thumb in her mouth and said around it, 'Phone, Mummy.'

'Mrs Delany? This is Martine from The Spa? You had a...'

'Oh, my gosh! I'm so sorry, Martine. I completely forgot.'

'Would you like me to reschedule your appointment?'

'Tell you what, I'll get back to you later when I know where I'm at. Please charge today to my account and do apologise to Tania for me.'

'I will, Mrs Delany, and not to worry, we'll look forward to seeing you soon.'

Gabrielle hung up and turned to Phoebe, pulling the delicate child to her saying, 'Anyway, Mummy would far rather spend this time with you.'

It was as good as, if not better than, even the very best massage Tania could offer.

She also still had those disgruntled thoughts to decipher. Something was up with her. That much was certain.

Jayne and Adam lay in each other's arms, both reticent but positively glowing in the aftermath of a morning of some torrid sex. It had been a while since they had melded so well. Obviously that time had given them both a renewed sense of impetus. In fact, it would have been fair comment to say this morning's love-in measured up to some of their initial couplings when they had first got together.

Jayne smiled at that. It pleased her. Adam was leaving later that day for Blackpool, they wouldn't have another opportunity like this until Jayne could get away from London during post-production on the documentary. She hoped this morning would stay locked into Adam's memory and take away the dangers of anyone else. A hope Jayne wasn't incredibly confident about but she intended to remain optimistic, all the same.

Now her post-orgasm contentment was fast wearing off, and cold reality waited, as ever, to jump on and trounce her warm fuzzy thoughts.

'Penny for them?' Adam said, touching her face.

'Oh, nothing. Just thinking how good you can be when you try!'

'Cheeky cow! I try ALL the time,' Adam laughed in response.

I know, thought Jayne. *Only too well, my love.* 'Shall I make you one of my gut-busting breakfasts to send you on your way?' she asked lightly, once again back hard and fast in the stark here and now of her crumbling marriage.

'Oh, Jaynie, yes, please!'

As she moved to get out of bed, Adam caught hold of her hand and pulled her back, wrapping a leg around her own. He gave her body a slow once over, then settled his eyes on hers, a deep longing gaze.

'But before you do...'

She watched as her husband drove away from the house, waving constantly through the sun-roof until he disappeared round a bend in the road. Jayne sighed. 'Que sera, sera,' she said aloud to herself. 'And there ain't nothing you can do about it.'

If this was the autumn of their relationship, so be it. Jayne knew she couldn't stop loving him 'just in case'. It didn't work that way. No, she would continue to feel everything in its full intensity until circumstances dictated that it was finally time to draw to a halt. She would know that moment when it came, of that she had no doubts.

For now, though, Jayne remained married to the love of her life, breaker of her heart. Jayne was still Mrs Adam Nash, and for all intents and purposes, that was exactly what she would project to the world. Until her position became untenable.

The phone rang and she ran inside to answer it. A crackle from his ageing phone told her immediately who it was.

'Just had to say you were wonderful, beautiful, this morning. I love you, Jaynie.'

'I love you too, Adam. Drive safely.'

Jayne smiled as she hung up. They were such lovely words that her husband had spoken, and with real love surrounding them. Even so, a familiar fast-freeze had already gripped her heart and started to harden it.

Oh well, there was still Daddy's birthday party in Perth.

Summer lugged a second load of bags up to her flat. She had hoped Giancarlo would have been there to help her, but upon news of his father's sudden death, he immediately left for Sicily. Not surprisingly, she hadn't heard from him since. Even so, for the first time in a long time, Summer felt terribly alone as she dumped the bags and went back for the final luggage run.

Her feelings suggested that she was really in love, at last, and Summer was finding it a strangely pleasant experience. So many new and different emotions, thoughts and ideals merged together in one big lump inside her, somewhere between her heart and stomach. The overall effect of which prompted what was, for this young lady, a unique sentiment – a wish that she wasn't imminently opening in a new show. That truly was a first. Instead, Summer wanted to be with Giancarlo, lending moral and emotional support, as he had done for her when George died. Show him the care she knew she could provide for him. Experience something, though tragic for her lover and his family, which would be so valuable to her as a person who was eager to learn about the responsibilities of a deep and meaningful relationship. A journey into a huge unknown.

Summer had simply never allowed herself to be so close to a man. Let him get within her precious inner sanctum, trusting him not to hurt her most vulnerable self. In opening up like this, she could let all kinds of previously barred feelings wander through her, some lingering longer than others, those Summer felt necessary to hold on to for a better understanding. In turn, she was beginning to discover things about herself that she had, until now, refused to face.

She thankfully dropped the last of her belongings in the small hallway and closed the door of the flat. 'Tea,' she said to herself in the gilt-framed mirror opposite, picked up two Tesco bags and headed for the spacious, newly fitted kitchen. As she entered, she stopped dead. There, perfectly displayed on one of the counters, was an open food hamper from Fortnum and Mason's. Nearby stood a bottle of her favourite pink champagne. She slowly moved to the fridge and opened it. Of course, it was stocked full of everything she loved and could ever have wanted. *Oh, Carlo,* she thought somewhat tearfully. *I just don't deserve you.* But she was planning seriously on becoming a woman who did.

Then there was the disturbance of a small consideration that fluttered into her mind. If Giancarlo had been away in Sicily, who the hell had put all this delicious fare in the flat?

CHAPTER TWENTY ONE

Doug stepped through the stage door. To him, it was like entering a home from home, maybe even his designated place to be, more than any other. A dear friend that welcomed the comedian with open arms and affection.

He felt safe within those arms as they slowly wrapped themselves around him, giving Doug an affirmative hug that said everything was going to be all right. Held in this mistress's embrace, everything always was. He understood her world. It was sanctuary from the real thing, the one that, in his most private candid moments, Doug acknowledged he wasn't very good at. Whatever might have been happening on the outside, however desperate one may feel about a personal matter, all of it ceased to matter as they passed through the stage door, a magic portal from one life to another, once again secure within this illusory domain.

The company manager, Phil Beauchamp, was waiting in the doorway of the stage door office. An attractive, small athletic man in his early forties, Phil had been in many chorus lines in the West End and, on the inevitable tours, had understudied for the star of a long-running musical and even replaced him when flu had struck. But as with the fickle hand of show business, apart from rapturous receptions from the audiences, Phil never got the professional recognition for his performance that was undeniably deserved. When it became apparent his career would progress no further, Phil, at one of an increasing number of loose ends one October, took up an offer to manage a panto for a friend who was directing, and never looked back. Now part of the formidable production machine owned by Buzz MacIntyre, Phil Beauchamp's career was finally on the up and up. He secretly still wished he could be out front, on stage, but at least he continued to work in the business, unlike many friends, and during a run would be able to draw in and stock up on the atmosphere and excitement of what he had almost left behind.

His face brightened as Doug appeared. 'Doug! How's it going?'

'Great, just great.'

'Come on,' Phil said, indicating for Doug to follow him into the depths of backstage. 'Let's show you around the dear old girl.'

'Sure, but hang on a sec...' Doug popped his head round the door of the tiny stage door office. A sixtyish, balding man had already seen Doug arrive and was moving toward him with an outstretched hand and broad smile.

'Mr Delany, pleased to meet you, sir.'

'Oh...just Doug is fine...and you are?' he asked, taking the man's hand.

'Clive Mawby. Welcome to the Opera House.'

'Thanks, I think you'll find we've got a blinding show for her.'

'With you in it, any show would be a winner.'

'Cheers, Clive! Listen, speak to you later.'

Clive nodded and mock-saluted as Doug gave a thumbs up and took his leave. Doug always made a point of introducing himself to the stage door keeper upon first arrival. It was worth it. Because with careful handling and the odd bottle or two of their favourite tipple, they became his personal security against pushy fans and unexpected guests when he wasn't feeling up to it, which was infrequent, but even Mr Happiness sometimes had a shit day.

'Anyone else arrived yet?' he asked Phil as they walked down towards 'number one' dressing room, situated almost side stage for the ultimate convenience for the top of the bill.

'Most of the girls and boys, with a couple of exceptions, but no doubt they'll show up later today, as will Adam. Probably still on the road. We've had to reschedule a couple of your rehearsal calls, Marcia wants to make some changes to one of the dance numbers, something isn't working... you know... typical Marcia, just before we're due to open! Hope that's okay?'

'No problem, just keep me informed, Phil. Oh, this is great,' Doug said as they entered the spacious and modern dressing room, fully equipped with its own shower room and toilet, fridge and television. Not to mention comfy sofa and what looked like new carpeting, and of course, enough square footage of mirrors to make one person look like a crowd. 'This'll do just fine. Where's number two?' he asked, referring to the dressing room reserved for next best in show. It would be where Adam Nash would settle in when he arrived.

'Just round the corner. Anything else you think you'll need in here?'

'Nah... but I'll let you know once I'm in. Maybe a decent bottle of Scotch on the dresser!' He laughed. 'No, this all looks fine. Just need to pack 'em in, now.'

'Amen to that!' The company manager chortled back. 'But I checked the advance bookings this morning and we've got full houses right through to August, already. That's including matinees. So it's looking pretty good so far.'

'That's excellent news. What about press?'

'There's a few interviews set up but I'll get back to you on those. There's plenty of excitement in the town about the show. How about I show you around the place?'

'No, you carry on, mate. I'll have a wander by myself.' Doug always preferred it that way. Get a feel of a theatre whilst alone. Size her up and see how they would get along together. So far, he felt he would get along with this dame like a dream.

'Okay, catch up with you later, Doug.'

As Phil left him alone in the dressing room, Doug took a lengthy breath in and slowly let it out, then made the few short steps to stage left, and walked out onto the boards. A couple of resident stage crew were fiddling with a piece of scenery suspended up in the flies. When they saw Doug look up at them, they waved and one said in a joking announcement, 'It's Doug Delany!'

'Hello, lads,' he responded while walking to front of stage, just behind the footlights. Below them, 'the pit', or 'orchestra pit' as it used to be known in days when they still put on shows that required one. Generally now, the orchestra was reduced to a 'band', as in the case of this production, with much of the music pre-recorded. Sadly, many shows now had no live music at all.

The stage itself was huge. No wonder the dance numbers were massive. A lot of surface to cover. Still, with what he'd heard about the choreographer, Doug was in no doubt she would provide the audiences with a spectacle. He wasn't looking forward to learning his few moves for the finale, though, when all the artists gathered for the curtain call. He'd also heard that Marcia Raeburn was a perfectionist, and here was Doug Delany with two left feet.

He looked out into the auditorium and its three thousand seats. There weren't too many of those to work in now, outside London. It was a tribute to Blackpool and her unending attraction that this town still boasted such a theatre, and he was going to be working it for the summer season. His last summer season.

Doug took in another profound breath, this time holding in the comforting aromas surrounding him. It was a sensory memory he could call up at any time, because it never left him. A musty mix of burnt dust on lights, old make-up and costumes, lingering sweat and exertion from all the performers through the years, and the scent of their successes and failures. For Doug, it was the most priceless perfume in the world. His world.

He exhaled slowly. Could he really let all this go? Give up the adrenaline rush as he stood nervously side-stage waiting to go on every night, and the cheers and applause as he walked out into the bright lights from the wings to start his routine? Was it going to be possible? Doug knew if he were to hold onto his wife, and in turn, his kids, he would have to make it possible. But, oh... how he would miss it. He would probably grieve as though bereaved. In the meantime, he would soak it all up, every single molecule. Store it away somewhere deep inside. Somewhere no one could find it and take it from him. Ever.

'Doug,' came a shout from the wings and Phil walked out on stage with another man, smartly attired in a grey suit. 'Like you to meet Kevin, front of house manager.'

'Kevin,' Doug smiled and held out a hand.

'Mr Delany...'

'Doug...'

'Pleased to meet you, Doug. She's a lovely theatre, isn't she?'

'Oh yes,' he replied, looking back out into the auditorium, eyes caressing every section of stalls, circle and boxes, imagining eager, happy faces looking back at him. 'I'm going to have a real blast this season.'

Summer continued to towel-dry her hair as she answered the persistently ringing phone.

'Bella! I'm back in London. How are you? Did you find everything okay there?' His questions were quick and excited.

'Carlo! God, it's so good to hear your voice.' It truly was. 'Everything was wonderful, but who brought it all here?'

'Ah... that's a secret!' he replied conspiratorially and then laughed. 'It was nothing, but a good surprise, yes?'

'Of course it was, thank you.' Summer knew not to press him further on the mystery. She was learning. 'So how were... things... how was your mother?'

'Mama was very strong, Bella. More than all of us, but then, she always has been. You know, after the service, at the house, there was a moment...' he paused, recapturing the image of his mother sitting in Paulo's chair, 'she looked so beautiful.'

Summer didn't know what to say, how to respond, or whether she should at all, so she waited. Giancarlo finally continued, his demeanour completely changed.

'Now I am back, I must see you!'

Summer's heart sank. 'Oh, Carlo, I want to see you too... but...'

'But? What is this... but?' His voice had suddenly become cold and clipped, the normally subtle Sicilian accent very strong.

Summer searched for the right words, ones that would let Giancarlo know how she felt about him now. At the same time, convince him that the reason they couldn't be together for a while was only the show. Marcia Raeburn, to be precise. A revision to a dance number, and rehearsals started at nine the next morning. Summer would be tied up at the theatre until at least the show opened now. Once the previews and opening night were under their belts, there would be more time for the rest of her life. The one she wanted to spend with Giancarlo. Summer so wanted him to realise she was no longer playing her usual mind-fuck games. This wasn't going to be another of her 'string him along' excuses, not calling when she knew she should, telling him she wasn't available when she was. Those days were well and truly over, but how should he know? It was only in the last couple of weeks she had realised that Giancarlo was a special gift, not to be misused. It was now up to Summer to get that through to him.

'Summer, I'm waiting?' he said, frost dusting each word.

'Carlo, it's the choreographer, Marcia. She's changing something in the show and we open for previews in ten days. I know you don't understand any of this and I don't blame you for thinking...'

'Don't tell me what I'm thinking,' he snapped like an alligator.

Summer recoiled. *Come on,* she said, calming herself. *You can do it. He's just upset from the funeral.*

'Carlo, please, listen to me,' she soothed. 'You can come up here whenever you like, but I'll be at the theatre all day, every day. And afterwards, I'll be shattered. What fun will that be? Trust me...' Those were big new words from her. For the first time, Summer wanted another human being to believe that he really could do that now. Trust Summer

Laine. 'All I want to do is put my arms around you and hold you close. I've missed you terribly. You believe me, don't you?' *Please...*

'I'm sorry, Bella.' His voice had reverted back to soft and tender. 'It's just the last few days. Forgive me?'

'There's nothing to forgive, Carlo. I understand. Look, when I know I'll have some free time, I will call you. It'll be soon, I promise.'

'That's fine. Till then, I miss you,' he said, blew a kiss to her and ended the call, then sat back on the bed and took a satisfied drag on his cigarette.

Giancarlo was pleased on several counts. Alessandro was in place, as per his instructions to his cousin before leaving for Taormina, and Summer would be protected in Giancarlo's absence, but more to the point, he would know every move his future wife made.

Then there was the lady herself. It seemed to him that she was slowly but surely becoming the woman he wanted her to be. The way in which she had immediately tried to placate him when he decided to test her loyalty, the genuine feel to her appeasing, all told him that she was closer than he would have dared to hope. He knew their time was drawing nearer but it wasn't now. Giancarlo would know when they had reached the perfect point of execution. He had a gift for these things. It was most important for him to be patient. Not jump too soon and possibly ruin everything. Summer was to be handled with the lightest touch, an influence so faint, she would not detect it.

Giancarlo would make his move only when he was certain that Summer could not refuse.

He smiled to himself and blew out a steady stream of smoke toward the ceiling on a slow exhale. Sometime soon, he would have the pleasure of seeing the joy in his mama's violet eyes when he announced he was to finally marry and complete his transformation to head of the family.

Doug had returned to his rental to start working on various routines. He had three spots to fill, two smaller ones at each end of the show, but his main act followed the opening dance number on curtain up after the interval. There were a few introductions for the dance routines and a couple of guests throughout the show, shared with Adam Nash. They'd have to get together over some golf and discuss who'd do what, and fine tune each appearance so they didn't clash with the jokes. Doug had heard good things about the ventriloquist and had loved the act he saw some years before with a rather wicked pig. He decided they should get on well. Then there was the task of personalising his act to suit Blackpool and her people. Make sure there was always a spare minute or two in case of any sudden topical news item he could work into the script for that day. He needed to keep up to the minute, be fresh, but always funny.

Taking a quick break, and Scotch to hand, Doug dialled home. There was no reply and he drained the glass. Gabrielle's absence set him thinking about the future, after Blackpool. He retained a very real sense of the gravity in his wife's voice during their conversation in the kitchen, her eyes had been burning into his when he had told her this would be the last full summer season. Doug was in no doubt there would be hell to pay if he were to break that promise. The cost would just be too dear, in every respect. But at what price for him?

He also knew Mrs Delany wouldn't stand for another indiscretion, thankfully those days were behind them. She would realise that in time. Doug wasn't stupid, he knew there would be some silly tart in the show who would do everything in her power to get his full attentions, and despite his newly developed principles on the matter, being Doug, of course he would be flattered and probably let her know that, in some trivial way. But he had set himself strict guidelines now, ones never to be crossed, for anyone. Even if she was just like that transcendent loveliness under the waterfall in the shampoo advert.

Doug truly believed he had turned a corner, that he was no longer the egotistical fool he had been. Gabs was worth more than all the extramarital sex in the world. She always had been and he understood that now.

Thinking back through all their years together and the countless liberties he had taken so blatantly at times, Doug shivered at how close he might have come to losing Gabrielle. No one had ever remotely been in the same calibre as his wife. When everything else around him seemed to exist on a wing and a prayer, his Gabs had remained constant. She was number one in his life and this husband would never forget it again.

CHAPTER TWENTY TWO

Gabrielle walked purposefully down Regent Street and straight to Hamleys. It was Alexander's birthday in a few days and she carried with her an extensive wish list from her son. Most of his preferences were computer-orientated and Gabrielle hoped some kind and knowledgeable shop assistant would help enlighten her before she made her choices. Despite being able to provide everything Alexander wanted without thinking about it, there was a strict code both she and Doug adhered to rigidly; that the children would learn the value of money and therefore, restraint. To appreciate what they were given and understand that just because you could, it didn't always mean that you should.

On that philosophical note, Gabrielle entered the store and felt a pang of girlish delight. Still an excitable child at heart, maybe rarely now but still occasionally, she looked about the vast toy palace, eyes keen to explore. With Phoebe safely in the capable hands of Doris for the day, this mother could be like her children and take time to drool over her own favourites, the cuddly toys, before reverting back to the adult self and carrying out the reason she was there. While slowly taking in the incredible array of play things, Gabrielle recalled a brief visit to New York with Doug, a surprise anniversary present prior to the birth of their son. During a walk up the fabled Fifth Avenue toward Central Park for the obligatory horse and buggy ride around the south east corner, they found FAO Swartz, New York's own First Lady of toys. Gabrielle insisted she simply had to go in and browse, so she packed a less than enthusiastic Doug off to the Plaza Hotel across the road for a drink, while she spent an indulgent half an hour looking at the most amazing toys she had ever set eyes on. The urge to buy a life-size baby giraffe and walk into the bar of the

Plaza with it had been huge, but at the last minute, Gabrielle had decided that even Doug's generous sense of humour didn't stretch that far. So instead, she bought a little white rabbit with long floppy ears and called it Mr Delany.

Gabrielle smiled at the memory, she still had that stupid rabbit but Phoebe was borrowing it at the moment, as had Alex and then Sasha, who had been quite indignant when Mummy told her she must give it up for her baby sister. Gabrielle suspected she'd have to fight both of them to get Mr Delany back. Then she considered how happy she and Doug had been on that long weekend and suddenly, as if pushed into a bright light from the soft tones of her memories, the carefree child instantly disappeared. Gabrielle dug out the list from her bag before going to find that knowledgeable assistant.

Alexander's carefully selected presents set aside ready for collection, she decided to have a quick wander around John Lewis's kitchen department and then grab a decent coffee and a sandwich. On the way up to the café, her mind was invaded by a certain Mr Maldini and his recent intriguing invitation. A wicked smile led to a wayward giggle. Two old biddies in the lift with Gabrielle looked at her with some suspicion. Knowing glances travelled between the two, although what, in fact, they thought they knew was open to suggestion. As the lift stopped at the top floor, they swiftly got out and began to whisper to each other while heading towards the café. Gabrielle pressed the button for the ground floor. What the hell, Angelo's wasn't too far away and she was famished, a plate of his delicious pasta over a ready-made sandwich, there was no contest. And anyway, she thought with impish mischief, this could be that little adventure she had previously deliberated about. That morsel of a secret life Gabrielle felt everyone was entitled to, however devoted they were to their partner. Harmless concealments that keep us individual and instil in us the essence of being free within the confines of living in accordance with society's expectations.

There was nothing wrong with going into the restaurant alone, many women dined by themselves; business women, mothers out with the children, or simply women like Gabrielle, who just wanted to feel as though they retained a sense of liberty, going against the code, risking a break from the normal constraints of an over-full life. Saturated with things that she didn't necessarily want but dutifully soaked up anyway, because as a wife and mother of three, it was what she was required to do. This would be a minor interlude outside that life. A defiant act of rebellion. How refreshing it might prove to be.

As she walked briskly towards Piccadilly, Gabrielle already felt empowered.

Angelo's looked packed to bursting as she stood across the road and viewed the hubbub through the windows. She nearly turned back, but something kept Gabrielle standing there, watching, thinking. Perhaps it was preferable that the restaurant was busy, remembering what Valerie had said, it might keep the proprietor's attentions strictly professional. Oh, but that would be no fun, would it? The whole point of her momentary disobedience was to play. For that, one needed someone to play with. Angelo Maldini seemed to fit the bill.

It wasn't as though the restaurateur was going to throw her to the floor upon arrival and ravish her there and then in front of the other diners... make wild passionate love to her while they all watched aghast... Gabrielle laughed out loud and several passers-by viewed her with a hint of wariness.

Now that WOULD be something to keep me going when Doug was up to his tricks again, she mused. Crossing the road, Gabrielle decided she would just pop in, see if he was there, take him up on his offer and that would be that. *Live a little, you deserve it, girl,* she told herself as the door opened and a pleasantly surprised-looking Angelo gently took her hand, guiding her into the restaurant while smiling like a Cheshire cat.

Amanda Jacobs breezed into the theatre and set about choosing her place in the girls' dressing-room. Not too close to the door, too much traffic, and away from the windows. Even in summer, Sara had advised her there could be a nasty evening breeze off the sea which would play havoc with her delicate chest. A bout of chronic bronchitis aged seventeen had seen to that. No matter how fit she was, Amanda was always susceptible to infection, especially in a hot sweaty dressing-room with a spiteful draft, so somewhere in the middle. It appeared most of her comrades had already been in, but there was a nice cosy place still vacant.

Selecting her spot, Amanda sighed, she had just learned from Phil Beauchamp that first rehearsal was the following morning. She wasn't best pleased. Now she had to call Jason and stop him coming down as arranged. He had a day off and had intended to spend it with her. Not now, and she knew he wouldn't take it very well. But what could she do? This was her life and he really should have been handling their relationship better. After all, he was working in theatre himself, there were times when he had to cancel and she had always understood.

They'd already had a heated conversation, started through her own frustrations at his changing attitude towards them as a couple. Amanda felt Jason was getting clingy, possessive, wanted to know where she was every moment of the day and night. Even so, he hadn't deserved what she had said, and she needed to apologise. It would have been to his face but now he would have to make do with a phone call. Amanda didn't want to lose him. Jason wasn't like the other men she had been with, and there had been a few. With Jase, what you saw was what you got; no hidden agendas, no secret egos in competition with hers, he was a regular stand-up kind of guy. Kept her grounded when she got a bit full of her own importance. Maybe it was time to finally commit herself, he'd certainly stuck around long enough, unlike the rest of the rabble. It was asking a lot, though, particularly with the show about to get up and running, and it meant Amanda had a lot to think about, not something she found easy at the best of times.

After placing some make-up paraphernalia on the cramped portion of dresser that would be hers for the next few months, Amanda decided to go for a long walk on the prom, take in some fresh sea air and clear her jangled mind. Try and work out how to break it to her already disgruntled boyfriend there was no point in him coming down to see her the following day.

The warm friendly ambience closed around her like a generous pashmina on bare shoulders on a chilly night, while Angelo led Gabrielle through the restaurant, and downstairs to a quiet table in one of the booths, normally reserved for his VIPs. Mouth-watering aromas wafted from the kitchen and she could feel her stomach doing its usual 'feed me' rumba. She hoped no one could hear it.

'Only the best,' Angelo beamed as he indicated for her to sit, while assisting in the removal of her coat. 'I will bring us something to drink,' he said and vanished into the restaurant again.

Get US something to drink, Gabrielle repeated mentally. *Hmm, so much for being busy... well, Val, this is where I find out if you're right!* Gabrielle made herself comfortable, fiddled mindlessly with the place settings and wondered why she suddenly felt really guilty, like a schoolgirl who had just bunked off lessons to meet up behind the bike sheds for a snog. She smiled at that thought. Why on earth she should be feeling disloyal to Doug was a mystery. She was only here for a quick lunch and probably an hour or so of Angelo flirting outrageously with her. What harm was there in that?

But hadn't she been down this path once before? Many years ago? In Bournemouth? Funny, the same uneasy sensations were beginning to surface. *Stop it,* she chided. *You were young and inexperienced then, this is now, you're a totally different person...* but that consideration pulled her up short. Was she? Would Doug's faithful wife have made the decision to come here? Food for thought, just as Angelo returned with a bottle of champagne.

'Oh, Angelo, this isn't necessary...'

'Gabriella! For you, only the best I have.' Then he leaned down and whispered into her ear, 'Don't deny me this pleasure!' His face lingered near to hers for perhaps a moment too long.

Gabrielle smiled sweetly, though her heart was jumping about and she realised that there was an element of adolescent excitement to all of this. As he popped the cork and poured the champagne, she swallowed to clear a tickle of anticipation. Angelo sat next to her in the booth and handed Gabrielle a glass.

'To unexpected pleasures in life,' he said and touched his glass to hers.

Gabrielle took a long sip. While the bubbles slipped agreeably down her throat, she knew this wasn't right, shouldn't be happening, but still she felt compelled to be there, with this man, drinking his champagne. Memories of secret liaisons with Doug flooded her thoughts, was it really that long ago since she had felt this way? Had they been through so much and their life become such that Gabrielle would never experience these emotions ever again with her husband? It was true that love, long term, could never retain those first heady days or weeks, when hormones and passions took you from one high to another, inhibitions abandoned, pure raw lust becoming the staple diet that could sustain you for far longer than any food or water. But shouldn't she be content in the life she had? It was better than most.

Or was it simply that she was surprised and flattered by another man's attentions after her time in a marriage fraught with its problems? Gabrielle had married young, Doug had been only the second man she had known sexually, and she had been his ever since. Were these the feelings of her lost youth trying to make a break for freedom after being suppressed for what seemed like an eternity, and at last seeking the thrills and distractions it had sorely missed out on? Whatever it was that she was encountering from deep within, Gabrielle felt intoxicatingly alive.

'So! What have I done to deserve your delightful company?' Angelo said, his arm casually settling around the back of the semi-circular seat, and in turn, Gabrielle.

Despite the champagne, her mouth was so dry with nerves, she could only smile and shrug like an embarrassed child. Even if Gabrielle could have spoken at that moment, it was unlikely she would have been able to think of anything intelligent to say.

While Amanda sat waiting for her tram back to Fleetwood, she called Jason.

'Hi, babe,' he breathed back down the line. 'All sorted at the theatre?'

'Yeah. How are you?' she asked, delaying the dreaded moment.

'Not bad, looking forward to seeing you.'

Now or never. 'Jase?' And Amanda told him, or tried to.

'I'm getting fed up with this, Mand,' he sighed. Jason only ever called her Mand when he was really pissed off. Because he knew she detested it. 'Can't I still come down and just see you in the evening?'

'Oh, come on, Jase, give me a break, I'll be knackered. And anyway, I've only just arrived at May's and, well... you know.'

'No I don't, what?' He was beginning to severely irritate her now. Sounding so bloody immature.

'It's just... Oh, for crying out loud, Jason, lighten up, will you? It's one day, for God's sake, we knew it wasn't going to be easy this summer. Let's be thankful we've both got work, eh?' Amanda realised she was being that short-tempered bitch diva again, not conducive to keeping this man in her life. Why did she find personal relationships so difficult? What was it about being intimate with a man that seemed to bring out the worst in her? Before Amanda's brain was fried with an overload of the deep and meaningful, she took in a long quiet breath, softening her voice. 'Come on, babe, let's not fight again.'

There was silence at the other end. *Come on, Jase,* she silently pleaded. Looking up, she could see the tram arriving.

'Jason, I've got to go, the tram's here. Please call me later? Jase?'

She looked at her display and saw that the call had already been ended.

CHAPTER TWENTY THREE

Summer added a banana to the various high-protein ingredients in the blender and turned it on. While she stood watching her own special 'workout' recipe mushing into a delicious and easily digestible smoothie, to an accompaniment of a high-pitched whirr, the phone began to ring. Knowing she was running a bit late, Summer grabbed a glass and poured out half of the thick creamy gloop, taking a few sips on her way to answer the call. It was Giancarlo, again. They had spoken twice already that morning, and with her heavy day ahead, he was now beginning to severely piss Summer off.

'I changed my mind. I have to see you, even just for a few hours tonight.' He was trying to sound whimsical and boyish, appealing to her sentimental side. It didn't suit him and certainly didn't wash with his girlfriend. She sighed to herself, finished the contents of the glass and checked the time, she simply had to get going, so no chance of putting him off. Too complicated.

'Whatever, Carlo, you know you can come up whenever you like. Just remember I'll be very tired, so don't go expecting... anything... you know what I'm saying.'

'Of course, Bella, I just want to be with you, that's all. Don't worry about me arriving, I have a key. I'll be there ready for when you get home, making you something to eat.'

'That'll be lovely, Carlo,' Summer replied in a resigned tone. The food thing would be very welcome. The company? She didn't have a choice, did she? 'Now I really must go.'

'Ciao.'

As they hung up, there it was again, that intrusive uneasiness creeping up from her stomach while Giancarlo's words echoed through her mind. *I have a key.* There was nothing essentially wrong with that statement, they were an item, it was normal to have access to each other. Or was it? Summer hadn't chosen to give her lover a key to this flat, unlike her London address. He'd had one before she did. Something didn't feel right about that. A deviation from the usual order of things. Her disquiet wasn't helped by the fact Summer had yet to hold a key to Giancarlo's home. Maybe this was how it was done in Sicily. Perhaps she should just carry on and stop asking these questions to which there would never be answers, as it would be impossible for her to ask the person with them.

This was her first committed relationship. Summer truly believed she was in love, even allowed herself to think she might need him, sometimes. But in giving way to such a need, was she sacrificing her independence? Something Summer would normally viciously protect, as she did her right to set boundaries, moving them only when she decided it was beneficial to do so. In pursuing a better self, trying to become someone she might really be proud of, the kind of woman a decent man would want to marry, and the woman Daddy had probably always wanted her to be, was she letting this man walk all over her?

Summer drank the rest of her smoothie straight from the blender jug, resulting in the usual milky moustache. She knew Giancarlo hated it when she did things like that. And maybe that was why Summer hadn't hesitated. She wiped her mouth with a tea-towel, another dreadful habit but she was in hurry... and threw everything else in the sink for later. *Or even Carlo,* she retorted to herself, seeing him standing looking into the sink, shaking his head at this house-husbandry sloppiness. With her rehearsal holdall slung over a shoulder, Summer opened the front door and paused to look at her reflection in the hallway mirror. A slightly fraught face with steely eyes studied her back.

She'd always known, even as a young girl, that she was up there in the attractive stakes, but that only ran to skin deep on any living thing. It was the heart and soul underneath this highly decorative exterior Summer was making her best effort to be beautiful. And it might take some time, more than was at her disposal, possibly, where Giancarlo was concerned. There would be hiccups along the way, that much Summer was sure of. Maybe forgiving him his suffocating adoration, especially when it was the last thing she required that morning, was a worthy first step on what could be a long and complex journey. And if she was brutally honest with herself, there were moments when Summer actually craved her lover's smothering nature, finding it a comfort, like a big woolly blanket to snuggle into and hide from the demons of her past that still managed to escape and torment her from time to time. When she was alone and in sombre mood. When she couldn't sleep at night. When self-hatred overwhelmed.

Safe in Giancarlo's presence, in his arms, or when held firm against his strong body with him inside her, those ghastly gargoyles of former deeds were kept securely shackled to the filthy walls of the foulest dungeons in her mind.

A shadow passed across her face and Summer shivered as she closed the door.

Gabrielle just managed to reach Sasha's school in time to pick her up. Thankfully, Alexander was at rugby practice and would be delivered home by the coach in the school minibus. It would at least allow Gabrielle to hide his presents without the usual shenanigans to keep him out of the way while she tried to conceal the revealing bags.

Lunch had been surprisingly enjoyable. Angelo had been charming, witty, but above all, completely respectful, apart from the odd casual touch on her shoulder and arm. Totally different to how Gabrielle had imagined the man would be. And those eyes, though almost black, they shone vibrant and expressive as Angelo spoke. Gabrielle had been rather transfixed by them at times, feeling as though she was being drawn into their inscrutable deepness. The longer they were together, chatting about an array of subjects, Angelo Maldini had transformed from a rotund, rather loud host, into an unusually attractive man. He had seemed genuine in his interest about Gabrielle, her own life away from Doug, especially life before the Doug factor, and that was a joy unto itself. He listened intently to what she had to say, sometimes agreeing, and when he didn't, politely putting his point across so not to offend. By the time Gabrielle realised she must leave to collect Alexander's presents and pick up Sasha, her bowl of pasta was hardly touched.

As he had seen her to the door, Angelo asked if they could 'do this again'. Without hesitation, Gabrielle had said yes. The logistics she would work out later. So an arrangement was made; a certain day, a certain time. 'Because we seem to have so much to talk about!' he had laughed warmly. She had no feelings of guilt, quite the opposite. For once, Gabrielle had thrown caution to the wind without the usual gauntlet of questions and emotions that would normally have resulted in her changing her mind. Back off. See sense. Not this time.

Drawing to a stop on the driveway, she looked in the mirror at her daughter, still blissful, bobbing her head and twirling a strand of hair as she listened to music. Gabrielle knew she would never jeopardise the security of her children. Their little lives and the big one she provided for them was sacred, to be protected at all costs. Even at the cost of their mother's own happiness, if necessary. But maybe, just for a brief moment, she might be permitted this little interlude. Like taking a pick-me-up tonic to see her on her way for the rest of her life as wife and mother. An away-day from her humdrum existence that would relieve whatever frustrations were sending her towards such an event in the first place. For too long, Gabrielle had been the dutiful carer of her husband and offspring, and though her role had been cushioned by the luxurious trappings of her husband's successful life, as with any full-time carer, this one desperately needed some respite care herself.

Gabrielle smiled ironically. Why was she suddenly feeling so profound about things? It wasn't as if Doug had ever stopped to think of the possible consequences of his own sabbaticals from their marriage, and Gabrielle was only going as far as lunch. Anyway, even if she did lose her mind for one stupid moment and something did happen, Doug wouldn't notice. Doug didn't see anything unless it was right in front of him, or in a script, or dancing on a stage. If Doug Delany wasn't involved, it didn't exist. Still, Gabrielle doubted very much that she would enter into anything other than a friendship with Angelo, someone to have a laugh with occasionally. After all, the man was married and had his own baby daughter. With everything Gabrielle had suffered herself as the wife of a prolific adulterer, she would never inflict it on another woman.

Doug was restless. He was on top of his act and raring to go, but he wasn't required at the theatre until the following day. And it was pouring with rain. Despite being an ardent golfer, even Doug would think twice before playing in such conditions. A light shower wasn't a problem, he actually excelled in a spot or two of drizzle sometimes, probably because he was thinking about getting wet and not his game. However, the weather outside the window was typical of the coastal north west in late spring early summer, so Doug had decided to cook a great big pot of the only thing he could, beef stew and dumplings. All right, it wasn't exactly the fare for this time of year and he could certainly afford to eat out every day, but there was something about the smell and warmth of a pot of the stuff when he was tired and hungry and wanted to stay in, especially when Gabrielle wasn't around. It was a comfort drawn from his childhood when his dear old 'mam' had made it their staple diet during rotten northern winters. Even now, when Doug wished his parents were still alive, wanting just to sit quietly with them in the 'parlour', not saying much, just being with them, a bowl of his mam's recipe always sent him there, anyway.

Unlike previous tours or summer seasons, Doug was already missing his wife and kids. It normally took a few weeks, or maybe just a bad day to prompt such feelings, but whyever he was experiencing these strange emotions, Doug realised he felt very alone, perhaps for the first time. He didn't like it one little bit, so setting about making his special pot of consolation would be the perfect antidote. For now. Then he had to work on getting his family up for a visit as soon as possible, and he knew exactly how Gabs would feel about that prospect. This new Doug Delany was proving a very difficult man to be.

As he mixed flour into softened butter with fast moving fingers, Doug recalled watching his mother doing the same and being allowed to have a go, then getting a clip round the ear for making too much mess. Although she'd had a hard hand that connected with a resounding thump on the side of his head, the memory still made Doug smile. And even though he had watched all those times and listened to her explain how to make them, Doug was never able to reproduce his mam's light and fluffy dumplings. After patting the mix into palm-sized balls, he set each aside on a plate and asked out loud, 'How do they look, Mam?'

'Too bloody stodgy,' he could hear her replying, as though she stood next to him, watching with arms crossed and the usual sarcastic look on her face.

'Aye, well, I'm doing my best!' he said with a cheeky grin on his own face. Then he wondered, was he? Doing his best? Not with the dumplings, his life. Could he stay on this new track for the duration of the imaginary marathon he had just entered? Yes, he could. Because this time, he had promised his wife from somewhere deep inside himself. An honourable contract to be the husband and father that Gabrielle wanted. And wasn't that what he wanted? Of course it was, it always had been, it was just... just the way he was. Correction, had been. This time, Doug was going to make damn sure he did his best.

He gently lowered his dumplings into the aromatic soup and stirred, then took a spoon and had a quick taste, savouring old familiar flavours. 'It's a goodern!' he said in a booming theatrical announcement to his mother, still standing next to him. He placed the lid on the pot and turned off the cooker. It was no use, he had to get out of the house, go for a drive or drink at the club, get to know the resident professional, maybe arrange a game. Anything to shake off the edginess he was feeling. Probably just pre-show nerves building, though the onset was rather more rapid and intense than usual.

He didn't make it to the golf club. Instead, the car seemed to automatically drive him to the theatre. He would sit incognito in the auditorium and see how the rehearsals were going, what delights Marcia Raeburn had created for the show, perhaps wander around the place and check out the bookings. It was what he was good at, made him feel better. Made him feel like Doug Delany again.

'... and five, and six, and now turn... up and, keep up with me... that's it... good... let's do it again.' Marcia's instructions from the stage area wafted through to the stage door office as Doug arrived and said hello to Clive, who handed Doug a couple of letters.

'They've already found me, Clive. They're tenacious!' Doug joked to Clive about his adoring fans. There were a couple, two ladies, who followed him wherever he went, and if they couldn't actually get to see him in the show, wrote copious letters to the theatre during a run. They were harmless, though, just lonely women to whom Doug was a light in their meagre lives. 'No underwear today, then,' he laughed, holding up the envelopes. Clive chuckled.

'I don't think we've ever had anything like that delivered here, so far,' he said.

'Oh... well... you'd better be prepared. My fans like to show me their affection in all sorts of ways, Clive!'

'Aye, Mr Delany, I can imagine!'

'Doug, Clive, it's Doug. Anyone else in apart from the girls and boys?'

'No, not at the moment, though I think Adam Nash is coming in later.'

'Right! Maybe I'll hang around for him. Thanks,' Doug said, indicating the letters and made his way to his dressing-room. He looked again at the envelopes and noticed one had very childish handwriting, Doug sat on the sofa and opened it. The letter was from Alexander.

Dear Dad,

I know you just left but I sent this so you get it when you get there. I think I will come to see you in the holidays if that's okay, Dad. Mum said you would take me up the big tower and to the fairground but you have to come on all the rides with me dad. Can't wait for my birthday. I gave mum a list so I hope I get whats on it.

Write back soon Alex xxx

Doug read the letter several times, his eyes watery. It was the first letter his son had ever written to him. The school fees were worth it, then. But this wasn't about that. The letter represented what Doug had begun with Alexander. It was confirmation that the route he was now taking was the right one. A timely reminder why it was important not to stray again.

It was his son's birthday. Although Doug knew Gabrielle would have made sure there was a card and presents from both of them, he wanted this birthday to be different. As he sat considering that, their afternoon at the pub flooded into his mind. Alexander was growing up faster than Doug had perceived, the letter showed him that. Not only had Doug lost what had gone before, never to be retrieved for another curtain call and encore, forever consigned to the mindful realms of what might have been between this father and son, but it seemed Alexander was fast getting away from him, even now. Thank God he had already reached out and taken a hold of the boy before he had moved too far into the distance to catch up with. It was imperative Doug never let go again.

He put the letter in a pocket and leaving the other fan mail on the room-length dresser, picked up his keys and left to go and buy a suitable present for the birthday boy. There were a few days left to get it there in time. Now all he had to work out was where on Earth would he find something to do with ducks?

Summer flopped in one of the front row stall seats, next to Amanda who was reticent. They were both tired from the hard work Marcia was throwing at them, but they also felt good. The routine was going well, and the choreographer wasn't as bad as they had expected.

'You okay?' Summer asked lightly of the solemn girl sat with head back on the seat, eyes closed. Amanda turned her face toward Summer and gave a tired smile.

'Yeah, just chilling, that's all,' she replied.

'She's all right, really, isn't she?' Summer said, casting a glance at Marcia, talking to a couple of male dancers on the stage. 'She could let up a bit, I guess!'

'Yeah,' Amanda agreed, then added, 'like someone else I know.'

'Oh?' Summer enquired politely.

'Oh! Don't get me started on him...'

'Him? Ah... say no more!' Summer laughed.

'Okay, people, everyone on stage, let's go through the whole thing and see how we get on. Come on, chop chop, haven't got all day...' Marcia bellowed into the auditorium and wings.

Doug was passing the stage when he caught sight of the ensemble getting into position to start a number, music sounding through the speakers, and he stopped. A few minutes wouldn't hurt. He placed himself where he could surreptitiously watch without distracting. Doug wished to keep on the right side of Ms Raeburn for when his own rehearsals started. Then his roaming eyes settled onto long blond hair, tethered in an ornate braid. A tall, slim but perfectly shaped body, and legs to die for. Then he found her face. She was stunning. Breath-taking. The most exquisite female being he had ever seen. But he had seen her before. This was the heavenly girl from the shampoo advert. The one washing her glorious hair under cascading water over a rock pool.

She was the dream.

Nirvana.

And so it was hopeless.

Every thought, each reworked emotion that had gone before, was immediately terminated. Firm resolutions, earnest intentions, final promises, all dissolved and ceased to be.

Doug Delany was utterly lost.

CHAPTER TWENTY FOUR

Doug browsed through the wildlife prints available in the art and crafts shop, but he wasn't exactly focused on the task. His mind was full of intangible thoughts and questions, and yet, numb at the same time. It seemed to drift from one state to the other as he slowly flicked pictures towards him while trying to find one with ducks as a subject matter. Any ducks would do. But it had to be ducks. His mangled mind was clear enough on that point.

Finally, he found a copy of a water colour showing a lake, a thin layer of morning mist lingered delicately just above the surface. More importantly, two ducks, similar to the ones at the pub, were in mid take-off from the water, necks stretched forward, wings fully extended. Perfect. Just perfect. Like her. *NO!* He screamed back at his mixed-up head.

Doug paid for the print and went in search of a post office to get a registered envelope and send the gift to his son, before returning to the theatre. He couldn't help it. Something he was unable to fight drew him there.

What could he do?

Events happen within a life that make no sense whatsoever, are so utterly alien to the dazed recipient, or maybe not in Doug's case, that the beleaguered person finds they can only follow the uncertain path suddenly laid out ahead of them. It requires no great thought process, in fact, soul searching is entirely removed from the equation. They simply need to put one foot in front of the other and blindly trust where they will be taken.

And so it was for Doug Delany. The newly created Doug Delany. The one who had made deeply solemn promises to his wife, and himself. The one with so much to lose. But as he walked through to the darkened auditorium and selected a rear centre stalls seat, Doug knew that whoever he had been not an hour previously, was gone. That identity had been unceremoniously snatched, never to be seen again.

What could he do?

It was beyond his control. Not that Doug had ever been blessed with copious amounts of the virtue.

He gazed at the stage and dancers upon it, all listening intently to the choreographer giving instructions and showing them moves they were to copy and learn, though Doug's eyes were not settled on Marcia, they regarded another. They watched the reason that his family no longer endured in this new life order, and as she carefully practised new steps, the subject of Doug's undivided attention was blissfully unaware of her power and its stranglehold upon him. Every minute, each second that she filled his vision, the further Doug free-fell away from Gabrielle and his children. The more lost to them he became. Destined to eventually disappear.

Whatever this meant, however he was supposed to go forward from this point in time, it didn't seem to matter anymore. The whys and wherefores, whens and hows, were all redundant, for this was a personal event so incredibly basic, so intense, Doug had no idea what was actually happening to him.

Only that wherever he ended up, it had to be worth it.

Adam arranged a few things in the dressing-room. It was more spacious than he had been used to for a summer show and he was feeling happy and contented. Even his marriage seemed to have taken a turn for the better, although he was under no illusions. Adam knew he and Jayne were treading on fragile ground, still... ever the optimist...

He recalled their parting sexual union and immediately stirred. A lustful smile crossed his lips as he played back some the more robust moments. They were still good together and theirs was a partnership worth fighting for, if he could find the mental capacity with the show about to open. But judging by the way in which Jayne had been with him in their last few days together, Adam suspected the relationship would stay on an even keel until the end of the summer when he could give more of himself. And of course, his wife had her work, so that would keep her occupied and not brooding at home like so many show business wives who seemed to give up their own vital lives for their more successful husbands. Always a mistake in Adam's way of thinking. Puts too much pressure on the poor bloke, what with everything they had to go through in their unreliable profession, anyway. So he was lucky in that respect. No, he was fortunate just to be married to the lovely Jayne. Shame about her father, but at least he wasn't burdened with the mother-in-law paradigm.

Adam couldn't deny that, somewhere in the recesses of his fickle heart, he still loved his wife as much as the day when he had proposed to her, backed by the sound of the Indian Ocean as it gently kissed the powder sands of a Seychelles beach. She had looked unbelievably gorgeous on that pink and violet evening, in a very simple chiffon dress, standing barefoot beside him. She had almost outshone their remarkable surroundings, which, considering it must be one of the planet's true paradises, meant his newly betrothed must have looked really quite beautiful indeed. Nevertheless, time had moved on from those amazingly brief but extraordinary moments, and the reality of their lives had taken its toll on them both. He acknowledged they were arguing more frequently now, his own selfish and idiotic behaviour the main reason, but it didn't mean there was nothing to be saved. There was everything about them to be salvaged. Perhaps this summer season would act as a needed break from each other, allowing them to both gather themselves and take stock of what strengths they had as a couple. It wasn't going to be easy for Adam, but he was determined to not become part of the merry band of show business divorcees.

He knew he'd been an egotistical bastard over recent years, and not just with Jayne. It was an affliction that had increased with each new success and elevation in his field. Adam also knew he wasn't the only one. Jayne was not alone in being the wife of a manic variety artist on a mission of fame and fortune, at the price of anything else of value in life. Like love and loyalty. Like life itself. So many just like him had, in their eyes, failed to reach the necessary echelons of recognition, turning to the bottle, and in more recent times, hard drugs. Some reformed but were never to work at their chosen vocation again. Some, a dear friend of Adam's being one, took the ultimate way out from their disillusionments. However bad it got, not that it was going to at all for Adam, not now anyway, he could never see himself taking such a terrible course of action. He was no Christian, original or born again, God forbid! And didn't follow any particular formal faith. Only the one that carried him through the most difficult times and he wasn't too sure what it was or where it came from. Even so, Adam would endeavour to see out whatever lifetime he had been allocated. Why rob the public of his talent? Why rob himself of their growing ovation? And in any case, he simply wouldn't cope with the adverse publicity such a death would generate, even from the other side. If there was one. And what about Jayne?... *Oh, do stop all this shite...* Adam chided, but he was in a certain mind-set and it led him deeper, down to a place where only his most private truths waited.

Probably the reason he would resist suicide was the fact he was essentially a coward. After all, Doug Delany strode out onto a stage without any props, just himself and his banter. Adam hid behind his boys. Though acknowledging his undeniably supreme gift for quite stunning ventriloquism, the point was the audience were focused on his other little characters, not his own. He was also aware that this subtle cowardice had infiltrated his personal life, and from quite an early age. So far though, or so he hoped, it hadn't manifested in his relationship with Jayne. If he had managed to keep it at bay, it would be because she was simply different from the rest of the riff raff. Better. Sure, there had been mindless affairs, but that was all they had been, nothing of any importance. Not to him, anyway. Apart from the one girl he broke with as soon as he had met Jayne. Well... nearly as soon as he had met Jayne.

His behaviour when ending this particular liaison had been, not to put too fine a point on it, the ultimate in spinelessness. Even by Adam's standards. They were only an item for a short spell, maybe four weeks, or maybe five, allowing him to ponder whether Jayne was a future worth breaking from the present. In that respect, he felt he had acted no differently to most other men in a similar situation. No, it was the way in which he chose to leave the girl that now rankled Adam's sensibilities. She had deserved better.

As they had been saying their good-byes after a fairly rampant evening together, strangely, which suggested to Adam that all women were psychic witches, she had asked him casually if she would ever see him again. He had been rather taken aback initially, did she know about Jayne? How could she? He hadn't said anything, acted differently. Had he? Maybe she had tuned into his silent thoughts as they lay together. Whatever. Adam would never find out.

So he said yes, of course she would see him again.

'Oh, not going to suddenly vanish into oblivion, then?" She had smiled enigmatically, eyes unreadable as she looked into his own and gently touched his face. Had she actually been trying to tell him that, in fact, she had beaten him to it and was ending their relationship? But why would she have? Adam had no great skill with women but he couldn't see what would have prompted it. Then again, he spent many years losing his girlfriends, one or two he had been very serious about, to other men who they invariably immediately got married to and lived happily ever after with. What exactly was it they had found in those men that they couldn't find in him? He seemed to have been asking that for years. Until Jayne came along.

'No,' he had replied to her second enquiry. 'Not for the moment!' he joked afterward, rather tackily, Adam now considered. Standing by his car as she watched from her doorstep, he waved and blew a kiss from the palm of his hand. 'I'll call you in a couple of days,' he said.

He would never know if she had been gently warning him that their time together was over. That she had made the decision for Adam but was giving him the chance to be a man and do the right thing. He would never know because Adam never called her again.

Christ! What an immature bastard, he mindfully reprimanded. And there, in a nutshell, was perhaps the answer to his lifelong question.

There was a sharp knock on his open dressing-room door. Adam's inward retrospective roaming instantly evaporated, probably as quickly as he had from many women's lives. He turned to see who it was, Doug Delany stood smiling from the doorway. Britain's top raconteur. The most influential person Adam had ever been blessed to work with. The man.

'Adam,' Doug boomed in his trademark chummy manner, the same one that had no doubt helped him reach the pinnacle of his career. It seemed a very long way up from where Adam was looking.

'Doug,' Adam responded warmly, if slightly nervously, as both men moved toward each other and heartily shook hands.

Summer and Amanda simultaneously smiled and sighed wearily, as Marcia Raeburn finally released them all for the day. There was a collective exhausted silence as she told them what time their call was for the following morning. Another early one. No doubt a few muted expletives did the rounds as everyone packed up and began to trudge from the theatre.

As the two girls made their way off the stage, Summer caught sight of Doug and Adam chatting animatedly in Doug's dressing-room. Cynthia's friendly warning drizzled into her thoughts and Summer stole a brief study of the man in question. He was taller than she had imagined and much better looking, although, she had to admit, she wasn't up close and the area immediately behind the stage was lit to its usual strength of just above dim. That said, she still sensed a powerful charisma emanating from his person. Not the other fella, Adam... something or other, he just looked like the normal run-of-the-mill variety 'turn' Summer had encountered from show to show. Big talent wrapped up in what amounted to jumped up little squirts. Then, without warning, Doug Delany was looking directly at her. Summer suddenly felt very shy under his gaze. It was only fleeting, and he soon returned his eyes to the ventriloquist. However, something bothered Summer about the way in which she had been affected. *How stupid!* she mused as she felt a cold shiver ripple through her.

'Wonder what they'll be like to work with?' Amanda asked in hushed tones as they walked on past, up to the stage door.

'From all accounts, and I only speak of Mr Delany,' Summer whispered, Cynthia's words echoing ever stronger, 'it should be... interesting!' Both girls quietly giggled.

Amanda had been pleasantly surprised by Summer Laine. She worked hard and was a team player, no prima donna tendencies as had been expected after Sara's detailed recollections. Perhaps Amanda's friend had been slightly economical with the truth, born of a rabid jealousy. Whether that was for Summer, or herself, Amanda wasn't too sure. Sara still didn't have a contract.

Summer appeared to be genuine and was actually quite funny, she had made the company laugh several times with surreptitious imitations of Marcia. Amanda was warming to her and hoped, maybe, Summer might turn out to be the friend she desperately needed. She and Jason had spat vitriol at each other down the phone the previous evening, when he had finally answered her numerous messages. They had both been on the brink of tears towards the end. A teetering truce was thrashed out and Amanda felt completely drained by it all. The day's rehearsal had been easy in comparison. She always found mental exhaustion far more debilitating than the physical version. Sure, the body ached, maybe even hurt, but when those natural endorphins kicked in, soothing muscles and causing the necessary amnesia that would allow the body to perform again, it was a pleasurable fatigue. Not so for her jaded mind.

Was Jason really worth all this hassle? Amanda truly wanted him to be. She had more feelings for him than any man before. Certainly, he was the first boyfriend to cause her a sleepless night like last night. Just what she had needed before today. She was always hopeless at relationships and it seemed, chronically inept at this one. Perhaps it was the depth of her sentiments for Jason that rendered her pretty useless in dealing with him at times. Yet when they were together... well, that said it all, didn't it?... When they were together. Then, Amanda and Jason were great. So what for the future? Time would tell. It always did.

'Fancy a drink before we go our separate ways?' Amanda asked Summer as they stepped out into a damp and chilly early evening.

'Yes, why not? I'd like that,' Summer replied and reached into her bag to turn off her mobile. Anything to delay going back to the flat where she knew Giancarlo would be waiting. She was still wired from the day's workout and needed to chill a little before succumbing to her other role. Yes, she would go home to console and care for, show her love for him and learn new lessons on her journey of self-enrichment. But for now, a short while, Summer simply wanted to enjoy being a professional dancer, one in a major summer show, have a laugh with a colleague and find out what the current gossip was.

It was what she used to live for.

CHAPTER TWENTY FIVE

Cynthia Hersh was hopeful. Her recent meeting with Moira Myers had been more open and constructive than the agent had expected. It was always best not to have any great expectations in her line of work, you might chance a little one here and there, perhaps even a slightly larger one in the case of Summer Laine. So Cynthia tended to work on the basis of how she felt about a client, how positively they sat in her mind, and found herself, generally, on the right track when seeking work for them.

Moira Myers had liked Summer's photos and résumé. Cynthia tried to enthuse for the girl's talent without falling into the trap of gushing about her to the casting director. Martin Thurlow did raise an overly-plucked eyebrow, and Cynthia heard the right noises coming across the office. Now she was playing the proverbial waiting game, and at that, Cynthia Hersh excelled. There weren't too many people in show business who never had to enter that agonising little arena. How long do you wait for 'the call'? When should you call them? Should you call them at all? When was it safe to assume you hadn't got the part? Or your client hadn't got the part? Had they lost your number? No, that was only at the 'getting desperate' stage. Cynthia never quite entertained that little gem. She was hardly scared of picking up the phone.

Still, it was an unavoidable torture requiring a steely disposition and iron will, and a strategy to deal with the more than often disappointment when either a negative call did come, or worse, the phone just sat silent for weeks after the interview or audition. That sick cold realisation you hadn't even impressed enough to warrant a quick 'thanks but no thanks' slowly infiltrated your being, your life, and once again you were cast adrift on planet unemployment benefit. And after all that, you continue to stick at it, the mission, the dream; that first night opening in the West End in a lead role, or heading the cast in a television series, or best of all, starring in a film with world-wide distribution. It drives you on, conveniently masks the otherwise obvious failings of such an existence, and the fact that so few actually achieve anything like moderate success.

Addicts, each one, even the agents, who are hooked on a slightly different concoction, but nonetheless still habitual users. Cynthia knew she could never have done anything other than something to do with the business. She was a born performer, it was just that these days, she was required to perform an altered dance, though dance it was, and she was damned good at it.

She was in no doubt about the outcome of her meeting, Moira would see Summer, even if only to keep her in mind for the future. Cynthia could live with that, especially with Martin Thurlow still in the background. She had heard on the grapevine that he was about to secure the backing he needed for his new film. She made a note to give his office a call. Summer Laine could soon be on her way to the hallowed one percent.

Some time had passed since she and Summer had lunched together and Cynthia realised she must arrange to go up to Blackpool to catch a preview show. She checked her schedule for the next few days. Tricky. A couple of meetings would have to be reorganised, but the agent felt Summer was worth it. She was actually looking forward to seeing her dance again, it was being in the vicinity of Doug Delany that irked. It was something Cynthia had been very careful through the years to avoid. Added to being in the same building was the possibility of actually standing face to face and having to make polite conversation. Not if she could help it, love! Oh, a lot of water had run under their bridges since that unforgivable moment in both their lives. The one when she lay in a state of intolerable degradation, disillusioned with life, and herself, on a small trolley bed, feet held unladylike and awkward in cold steel stirrups, while an anonymous doctor removed their baby from her body, killing it. But he hadn't been its murderer, she had. And so had Doug Delany. He had waited in the car outside the clinic, well... HE couldn't show his face in there, could he? She was even booked in under an assumed name and paid with cash. Doug's cash. His thirty pieces of silver.

After that season, both their lives had progressed onto good things, for Doug more than even his egotistical mind could have imagined for himself. Cynthia had taken some time to recover and regain a composure to her shattered personal life. It was at that time she decided to leave stage and television and become an agent. She couldn't complain now, the Cynthia Hersh Agency was one of the most prolific at providing the industry with some of the best talent in the country. She received great respect from everyone. People clamoured to be on her books. Only a shrewdly chosen few were. So it would be interesting to see just how much 'respect' Doug Delany might show Cynthia now. Any trifling amount would be an improvement on zilch.

If Cynthia was candid with herself, deep down, did she really care anymore? Not on her own behalf, maybe, but for her special girl, for Summer Laine, more than ever. She simply couldn't cope with the guilt if she let Doug destroy another fine talent. Cynthia had been lucky, she'd been tougher than she had given herself credit for in the beginning. She had carved another career out of the broken pieces of her life. Could Summer do the same? Cynthia knew the girl was far more mature and advanced in the knowledge of men than she had been at a similar age. There was also the simple truth that it had been Cynthia who had made the ultimate decision in Scarborough. Apart from Doug's selfish pontifications, the baby grew inside her body, not his. She had made the final devastating choice.

She lit a cigarette. This line of thinking was bringing on one of her 'nicotine fits', she was becoming shaky. Usually a good time for a fag. So what if Doug did embark on a liaison with the lovely Summer? And would she want him, anyway? There was always that angle. And then again, what if nothing happened at all? Cynthia considered. All her fervent speculation and conjecture was about an event that might never happen. Even if it did, it was unlikely the headstrong and modern Summer would let herself get pregnant, however carried away she might get with him. At this, Cynthia smiled and laughed softly as she blew smoke across her desk. Was he up to it these days? She bet those ageing knees were a bit stiff and wondered just how long he could keep it up now. Her gentle laugh became a vociferous guffaw which caused an involuntary fit of coughing.

There was also the slimmest possibility that Doug Delany had changed. She had thought about that several times but always came to the same conclusion; not likely but truth can be stranger than fiction. He was certainly highly regarded in the business and did seem to carry himself with an air of a man who had fought many demons and won. Cynthia pursed her lips for a moment as she pondered that morsel. Perhaps the delightful Gabrielle and the arrival of his children... she found herself taking in a sharp cold breath... maybe they had tempered the womaniser. It wasn't impossible. Just improbable that a man, any person, could truly change that much. Move on that far from where they used to be. But hadn't she? Moved on? Then why was she rewinding through her life to when Doug Delany was in it? And did the reason for her going to Blackpool have more to do with making sure Summer wouldn't fall under his seasoned grasp, and not just to appraise her client's performance?

Oh, to hell with it all! she huffed to herself. *You're her agent, not her bloody mother!* Cynthia picked the phone and punched a number.

Summer watched as Giancarlo drove away. When she had eventually arrived back at the flat the previous evening, he had prepared one of his sumptuous suppers and was in an unusually mellow mood. It was all a pleasant surprise and Summer quietly wished that she had made her way home earlier. Whilst Amanda had been great company, Summer knew that when Giancarlo was in one of his rare tranquil temperaments, there was no other place she would rather be. Unfortunately, the man was hard to read or predict at the best of times, so Summer could only luxuriate in such a cosy ambience whenever she happened to stumble across it, which wasn't too often, but frequent enough to remind her of why she stuck with this intricate character. Now if he asked to visit again, Summer wouldn't hesitate.

He had even been a gentleman of restraint, simply holding her close in bed as he talked affectionately about his 'mama' and Taormina, and how one day, he would return. Thoroughly spent from the long day and satiated on fine cuisine and company, Summer had been slowly drifting off into deep and peaceful slumbers, not paying too much attention to his soft and lyrical musings. By the time Giancarlo spoke of his desire to make enough money so that he might be able to 'go home' with a wife to complete his days there, she had been fast asleep.

The phone rang. It was Cynthia.

Giancarlo felt happy and contented. A state of being he always sought but was infrequently blessed with. He was now more sure than ever that he would be able to secure his personal future very soon. This impromptu visit had been enlightening.

He wasn't angry that Summer had spent time with her girlfriend before joining him at the flat, though perhaps he would have preferred that she had chosen a better venue to have a drink. Giancarlo was no lover of the English pub, the London variety were bad enough, but here... still, he had to allow her these little freedoms. It was important. Imperative if he was to instil in Summer the perfect inclination that would prompt not only a positive response to his proposal of marriage, but one that she was hungry to provide him with.

As he turned onto the motorway, Giancarlo smiled. Their future was almost their present. Not long now. A life together that he believed was destined. An alliance that, in time, Summer would come to understand and accept as the only future.

The pool installation suddenly wasn't quite going to plan. The work had fallen behind, and Gabrielle was less than pleased by the whole situation. She was bouncing rapidly between apathy and seething, like a small rubber ball thrown into a confined space.

Jim was permanently apologetic, although the problems were not all his fault. The main contender for Gabrielle to throttle was the designer tile company that she had ordered from. 'Apparently' the supplier in Spain had been delayed and this meant a knock-on effect with delivery from the English depot... blah blah blah... Meanwhile, the pool itself was causing a few tantrums among Jim's workmen, and Gabrielle was beginning to wish she hadn't nagged Doug so much to get the bloody thing in the first place. *It's for the children,* she had to keep telling herself.

Her main concern was that she had arranged a charity luncheon at the house to coincide with the work being completed. A sort of upmarket 'bring-and-buy' with drinkies around her new pool. The luncheon was to take place in three weeks' time. Every assurance had been given by all parties that the project would be finished 'to the highest standards' well beforehand. So why wasn't Gabrielle entirely convinced? In any case, there wasn't an awful lot she could do, so she forced herself to forget all about it on the drive into town. It was that certain day, and getting close to that certain time.

Lunch with Angelo again.

She had spent serious quiet time pondering whether she should go at all. Would it be tempting some kind of horrible fate? Or had she already crossed that invisible line and was now too far in to change the eventual outcome? What the hell could happen? She was only meeting the man for a friendly lunch and a chat, maybe some laughs, and Gabrielle knew she definitely needed a few of those.

Wasn't a married woman allowed male friends? Surely it couldn't be an absolute truth that men were incapable of having a mere 'friendship' with a woman? That their side of the relationship would always have certain sexual undertones? But then, was that not also true of the women in such a friendship? Did any woman really embark on just a platonic companionship with any man? It had been so long since Gabrielle could remember being in such a situation that it was quite possible she never had. Could it not then be said that somewhere, hidden deep inside each of the parties, was, in fact, a basic carnal desire? Perhaps but more than likely not, Gabrielle quickly decided, closing down her meanderings as she finally found a space in the bowels of the car park. Time for the ritual wrapping of car keys around her hand in knuckle-duster fashion and a heightened state of alert as she made her way to the street. You could never be sure what might be lurking in those stench-ridden shadows. Then she laughed at herself. Maybe something was trying to tell her this was all a big mistake, that she should turn back now and run away as fast as she could. Stuff and nonsense. Gabrielle was determined to enjoy herself once again and anyway, her taste-buds were already jostling for position as she recalled having not had much of her meal the last time around.

Strange. Even slightly worrying. Angelo's looked deserted. It was deserted. Windows dark, no one in sight, had she got the wrong day? Or perhaps something had come up when she had been already en route. Then, Gabrielle saw movement from behind the door and it opened. Angelo stood in the entrance, dressed in smart but casual attire and smiling warmly.

'Welcome,' he said standing to one side to allow Gabrielle past.

'Where is everybody?' she enquired lightly, trying to hide a sudden onset of the jitters. Warning sirens began screaming in her head to 'leave now!'

'Right here,' Angelo responded by indicating the two of them. 'Today, we have a private lunch.'

'I see!' Gabrielle said, knowing she really should listen to her highly vocal intuition and turn tail, but instead, she followed Angelo down the staircase to a subtly lit lower restaurant floor and a table perfectly dressed with candles and chilling champagne. Even a long stemmed red rose was set carefully in the centre.

'Please... sit, Gabriella. I have it all prepared.'

'All this just for me?' she asked like an awe-struck little girl. *Leave now!* an urgent voice echoed throughout her whole self. 'How lovely!' Gabrielle found herself saying to Angelo as he sat beside her and poured the champagne.

Valerie sat at her dining-room table with the cards. She had been learning more about them since her reading for Gabrielle. There had also been moments when Valerie nearly threw them away, but those confused feelings subsided and were replaced by a desire to know more. To truly understand the Tarot. It seemed important.

So here she was, finishing a personal reading, something Valerie did fairly often, mainly as a study tool but also it helped her through her difficult days, especially those at a certain time of the month. It was preferable to those irrational contemplations about murdering her husband. Again. Luckily for him, they only ever exhibited themselves as one of her sudden, volatile and quite asinine rows. The messages the cards suggested were not always what Valerie wanted and occasionally, she still viewed them rather sceptically. As time had gone on, she began to 'feel' their meaning, even knew when it was the right time to create a spread, taking comfort from them like a cup of tea with a friend. The Tarot calmed her. Just like today.

As she gathered up the pack and started to wrap them in a delicate silk scarf bought specially, Valerie's harmonious thoughts were suddenly filled with her friend, Gabrielle Delany. Valerie frowned briefly, wondering why, then recognised the sensation of needing to set out some cards. This time, though, the feeling was tempered with something Valerie had hoped was consigned to the past.

There was an air of foreboding in the room and the scarf seemed to have become very warm in her hands. It reminded her of the day when she thought she had released some dreadful entity into her domain. The same day she had first read the cards for Gabrielle.

Still uneasy, Valerie removed the scarf, set it aside and slowly shuffled the cards, deciding to pick just three. This she did at random and placed them in a line from left to right, pausing to look at them lying in front of her for a few moments. Then she turned over the first card to the left. The Knight of Wands. She turned the centre card. The Lovers. Finally, holding her breath, Valerie turned the final card. The Ten of Swords.

She studied the cards for a while before consulting her various books. It was impossible for Valerie to know for certain what the cards were trying to say for Gabrielle. Without the presence of the person for whom she had chosen the cards, or their knowledge of this extemporaneous reading, the meaning could be interpreted in all kinds of ways. Wrongly. Valerie even considered the cards may hold a message for herself. But in the instant of thinking it, she knew they did not. The reading was most definitely for her unsuspecting friend.

So just what advice was held within these three cards?

The Knight of Wands led Valerie to a vibrant man, someone with a zest for life, a man who can lead and guide, who believes he knows what is best for everyone around him. He makes things happen. Who the hell was that? It didn't feel like it was Doug. So who could it be? He would probably end up being someone of influence in Gabrielle's life. But was he good or bad for her?

Onto The Lovers. Always an interesting card to come up. It never failed to make her querents respond to it in a uniform way, most thinking immediately it referred to their love life, which it did, but in an unconventional way. As Valerie was learning more and more, the Tarot were never obvious. One had to think carefully about what they were saying, sometimes it took a while for their message to ring true. Good aspects of The Lovers were being able to relate to those closest to you with loyalty and understanding, being able to understand yourself and your desires so that your relationships were built on the true self. The Lovers also advised against allowing ourselves to stagnate in a friendship or intimate relationship. To not let problems and negative events rule how we might act in the future. Valerie thought of Gabrielle and Doug. It was perhaps the one card that was most relevant to them as a couple. Yet, with The Knight of Wands sitting next to it, what did that mean? Valerie shook her head and cleared her mind. On to The Ten of Swords.

This card, coming after the other two, gave Valerie cause to stop and reread her book of explanations. An iciness seemed to have settled over her. She wasn't sure she really wanted to carry on but she knew she must. It would be impossible to dismiss the cards now. It was too late. Their message was there for her to find and it could be that Valerie would have to tell it to Gabrielle. She didn't relish the task but Valerie also suspected she would not be allowed to keep this bulletin from the Tarot to herself.

The Ten of Swords showed a great loss, something ending, of taking stock and moving on. Change and reorganisation after a period of suffering or hurt. The possibility that whatever is to happen to us, cannot be stopped. But maybe, with the right frame of mind and application in the aftermath, we might go on to live a better life.

Valerie sat quite still for some minutes, mulling over what she had been reading. Her eyes wandered from card to card, trying to put some order to them in her mind in relation to Gabrielle, finding a suitable way of explaining it to her friend so that she would not scare the living daylights out of her again.

It would not be easy. For either of them.

CHAPTER TWENTY SIX

Angelo spoke lovingly about his baby daughter, Luisa, while Gabrielle tucked into a fresh fruit salad. Despite them talking non-stop for the best part of ninety minutes, she had managed to eat baked aubergines and now this delightful concoction to freshen her palate.

'I couldn't have imagined it would be this way, already having my other two, but, I suppose, coming so late, she made me feel young again!'

Gabrielle quickly dabbed her mouth. 'Oh, Angelo, you aren't exactly ancient!'

He shrugged and smiled shyly. 'But I feel so sometimes, Gabriella.'

She sipped water and regarded the man. He had always added the 'a' to her name, much to Doug's irritation. However, Gabrielle noticed her husband had never once corrected Angelo. So why should she? In a funny little way, she rather liked the melodic inflection it gave as he would say her name with his tuneful accent. It seemed to give it a phonetic depth, otherwise lost on the English tongue.

'Little Luisa must have been quite a shock for Donatella,' Gabrielle said with a sympathetic and knowing smile. The thought of having a baby in her mid-forties made her positively cringe. She adored her three treasures, but frankly, they were quite enough, thank you.

She saw an ephemeral darkness pass over Angelo's eyes at the mention of his wife. He had managed not to speak of her at all during their conversations, even when referring to Luisa. Gabrielle wondered if perhaps she had just made a huge faux pas. Then, Angelo's face seemed to brighten again, eyes fixed somewhere across the room and he laughed softly, some private recollection amusing him.

'I think you can be sure of that!' He paused. 'Coffee?' the question asked with a touch of his hand on her forearm.

'Yes, just a quick espresso. I should be getting back.'

'So soon?' he asked, the slightest intimation of disappointment in the tone, yet smiling broadly at the same time.

'My children,' Gabrielle said with mock resignation, her own eyes lifted towards the ceiling as if to say, 'what can you do?'

Without warning, though maybe there had been and Gabrielle had chosen to dismiss it, Angelo moved close to her and stroked a strand of hair away from the side of her face. Although it was gentle, like the brush of a butterfly wing, his touch made Gabrielle flinch and he stopped.

'You are very beautiful, Gabriella,' he said, a certain timbre to his voice causing tiny hairs to rise at the back of her neck. The earlier subconscious echoes of caution now taunted her. *Told you so!... Too late now...*

'Don't fight it,' Angelo was saying into her ear, his breath sultry and suggestive as he kept his mouth close to her neck, a hand now crossing her chest and taking a shoulder, turning Gabrielle to face him. 'It will be our secret...'

'NO!' Gabrielle cried. *Shit!* She thought.

In what seemed like the time between one film frame and another, no time at all, Angelo had her pinned down on the semi-circular booth seat, his mouth now roughly working on hers. Gabrielle was frozen for a few seconds, desperately gathering her scattered wits together, deciding on the right response and knowing she had to be damned quick about it, because his hands were beginning to deftly explore parts of Gabrielle that hadn't been touched by another man since she'd married Doug.

Think! Come on... this is serious! she screamed into already frantic thoughts.

'Angelo, NO!' she finally said ferociously, drawing her face sharply away from his. It caused him to pause for a split second, time enough for Gabrielle. She ripped herself away from under his considerable weight and sat up, casting a look full of anger and disgust in his direction. 'Just what the HELL did you think you were doing?' she spat. Yes, it immediately seemed like a stupid question but it was one that Gabrielle felt needed to be aired at that point in time. At least it might give her a couple of moments to wonder what the hell SHE had been thinking of by taking lunch with this man alone in his empty restaurant. During the silence that followed, she fumbled around under the table, finding her bag and trying to straighten her attire to a more suitably acceptable state. The longer Angelo remained reticent, the more furious, probably fired by her own senseless actions, Gabrielle became. 'How could you do this to me? I'm a married woman, for God's sake! I love my husband very much.' And at that particular unfortunate juncture in her life, Gabrielle truly meant it. The 'thing', now pulling himself up next to her, still not meeting her eyes, had, in one ridiculous instant, shown her just how idiotic she had been. What a terrible risk she had taken. Suddenly, Gabrielle was utterly terrified that Doug was somehow going to know what had happened, that she would lose him and the children. The children. Their little lives, essential little lives, would be thrown into emotional turmoil, their comfort and security would lie in tatters. Oh, dear God! What had she done? Nothing was worth the churning up of these heinous thoughts and the swell of such vile possibilities. Consequences. It was a state of unbearable flux that Gabrielle had never dreamed of ever being in. She was not a woman who had affairs, could even contemplate one when push came to shove, and push had very nearly come to a lot more than shove a few minutes before. Gabrielle shuddered. What if she had drunk more of the champagne that Angelo had persistently offered? What if he had overwhelmed her? Or more to the point, overpowered her?

Gabrielle felt sick.

She pictured God looking at her from his heavenly domain, eyes saddened and head shaking in disapproval, his angels with their backs turned to her, and she wasn't even Catholic! Even so, Gabrielle closed her eyes tight and said a silent prayer, hoping He would forgive her. But in truth, the hardest thing would be for Gabrielle to forgive herself.

'Gabriella...' Angelo said but was cut off by a vicious verbal slap.

'Gabrielle,' she countered, with heavy emphasis on the 'elle'. 'I think at least I deserve for you to get my fucking name right for once!'

Angelo's eyebrows shot up at her expletive, but his demeanour remained one of absolute shame. 'I am so sorry...' he began.

'Yes, well... I should think so too,' Gabrielle said, her voice calmer now as she concentrated on fixing untidy hair.

'Please, I don't know what happened. I have never done anything like this before...'

Yeah, right! Gabrielle said silently to herself in a small hand mirror through disbelieving eyes.

Angelo continued regardless. 'I have made a terrible mistake.' Then he shook his head before placing both hands on each side of his face and letting out a deeply remorseful sigh. Gabrielle shot him a quick glance and considered her options.

She could try and make him feel even smaller than he quite obviously felt at that moment, and then make an exit that might make even the inimitable Bette Davis proud, or maybe she should accept her part of the blame for this awful situation and deal with it in a more grown up manner. After all, Gabrielle had accepted his invitation without a second thought. That had come later and had been summarily ignored. Every time she had deliberated about the scenario, she hadn't failed to come up with a good reason to go ahead with it.

Perhaps she had been rather cavalier in her attitude, and Gabrielle knew exactly what that trait had been born of; mainly Doug's sordid little antics, but did she really deserve to be where she was now? How come so many women seemed to have quite carefree extramarital liaisons and appear none the worse for them afterwards? Or were they? Did their affairs, in fact, cause them the same internal pain as Gabrielle felt now, but were they thick-skinned enough to hide it from the world, and perhaps themselves? Whatever their reality was, it wasn't how Gabrielle wished to conduct hers.

This still didn't help her with handling Angelo Maldini. It also didn't tell her how the man himself was going to react. Could she trust him? That seemed unlikely. Gabrielle could barely trust herself. Was she already poised on the steps of the divorce courts? And worse, about to be thrust unflatteringly into the public's attention via the tabloids? That was one nasty reality a disgraced Mrs Delany could never avoid.

The children, she thought simply. *The children.*

'Look,' she said, forcing him to meet her eyes with a long cold stare. 'Let's be adult about this...' *Please...* 'We'll put this down to too much champagne and leave it at that, okay?' Angelo nodded as though he had been waiting for her to make the first move. Something Gabrielle was well used to with Doug. She was suddenly struck by the similarity of the way both men dealt with the immediate aftermath of being 'found out', only, in this case, was it not Gabrielle who had 'found out' about herself?

'*Si,*' Angelo finally said. 'But I have no excuses, Gabrielle.' He was careful to say her name correctly this time. 'All I can say is that, maybe, having Luisa has made an old fool a little crazy...'

'Stop right there,' Gabrielle said, 'you don't need to tell me about what having a young baby in the house does to a marriage. I've had three, so I know EXACTLY what it does to the father. Believe me, I know. That said, I'm not letting you off the hook so easily!' And she laughed, not really knowing why. There was a palpable wave of relief from the man beside her as he looked at her and laughed too.

'No one will know about this, Gabrielle,' he said, serious once more. 'On that, you have my word, and my word you can trust.' His sombre eyes bore into hers. Gabrielle felt he was being truthful, but something about what he had said irked her. She let it go. Too much going through her frazzled head already. 'And I want to say this,' Angelo started again. 'I cannot expect you to grace my restaurant again, though I hope, maybe, in time you will... with your friend... or even your husband,' he added quickly. 'There is little I can do to make this... right... but I have...' he trailed off for a second, Gabrielle waited. What was coming now? 'I have friends, many friends, who I can call on at any time, should you need help.'

'Help?' Gabrielle asked.

'Perhaps in the future, you or your husband might need some... help,' Angelo smiled, mainly to himself, as though he couldn't think of any other way of explaining it. 'If ever you are in trouble...'

'What? Like now?' Gabrielle jested, trying to lighten the sudden heaviness of the atmosphere. Angelo allowed a wry grin to pass across his lips before saying, 'I am always here. If you need my help, call me. With anything. Do you understand, Gabrielle?'

'I think so,' she replied, not wanting to believe he was actually saying what she thought he was saying. That only happened in the movies, surely? 'It's a very kind offer,' she managed, anyway. What else could she say? But it seemed to do the trick because he looked quite satisfied with her response.

In the car on the way home, home where her life was, her very good and decent life, a life that even with her husband's wandering manhood, Gabrielle knew others would lie down for, she forced herself to go over every single minute of the last two hours. Each sentence, every word, all Angelo's passing incongruous touches, her reactions. She eventually found herself smiling a rather lascivious little smile.

However close to a personal catastrophe she had taken herself, however stupid and reckless she had been, there was one overriding thought that kept popping its impish head round the corner of these meanderings; after all the traumas of her sometimes sham marriage, bearing three children, and however ragged she felt around the edges,

Gabrielle realised with some degree of self-gratification that, although she may have to concede it had been a consummate Latin lech, she could still pull.

Doug breezed into the theatre. There was a technical rehearsal and though they could be incredibly boring and tedious at times, especially for someone as vibrant as Doug, he was just pleased to be finally getting on with the show. Also, he knew the whole company was expected to attend, and therefore, she would be there too. Somewhere close by. Her loveliness still took his breath away. But would he be able to approach her at all? Find the right way to begin a conversation?

She seemed quite different to the rest. Though this particular collection of dancing girls was well above average, Doug felt in his bones that the subject of his endless musings was set apart, and it wasn't a subliminal mechanism to provide a reason for his unexpected change of heart. Doug just knew the girl was from better stock. The way she carried herself, interacted with the others. Simple genetics. For the first time in his life, it seemed, he was having to summon up courage to speak to her. She had actually managed to make Doug lose his nerve. Unheard of! His precious powers of prowess had gone walkies. In the nanosecond he had allowed Gabrielle to streak across his mind, Doug realised that even she, his meticulously chosen wife and mother of his children, had never provoked such a response from him.

It wasn't long before Doug caught sight of Summer chatting and joking around with another girl, nice enough but she wasn't even in the same league, sorry, love. They didn't notice him peeking at them from the wings as they stood on the opposite side stage, but Doug was determined he would be noticed at the right time. By the right one.

He watched her. She looked refined, almost too cultured to be in this show. Oh, it was a great show, hell... he was in it, wasn't he? No, it was just... she was the type who should be in films, gracing the big screen with her unbelievable presence. It oozed from her like the sweetest golden honey from a very special honeycomb. Whatever it was that she unknowingly sent out from her person, into the world and straight to Doug, it intoxicated him, like nothing else he had ever known.

Back in his dressing-room, he began to imagine how he could start up a light conversation without seeming too eager. She looked intellectual. Not one of Doug's greatest attributes but he wasn't an idiot. Bless them, before he chose his path in life, Mr and Mrs Delany, not exactly academics themselves, had managed to give their son a good enough upbringing that he had passed his eleven-plus and made it into the local grammar school. What could he possibly say that would interest this girl enough to give him her attention for a few minutes? Something that might enable him to hold her undivided attention for more than a few minutes? Suitable to the point that, eventually, it wouldn't only be her mind that he was able to hold.

'Doug?' The voice cut into his thought process like a hot knife through butter. Doug looked up from the sofa and saw Phil Beauchamp in the open doorway.

'They want to start on the lighting for your spots first, say, five minutes?'

'Sure, be right there.'

Alone again, Doug let his wife into his thoughts once more. His faithful Gabs. The one woman who had stayed through thick and thin. Had given him everything that she was. His stable raft on the turbulent sea of his life. Then, like a beautiful shell cast into an ocean, her face slowly faded as it sank back into the cold depths of his subconscious.

CHAPTER TWENTY SEVEN

As Phoebe played quietly at her feet and Gabrielle prepared some lunch, Valerie wondered just how she was supposed to open up the subject of the Tarot to a friend who had not exactly reacted well the first time around. When Gabrielle had asked her for a second explanation, she had listened intently, made a newly-informed comment now and then, and simply hadn't mentioned the matter since. So Valerie tried to make a swift analysis of how Gabrielle might take the revelation of her recent reading, and decided all she could do was hope for the best. Even so, held within her was a sense that there was something ominous in the message she carried from those three cards. It wasn't going to be easy, trying to instil in a cynic the significance, as Valerie believed, of that communication, whilst also attempting to make light of the very same. Gabrielle had been fairly confused in the first place, and here was the actual Tarot teller in her own state of mystification.

Phoebe now stood next to Valerie on the sofa, patting her gently on the shoulder and saying something that Valerie hadn't quite caught. Her thoughts suitably stowed for later, she smiled at the child. 'What is it, sweetheart?' A Barbie doll was thrust in front of Valerie's face and she took the offering. 'Why, thank you, Bee,' she said. Phoebe produced another, but in different clothes and with another hairstyle, haphazard might have been a good description, but the little girl looked remarkably pleased with herself.

'Are they sisters?' Valerie asked in that voice she used especially for cute three-year olds.

'No,' came the simple but firm reply. Phoebe clambered off the sofa and ran away into the kitchen, obviously to explain to mummy what she had been doing.

Valerie smiled. She fondly remembered when Elsa, her own daughter and Sasha's best friend, had been this age.

Where had the time gone? Three years seemed to have flashed past in the blink of an eye and yet Valerie's life, apart from the recent inclusion of a celebrity friend, to all intents and purposes had stayed in some sort of suspended animation. Perhaps it was her own doing, perhaps not. That feeling of having let herself down came to nag again, it seemed to drop in for a moan more often now, and Valerie knew she alone had the power to do something constructive to change the way she lived her life. Not an easy task when you are half of a well-established partnership and dedicated parent to young children. This with the addition of a highly successful ex-Olympic sportsman for a husband, who had managed to carve a second productive life for himself since his retirement from competing. Valerie was still chipping away at her first. The apparent injustice of that fact sometimes burned like the sting of a scorpion.

'Val? Come on through,' Gabrielle called from the kitchen. Valerie realised her eyes were watery with the beginning of tears and she quickly blinked, wiping away the evidence with her hand. She really had to address these issues, and soon. However, in the meantime, Valerie put her emotions down to being in her 'ratty' week, just before her period.

Checking herself in a mirror as she made her way to the kitchen, Valerie comforted the weepy child inside with a brief smile. *You'll be okay,* she counselled mindfully, and walked into the kitchen with a bright expression, to face Gabrielle and an uncertain afternoon.

As usual, Gabrielle had prepared something simple and yet exquisite. Phoebe sat in a highchair while her mother softly negotiated on the Barbie doll still clamped in a stubborn hand. Eventually, Phoebe relented but didn't look at all happy. Gabrielle glanced at Valerie and gave an exasperated upwards bob of her head as she placed the doll carefully out of sight behind the chair. Just as Phoebe was about to burst into a cry of frustration, Gabrielle put a bowl of spaghetti hoops on the chair's plastic tray, and little defiant eyes concentrated on it. The quivering bottom lip seemed to magically stop and where once she held her precious toy, Phoebe now had her spoon and was going in for the first mouthful.

'She's very good,' Valerie said.

'It took some time, but, I have to say, Bee's been the easiest out of all of them.'

'Lucky old you!' Valerie laughed with a degree of jealousy, her own two having been absolute nightmares about food. Her son still had an aversion to green vegetables, saving his most intense loathing for the inoffensive pea.

'Although, I'm not being entirely honest with you,' Gabrielle replied, looking at her friend with a glint in her eye. 'Doris had a hand in the process.'

'Ah, that explains it, then!'

'Are you suggesting I alone couldn't have achieved this with Bee?' Gabrielle asked through a fake indignant smile as she poured wine.

'Not at all,' Valerie responded in a similarly joking derisory tone. 'But maybe you would have had to be married to a magician and not a comedian!'

'Sauce!' Gabrielle chortled, just as Phoebe accidentally tipped her bowl onto the floor, creating a clatter and a lumpy orange pool, the bottom lip starting to wobble again. Valerie waited for Gabrielle to explode, recalling the reaction to a few footprints from the builders, but instead, she calmly cleared it up and gave her daughter another helping in a fresh bowl. Not even a bad-tempered sigh or tut. Valerie quickly looked at the floor, it was the same prized terracotta as before. Amazing! Only Gabrielle's own flesh and blood could have prompted such a different response from a woman who had appeared before to get a trifle deranged about marks on her new tile floor.

They finally got on with their lunch, chatting non-stop as these two friends normally did, except for one thing. Gabrielle's visit to Angelo's. She felt it was best left in the mental box she had packed it in, ready for airing in private when she felt capable. As much as Gabrielle trusted her lunch guest, certain things were not for discussion, often surmising it was not always right or even healthy to be utterly truthful at all times. With anyone. The less people who knew, the less possibilities for Doug to find out. Somehow, Gabrielle was sure Angelo would keep his word. She didn't know why, it may have been the other thing he said, which still caused goose bumps, but with him, she knew her secret was safe. So that just left herself. Not a problem. If there was one thing Mrs Doug Delany was good at, it was keeping her mouth shut.

During their conversation, Phoebe fell asleep in the highchair. Gabrielle quickly took her upstairs to put her down for an afternoon nap and returned to the table.

'She'll be down for about an hour,' she said as she sat down again, a satisfied and relieved smile on her face.

Valerie realised this was about as good an opportunity as any. 'Gabby?' she started. Gabrielle raised her brow. Valerie took a deep breath. 'You remember that silly Tarot reading I did for you?' she said with a shy smile, trying to appeal to the humorous side of her sceptical friend.

'I do indeed!'

'Well... the other day...'

'Oh, hello! What's happened now?' Gabrielle broke in with a laugh, eyes fixed on Valerie, waiting patiently and looking interested, if in a somewhat mocking way.

'I did a reading for you.' There, she'd got it out. Now it was Valerie's turn to wait.

'For me? But how could you if I wasn't there?'

'It was a sudden thing... I sort of "felt",' she made the ditto sign with her fingers, 'I had to.'

'Excuse me?' Gabrielle asked, head cocked to one side in contemplation, not sure she was getting this right. 'You felt you "had" to do a reading for me? Whatever for?'

Skirting around that question, Valerie quickly went on. 'I only picked three cards from the pack... at random,' she said, feeling it was worth mentioning. There was stony silence from across the table so Valerie continued. 'The Knight of Wands, The Lovers and The Ten of Swords.'

Gabrielle gave a small sarcastic smile and lifted her hands in a shrug, her face saying mutely, 'and I'm supposed to know what that means?' Then she said, 'So do tell... what dreadful thing is going to happen to me.' As the words left her mouth, Gabrielle nearly died. Whether the cards had been meant to warn her or not, and even though she didn't really believe in them, a dreadful thing had, in fact, already happened.

Valerie watched Gabrielle closely, realising there had been a subtle change in her. She no longer met Valerie's eyes and seemed suddenly distant. Without knowing it, or for the same reasons, both women experienced a deathly chill that permeated through to the bone. There was a momentary pause before Valerie began to give Gabrielle an explanation while feeling as though she had tiny spiders crawling all over her skin.

'These three cards...'

Funny, he had never been one to dwell on matters like fate.

Maybe once or twice during the early days of his career, but for a long time now, Doug had reasoned that you made your life what it was. If there was one sentence that pissed Doug off the most it was 'Aren't you lucky'. That really made him mad because Doug believed that with diligence, application and damned hard work, you made your own luck in life. Somewhere within that mix were also sacrifices, but he didn't ponder too long on sacrifices. Life was too short to worry about them. An often silent but wise old man, his father, had once said, 'Regret nowt, lad, what's done is done, only think about what's to do.'

Doug couldn't recall much of what his father had said through the years but he had never forgotten that small snippet of advice. At times, it was difficult to act upon it and recent weeks had made it harder than ever. But fate was an idea that Doug tended to avoid. It was easier that way. If everything that happens to you is preordained, therefore giving you no control over your life, the insecurity that notion would bring to bear would be intolerable for such a man. He had quite enough trouble just dealing with his life as it was, the non-theatrical part mainly, so any talk of kismet was instantly dismissed as paranormal psycho-babble.

Despite this, Doug admitted that even with his realistic approach to things, there had been moments, tiny fragments of time, when, however hard he tried to rationalise his feelings, destiny had seemed the only reluctant explanation. Brief, unforeseen events that trampled over his stoic sensibilities, prising him open to the possibility that our lives just might be a little further removed from the interference of our perceived control.

And so it was for Doug when a lunch-break was called, much to the relief of the dance ensemble who were quietly ready to throttle the lighting and sound technicians. Of course, they were only doing a bloody good job and making sure the show would be presented at its very best, but honestly! This wasn't the West End, for God's sake!

For all his worrying about how to approach his divine young woman, all Doug had 'to do' was be in the right place, at the right time. On so many occasions in answer to questions on his overwhelming success, Doug would say it was due to precisely that. With a little element of natural talent thrown in for good measure. To this day, he still spoke of that fortuitous meeting with Harold Hall and told all and sundry who would listen.

There he was, standing in the stage door office, chatting to Clive about golf, when who should step into the doorway but Summer. She smiled sweetly at Doug, but quickly, maybe a little too quickly, turned her attention to Clive, who was more than delighted.

'Any messages for Summer Laine?' she asked.

Doug took in her well-spoken voice on a breath, letting its delicate tones spread through him like a warm elixir.

'It's just my mobile's on the blink and I'm expecting a call from my agent. She's got this number.'

'Nothing as yet, Miss Laine, but I'll fetch you if your agent calls. What's the name?'

'The Cynthia Hersh Agency. It'll be Cynthia Hersh calling.'

Doug nearly shit a brick but kept himself composed all the same. His chest felt suddenly restricted and breathing was becoming a chore. Thankfully, Summer and Clive didn't notice.

'Got that, Miss Laine,' Clive said with a broad smile while making a nifty scan of Summer from head to toe.

She turned to leave, presenting Doug with another demure smile and an opening. Recovered from his sudden catapult back to a distant past, he asked, 'Cynthia Hersh?'

Summer stopped and looked at him. Doug felt his knees turning to jelly. Close up, she was the single most naturally beautiful woman he had ever seen.

'Yes,' she replied. 'Do you know her?'

'Oh, years ago now,' Doug said nonchalantly, trying to keep unwelcome foul memories from flooding into his head. 'What a lucky lady to have Ms Hersh for an agent.' Doug was heavy on the 'mizz'. 'She's a tough old boot but one of the best in the business,' he finished, unable to move his gaze from Summer's now-interested eyes, inviting him in as though drawn by a spell.

Summer smiled enigmatically at his description of Cynthia, remembering the agent's own advice about Doug Delany. 'Yes, I suppose she can be a bit brash. I think she's great. What a small world! Fancy you knowing her!'

I wish to God I never had, Doug thought ruefully. 'So!' he said with renewed vigour. 'Summer, wasn't it?' Doug held out his hand.

'Summer Laine,' she replied and took it. The mere touch of her soft skin on his produced a silken shiver that Doug luxuriated in as it rippled through him.

'Pleased to meet you. Doug Delany.'

'Yes... I think I knew who you were!' Summer retorted with a cheeky grin.

Doug now felt regressed to the mental and emotional age of about twelve. Oh, but other parts of him didn't. 'Hey, can I buy you a coffee? We can talk about our mutual friend,

Cynthia,' he said. Not that Doug relished the thought of having to discuss anything to do with the woman but it was the perfect way to open up that conversation with Summer he had been thinking long and hard about. Strange how these things just suddenly crop up. Fall into place where you least expect. It was one of those Harold Hall moments again.

Kismet.

'All right,' Summer finally replied. 'Why not?' Then she turned back to Clive and said with a flirtatious beam, 'Thanks, Clive.'

'Oh, not at all,' he came back. Clive had been thoroughly enjoying this little *tête à tête* between Doug and the gorgeous thing standing not two feet away. So everything he had heard about the bloke was right, he was indeed a fast worker. But Clive had to hand it to the comedian, he didn't go in for tat. No, sir! She was about as up market as Clive had ever encountered for a chorus girl and Doug had shown excellent taste. *Good on yer!* he thought admiringly.

'See you later, mate,' Doug said to Clive as he stood back to let Summer pass through the doorway, the gentlest touch of a guiding hand in the small of her back.

'I hope I'm not keeping you from anything,' Summer said as they made their way out of the stage door and into a damp chilly westerly sea breeze.

'Absolutely not,' he replied, the warmest of smiles cast in her direction.

Quite the opposite, my love.

'So, in a nutshell, there's this important man in my life who I may or may not already know. Something about my love life... huh!... and some catastrophic event in the future. Am I right?'

'Well,' Valerie said. 'That would be simplifying it on a grand scale but, I suppose, yes.'

'Oh, Val,' Gabrielle said with a long sigh and paused before continuing. 'Come on now,' she placed a hand on Valerie's, 'you don't really believe all this twaddle, do you?'

Suddenly, Valerie sat up very straight and looked Gabrielle deep into her taunting eyes. 'Don't patronise me, Gabby,' she snapped. 'I haven't forgotten how worked up you got before. Calling me to come over and explain it all again.' On that, Valerie withdrew her hand.

'Val, please, let's not do this, eh? Let's just forget the whole thing.'

'That might be easy for you. I can't.'

'Look, don't get me wrong, Val, but quite honestly, when you said "These three cards", I couldn't help but think of the three witches at the beginning of *Macbeth*, you know "When shall we three meet again"?' There was deathly silence from Valerie, so Gabrielle went on in the hope she could smooth over the very tense atmosphere that now prevailed. 'I know I sound like I'm taking the piss but...'

'Listen,' Valerie said as she stood, her chair scraping the terracotta. 'I understand where you're coming from, Gabby, but it's getting late, I should be getting home for the kids.'

'Oh, Val, don't go like this,' Gabrielle genuinely tried.

'No, I think it's best. I'll call you sometime.'

Valerie saw herself out before Gabrielle could even get to the door.

Sitting next to Phoebe's bed, her sleeping child so peaceful and carefree in her little dreams, Gabrielle considered the cards that Valerie had talked of.

She had played the ardent non-believer because it was the easy route to take. To have allowed Valerie to know the truth of how she felt would have been to show weakness. And Gabrielle could not be weak. Not now. Not in the light of recent days. She had been incredibly disturbed by the cards and their possible meaning. As Valerie had explained each one, the more Gabrielle felt like hiding under a rock and never coming out.

Was The Knight of Wands Angelo Maldini? If not, who? Without having to justify herself, Gabrielle knew in her heart it wasn't Doug. Dear old Doug. He was many things but never the type of man of which Valerie had spoken. The

Lovers card had caused a few private sniggers of mirth. Then unbearable feelings of regret. The last card, Gabrielle chose not to think about too much. At that point, those old Shakespearean hags seemed to have set up camp in the forefront of her imagination, an evil smirk on each of their disgustingly ugly faces.

Gabrielle let her eyes settle on Phoebe's innocent countenance, filling her whole vision with it, until all the others were gone.

CHAPTER TWENTY EIGHT

Doug didn't say much.

It wasn't something that happened too often, either. But it had suddenly dawned on him that in just listening for a change as Summer expressed her love of music, dance and theatre, he was, in fact, learning far more about her than he might have, and in a very short space of time.

Usually prone to jumping feet first into someone else's chat, rapidly turning the conversation round to all things Doug Delany, he ultimately took little away with him afterwards. And no doubt left the other party rather miffed and feeling a bit short-changed. This time, strangely, it felt completely natural to simply acquiesce and quietly munch his way through a prawn sandwich and sip on a black coffee. Keeping eye contact to a maximum, another social interaction that Doug was less than proficient with, his gaze normally on a permanent scan of his surroundings, checking out if anyone was looking in his direction. Of course, in the case of Summer Laine, Doug had no problem with directing his eyes onto hers and nowhere else.

Every now and then, he would make a brief interjection with a nod of his head or suitable expression, but for the most part he remained silent. She was in full flow and Doug just wanted to listen to her fluent voice. The words she chose and how she formed her sentences, gave the right amount of weight to certain points and made the occasional witticism. Summer spoke of how her career had filled a gaping void in her life, gave her a sense of worth and made her supremely happy. There was little else in her life that could make her feel quite the same way.

Doug knew exactly what she meant.

He could also see that with careful handling, and she had the perfect agent for that, Summer Laine might be a star in the making. There was 'that thing' about her. Ironically, as

253

far as he could tell, she didn't even realise it. And that drew him closer to her than anything. She was a breath of fresh air and he sucked it in, deep inside.

After about half an hour, there came a pause between them and it seemed a spontaneous end to their lunch. Summer thanked Doug for the coffee, it was all she'd had, saying she had better be getting back in case Cynthia called. Doug smiled to himself, funny, they hadn't spoken about the old lesbian baggage once.

'Thanks for the lovely company,' he said, then immediately hoped it hadn't sounded too familiar, giving her the impression he was some sort of fawning sycophant.

He had asked countless girls 'for coffee', it was his most successful ploy. This was also how he had met his wife. But generally speaking, these little window openers were of little significance in themselves, it was what they helped lead to. And not a great deal, if his long memory served him well. Although, Doug had to concede, Gabs had been different. Must have been. She became Mrs Doug Delany. So surely she had caused similar feelings within him? Otherwise, why did he give up his precious free and single status for her? Maybe he had simply forgotten, and what he was experiencing now was only a recurrence of the sentiments that must have hit him for six during that previous momentous event.

Doug's thoughts meandered back to their sneaky trip to a café on the prom at Bournemouth. Gabs had been somewhat shy in his presence, and of course, that had endeared her to him even more. She had also been a youngster and Doug smirked at the thought that he had been, and in a way still was, a damned dog. He recalled how ordinary Gabs had seemed, set apart from her peers. Presenting as a 'real' person, unaffected by her theatrical experiences. But however hard Doug tried to pass off his present feelings with those he had been through with the girl who became his wife, he knew in his heart that this was different. He had never been in this place before.

And that was the basic truth of it.

Then again, Doug was on the threshold of sixty. Perhaps the dreamy Summer had unwittingly happened along at a point of his life when, as a man, he was wallowing in the dodgy middle-aged years. Unbeknown to him, until now, had Doug been subconsciously worried about hitting the big six-O at breakneck speed? Even while enjoying his most exalted place in show business, and if he was honest, his personal life?

Doug knew as he had become older, he had recognised the change in the respect he got from people, whether the public or amongst his colleagues. Maturity, as seen by others, had imbued a sense of authority about him. They seemed to look upon him differently. In a better light, maybe. Were more willing to sit down and listen to his act because they felt it now carried the necessary life experiences to make it one of the very best comedy acts around. Some had even said to Doug that at sixty, he would be in his prime. Unfortunately, some had said that to Doug when he was about to turn fifty. Fickle folk.

If he was in the throes of a mid-life crisis, did that mean Doug Delany was still an ordinary bloke after all? His dad would certainly have been pleased. He had always been highly suspicious of his son's chosen profession and how it had slowly but surely changed him. As he saw it.

No, was Doug's succinct answer to that.

What was happening to him now was... exceptional. Special. She was... extraordinary.

And Doug wanted her.

Giancarlo sat very still in his office above a bustling Carlo's, trying desperately to rationalise his crazy thoughts.

Of course, he understood only too well the reason that Alessandro had to take a trip back to Sicily. It was all part of the man's 'business'. Giancarlo knew such operatives had to disappear from time to time.

This was nothing new.

What was unfamiliar to Giancarlo was the fury he had almost found impossible to hide down the phone line. He had indeed found himself having to apologise more than once to Alessandro. Not something Mr Scarlatti was used to. And not being able to keep his personal feelings in check during business was unforgivable. It would never have happened to his father. Paulo would be very disappointed, and in turn, Giancarlo was more so.

And what had prompted such a lack of self-control? The fact that Summer was now 'alone' in Blackpool. Giancarlo no longer with the luxury and security of a second pair of eyes and ears to keep her safe. But he could trust her, couldn't he? Hadn't he accepted that as fact when he also decided to make her his wife? So what was it about this situation that was making him so demented? After all, Summer would only be away from him for a few months, and he could always go up to see her whenever he wanted. But as it would be for her, the summer would also be a hugely busy time for Carlo's. So it seemed, whichever way he turned, everything was conspiring against him.

Giancarlo knew there were other quite capable people he could call upon to replace Alessandro, but he was the best in his field and had assured Giancarlo that he would return just as soon as it was safe again. So Giancarlo would wait. Something else his father had taught him; never lower your standards. Never settle for anything other than the best. Was this not the very reason choosing Summer? Paradoxically, she seemed to only bring out the worst in him. Sometimes, Giancarlo had caught his father ranting like a madman in his study, gesticulating wildly, some poor minion receiving the full force of his frustrations, usually Fabia. But Paulo always calmed himself before making any decisions. It was as though he would flick a switch and the madness evaporated from him like breath on a cold mirror. Giancarlo would now try to do the same.

In the meantime, he could put his mind to rest by calling Summer at the number she had given him for the stage door of the theatre. Giancarlo would also see to it that she received a new mobile telephone without delay.

Doug browsed through some of the fan mail while he waited for his next call. It was the normal stuff that also arrived at his fan club; notes of undying admiration, requests for signed photos, things like that. Phil would take care of most of it but there were some fans that Doug liked to deal with personally. Such as his two VIPs. Betty and Vera. These two had followed his career from the early days and even now would write to him wherever he was.

In particular, Betty Winton, Doug's first real devotee. She had been a camper at Butlins in Pwllheli during his first appearances there. *Ahh,* thought Doug as he read her latest 'news' letter, fondly recalling those heady days being newly managed by Harold Hall, and Betty volunteering to come up on stage unsuspectingly to be the brunt of some silly slapstick. She had taken it all in good faith and with an enormous smile, even when he was causing much laughter at her innocent expense. Doug chuckled at the memory. The poor cow probably had no idea what was going on the entire time, completely ignorant, just lapping up her few minutes in the spotlights.

He understood exactly how that felt.

Betty had been in touch ever since. Doug was even asked to attend her husband's funeral. Frank had suffered with angina for years but died of a heart attack very suddenly. The request was carefully declined. It would not have been appropriate. Where would it have ended? How many others, once hearing of Doug turning up to a fan's funeral, would jump on the bandwagon? But not only that, Doug felt his celebrity presence would detract from the solemnity of the occasion. Frank deserved everyone's full attention on that terribly sad day. Instead, he sent a huge wreath to the church and a generous donation to the British Heart Foundation, as Frank had requested of family and friends in his will. Betty had been very gracious in her thanks. Now, she was just a lonely old widow, who probably still had a secret crush on him, so Doug would write to her from time to time. Send her a few words of cheer and a saucy tale to lighten up her companionless melancholy existence.

The call came. Doug had a quick glance at himself in the mirrors before leaving the dressing-room. All right, this was only a technical rehearsal, no one was in full schlepp, in fact, some were positively scruffy, but this was Doug Delany, folks! Behind closed doors at home, he could relax and pig out as much as he wanted. And he usually did. Here though, in his other home, that simply wasn't possible.

While he took his mark on front of stage, his three spots would take place there in front of the main curtain, allowing for scenery changes, Doug caught sight of Summer and her friend in the shadows of side stage to his right. They were talking but something was definitely wrong.

'Doug?' A lighting technician called from the auditorium. 'How's that?'

'Fine,' he called back.

'Okay, go to your next mark and wait a sec, thanks.'

Doug walked to the centre of front stage and stood obediently. He hated this process but it was absolutely necessary. Without these experienced technicians, working on lighting and sound, there would be no show. A few of the nameless, faceless production staff that were so essential to theatre but, unlike their counterparts in television and film, rarely got any recognition. Apart from some small mention on the back pages of the programme which your average theatregoer never read.

Once in position, Doug looked back into the wings. The two girls were gone. He suddenly felt incredibly agitated and impatient to leave the stage. He wanted to find Summer. Ask why she had been crying.

Amanda mutely passed tissues from a box as she listened to Summer recount her recent telephone conversation with her boyfriend. He sounded so typical of his kind to Amanda. Not that she had ever been out with anyone from the Latin countries. In her opinion, they were always possessive and jealous in the extreme. Until they married you. Then, quick as a flash, they completely lost interest, having taken all your youthfulness and feminine zest, consigning you to a thankless role of wife, housekeeper and breeding machine, while they themselves sought new, unspoilt pleasures of the flesh.

Why on Earth Summer was involved with this guy, Amanda couldn't imagine. This girl that could have any man she wanted, and generally did from all reports, why had she settled for this Sicilian control freak? Still, perhaps he was a diversion from Summer's usual choice. A welcome break from those sickening bastards masquerading as producers and directors, and of course, the odd rising personality or two. Amanda mused to herself that Adam Nash seemed to fit that particular bill quite well. Perhaps she should open up a 'book' on the two of them, with the other girls. Then she stopped herself. The truth was, she actually liked Summer. A lot. Sara had been quite wrong in her evaluation. But Sara hadn't exactly been coming from the same direction. She infrequently was.

Amanda surmised that, with Jason still off on one, not returning her messages and beginning to make Amanda rethink their whole relationship, she really did need a friend. And from the snotty weeping girl beside her, it looked as though Summer might need a friend as well.

'... I mean, I've been trying so hard to make him see that I really love him. But he just doesn't get it because he's so bloody complex,' Summer was saying as she gratefully received another Kleenex.

'Well, he's no different to any other man in that respect, love,' Amanda replied, resisting a fleeting thought of what her own boyfriend might be up to in his fit of pique. An unexpected stab from the green-eyed monster pricked her thoughts. 'Maybe he cares about you too much. I suppose Jase is the same, but really, of all people, he should know better because he's in the same sodding business.'

But wasn't it because Jason had been different to all the others 'in the same sodding business' that she had gone out with him in the first place?

Summer wasn't listening to Amanda and continued regardless. 'Carlo should understand me by now. He knows my past. Well... most of it. I don't understand why he was so nasty to me. Just because I wasn't in the theatre when he called. I mean, I have a fucking life apart from him, for God's sake!' She blew her anger out through her nose and reached for another tissue. 'Anyway, he seemed pissed at something else, not just me, but I'm the one that got it, aren't I? Like... I really need this crap right now. My agent's coming up for press night and as it was, she called right after him and I nearly bit her head off for no reason.'

'She all right?' Amanda asked, knowing some agents didn't have the greatest sense of compassion.

'Yeah, she said not to worry, she knows what it's like. Actually, she told me to put him onto her next time.' Summer smiled at that scenario. 'That would be worth getting tickets to!'

Both girls laughed.

'Come on, better get back in case we're needed,' Amanda urged, the professional suddenly kicking in again.

'Oh dear!' Summer said, having seen her red soggy face in the mirror. 'Mess or what?'

Doug locked his dressing-room door and was on his way to hand the key into Clive when he saw Summer returning to the stage area. She saw him and acknowledged with a brief, if somewhat uncomfortable smile. He went over.

'You all right?' he asked in a gentle tone.

Amanda glanced between the two and raised a brow. 'Yes, she'll be fine.' she said, not wanting to get left out.

'And you are?' Doug enquired with a smile, but also the suggestion of mild irritation coating his words.

'Amanda Jacobs,' she replied. 'Pleased to meet you.' Amanda gave him her very best smile.

'Likewise, Amanda. Could you give us a minute?' Doug asked, a polite but firm cue for her to bugger off.

Bollocks! she thought and resentfully excused herself after Summer had indicated it was all right with an almost invisible nod of her head. Maybe she had got the wrong man for her sweepstake. Was her new-found friend back on form and going for the top of the heap?

With Amanda Jacobs out the way, Doug softly touched Summer on the arm. 'What's up, love? Can't have one of the ladies in my show unhappy, can I?'

'Oh, nothing really,' she responded without looking at him, eyes firmly at her feet. *How embarrassing,* she thought. Then looked up and said, 'But thanks for asking.'

She seemed so vulnerable in that moment. Standing there, so in need of a hug. The urge to put an arm around Summer and draw her close was agonising in its intensity, but Doug fought it. He had to. This wasn't the time. Or place. Not yet. Not here.

'Listen, don't get me wrong,' he started. Summer watched him, wondering what was coming. What could he say that she might 'get wrong'? Doug went on. 'Seeing as we seem to be living so near to each other,' he still hadn't got over that one, when it became apparent in the pub, 'I wondered if you would like to pop in this evening for a drink? The house is great but gets a bit lonely without the kids!' he laughed. Careful not to mention the mother of those kids.

Summer was slightly dazed by the invitation. Something in the back of her mind was chomping at the bit but wouldn't release itself from the starting gate. 'Oh, I don't think so,' she said. 'But it's really sweet of you.' Then felt she had sounded ungrateful. 'Maybe another time, perhaps,' she added quickly, hoping he wouldn't be offended by her rebuff.

'That's fine,' Doug said without a hint of affront. 'Not to worry. Another time, as you said.'

He knew not to push it. There was a long summer season ahead of them. There would be other opportunities. He'd make sure of it.

Summer turned to go, then paused. *Why the hell not?* she suddenly asked herself. *Heaven knows what Carlo gets up to when I'm not around.* Summer had seen the women in the bar and restaurant, clocking him, flirting outrageously, even when she was right there with him. He was totally gorgeous and unfortunately, like most of his peers, he also knew it. *I didn't deserve his diatribe earlier, and Doug is just trying to be a pal. There wouldn't be any harm in just having a drink at his house. He's obviously very married, just mentioning his children and everything...*

But there was still that niggling something in her head. Summer ignored it. 'Actually,' she said, turning back to face Doug. 'Can I say yes?'

Doug's heart lurched and then settled back into a slightly increased rhythm. What had changed her mind? Whatever, or whoever it was, he was highly delighted. 'Of course you can,' he smiled warmly, trying not to sound too relieved. 'And if you're hungry, I've something on the go already.'

'What time shall I come round?'

'Anytime. I'm off home now, in fact.' He reached into an inside pocket of his sports jacket and produced a card. 'Here,' he handed it to her. 'That's the house number, give me a bell before you leave and I'll direct you. I look forward to it, Summer.'

'Later then,' she said.

'Later,' Doug replied.

Summer made her way back to the rest of the ensemble who were gathered in the front stalls.

Cynthia's words of caution were completely forgotten.

CHAPTER TWENTY NINE

The phone rang again and Doug stood looking at it for a moment. Perhaps she wasn't going to come, after all. Changed her mind, once more. Women were prone to do that, weren't they? On the fourth ring, he picked it up.

'Hello!' Doug said in his usually loud and enthusiastic manner. Something he had perfected over the years. Mainly for the benefit of answering calls from agents, colleagues and the press. Now though, it was how he answered all calls. But Gabrielle was used to it.

'It's me,' she said. 'How's things?'

'Gabs!' Doug replied, genuinely pleased to hear from her. Or was it because it hadn't been someone else? He glanced quickly at his watch. A nervous tick caught in his throat and he cleared it. 'Sorry, love, frog in the throat. Fine! Rehearsals are going really well. Full dress in a couple of days, then the press review. How's the kids?' Doug then remembered it had been Alexander's birthday. All day. He hadn't called. 'Did Alex like his picture?' he said to cover quickly. Gabrielle opened her mouth to speak but Doug jumped in, 'Sorry I didn't call him this morning. I had a really early call at the theatre.'

'No problem,' she finally managed to edge in. 'He loved the duck picture. He's been so taken up with organising his friends coming over this evening, he hasn't said anything.' While she was saying all this, Gabrielle was quietly deliberating the truth. Doug had simply forgotten. Just like all the other times. Not only that, she knew it had been some years since he had been given an early rehearsal call. Interfered with his golf, you see. 'It was very thoughtful to send him the extra present, Doug. Not like you! Were you feeling all right at the time?' she mocked but secretly was rather impressed with this outstanding effort.

Doug paused a second before answering. 'I know what

you're saying, but I'm trying my best, you know that. Anyway,' he said, getting off the subject, too complicated and there wasn't much time. 'When are you coming up?' That usually brought their phone calls to a rapid end.

'Soon, actually,' Gabrielle replied. It hadn't been the response Doug was expecting. 'I'm trying to arrange something in a week or two, get permission for Alex to have a Friday and Monday off, make a long weekend of it. The school is usually accommodating under the circumstances. I'll keep you informed.'

Doug's mind was in an uncomfortable state of flux. 'So, I guess that means you won't be up yourself for the opening night, then?' He always asked her about tour opening nights, knowing precisely what she would say.

'I'm thinking about it. Maybe it's time I showed a bit more support and all that,' Gabrielle said, rivulets of guilt dripped undetected off each word. Angelo Maldini, Valerie's Tarot cards, and three boil-infected faces swirled around in her head like ingredients in some warped psychological blender.

Was this for real, or was Gabrielle just winding him up? Doug was at a loss. He also looked at his watch again. *Great!* he said to himself. A heavy sinking feeling descended as Summer's face drifted across his mind. *Of all the moments she chooses to play the dutiful showbiz wife, she picks this one. Women! Always changing their minds.*

Doug felt a thin layer of sweat beginning to emerge on his forehead.

'Well, if you do want to come for opening night, of course I'd love it. I'll make sure you get the best seat in the house, as always.'

'I should think so too! Anyway, darling, I'd better go, Alex's mob are arriving any minute. Speak to you later tonight?'

Darling? thought Doug. Was SHE feeling all right, never mind about him? Perhaps this being his final summer season was having a good effect on her. Or maybe for the first time in ages, absence was having its most-quoted impact. It had on him, for a while, but that was then. And 'then' seemed a very long time ago to him now.

'Sure, but look, I've got Adam Nash coming over this evening, so I'll call you, yeah?'

'Of course, have a nice time. Bye.'

'Bye, love.'

Doug sighed as he hung up, putting a hand to his mouth as he pondered deeply. Then, in a blink of an eye, he snapped out of it. A second later, the doorbell chimed.

He checked himself in a huge antique mirror above the fireplace, breathed slowly in and out for a couple of beats and struggled to banish an impromptu attack of uncertainty. Should he?... Shouldn't he?... *Fuck off...* Turning to leave the sitting room, Doug took one last look in the mirror. There was something concealed behind his eyes. A semblance of something he couldn't pin down. A truth he wasn't prepared to face?

Doug had always known he lacked any real form of self-control. Only when it mattered. Only in the glare of the footlights. His past was scattered with mistakes of varying severity because of it. He was ultimately a man of weak will but also great desire. He was stupid, irresponsible, a cheat and a liar. A philanderer without bounds. He'd even called himself a damned dog. Though, that was perhaps detrimental to the whole canine species.

Doug knew all these things. He also knew he probably needed help.

Maybe this woman, an embodiment of his supreme female, would be the one to finally put him in his place. Silently, and at odds with his rampant thirst for her, Doug pleaded that Summer Laine might save him from himself.

He answered the door. Summer stood smiling, still with that self-conscious air about her. It made Doug crave her even more.

'I come bearing gifts,' she said, holding up a bottle of white wine and laughing gently through a demure smile. The porch light danced like fairy-dust in her hair as she flicked it from her face.

'That wasn't necessary but thank you anyway. Come in.'
He let Summer past him and closed the door. 'Here, let me
take that,' he said putting a hand on the bottle, 'I'll pop it in
the fridge. I've got one open, or would you prefer
something else? Red perhaps?'

'Oh, white wine would be great, thanks. Lovely house,'
Summer said. It was nearly the size of the mansion her flat
was part of.

'Yeah, well, I try to make myself comfortable while away
from home.' Doug smiled as they walked into the sitting
room. He made sure not to look in the mirror. 'You make
yourself at home while I get us a drink.'

But Summer followed him into the kitchen. As Doug was
placing Summer's bottle of wine in the fridge, he saw it was
a very exclusive Sancerre. *Blimey! She must be from a
better background than I gave her credit for!* 'This is a
nice bottle of plonk,' he said, indicating the Sancerre while
bringing out a modest but quite decent Sauvignon Blanc.

'Oh, don't make a thing of it. Anyway, it was a present of
sorts,' Summer replied dismissively. 'Something smells
delicious,' she said to direct the conversation away from
the wine that Giancarlo had left in the flat, along with
many others of similar pedigree.

'It's a stew I've made. Always have one on the stove when
I'm touring. Easy and quick to snack on.'

'Good idea, Doug,' Summer said as she lifted the lid of
the pot. 'Gosh! Dumplings as well! Is there no end to your
talents?' she laughed.

Doug smiled at her sarcastic tone. So she was feisty as
well, was she? Someone who could give as good as she got?
He liked that. He liked that a lot in a woman. He had liked
it in Gabrielle...

'Would you like some?' he asked as he poured them two
glasses of wine.

'Yes, please.'

Summer fondly recalled her mother's superb Irish stew,
but if you didn't get your mitts on it before her father, you
were left to scrape the pot. That was if he was feeling

generous and her brothers weren't in an unyielding line behind him.

Two bowls of mam's finest later, or, two and a half if you counted Doug's second helping, he could never eat just one serving, they were sitting opposite each other on matching sofas, a smoked glass coffee table between them. Both held their wine in hand and Frank Sinatra embellished the relaxed ambience. Summer started to speak just as Ol' Blue Eyes started to sing *I've Got You Under My Skin*. Doug found himself having to hide an involuntary swallow as the words came at him like a plethora of fists, beating on his conscience without mercy. Eventually, in what seemed like minutes and was actually only seconds, Doug brought himself back to the sitting room and his lovely guest, who was talking animatedly about some film producer called Martin Thurlow and a possible audition for him. It only went to prove to Doug that his earlier presumptions about Summer were correct. Perhaps her stardom was closer than even she suspected. Sadly for Doug, not having had much time to go to the cinema over the years, first because of work, then because of fame, he hadn't the slightest idea who this Thurlow bloke was. All Doug did know was that he envied any man who got to be in her company for longer than a quick drink.

Of course, Summer being on the brink of a film career didn't surprise Doug. She was in the tenacious clutches of Cynthia Hersh. That woman only gave up her time for those who deserved her special guidance. She only took on the best. Funny then, that Cynthia hadn't ever contacted Doug to sign him up. Not that he could have let himself be on her books, in any case. It was an irony though, two of the most successful people in their fields and keeping as far away from each other as possible. Until now. It seemed as though they were, in fact, to meet once again.

A grubby old regret pushed at him from another time that seemed so distant, it could have been from another universe. An audible sigh escaped from him as he shoved the unwanted penitence right back.

'Big sigh?' Summer said.

'Sorry, love,' Doug replied, feeling somewhat embarrassed. 'Miles away.' Realising how that must have sounded, he qualified with, 'which is terribly rude in your delightful company!'

Summer gave him a 'give me a break' look and a wry smile threatened to find its way onto her lips. Doug tried not to concentrate on them too obviously, or for too long. Just the mere thought of his own brushing against them... 'Another drink?' he said, almost jumping up off his sofa. Moving about would help him cope with the increasing sexual twitches.

'No thanks, but a mineral water would be good.'

'I agree, love the stuff myself. Keeps the old voice box clear in the theatre. It gets pretty dry out front, as I'm sure you know,' Doug said. A referral to the desert dry air on stage. A result of no windows, air conditioning or heating, depending on which season, hot spot lights and the ever-present dust. He always kept honey, fresh lemons, a bottle of pure glycerine and a kettle in the dressing room. The eighteen-year-old single malt was kept for after the show. But never a matinée, of course.

He brought in two tumblers and a bottle of Malvern, placing them on the table in front of Summer, then saw an opportunity and seized it, sitting next to her.

'There you are,' he said, handing her a glass of still water.

'Thanks, Doug,' Summer replied as she took it. Their fingers touched for an instant and they glanced at each other. Something seemed to transpire for both, but neither made it apparent.

Doug smiled sheepishly, drawing his hand away quickly in a jokey gesture, as though it had been a forbidden contact. Inside, he was a mass of contradictory thoughts and feelings. Almost too much to bear. Overall, he simply wanted to lean across and kiss her.

Summer sipped her water.

Somehow, amazingly, she really liked Doug Delany. There wasn't any discerning reason that she could latch onto, but something about the man was extremely attractive. Quite unexpectedly so. Doug was not handsome in her opinion, his attraction came from within. He was funny, not just when he was giving some of his well-practised banter, no, there seemed to be a completely natural sense of humour that emanated from him. Doug appeared to be kind and thoughtful. He could even cook! That WAS a revelation. Who'd have thought! At home, in private, Doug Delany was nothing like his professional persona. There was the occasional smattering, perhaps, but nothing like one would have imagined.

Summer had enjoyed their time together immensely. Far more than she had thought she might, while driving to his house. Far more than, perhaps, she should have. She wondered how many messages would be on the answerphone at the flat. How much of their content would be in rapid, furious Sicilian? Her sudden thought of Giancarlo made her feel cold. She quickly rid him from her mind. He wasn't going to spoil this restful evening for her. Even so, this seemed like the right time to leave.

'I really should be getting home and catch up on some sleep for tomorrow.'

'Oh, okay then,' Doug said, desperately trying to hide his disappointment. 'Maybe we could do this again, sometime.'

'Love to. It's been a really nice change,' Summer replied. That sentence, she realised, needed some explanation, not only to Doug but to herself. Now was not the time to get into it, though.

Doug led her to the front door. As she walked through to the hall from the sitting room, Summer realised there were no pictures of his family. Rather odd. Maybe he kept them privately upstairs, in the bedroom. She was sure he would have at least one in the dressing room. They usually did. Normally some rag-end snap that had been stuck on numerous mirrors. In many cases, just for show. To save face. Image.

He opened the door and she stepped onto the porch.

'Bit chilly tonight,' Doug said, rubbing his arms and

hunching his shoulders in a rather comical way. It was subterfuge. Anything to delay her from leaving.

'Yes,' she replied. 'But it seems to me it's always chilly up here!'

'That's the Irish sea. Nasty old wind comes off it most of the year. Still, my stew should keep you warm for a bit!' He wished with his whole heart, no room for anything... or anyone else... that it wasn't only his stew that could be keeping out the cold. 'Drive carefully, won't you?'

'I will. It's only round the corner, really.'

There was a pause, both standing reticent, looking into each other's eyes. Doug just couldn't help it. He leaned over and placed a light kiss on her cheek. 'Let's do this again, soon,' he said, still holding in the delicate scent of her as he spoke. It was as though they were the only two people on the planet in a hazy, shameless moment.

Summer regarded Doug. Something in his soft touch had caused an unfamiliar sensation to invade even the tiniest and most concealed facets inside her. It lingered, like incense, filling her with a sweet warmth Summer had never felt before. She almost felt like crying because in that very instant, she realised Giancarlo had never made her feel this way. But she loved him. Needed him. *What are you doing? You shouldn't be here.* Doing what? Summer got her answer.

Doug's lips settled gently on hers.

Like images of flash photography, Doug's mind was a fast-moving picture-board of Gabrielle, the children, Alex at the pub... ducks... *Stop me! For God's sake, say no...* He honestly cried, waiting for a rebuke, a hand pushing him away, angry words and footsteps down the driveway as she left. None of them came. So he kissed her again, firmer, lips slightly parted. Summer responded. Already condemned, Doug went for broke.

'Come back inside,' he whispered, voice shaking.

'I shouldn't...' she started but found herself being guided tenderly back into the hallway and Doug closing the door behind them.

He enveloped Summer with his arms and drew her into him, feeling her body pressing against his, like a customized glove. Her arms slowly sought their way around Doug and he buried his face into her neck, every part of him feeling unbelievably alive. It was as though he were on fire, and whether they be the flames of the hell he was surely to face, he, Doug Delany, married, three children, abandoned himself to them. Summer was beyond anything he could ever have, or indeed had, imagined.

Doug lifted his face and looked into luminous probing eyes before kissing her again, this time deeply, longingly and without conscience.

Summer's mind was a wildfire of thoughts and questions. So many questions. She searched for something to help her stop what was happening. But Summer didn't know what was happening. So what was it she was looking for? Suddenly Giancarlo was there, they were making love, he was saying he loved her... then his face seemed to float away and was replaced by Anthony Wiggins. *No! Not even you.* Nothing would make her let go of Doug. She wanted to be free. Live her own life. On her terms. And these were her terms.

Summer wanted to be able to breathe again.

Slowly, almost gracefully, they sank to the floor, assisting each other in removing clothes. It became more ravenous, their kisses now uncompromising and intense. Desideratum. Incoherent sounds of desire issuing from both of them. When he entered her, Summer let out a strangely distant moan, as though she wasn't there with him at all. Doug almost came immediately but called upon every ounce of experience to hold back. It felt on the verge of painful. Blissfully agonising. A suffering he would have been willing to die to. Summer joined with him so perfectly, Doug considered they might even have been meant for each other.

'Oh, my love,' he breathed, finally unable to prevent his hedonistic detonation any longer. 'My sweet, sweet love.'

They came together.

CHAPTER THIRTY

Cynthia checked into Blackpool's Grand Hotel. Although it didn't quite hold the same regal ambience as the Grand Hotel in Brighton, it still managed to adequately pass all of Cynthia's comfort criteria and in any case, she was only there for the one night.

She decided as soon as she had checked in, to have a shower and scrub away the frustrations of the hellish journey she had just endured. Cynthia was thankful she would not have to repeat the fiasco again anytime soon. Before heading for her 'double room with sea view, television, tea-making facilities and mini-bar', she felt it necessary to hit the main bar of the hotel and order a large vodka and tonic, no ice, never knew what lurked in the tap water, and plenty of lemon. While waiting, she also lit up a much-needed fag. Within seconds, Cynthia felt abundantly better.

After freshening up, she would pop along to the theatre to see Summer before going to front of house and taking her seat in the auditorium, maybe sneaking another drink beforehand in the theatre bar. Cynthia didn't normally need to oil herself up like this, but then, this was going to be a very interesting few hours.

Suitably spruced up and considerably calmer, Cynthia took a stroll along the promenade. She had taken rather longer to get ready than usual. More care over her hair and make-up, which she rarely wore now. And was pleased with her decision to bring a very fetching Harvey Nicks trouser suit, just in case. All because of Doug Delany. Silly really, when she thought about it. After all these years.

As she walked along, Cynthia gazed out onto the flat, dull-looking sands and the hundreds of holidaymakers at play. She couldn't remember the last time she had taken time out. In her line of work, it was almost impossible, especially when you were one of the top agencies and had some highly sought-after talent on your books. A call that went unanswered generally didn't come again. Well, it had been like that in the early days but Cynthia had not been able to let go of that motto. Somehow, seeing all those people enjoying themselves caused an involuntary urgent need of tropical sunshine, white sand beaches and crystal blue seas. She had been meaning to go to the south of Spain to search for a villa. So, it wasn't the Tropics but it was close enough by air to London to get back within a few hours if necessary. Perhaps she should just go and get a ticket and get her very white bum over there.

Cynthia's eyes settled on a group of donkeys being led along the beach below her. Some walking, one or two in a jerky trot. Small children bobbing up and down in heavy-looking saddles, their heads rocking about like the puppets in *Thunderbirds*. The prospect of very sore bottoms in the morning. While she smiled at this, Cynthia had never ridden a donkey. Refused outright as a small girl when once brought here by her grandparents on a rare holiday away with them. She had never quite gone in for the full-on 'save the planet and care for the animals' movement, but even as the hard-bitten woman she was now, Cynthia didn't like to see animals treated poorly. The donkeys looked forlorn and weary. In need of a peaceful green field, hay and fresh water. There was a wonderful sanctuary for them in Devon somewhere, and Cynthia wished she could magic these sad little creatures away there. She made a mental note to send the sanctuary a donation when she got back.

The Opera House loomed large across the road. There were a few people milling about the entrance but the main gaggle would arrive about half an hour before curtain up. Cynthia rang the bell of the stage door. In more provincial theatres, it was often left unlocked, but with all the big names, and especially Mr Delany on the bill, this stage door would remain firmly locked against any undesirables. And to delay the odd wife, girlfriend, or boyfriend for that matter, so that no one was found in an uncompromising situation. The door was quickly opened by a pleasant old chap and Cynthia was ushered in once she'd made herself known to him.

'Just wait there a minute and I'll call her down, Miss Hersh,' Clive said and ducked into his office to make a Tannoy announcement.

'Summer Laine to the stage door, please.'

While she waited, Cynthia cast her eyes down to the darkened stage area, anticipating what it was going to be like, coming face to face with her nemesis after all this time. Would the Cynthia Hersh that existed now deal with him in a way that the other Cynthia wouldn't have been able to in a month of Sundays? Polite but curt, brief but significant? Or maybe this occasion called for a more... sophisticated approach. Yes. Something he wouldn't be expecting from her. But exactly what would Doug be expecting from her? Whatever it might be, Cynthia wasn't about to let him see that the pain had survived in a watered-down version and that his self-serving and thoughtless actions of long ago had made her the woman she was today. Not the successful agent one. They both had played a part in that. She meant the hard-headed, forceful and somewhat mannish one she was inside. The private Cynthia. Quite removed from the young dancer breaking into acting she had been in Scarborough.

But was she not still an actress? Surely somewhere within the clusters of ageing cobwebs, the performer lay doggedly waiting. Faithfully waiting for that new opportunity. A chance to shine once more. A bit rusty perhaps but shine she would. *Better freshen up the make-up, darling,* she advised. *You might have to go on sooner than you think.*

Into Cynthia's field of vision came a familiar form. She focused and saw Summer approaching. She looked fantastic. Radiant. Unusually so, even for her. There was a smile the size of the Forth Bridge across her face. Something stirred in the agent.

'Hi!' Summer said when she saw the agent. On reaching

her, Summer gave Cynthia an affectionate hug. 'I'm so glad you made it here.'

'Been looking forward to it,' Cynthia responded. 'Have we got time for a quick chat before the show?'

'Sure. Come up to the dressing-room, the other girls won't mind. Some aren't in yet, anyway.'

They started to walk down into the theatre. 'You're looking very pleased with yourself, young lady,' Cynthia said in playful tone. 'It's obviously been going really well for you.'

'Better than I could have imagined,' Summer replied.

There was something in her voice. Cynthia stopped and touched Summer's arm. She turned.

'What is it?' Summer asked.

'Have you met someone?' Cynthia enquired with a slightly sarcastic smile, keeping constant eye contact.

'No!' Summer came back with an air of real surprise. 'Why ever would you ask me that? Anyway, you know I'm with Carlo. Remember?' All innocence and indignation. But Cynthia knew Summer too well to be taken in.

'Of course, sorry.'

While they climbed the steps to the first floor, Cynthia felt a strange sense of foreboding. It seemed to have been suddenly dropped over her like heavy blanket. Whatever it was, she didn't like it one little bit. It felt sickeningly too well-founded. Cynthia hoped that concentrating on telling Summer that Martin Thurlow's film was back on track would help keep this unease at bay.

The show was outstanding. Even Cynthia Hersh had to allow. She had enjoyed it immensely. The vent had been terrific, even by Cynthia's rigorous standards. Adam Nash, or rather his puppets, were very well balanced and Adam's incredible skill was unequalled. Cynthia had a soft spot for the disagreeable Rasher. A pig after her own heart. Of course, Summer had not only been a joy to the eye but had danced with a renewed vitality. It was therefore no surprise that Marcia had given Summer a lengthy solo feature as accompaniment for the guest appearance of a young aspiring tenor, who was becoming quite well known after releasing a contemporary album. Unfortunately, it all just seemed to confirm Cynthia's private suspicions about her.

The greatest revelation to the agent was Doug Delany. He looked pretty damned good. Much better in person than on television, before Cynthia would swiftly change channels. That was when she had time to watch the box. Not often. Still, she had to admit, she was sitting just forward of centre stalls, generally the best place to watch a show, and he was in the kind and wrinkle-fading spotlights, wearing a light make-up so as not to appear like a ghost to the audience. It wasn't a true representation. His main act had been very good indeed. Cynthia even found herself laughing quite heartily at some excellent observations about life in Blackpool. The locals seemed to take it in the spirit it was meant and kept interrupting with spontaneous applause.

He had come a long way and had obviously been very prudent in studying how comedy had moved with the times. His script was spot on. Although, those that knew him of old could easily still catch the essence that was purely Doug.

As she left the auditorium and made her way backstage again, Cynthia felt more relaxed about actually meeting him once more. Perhaps having to confront fears and bitterness from the past had, in fact, helped her to realise that time had been a great healer as the old adage promised and previously ardent bad feeling was now merely a distant memory. Maybe this wouldn't be such an unpleasant evening, after all.

Adam slumped into an old armchair in his dressing-room, wiping his brow with a towel, careful not to disturb the make-up. There was still a press and photo call to come.

He dialled a number on his phone and waited. On the second ring, Jayne answered.

'It's me,' he said.

'So tell me how it went,' she replied eagerly.

'For a preview, really well I thought. Got to get used to the sodding dance number we all have to do at the end of the finale, though. What a nightmare. Doug and I kept looking at each other. We both had to keep from cracking up. Otherwise...'

'It was good,' Jayne finished for him.

'It was good. So! How's it going with you? Finished at the conference?'

'Yeah, thank God! What a load of old wankers! Honestly! I thought you lot were bad enough...'

'Hey! Steady on!' Adam laughed. 'Anyway, seeing that the show looks like a success, are you coming up for the opening night?'

There was an ominous silence, then, 'Oh, Adam, I can't. I really tried, but there's so much work to do on editing and stuff. I just can't get away. I'm so sorry. I should have called you sooner but you know how it is.'

Yes, he did. But she sounded genuine and that was all that mattered. He knew when she could, Jayne would be up to see him. It was still a shame, and not the first time, although Adam was content in the knowledge this absence would truly be down to her work. No hidden messages.

'That's all right,' he said. 'I understand.'

There was a knock on the door and someone was calling for him.

'I've got to go, the local press awaits! Talk to you later.'

'Have fun!' Jayne said in droll tone. She couldn't think of anything more boring and arduous than a local press and photo call.

Adam smiled at her comment after he ended the call. Then he quickly checked himself in the mirror, put a dab or two of Max Factor back on his forehead and opened the dressing-room door. Before leaving, he turned back and glanced across to Floppy and Rasher, propped up on their cases.

'Well done, boys.'

Cynthia fought her way through the inevitable throng and found Summer talking and laughing with some of the other girls. They all stopped as she approached. She liked that effect she had.

'So? What did you think?' Summer asked, a girlie grin on her face.

'Darling, it was great.'

Summer tilted her head and laughed. 'No... Really?'

'Really!'

The girls all looked at one another with raised eyebrows and a few nods of self-congratulation.

'Pleased to meet you,' Amanda Jacobs beamed with hand held out. She wouldn't get another chance.

'And you, dear,' said Cynthia while giving a perfunctory shake of her hand. She tried to remember which girl this was, but apart from Summer, they had all seemed so... average. Good, but definitely average.

'Come on,' Summer said, sensing her agent wanted them to be alone. 'I'll get you a drink.' Turning to the others, she smiled. 'Catch up with you later.'

They all mutely nodded, eyes still on Cynthia. Cynthia Hersh! The general consensus was that Summer Laine was a lucky bitch.

Cynthia watched as Summer deftly made her way through the company towards the drinks that had been laid on for a small celebration. The big party came after opening night and was usually held at some hotspot venue. Sometimes, and mostly in smaller theatres, the party would be held in the theatre itself, on the stage. Thankfully, Cynthia would be long gone by then. She couldn't abide them. Never could. Found them excruciating when she had to attend one. There was so much obsequious crap flying about, it was advisable to turn up in a wet suit.

As she admired Summer for her excellent handling of everyone, such maturity in someone so young, a little smile crossed Cynthia's face. She was reminded of someone else from a very long time ago. Though, it had to be said, Summer would have easily beaten her hands down.

'Hello, Cy,' a voice caught her from behind. Cynthia felt herself shiver and turned to meet eyes that had once lovingly held hers as they had made love.

'Hello, Doug,' she replied as breezily as she could muster, her heart rate increasing by the second. Cynthia was in slight shock from being suddenly so physically close to him. It had taken an unexpected grip and she fought to keep it hidden. But she needn't have worried. Earlier instructions had been paid heed to. The make-up had been retouched and that other self was just emerging from the wings, out into the lights for a long-awaited resurgent performance. 'So how are you?' she asked, easing into the routine.

Doug seemed to be studying her. Perhaps comparing notes with the Cynthia he walked away from.

The one that had briefly carried his first child.

'Just fine. You look lovely this evening, I must say,' he said. For a split second, Cynthia thought he might even be serious.

'Oh, I see you two have met, then,' Summer said as she returned with a glass of wine.

Doug looked from the agent to Summer and back. Cynthia turned to ice. She knew that devastating look. Every memory of Scarborough rushed through her head like the violent torrent from a breached dam. *Oh, dear God!* she cried silently. It was too late. There would be nothing she could say or do to change anything now.

Cynthia took the wine from Summer and saw that the girl quickly stole a glance at Doug. She saw things in Summer's eyes that had once prevailed in her own.

So he had already snared her. Summer was now part of a hunt he had been on for years. He wouldn't let her go until she had been suitably skinned. Then, without warning or much ceremony, her carcass would be tossed out for the hounds.

The best that Cynthia could hope for was that Summer's huge ambition to become well known would carry her through. She had always sensed that Summer was beyond her years and this might just prove invaluable when she realised that Doug was simply toying with her. And yet, Cynthia had seen how Summer was behaving. How happy she seemed. Those eyes.

'Enjoy the show, Cy?' Doug asked.

Cynthia wanted to grind her fist into his smarmy face and deck him. 'The show was excellent, Doug. But you know, as much as I'd love to stay, I really have to get going. Driving back tonight.'

'Oh?' Summer said frowning. 'I thought you were...'

'No, I got a call as I arrived,' Cynthia cut her off. 'I'm needed back in London for an early meeting.'

'Oh, that's a shame,' Summer replied, looking as though she wasn't pleased but accepted Cynthia's rapidly improvised explanation.

'Well, it's been... illuminating... meeting you again, Doug,' Cynthia said carefully. 'I hope the show does well. I'm sure it will.'

'So am I,' Doug retorted. He didn't quite know what illuminating meant but knowing Cynthia Hersh and the way it had been said, it had to be an insult. 'It's been...' but he wasn't able to come back at her. Phil Beauchamp was beside him, whispering something. 'It looks like I'm required elsewhere. Safe trip back, Cy,' he said, the delivery of her name was saturated with derision. He winked at Summer and followed Phil to the other side of the stage, vanishing into the wings.

'You take care of yourself,' Cynthia said, touching Summer's face briefly. 'Don't let yourself be... well, I think you know what I'm trying to say. I'll keep you updated about the audition.'

'I can't wait!' Summer breathed excitedly. Then said with a smile, 'And I'm with Carlo! Don't worry yourself!'

Cynthia left the theatre and went for a very long walk in the cold night air. She could feel sea spray settling on her face, lips tasting salty. She welcomed the sensation. It suited her mood. The private lives of her clients were only her business when they interfered with their work. Or a story got out that was big enough to warrant damage limitation in the press. Until then, this agent kept her nose out. But this time, it would be difficult because her own personal experience was muddying the waters.

It was time to go back to the hotel room, watch some banal television soaps while getting sloshed and shut it all out of her mind.

Adam, finally released from the photo call, wandered through the company, collected a lager and wished that Jayne could have been there with him. He felt uncharacteristically lonely and couldn't seem to shake it off.

'I thought you were marvellous.'

Adam looked up from his feet. Amanda Jacobs stood smiling at him.

'Quite fantastic. The best I've ever seen,' she said enthusiastically.

'Thank you very much,' Adam responded, puffing himself up a bit. He had no doubts that he was probably the best ventriloquist in the country at that moment, but it never hurt to hear it. And if he were typical of his kind, he could never hear it enough. 'You're Amanda, aren't you?' he enquired of the bubbly petite blond.

'Yes!' Amanda replied, impressed that he had actually known who she was. Gosh! 'So how do you think the show went?' she asked.

'Very well.'

'Do you think we'll get good reviews?'

'Don't see why not,' Adam said. *I know I will.* 'But then, you never can tell!' He laughed and took a swig of lager. It wasn't the brand he was used to and the dryness of the brew bit nastily. He cleared his throat, reminding himself not to touch that cat's piss again.

'I'm looking forward to opening night now,' Amanda said. 'Got anyone coming up for it?' Jason was apparent in her mind. She knew he wouldn't be there, not only because of his work but because they still weren't speaking. Or rather, he still wasn't speaking to her. Sometimes her mother would make the effort, but it seemed Blackpool was too far away this time.

'No, not on this occasion,' Adam replied. 'Still, there's been a few!' he smiled. *And there'll be a few more if I crack this season with Doug Delany.* 'Sometimes I prefer to not have anyone I know out front on opening night. There's enough pressure as it is!'

'I can understand that one!' Amanda smiled.

There was the briefest of charged pauses between them before Adam suddenly said in a hushed voice, 'Fancy a drink away from here? Get some fresh air?'

Amanda hid a nervous intake of breath and reflex swallow. 'Yes, that would be great.'

'Tell you what,' Adam said, looking around them. 'Best meet outside, say, ten minutes?'

'I'll be there.'

CHAPTER THIRTY ONE

'Hey, sleepy...'

Summer opened her eyes. Doug stood beside the bed holding a tray. He was wearing a loosely fastened robe and nothing else, except a radiant smile that lit up his face all the way to twinkling eyes.

'Breakfast,' he said softly.

Summer stretched and yawned with abandon as he settled the tray on the bed, dropped the robe where he stood and clambered back into bed.

'Boiled eggs, toast, orange juice and coffee,' he announced unnecessarily. Doug was proud of this supreme effort and just felt like saying it, perhaps as a form of self-endorsement. He certainly looked very pleased with himself and Summer noticed. She smiled to herself.

'Free-range eggs and wholemeal bread, I hope,' she said in matronly tone, a serious expression on her face. Then seeing Doug quickly glance at the tray, his little mind working overtime, she broke into an audacious grin and laughed.

'You... are a cheeky little mare!' Doug teased as he snatched a half slice of toast, nearly stuffed the whole lot in his mouth in one go and started to chomp.

'Couldn't manage the whole piece, then?' Summer taunted while she carefully removed a dribble of melted butter from the corner of Doug's mouth with a finger, then licked it provocatively.

Doug threw the corner remnant of his toast onto the tray and made a grab for her.

'Watch the tray!' she warned as he began to tickle her ferociously. Her fits of giggles turned into laughing screams for mercy. Then suddenly, Doug stopped and gazing into her face, said, 'God! You're fabulous.' His eyes slowly lowered to her small but perfectly curvaceous breasts, he lowered his head and gently kissed one. The nipple instantly tightened in response. 'Quite fabulous,' he repeated quietly, mainly to himself, closed his eyes and nuzzled his head into her chest, drifting with the hypnotic regular beat of her heart.

'You're not so bad yourself,' Summer replied pensively while delicately, she traced the contours of his ear.

'Can we just stop time here? Right now? Stay in this moment forever?' Doug breathed dreamily. He considered the relevance of the title to a certain musical. The same one he often recalled a particular song from. But Doug didn't feel like a fool when he was with Summer, quite the opposite in fact and if ever there was a moment he wanted to stop the world so he could get off, this was the one.

Summer was reflective and reticent. How many times had she asked that same question? Had the same wish? In her case, it was usually because of something unpleasant happening in her life. Or downright malignant. But whenever she had harboured Doug's present yearning and told the heavens so, the seconds just ticked on... and on.

'Come on, silly,' she said. 'It's getting late. I've got things to do.'

'And I've got a phone call to make,' Doug said, breaking into her sentence while straightening himself up.

'Oh?'

'Surprise!' he replied with an enigmatic grin.

'I hate surprises,' Summer said. She'd had enough of those for this lifetime.

'Ah yes, but you'll like this one!' Doug retorted undeterred.

'Will I now?' Summer responded, faintly sarcastic, as she reached for a slice of toast and the orange juice.

'Oh yes!'

Doug ruffled her hair and patted her head affectionately before getting out of bed and pulling on his robe.

'Woof!' Summer said, bringing her hands together in an imitation of a begging dog.

'Careful! Don't give me ideas!' Doug playfully warned,

eyes flashing with mock menace. 'Just tuck into that lot and I'll be back in a minute.'

Summer gave him a mischievous smile while munching on the toast. Doug blew her a kiss and left the bedroom.

She sipped orange juice and sighed, feeling unbelievably relaxed. What was it about this man? What secret ingredient had he invisibly added to the compound that was her life, and bound it together so wonderfully? It was as though this was where she had always meant to be. Everything, each experience, had brought her to this point. But how could this seasoned comedian, of a certain age, have torn down all her intricate defences with the equivalent force of an infantry on full battle advance?

Maybe because it had been done for him.

By another.

Giancarlo.

Ironically, for all his skill in dismantling Summer's fortress battlements, it seemed he had not then taken full advantage of her exposed state. Thus, when she had been thrown into a theatrical lion's den, the head of the pride had smelled her willingness and taken his chance.

Was it all as simple as that? Surely not. And it didn't feel like it to Summer. There was something special that happened when she was with Doug. Inexplicably intense. Consuming. A feeling so profound it was difficult to breath sometimes. Had she truly never felt this way before? She searched inside for the tiniest clue that she had. Try as Summer might, no case-closing evidence could be uncovered. Because it didn't exist. Just like this sensation rushing through her now. A notion that this was how it was supposed to be. That for all her efforts in building a special relationship with Giancarlo and the work it took to understand him, in the instance that Doug had kissed her for the first time, there had been no resistance. No complexities dampening the moment. Everything had naturally fallen perfectly into place. She didn't have to try with Doug. They just 'were'.

He was also a married man with children. And a much-loved image. But Summer knew that. She had always known that.

What could she do?

It was impossible to control such basic compulsions. No one could. At the end of the day, with all the embellishments of human life removed, they were just a man and a woman.

Should she finish with Giancarlo? End their relationship now? Seeing as he wouldn't stay out of her thoughts, Summer decided to give in and contemplate their future. Could she honestly bear the consequences that action might cause? Especially in the middle of a demanding summer season when she would need all her strength? There was the flat to consider, of course. Doug's house would certainly be a joy to live in, especially with him, but it was a family house. For the family man. Summer was under no illusions about that. Or the fact that it would take a difficult journey down a long road before he might sacrifice his wife and kids for her. If ever. Even so, the passing thought of her and Doug as a legitimate item sometime in the future hung tantalising in her mind.

There was also the small matter of his age but Doug was in great shape. Although the difference in stamina between him and Giancarlo - there he was again - was apparent to Summer. Not unexpected. It was the whole experience of Doug Delany that attracted her to him. In any case, he was a wonderful lover; unassuming, gentle and affectionate. Where Giancarlo was strong, sensual and ardent in his technique, even dramatic, Doug was unhurried, more precise. Thoughtful. After their torrid coupling on the hallway floor, their lovemaking had been exactly that; making love, not just sex between two lonely people. There was a psychological connection Summer had not felt with any other lover. For the first time, she was not expected to perform. Doug always made love to her. When Summer reciprocated, she found it was with a new sense of really wanting to please him, give willingly of herself, rather than feeling she had to.

The difference it made was unprecedented. Under Doug's expertise, her orgasms transcended anything she had ever felt before.

Doug returned to the bedroom with a huge smile and an air of excitement. Then he looked at the tray of breakfast and saw that only two pieces of toast were gone, one of them being his. 'You haven't touched it,' he said with real concern. 'You must have something, love. Most important meal of the day. And it's going to be a big day tomorrow. Got to keep your strength up.'

'Oh, do stop!' Summer laughed. 'You sound like an old woman! And anyway, is it you or the show I need my strength for?'

'Right!' Doug said. He purposefully removed the tray from the bed, paused for a second and then pounced, lunging for Summer. 'I've had enough of this insolence, young lady, come here...'

They play wrestled for a moment, then Summer said in the middle of it, 'Hang on a minute, what's this "surprise", then?'

'Ah, well, you'll need an overnight bag.'

'And?'

'Don't make any plans for next Sunday.'

'Don't be so bloody obtuse! Tell me!'

'I hope you don't get air-sick...' He was giggling now, knowing this was infuriating her.

'Doug!' Summer said and slapped his chest.

'Ouch! That hurt!' He clutched his chest in false pain.

'That's nothing compared to what I'll do if...'

'Oh, for God's sake...' He pulled Summer down on to her back and moved himself on top. But then he saw something in her eyes and became still, gently moved strands of hair from her face and stroked her flushed cheek. When he spoke, his voice was hushed. 'You really don't like surprises, do you, love?' he said softly. 'Why?'

Summer held his gaze. 'Baggage. Not for discussion.' The coolness of her reply caused Doug to raise an eyebrow but he didn't attempt to delve. Maybe in time...

'Next Sunday, I'm taking you to the Isle of Man.'

'Isle of Man?'

'Mmm... a friend of a friend is a pilot and does private flights from Blackpool airport. It's not far from here. We'll spend the night and return on Monday morning. I would have made it for this Sunday but... with the opening night... it'll be difficult...' Doug's voice trailed off as he thought about Gabrielle.

'Oh, Doug,' Summer smiled and put her arms around him. 'That sounds wonderful. Next Sunday will be fine,' she said in an attempt to let him know she understood his dilemma without having to go into detail. 'Thank you.' Studying his adoring eyes, she melted back into their moment again. 'I'm sorry.'

'For what, my love,' Doug enquired and kissed her gently. 'Why should you be sorry?' He brushed her lips again.

'For spoiling the surprise.' She responded to his attentions by caressing his lips with hers.

'Doesn't matter,' he said huskily and they lost themselves in a deeply passionate embrace. Doug was instantly erect and revelled in its fullness. It had been a very long time since he had achieved those of any similar fortitude. Maybe years. But then, this woman was something so special, with her they just seemed to happen voluntarily, so was it any surprise to him?

The only wonderment to Doug was that he might be falling in love.

Giancarlo slammed the receiver down. It bounced off its cradle and clattered onto the desktop beside the telephone. He picked it up again and set it back properly. Sighing heavily, he grabbed a small coffee cup and in a sudden violent impulse, hurled it across the office. It connected with the door in a sharp smash and disintegrated into pieces. A dark splatter of espresso decorated the highly polished wood in an abstract splodge, while gravity began to draw tiny rivulets towards the floor, complete with coffee grounds. Only the remaining saucer broke the restored equilibrium as it continued to wobble, coming to a stop with a brisk final series of increasing rotations.

Giancarlo looked at the saucer for some moments, then put his hands to his face and muttered rapidly in a rage so intense, he could feel the stirring of a foul secret element within himself that had only been let loose once during his life. Acquaintance with the mortal danger it threatened for any person who provoked its shameful emergence suddenly brought Giancarlo to his senses. Shaking off the familiar chill clarity it bestowed, he removed his hands, and distressed eyes rolled towards the ceiling in a desperate incantation to God. It was a reflex response but one he knew would never be answered. Not by Him. Giancarlo had forfeited any affinity with Him in the instance he allowed this evil self to be unleashed. But for Giancarlo Scarlatti, it had been a necessary evil. An initiation of sorts. A test.

He still prayed.

Where was she? Why did she not return his calls? How long could she punish him for getting angry with her? Perhaps she was sick, lying in bed, unable to pick up the phone. But somewhere buried deep in his ragged meanderings, Giancarlo knew Summer wasn't ill.

If only Alessandro had been there. If only he himself could have been there but he couldn't be, could he? Carlo's was unseasonably busy, much earlier than the expected summer rush. It seemed the word had finally gone round that this was the place in which to see and been seen. It therefore made it impossible for Giancarlo to leave London. So he had to find a way to deal with this woman who rendered him a mad man at times. A ranting, unthinking sop.

The head, my son...

Gabrielle had another go at choosing the outfit she thought most appropriate and more importantly, would be the one that suited her mood on this spontaneous occasion. She hadn't attended an opening night for quite a while. Not those on tour, anyway. After coming away from them, leaving Doug to God knew what, Gabrielle had decided long ago it wasn't worth the strain on her emotions and sanity. And in direct consequence, the children.

Having them, two now with school terms to consider, it was easy to make believable excuses to those who made an issue of her absences. Doug had protested in the beginning, but even he gave up. He knew the truth. In pressing for a change of heart, he must have realised he would be making a rod for his own back where his little whores were concerned. So now he left Gabrielle alone.

No wonder he seemed so surprised! Gabrielle thought as she recalled his reaction to her decision to show up for this opening night. Of course, he would never know the real reason Gabrielle was suddenly so willing to resume playing the type of wife she should be to a man like him.

And Doug could never know.

So she wanted to look dazzling. Cause a few heads to turn. Show Doug what he already had, as opposed to what he could have. Prove to herself that she was still the formidable show business wife most saw her as. The one she projected when working on his behalf for the Variety Club and various other charities.

The public Gabrielle Delany.

Her eyes settled on the dress she kept finding herself going back to. It was a full length black silk-jersey creation. Bias cut across the chest and one sleeve falling from the higher shoulder, it was fitted to the waist, then fell simply to the ankles, two modest slits on the sides to just above the knee. A creation from one of London's premier designers with a boutique in Beauchamp Place. It had cost Doug an arm and a leg, but he was feeling 'remorseful' at the time and like a retaliatory hawk, Gabrielle had swooped in on her opportunity.

To complete the look, from the bare shoulder Gabrielle would casually drape a long black chiffon scarf, embroidered delicately in silk thread with tiny red rosebuds. To finish, she had a pair of elegant black strappy shoes and matching envelope bag. Jewellery was to be kept simple and complementary. An ensemble of droplet diamond and ruby ear rings and bracelet.

Hair up but soft.

Perfect.

There was a gentle knock at the door and Doris Green popped her head round.

'Making tea, dear. Would you like a cup?'

'Oh, Doris, that would be lovely. Thank you. I'll come down for it.'

'Right oh,' Doris said and was closing the door when Gabrielle stopped her.

'Doris, come in a minute. Tell me what you think.'

Gabrielle laid out the dress and scarf and placed the shoes and bag beside them. Both women stood in silence for a moment, considering. Then Doris spoke.

'I would say you will be the loveliest thing there,' she said with a warm smile. There was the faintest suggestion of a motherly 'you'll be fine' in her eyes.

Gabrielle smiled shyly and nudged Doris. They both laughed.

'You know, dear, you could turn up in sackcloth bound with string and still outshine anyone there,' Doris mused and winked at Gabrielle. 'I'll go and put the kettle on.'

'Thanks, Doris, and not just for the tea... you know? You will be okay with the children for the whole weekend, won't you?'

'We'll all be just fine. You go and have yourself a good time and don't be worrying. Alex is being very helpful. I'd say he's grown up a lot recently.'

With that, Doris left the bedroom and soundlessly closed the door behind her. Gabrielle looked back to her final choice still lying on the bed. She sighed. Her son certainly did seem to have had a maturity spurt in recent weeks. Could it be the renewed interest in him shown by his father? The duck print was already on the wall above his bed. It was difficult to know, really. Perhaps it was just his age. They were all growing up so fast these days. Too quickly. And where was Doug? Still, at least Alex would have his two weeks during the holidays to be alone with his father in Blackpool. Hopefully Doug would redeem himself then. Maybe she would have a gentle talk about it to him over the weekend.

After opening night and the after-show party was over. There would no point in raising the subject before then. Gabrielle gave way to a wry smile.

No point at all.

CHAPTER THIRTY TWO

And so, finally, it was upon them.

All the auditions, elation from the phone calls, signing of precious contracts, exhausting rehearsals, costume fittings and the search for digs... all of it... led up to this.

Opening Night.

Now, it was the silent anticipation, the private insecurities, the excitement and then terror of failure, getting something wrong, the whole thing going wrong, forgetting a line, missing a cue, tripping over a step.

They had all messed up over the last few weeks. Now there would be an audience to see it. But these were professionals. This was their job. Their life. Even with all their natural talent, training and preparations, they were all still nervous as hell. And that was good. It got the adrenaline pumping. It focused them. A performer who could stand in the wings without doubting their readiness to go on, feeling sick at the possibility of not being the best they could be, was a performer who knew it was time to give it all up.

While the electric buzz of the audience arriving filled the front of house, chatting over drinks in the theatre bar or taking early possession of their seats, backstage was alight with a nervous energy unique to that realm. Individuals putting on brave faces, hiding their numerous uncertainties, but who would nevertheless join together in a collective performance of the highest quality.

To that end, they had all made sacrifices. Life offerings that, to these people, were worth the euphoria and ecstasy of stepping out from the darkness onto the stage.

And into the magic.

Gradually, the initial furore and excited chat of the dressing-room had descended to just a few hushed conversations from time to time. The girls had got down to the intricate business of getting ready for the show. It started with the make-up. A fascinating process to observe for the non-performer. Each girl with her own special technique, preference of products and artistic flare. Skills learned from the different requirements of every show they had worked on.

Theatrical make-up, especially that of female performers, is necessarily extreme. Close up, the kaleidoscope eye colouring, masses of mascara and enormous canopies of false lashes, give them the appearance of walking Picassos. Of course, once out on stage, under the bleaching effect of the lights, their careful applications look perfect.

For the male dancers, make-up is also essential but in a more natural way. They will have less eyes on them for their looks, more for their strength and skills when dancing with their partners. The guys come into their own during feature numbers choreographed just for them. Then they can prove their merit to the audience. In some cases, it becomes apparent the males of a dance ensemble are, in fact, better than their female counterparts. More chutzpah. More pizzazz.

'I never thought I would be so nervous! I can't seem to get my lips right,' a meek voice said into her mirror that was bordered by several brilliant, and annoyingly hot in midsummer, bare light bulbs. Heads turned to look towards the owner of the voice. It was Pip Levy, and this was her first big professional show. She had worked at Pontins and on a cruise ship out of Miami, but this was huge in comparison.

Summer was sitting next to her and recalled how hard she had worked at the auditions. Marcia had been quite tough on the poor girl during rehearsals but she had come through it, albeit a bit frayed around the edges.

'Oh, you'll be fine. We're all nervous. It's just we've all found ways of dealing with it. You will too. Give it time.'

Levy smiled her thanks to Summer and drew in a long deep breath to steady herself, whistling on the exhale.

There was a sudden stony silence among her peers. Then Summer put a hand on her shoulder.

'Never whistle in the dressing-room. Don't you know that?'

'No,' she replied, wondering if this was the beginning of some practical joke on the new girl. 'Why not?'

'You just don't. Anyway, go outside, turn around three times and say "shit". Then knock before you come in again.'

Levy grinned at Summer and began to giggle. But Summer's face and the continued silence in the room made her realise perhaps this was for real. She stood up and took her walk of shame to the door, giving the others a droll look before closing the door behind her. As she started the embarrassing but obligatory triple twirl, one of the wardrobe ladies came up to her and laughed softly.

'You didn't, did you?' she asked with a sympathetic smile.

After completing her turns and saying 'shit', she knocked on the door. 'Apparently I did!' she replied as a collective voice from inside said 'Come in'. The wardrobe lady followed Levy into the dressing-room, with an adjusted costume for one of the girls.

Summer completed her make-up, a new variation on her usual creation for such a show. Now, time for the hair.

She was trying not to think about recent events, and those to come. It was difficult, what with the opening night and all that entailed. In a sense perhaps, Summer had no right to be feeling the way she did. When involved with a married man, at various points during such a liaison, the wife will have to take precedence. It followed a natural order of things. Whether that order culminated in a stronger marriage or the divorce courts, was purely down to those involved. It was a tough cookie that took her man back after the all-important trust bond had been snapped in two. How deeply that belief system is held within her heart will determine their revised version of their marriage. If it should survive at all.

Summer suspected Doug's wife fell into the category of those celebrity wives who had learned how to turn a blind eye or manage to live in that much kinder perpetual state of complete denial. Perhaps their fabulous lifestyles or the constant threat of public humiliation, should they cause their glass pedestals to shatter, were simply too much to risk for a modicum of self-respect.

Summer knew all about self-worth, life with it and a nasty little existence without it. She was in no doubt which way of being she preferred.

There had been no pictures of Doug's family in the house. Anywhere. Unusually, none in his dressing-room either. His excuse of 'to protect their privacy... especially the children...' seemed genuine, but Summer suspected that maybe even Doug Delany suffered from the occasional bout of guilt. Perhaps it was just easier not to have the faces of his wife and kids looking at him in case he fell foul of one of those moments.

Summer wondered what Mrs Delany might look like. She had either never seen a photograph or was uninterested when she had. Summer had surreptitiously asked around. Of course, the best person to get an accurate picture from was Cynthia but that was not an option. Summer knew the agent had known the truth during that after-preview soirée, but like the consummate professional that she was, Cynthia had kept her mouth shut.

Luckily, one of the male dancers had worked on a television show with Doug and told Summer that his wife was very attractive and had seemed to be quite pleasant, although he had not been in a position to speak with her. He also informed Summer that Mrs Delany had once been a dancer herself. It was how she and Doug had met.

Something about that last little snippet of gossip irked Summer and she didn't really know why. Her sudden unease at this recollection worked its way through to her fingers and a large grip she was fastening into place slipped, scraping spitefully along her scalp. 'Ouch!' she exclaimed and in a fit of pique, flung the grip onto the counter. Then Summer breathed in and used a relaxation technique taught at many drama schools, imagining all her ill thoughts as an entity that would flow out of her upon the exhaled breath. She let it go very slowly, eyes closed, concentrating on the image.

'You all right?' Amanda Jacobs asked after seeing this through her mirror across the room.

Summer opened her eyes and gave her friend a pained smile. 'Yeah,' she replied with a sigh. 'I'll be fine.' She selected another grip from a bag full of every type, size and colour and returned her mind to what was really important.

The show.

It was a resounding success. The rapturous reception from the audience was lengthy and continued through three curtain calls. It was some minutes after the last one before Doug, as star of the show, could say the usual words of appreciation. Not just for the audience but also the production staff, crew and band. And of course, Blackpool for having them. That always went down a treat.

Gabrielle sat pensively while browsing through the programme, waiting for the crowds to leave their seats before making her way backstage. And to Doug.

The show had been much better than she had expected. Quite enjoyable. The presentation was energetic with no unfortunate dips as in many seaside productions. The dance numbers had been interesting for Gabrielle and she believed the ensemble had worked extremely hard. They were a talented bunch. There had been a few fleeting moments of wishing she could have worked under the sublime Marcia Raeburn. They didn't last long.

But it wasn't nostalgia for her earlier career that dampened Gabrielle's enthusiasm for leaving her seat and joining the celebration backstage. It was something she had seen. A mere passing glimpse, but it had been there. A suggestion of impending danger. The same feeling she could almost put her trademark on. All Gabrielle's hopes that some redundant moral light bulb had finally been turned on inside her husband's head and he'd seen the glow from it, hopes that Doug had truly meant all those promises he had made a few weeks before, were shattered.

Whatever plans she may have made for them as a family after Blackpool now lay as worthless scraps at her feet. In her mind, Gabrielle could see herself slowly treading on those bitter remnants, one foot at a time, and grinding them into a pathetic dust, to be blown away by the chill wind of her realisation.

As she finally walked down to Doug's dressing-room, Gabrielle briefly caught sight of the inside of Adam Nash's dressing-room. She had adored the sweet, slightly thick elephant but now decided the hard-hearted pig was more fitting to her mood. With the door slightly ajar, Gabrielle noticed young female legs crossed demurely, and unless Adam's wife had attended the show in theatrical fishnets and black tap shoes, she settled on the obvious explanation. Gabrielle shook her head, a priceless expression of her face.

Was it written in their fucking contracts?

Doug's door was fully open and he was standing in just his underpants while removing make-up. Gabrielle instinctively looked directly at his privates and matter of factly considered whether he already had or was about to. Doug saw her in the doorway and with half his face smeared with Vaseline, smiled and said, 'Gabs! Oh love, come in. What did you think? Good, or the same old crap?' His question was posed with an air of truly wanting to know and... not.

'The show was very good, honestly,' Gabrielle said, really meaning it, right up to and until the final few bars of the finale. Then she mused... *the same old crap? Yes Doug, it's the same old crap.*

'Oh, that's great!' Doug replied as he wiped his face with tissues and went into the shower room. He turned on the shower. 'What did you think of my new act?' he enquired, stepping into the cubicle.

'Very amusing,' Gabrielle said from the sofa.

'Great!' Doug said emphatically again. It was obviously

his word of the moment. He usually had one. Never 'faithful' though, Gabrielle mused sarcastically as she scanned the dressing room for the usual evidence while Doug was having his shower. There was none. *Early days then*, she said quietly to herself. *Early days.*

Doug emerged from the shower with a towel draped around him. He went straight over to Gabrielle and she stood. They embraced. His skin was still warm and damp and he smelled of his favourite shower gel. Gabrielle let him hold her tight, despite overwhelming reservations. This was not the time or the place. But she would find one. When he came home at the end of the season.

Doug gently kissed her and Gabrielle responded. All part of the game they played as Mr and Mrs Doug Delany. One day, it would all come to an end. And Gabrielle would be declared the winner.

'It's so lovely to have you here,' Doug said and kissed her again. 'And you look...' He stood back for a moment, regarding his wife from head to foot, and back. 'Stunning!'

'Thank you,' she replied simply.

'Sit down,' Doug instructed. 'I'll get dressed and we can go and join the others. I can't wait to show you off,' he said smiling at Gabrielle through the mirror.

She sat contemplating the truths and complexities of that statement and the thought of being in close proximity to his newest floozy. Gabrielle could recall her face quite clearly. Although at a distance from the stage and knowing she was somewhat disguised by performance make-up, the girl had appeared to be rather beautiful. A cut above the rest and not just in this show. She also remembered it was the same girl that had a solo ballet number as accompaniment to the young tenor, Jamie Thomas. His wonderful renditions of *Granada* and then *Maria* from *West Side Story* had given Gabrielle goose bumps. Ironically, at the same time, she had also thought what a fluid and delightful dancer the girl had been.

During the after-show party, Doug was remarkably attentive to Gabrielle. Never left her side for a minute and she found it faintly amusing. But it had been there again. Another soul-chilling stolen glimpse. The girl was indeed naturally breath-taking. Equally, she seemed to have a good understanding of the situation, keeping a fair distance between herself and them. Apart from the occasional discreet look cast in Doug's direction.

Summer had mixed emotions about seeing Doug's wife. The woman had kept herself trim and was far more attractive than she had imagined. Younger and yet very self-assured. So many wives seemed like terrified wallflowers on these glitzy occasions, almost trying to become invisible. Not Mrs Delany. No, this wife was very comfortable in who she was and made sure everyone knew it. Done so charmingly with a smile as bright as Venus in the early night sky, but Summer could sense a protective hardness underneath this carefully crafted act. Summer also noted how Doug clung to his wife like a limpet. That grated a little. Or rather, a lot, but he had gently warned and then assured Summer about how things might appear during this evening. Told her not to worry. It was only for the weekend.

As Summer secretly regarded Doug with his wife, deep down she hoped with all her heart that their impression of togetherness was just for appearances.

On the following morning as Doug stood waving goodbye from the gates, Gabrielle eased the car away in the knowledge she had a grim task ahead. How to find some plausible explanation for why her son would not be spending any time away with his father during his summer holidays. Gabrielle knew it was going to be almost painful to lie to Alex. He had been so looking forward to his two weeks but now aware of the possibility, there was absolutely no way she would let him be exposed to his father's infidelities. Gabrielle knew that probably, Alex had already been with his father during other sordid little affairs, but their son was becoming quite an observant little soul now. He didn't miss much these days, however Doug might try to hide the truth during his short stay, and Doug was a master of that. The boy would just know, and his mother was determined to protect all her children from that reality for as long as she possibly could.

She also had a gut feeling that Doug would put up little resistance.

Gabrielle turned on the radio and found herself listening to Gloria Estefan singing *Cuts Both Ways*. The words seeped into her one by one.

A tear drizzled onto Gabrielle's cheek.

Then, slowly, she began to laugh.

CHAPTER THIRTY THREE

As the small aircraft travelled bumpily along the runway and finally lifted into the air in a swift steep climb, Doug fondly recalled a time back in the late Eighties when he was enjoying the first real rewards of making it into the big time.

He had invited a couple of mates to 'do Le Touquet for lunch'. A small airport on the coast halfway between Calais and Dieppe, and one of the prerequisite jaunts before being accepted as a member of the dubious club of young upwardly mobile young things for which the decade was infamous. Doug remembered sitting in a similar seat to the one he was in now, being the tallest and needing most leg room. On their approach to Le Touquet, the pilot asked if Doug would like to have a hand in the landing, although he, the pilot, would ultimately keep control, Doug could at least get a feel for the aircraft during descent and touchdown. A few joking but serious words of 'Don't tell the CAA or there goes my pilot's licence!', some goading from his mates, and Doug nervously put his hands on the second yoke.

Under his 'assistance', their plane had come in for a rather ungainly landing, bouncing twice and prompting a droll retort from a laughing pilot of 'Greaser!', apparently flight deck speak for someone who makes a naff landing. Of course, his two guests couldn't let that one go and teased him mercilessly all the way through lunch in Le Touquet airport, where, amazingly, there was an excellent restaurant that was packed to capacity.

Doug drifted back to the present, reached through the gap for Summer's hand and held it tightly, occasionally stroking his thumb across her fingers. He wasn't nervous. In recent years, he often used private flights to get around the country, especially for special events arranged at short notice. And always for a quick round at St Andrews or Gleneagles. The reason he wanted to hold Summer's hand was his incessant need to have physical contact with her. It was a drug that he craved like the most prolific addict, even a mere brush against her as they passed each other back stage would be a temporary fix to get him through to the next real hit.

They had to be careful. Make sure no one knew. For once their affair was uncovered, it would be into the tabloids quicker than the speed of light, with some faceless little dickhead a few quid richer. Sometimes the forced separations to perpetuate their deception was agony. Other times, he enjoyed their furtive game. But he knew there was a need to be away from the theatre, from Blackpool, away from telephones, interruptions and on neutral ground, if he and Summer were to really discover each other. Though, in the instant he had first dared to kiss her, Doug had sensed that they were two halves of the same creature and that there would already be in place a profound understanding of the other.

The plane levelled off and after a brief dialogue with air traffic control, Terry Cayley started to give them some technical data, something it seemed to Doug that every pilot had the propensity to do, whether on a private flight or commercial. So they were in a Cessna Turbo Stationair, cruising at an altitude below the aircraft's maximum of 17,000 feet, and at a speed less than the 178 knots the plane was capable of. ETA at Ronaldsway airport, Isle of Man, was approximately 10.45am. 'So just sit back and enjoy the ride,' was the finishing advice.

Doug was grateful to his friend and popular impressionist, Andrew Edwards. It was one of his two holiday homes they were en route to, and Terry was a friend of Andrew. Doug had been truthful about the reason for asking this favour. He knew his mate would keep it to himself because there had been occasions when Doug helped Andrew Edwards in a similar fashion. Normally giving him the use of his digs when on a home visit while on some tour. Doug considered Andrew's reasons and sympathised, as he often had before. Linda was an absolute sweetheart, maybe a bit common-sounding but that had never mattered to Doug, in anyone. It wasn't how you sounded or produced your vowels, it was who you were. The person. In his world of constant superficiality, Linda Edwards was a good soul. It was just that perhaps she had sat for too long in the sun at their flat in the Algarve, close to Doug's sprawling villa, and her face now looked, if he was kinder than usual, like a patch on a well-worn leather sofa.

But he didn't have that excuse, did he? Gabrielle was still in her prime and he had to admit, looked quite impressive on opening night. As he thought of her, Gabrielle's face seemed to emanate from the startling white puffs of cloud that Terry negotiated from time to time. Doug felt as though he might be able to reach out and touch them, leaving a dent in their cotton wool softness that would immediately plump back out again. When they headed straight for an accumulation, it was hard not to feel as though they were about to collide, but at the point of impact, they merely entered a mist and the cloud silently rushed past them as the suspended water vapour it always had been.

'Free as the birds,' Doug said wistfully.

'Repeat that?' Terry responded.

'Oh, sorry, mate, just admiring the view,' Doug explained, having forgotten they were connected by mic headphones.

'Roger that,' Terry said with a knowing smile. He had notched up thousands of air miles but Terry Cayley still adored to be up there, as Doug had said so well; free as the birds. He didn't know many pilots who didn't feel the same, even after many years of flying. There was something almost spiritual about being disconnected from terra firma and looking down on it all.

Doug sighed quietly and without taking his eyes away from the horizon, gently squeezed Summer's hand. She returned the affectionate signal.

He would never be free, though, would he? Could never be. Whatever happened between him and Gabrielle, he would always have the children. And Doug could never be free of his three kids, nor would he want to be.

But somewhere inside him, there beat desperate frustrated fists as Doug considered how all his other affairs had been necessarily finite, and how distressed he became at the thought of losing Summer. This was something significant and Doug wanted it to last.

In his perfect world, he would be able to gently let his wife go, with ample access to the children, and then share the rest of his life with the woman sitting behind him. A woman he adored. Completely. Together they would go places beyond his wildest imagination. With her, he was a whole being. No other person had made him feel so. Only performing in front of an audience had ever instilled such a sentiment. In Summer's arms, he could also pretend to be young again, with an exciting future ahead, rather than a tangled past dragging heavily behind.

Why did it all have to end? Couldn't he find a way that wouldn't hurt anyone? Surely there was something he could think of? Some plan. Doug looked into the endless sky and sought inspiration.

Summer gazed out across the wing and down to the sea. The occasional ship or ferry appeared tiny from their altitude. It made her ponder just how insignificant we all are in the scheme of life on earth. All her worries, personal battles, ups and downs, good times and bad, even her hopes, mattered not a jot, except to the constant inner child that lived inside her head. But there was something, or someone, who did matter.

Doug Delany.

He had kept his promise. It truly had all just been for appearances. Apparently she, Summer Laine, did mean something to the esteemed entertainer. A lot, it seemed. The trouble he must have gone to for this trip to the Isle of Man proved that she meant more to Doug than Summer had previously thought, even when he had initially mentioned it. Her mind went back to the first time she saw him again after the opening night weekend, and his wife was on her way back to the Home Counties. The intensity of the encounter had been almost unbearable, and as they had cuddled into each other afterwards, both had privately wept. It was an extraordinary emotional experience that was disturbing and beautiful at the same time. Summer would never forget it.

In contrast to all the obsessive pandering she received from Giancarlo, Summer knew Doug's attentions were born of a different want. For a man with his reputation and yes, celebrated family, taking her on a private flight to some secret location was, in Summer's estimations, a big deal. For Giancarlo, it would simply have been another cog in the wheel of his need to prove how generous he was, make Summer grateful in some obscure way for the money and gifts he lavished on her. And yet, maybe she was being unkind, even unfair, to her wealthy but immature Sicilian. She knew he cared deeply about her. That was one of the few certainties about Giancarlo. And after all, had she not previously played with the notion of becoming the woman he craved her to be? Or, indeed, of being his wife?

Her thoughts returned swiftly to Doug and the way in which he simply let her be whoever she was. He didn't ask her to change or modify the original. Doug Delany just wanted Summer Laine.

For her, there was nothing more irresistible in a man.

After they landed, a near-perfect manoeuvre by the pilot, and while taxiing to the terminal, Terry said, 'I've arranged the usual car for you, he's very discreet. We've got an oh nine hundred take off slot on Monday, so Kev will arrange with you a suitable time to pick you up. The weather forecast for the next few days is good so I don't anticipate any delays, but I'll let you know in good time if there are.'

'Thanks,' Doug said, impressed with the arrangements. Andrew Edwards had obviously become quite accomplished in organising his own extramarital shenanigans.

'Have a nice stay,' Terry said with a sly wink at Doug that hid a jealous silent comment of 'lucky bastard!'

Doug, ignoring the underlying message, simply said, 'We will, thanks. Great flight, by the way.'

The private cab drove them through picturesque scenery to Port Erin on the south west coast of the island. It was nestled in a quiet bay and away from the main tourist attractions along the east coast around the towns of Douglas and Ramsey, and the ever-crowded Snaefell mountain railway that although spectacular, was an excursion that was out of the question for Doug and Summer. As was staying in one of the main hotels on the island. These were risks he just couldn't take. His face was too well known and with a lifetime of wearing a public mask, this was one occasion he didn't want the burden of any disguises, even in the literal sense. Doug Delany wanted the freedom to be himself for a change.

But maybe, with a little more help from his friend, there was one place he might be able to sneak them to.

The flat was delightful, just as Andrew had described it. Doug smiled as he remembered his friend also saying, 'But try and leave it exactly how you found it, mate. Linda's a hawk-eye. She'll even notice the pile of the carpet facing the wrong way!' But Doug was used to that level of OCD with Gabrielle, so he was well prepped.

'This is lovely,' Summer said dreamily while standing looking out of a window across to the quaint Port Erin harbour, complete with whitewashed lighthouse at the end of the harbour wall. It reminded her of the small inlet in County Kerry where her father moored a boat. In fact, the island was very similar to his homeland. But then, the Isle of Man did sit in the middle of the Irish sea.

'So are these,' Doug said with a broad smile, holding up and jingling a set of car keys. 'Andy said we could use the car if we wanted.'

Summer regarded the keys, raised an eyebrow and turned back towards the view. 'Do we want to go driving around?'

'No, but I would like to take you to a special little place later. It's not far from here and if we go late enough, there shouldn't be anyone there.'

'Oh? Where's that?' Summer asked, looking back to Doug and smiling.

'Surp...'

'Surprise! I see! Another one!' she laughed.

Doug said affectionately, 'At least this one's made you smile!'

'No, you make me smile, Doug,' Summer replied to the window pane.

He walked over to her and slipped his arms through hers, nuzzling his chin into her shoulder. Doug breathed in the subtle floral notes of the L'Air du Temps perfume Summer always wore. He mused whether she even realised it might be the ultimate perfume to compliment her name. 'Happy?' he whispered into her neck and softly kissed the silkiness behind her ear.

'Very,' she replied restfully and brought a hand up to touch his face. There was a natural pause, both gazing contentedly out of the window, then Summer slowly turned in Doug's embrace and after tracing his lips with a finger, grazed them with hers. 'Where's the bedroom?' she murmured, lips still close to his, enticement sparkling in her eyes.

'Follow me,' Doug said, his voice sonorous and velvety with anticipation. He took her hand without breaking eye contact and began to lead Summer away from the window, then stopped beside their bags. 'Here, take these,' he instructed, rummaged in a bag and handed her two champagne glasses. 'And I'll take this,' he said, revealing a bottle of Moet. 'For afterwards.'

In an unexpected movement, Doug scooped Summer up into his arms, the neck of the champagne bottle still gripped securely in his hand, and carried her to the bedroom.

The car drew to a gentle halt near a farm track and

footpath that led into a wooded area. Summer looked around them and frowned, a questioning smile on her face.

'Okay, where are we?'

'Ah... that's for me to know...'

'And me to find out,' she finished for Doug in a mock sigh of exasperation.

There was a wicked glint in his eyes as he retorted, 'All will be revealed in good time, young lady!' He gave Summer a jokey patronising pat on the leg. She cut him a sarcastic look and both got out of the car.

It was dusk and Doug had been accurate in his assessment, there was no one about.

'It's just a short walk from here down this footpath,' he said and took hold of her hand. 'Come on, doubting Thomas!'

After a ten-minute walk through a peaceful wood, they reached a small ancient stone and flint bridge that spanned a rocky stream.

'Now,' he said, drawing them both to a stop at the entrance to the bridge. 'You can't pass by it or cross over it without saying hello to the fairies.'

His face and tone of voice were completely serious.

'Hello to the fairies?' Summer asked with her head cocked to one side and a wry smile as she looked up into Doug's eyes.

'This...' he replied with an outstretched arm, 'is the famous Fairy Bridge. The locals are quite superstitious about it. None of them will drive past on the road back there, or walk across it without saying...' he paused to recollect the correct words, 'laa mie,' he said, looking very satisfied with himself. 'It roughly means good day. The islanders say that if you don't greet the little people, they will cast a spell of great misfortune on you.'

Summer pulled a cynical face and said dryly, 'You are utterly mad, you know.'

'Takes one to know one!' Doug replied.

'Okay, if you insist! We'd better say laa... what was it?'

'Laa mie.'

'Better say "laa mie", then!'

They looked towards the centre of the bridge and through fits of giggles, said it in unison. Then Doug reached out and pulled Summer roughly to him, wanting to take her right there and then but, under the circumstances, settled for the pleasing feel of her body contours pressed against his. As they held each other and looked down onto the clear waters of the fast-moving stream, Summer suddenly said, 'Let's make a wish.'

'A wish, my love?'

'Aren't fairies supposed to grant wishes?'

Doug thought for a moment. 'I suppose so.'

'Let's make our wishes together. On the count of three, close your eyes and make one,' Summer said, her voice having taken on the character of an excited young girl.

Doug smiled lovingly at the complex woman in his arms. She of many facets. Someone who would probably take a lifetime to know and understand. If that were ever possible. There was an enigmatic quality about Summer, and Doug sensed she would always keep part of herself forever secret. But then, didn't we all?

'So,' he finally said breaking their reticence. 'What did you wish for?'

'Can't tell you,' she answered stubbornly. 'Won't come true.' Summer placed a quick kiss on Doug's cheek before skipping away over the bridge in a childlike imitation of its mysterious legendary sprites.

Doug watched her silly dancing gait and laughed to himself.

God, she was wonderful.

And in that defining moment, Doug knew he was hopelessly in love with Summer.

Part Three

THE FINALE

CHAPTER THIRTY FOUR

Three months later...

The break-up of the family was imminent.

It was the last week of the run and a time of mixed feelings. On the one hand, the company was already winding down towards the final performance. An air of wanting to be done with it and get on to other projects. Hopefully. And some would indeed already have new work waiting for when they had taken their last bow in Blackpool. For the others, a period of rest 'in between jobs', most likely being a nuisance to their agents, searching *The Stage* newspaper for auditions and of course, many taking casual jobs to pay the bills. On the other hand, emotions in some would be running high. Friendships made during the summer season, even those of a more intimate variety, cemented with their shared experiences in the theatre, would now either be proven and many who met in a show would enjoy marriage and a long, happy life together, or slowly draw to the inevitable conclusion. Some might linger for a while after the last piece of scenery is stripped from the stage and packed into the final removal truck, and the theatre becomes 'dark' for a time between productions. Most of the pairings were destined to fail from the start, transient by the nature of the business from which they were forged. But each participant had known that. For many, this would not be their first and for them, it was simply a need for a friendly smile or conversation, or a warm yielding body to comfort them in the lonely, dark night hours. The unattached would take with them just their memories and no hard feelings. For those that should have known better, and rarely ever did, would not only take their recollections but deceit and maybe even turmoil home to the ones they had left behind.

On the final night, there would be much laughter and many tears, collecting of phone numbers, satisfaction of another job done well, worries about the immediate future and where the next pay check was coming from. And when.

For the rare, long-running show companies that met each season for another run, longevity brought a real sense of belonging, and friendships nurtured here would last a lifetime.

Giancarlo almost bounced into the bar area from his first-floor office, a smile on his face as broad as his Latin ego. Fiona saw this as she prepared two cappuccinos and was pleased. Perhaps relieved was a more accurate assessment. He had been like the proverbial bear with a sore head for what seemed like forever, in fact, since Summer had left for Blackpool. Although there had been occasions when he seemed more relaxed and upbeat, they were infrequent and Fiona had probably seen every emotion from him she deemed possible from the male of the species.

There had also been times when she seriously wanted to tell Giancarlo where to stick his job, but somehow, common sense had prevailed. Just. Usually after copious alcohol alone in her flat and much ranting and raving like a drunken banshee, the main result of which was scaring the shit out of her Abyssinian cat, Sandy.

Fiona watched Giancarlo greeting the two regulars who waited at the bar for their coffees. He appeared genuinely happy for a change. The relevance of Summer being only a few days away from coming home had not gone unnoticed by Fiona.

Giancarlo chatted for a few minutes to his customers and then informed Fiona he was going out to meet his niece who was visiting and would return after lunch. In truth, his 'niece' was an old flame who had travelled to London, from Paris where she was working, at his request. An Italian haute couture model with whom Giancarlo had enjoyed a casual relationship for many years. He had selfishly rekindled their friendship on an impulsive diversion to

Milan, where Laura was based, while returning to London from a trip home to see his ailing mother.

Since the death of his father, Fabia had not 'given up' as some might suspect, but her spirit seemed more distant now, maybe already making its way to where Paulo's waited. There was a peacefulness about her, a look in her eyes, that was not just that of old age but more, maybe a feeling that she could now leave this plane for the next, and everything and everyone would be fine. Her reason for being here was drawing to a close. Her work was done. Lessons learned. Slowly, Fabia was making a dignified private journey towards the shadow of this world and the light of another.

Giancarlo and Laura had met several times during the summer months when her hectic schedule allowed, mainly in London so that Giancarlo could be close to his business. Laura had been surprised to see him after so long without contact when he arrived unannounced in Milan and had called her. Even so, she was more than happy. Laura loved her intricate and volatile Sicilian. She had from the first day they had met while she had been on a trip to see for herself one of the regular eruptions of Mount Etna. Gloriously awesome and conversely, quite shocking, a reminder to the rest of us that we can only try and live in harmony with this celestial orb because she will, when we're least expecting it, fight back. And win every time.

Laura had gone with friends to a happening restaurant in Palermo and Giancarlo had been there. He sent a note to her table and when the Mediterranean sun rose up over the east of the island the following morning, they had already become lovers.

Giancarlo ceased all contact when it became apparent another woman had entered his life. Not normally a reason they would stop being in touch with each other, but this woman had obviously been important enough for Giancarlo Scarlatti to completely break with Laura. She understood. In a very grown up way. She had always known they would never be more than they were. Though, in her more impressionable heart, Laura felt differently. Often she would imagine them as something more significant, with a beautiful home in Taormina, and eventually a family of their own.

In her sometimes mixed up model's mind, it was always crystal clear on the subject of Giancarlo. They could never be. But Laura still played with the thought from time to time.

Giancarlo drove towards Berkeley Square where they were to meet at their favourite casino for lunch and a little blackjack. As usual, he would try and let Laura win. Not easy with a good dealer and the necessary concealment from various hovering inspectors and security cameras of his attempts to count the cards. He smiled to himself, not at the thought of seeing Laura again but at the knowledge that Alessandro was back and already arrived in Blackpool.

It was late in the day in respect of keeping a watch over Summer during the last few months, but at least he would now get the measure of what had been going on in their time apart. Further apart than Giancarlo had expected. When Summer had called a few days after their verbal slanging match on the telephone and had said that she 'needed some space', Giancarlo had almost crushed the telephone receiver with his bare hand. He wanted to jump in his car and go to her, bring her home and teach the silly girl a few things. Instead, he had graciously allowed Summer this 'space' and in turn, used his visit to see Fabia to chill out and get a grip of his unfathomable rage. Make a final decision about what he truly desired. Find out whether he felt Summer was still worth fighting for. Try and prepare himself for what personal struggles might lie ahead if he decided she was.

In the serene magnificence of his native land, Giancarlo had made his choice. But he also knew he would need a... distraction, through the following months. After all, he was an archetypal red-blooded male, it was necessary to grant himself a little... entertainment. Laura had proved to be an exquisite recreation while he quietly considered his best course of action with Summer, his mind never clearer than in the immediate aftermath of uncomplicated and competent sex with the sweet girl from Milan.

Now, the time had come for Giancarlo to spring clean his life and rid himself of appendages that had reached their sell-by date.

The end game was about to commence.

'... And that's it in a nutshell, Doug. Us, or the rest of your life making amends to the children for what will be, how shall I put this? a very... messy divorce. You can be assured that I'll make it my mission to cause you as much suffering as possible. And let's not beat around the bush, Doug, I know exactly where to aim for. We both know where that is, don't we? You may well see Doreen Davis as a Welsh witch but as I said, push me far enough... and this is quite far enough. The end of a road we've been on for far too long. Maybe it's partly my fault, but that's something I'll deal with in time. Right now, it's time to take a new road. The question is, Doug, will it be together as a family? It's entirely up to you.'

Like hell it was...

A deafening silence stretched down the telephone line between them, thick with something close to mutual temporary hatred. Though as George Bernard Shaw once wrote, *if hate is akin to love...* And it was the love Doug and Gabrielle Delany still had for each other that gave rise to the severity of this moment in their floundering marriage.

Gabrielle realised that for once she had actually rendered her husband speechless. Were there prizes for such events? She knew she deserved more than a medal for what he'd made her put up with. Although it was never far from her mind that she herself was also responsible for the mess they were in. But for the children's sake, she had to make a final last-ditch attempt to make their father see sense. Come to terms with the fact he owed it to his family, his wife, to actually be the man his carefully honed image, projected to his mainly female audience, suggested. And they were Gabrielle's most lethal ammunition if Doug should choose life without his family.

Of course, it had always been her decision to make. Right from the beginning of their relationship. One of the more unreasonable hidden responsibilities of being married to someone like Doug. A person so wrapped up in their craft and the fame and fortune it can bestow, and once having been bestowed upon, rabid in their fight to retain it all. The same people who, when faced with issues in their real life, the one they all seemed to shy away from as much as possible, could barely negotiate their way out of a paper bag.

But she didn't want a divorce. It was the worst-case scenario. Not just for her. For their three offspring. So she had made a pact with the devil. If she could just get Doug to give up this latest floozy and make his best effort at being a real husband and father, then for her babies Gabrielle would remain a loyal, allowing for her near-miss indiscretion, and faithful wife. She would be adoring when adoring was required, and smile and dazzle as befitting the wife of Mr Show Business.

The thought of this wasn't too harsh on her, because Gabrielle was in no doubt that one day, and one day soon, she would have her day.

However, in the meantime, the fact remained that this wife had already nearly given all of herself to Doug's cause and she simply would not allow him to suck out what was left of the fragile remnants that represented her soul. The one that had started out so dynamically as the bright and ambitious Gabrielle Weston. What use as a mother would she be if that mother was mentally and emotionally depleted and had no self-regard or sense of worth?

This phone call was the considered action of a woman trying to save her family, and the only life she now knew. Looking into a future after divorce, all she saw was devastation and desolation. But for now, Gabrielle still held on to a hidden strength which, despite being reduced to a pitiful level from the original, would be enough to sustain her through this ultimate test of their bond. She had thrown down the gauntlet of their marriage. If Doug decided to pick it up and hypothetically slap her twice across the face with it in true gentlemanly duelling fashion, he would find himself dealing with a determined woman and protective mother scorned. One that would not only make her husband suffer financially, but, horror of horrors, professionally too.

A good proportion of Doug's most faithful audience consisted of many women just like Gabrielle. In failing marriages but without the wherewithal or mind set to do anything about it. Probably so crushed by their failure to hold down a decent marriage, they stay within its soul-destroying confines until their control-freak husbands eventually walk out on them without even looking back to say goodbye. Gabrielle would therefore be some kind of crusader on these women's behalf. Her mission: one that rejected women everywhere know and carry out so well, and founded when hell begot its fury.

'Say something, Doug,' Gabrielle suddenly said with dripping sarcasm.

He tried to speak but his whole world was crumbling around him. Piece by piece, crashing to the ground in an emotional dust that was slowly choking him.

So she had known all along. He thought he might have been clever enough this time. Or maybe it was because he hadn't really thought about it very much at all. So totally consumed with Summer, he hadn't realised how his cancellations of normal home visits and lack of invitations to Blackpool must have seemed. So taken up with hiding the truth from those around him at the theatre, Doug had forgotten the instinctive infidelity radar Gabrielle possessed. There had been Alex's two weeks that never happened. The lack of phone calls from Gabrielle.

What a fool he had been. Once again. At least he was consistent. But now his wife had called time. Pulled the rug. Stamped her foot. The problem was, unlike with all the others who had meant less than nothing to him, he was being asked to let someone very special go. Remove her from his life, throw her overboard and cast her adrift. Then sail away. Forever.

From the love of his life.

Doug did still love Gabs. Thought the world of her and the children. Cared deeply about them all. He just didn't love Gabs in the way he loved Summer. He never had. Of that, Doug was quite sure. Could he love two women at the same time? And with Summer, was it love at all? Of course it was. How could he deny the power of the time they spent together? The depth of passion and intensity during their lovemaking? The way she would look at him. The way he felt when he looked at her. But maybe it was merely raging lust that he had mistaken for love. Perhaps Summer, with that body to die for, had only released the sleeping young stag in Doug once more and in his advancing years, the sensations were super-magnified. Could it be he subconsciously felt that the longer he clung on to those unbelievable sensations, the longer he could pretend to keep the ageing process at bay? Give the finger to time and the cruel tricks it plays on a human body?

Questions. Too many questions. It seemed his whole life over the last few months had been a fucking question. Yet, in the cold light of day, this day, when he had been asked the most probing one of all, whatever had gone before this moment could no longer serve any purpose. Because there could only be one answer if Doug-keep-em-rolling-in-the-aisles-Delany was to survive.

There had only ever been, and was only ever going to be, one honest love in his life.

His thoughts finally homed in and clarified on that succinct point of realisation with the precision edge of broken glass. The crux of Doug's truth.

As if by magic, the words that had escaped his earlier rambling mind seemed to slip off his tongue with extraordinary ease.

'I'll end it today.'

And then Doug hung up.

He opened the door and Summer beamed at him. She looked fabulous. All Doug could muster was a wretched sinking feeling. He welcomed her with a brief kiss on the cheek and said, 'You look gorgeous, as ever, love,' then turned and walked without another word into the kitchen. Summer followed. Something didn't feel right. There was a taut atmosphere around Doug that imbued a slimy sense of foreboding.

'Doug?' Summer said as she joined him by the centre island where he was opening a bottle of wine.

Doug glanced quickly at her but found it impossible to hold her searching gaze. He returned his focus to the bottle. Summer put a gentle hand to his face.

'Sweetie pie? What's wrong?'

The contact of her softness on his skin caused Doug to close his eyes. He could feel burning tears welling up behind them and fought hard to keep them inside. Doug sighed and turned to face Summer, the corkscrew still in the cork that was stuck halfway out. Doug rested his hands on Summer's hips and drew his eyes from his feet up to where they met hers. Full of questions. More questions. But beautiful, all the same. Eyes he would now have to take a mental photograph of and hold somewhere within him. A secret place that would yield it to him whenever he needed to look upon them again.

'Summer,' he began, but his emotions were so near the surface that his voice broke away from him and he swallowed back a wave of desperation. Doug turned back to the wine and continued to open it.

How could he possibly tell her? What suitable words were there to make this terrible task less traumatic for both of them? How in God's name was he supposed to deal with this situation? *Like a man,* Doug heard his dad's gruff northern voice echoing through his thoughts.

Aye, Dad, but what kind of man?

Summer would never understand what she had come to mean to Doug. What she would always mean to him. She had freed a part of him that he had never expected he would have been able to let see the light of day. A part of himself so long locked away, Doug had never even shown it to Gabrielle.

It was his vulnerability. His playful childlike identity. One hidden from the world and even himself. Doug had forgotten it even existed any more. Then Summer came along and released it from the shackles of social expectations. Now, he was at the point of becoming used to this more open character, with a willingness to act as the moment might warrant, rather than how he should under the burden of constraints that came with who he was. Had become. But his wife had called, 'Cut! It's a wrap!' and Doug faced the prospect of burying this essence for the last time.

Well, he didn't want to. It was as simple or as convoluted as that. With Summer, he thought differently. Felt differently. Looked upon the whole world differently. With Summer...

There was only one way Doug could handle this. He'd used it many times before in other challenging situations, although this one was the mother of them all. Short, sharp and done with. It was brutal, not only to the recipient but also for the man dishing it out. It was all he knew.

Summer didn't deserve it. She didn't deserve any of this. And it had been Doug himself, his own self-centred needs, that had drawn her in. Now he must strike the crucial blow but whereas she would eventually recover and carry on, he would be left in a heap on the floor from the might of the impact. Held down by the weight of never being able to forgive himself. He would take this moment to his grave with him. And beyond.

'Doug, you're scaring me. What's wrong?' Hands on hips and a hard look in her eyes, Summer stood a little taller. Doug considered she would need that type of fortitude. He hoped she had bucket loads.

'Let's go into the other room,' he said, picking up the wine and some glasses. Summer watched him go and found it becoming increasingly difficult to breath normally. There was the suggestion of a tremor throughout her body and a feeling of dread permeating her churning thoughts.

He couldn't possibly...

When Summer walked into the sitting room, she saw Doug standing at the fireplace, his back turned to her, looking deeply into the empty grate while slowly swirling the wine in his glass. She looked to the table and noticed hers had also been filled and sat forlorn and alone. Summer sat on the edge of the sofa and took a fair gulp of the red wine. It immediately tasted too dry and left a lingering bitterness on her palate. She shuddered. A portent of things to come?

Suddenly, Summer clunked her glass onto the coffee table and threw herself back into the cushions saying, 'For fuck's sake, Doug! What's going on?'

'It's over,' he replied too quickly in a small, distant voice.

Summer felt her stomach flip and settle heavily like she had just swallowed a ball of lead. Her heart was thumping, and the mild tremor had increased to a cold shiver.

'I don't understand...' It came out as a whisper.

'Us. You and me. Over,' Doug said with more force. The suddenness of this retort caused his body to jolt and wine spilled onto the Chinese rug below. 'Fuck it!' he exclaimed, watching helplessly as purply-red splatters seeped into the green and pink head of a fearsome dragon. Doreen...

'Why?' Summer almost screamed as she jumped up off the sofa, arms lifted in a gesture of exasperation. 'Tell me why, Doug!' her voice now a quivering, shrill yelp.

Doug turned and finally looked straight at her. He couldn't hold back any longer. It had to be done. Here and now. No turning back. Get it over with. He found himself looking at Summer who just stood very still, watching him. Waiting. But she knew what was coming.

Doug wrestled with his ragged emotions. He was useless at this kind of thing at the best of times, but this... this needed calm. The calm he reached for when standing in the wings, about to go on for an opening night.

Doug wiped the dampness from his cheeks with a rapid swipe of both hands. He focused in on Summer whose face wore an expression he had never seen. It shouldn't have been there. Didn't belong.

'Summer,' he said softly, 'Sit down and let me explain.'

She stared at him for a tense second, then slumped back into the sofa, lying her head back, looking up with eyes concentrated on an ornate Victorian ceiling rose that surrounded the light.

This was it, then. She was about to be thrown away like an old stage prop. Oh really? Just like that? After the Isle of Man and everything that Doug had said to her? After a summer of being inseparable, almost to the point of being found out?

After last night?

Oh, Summer would get over it. Hell, she'd managed to get through a lot worse than this, hadn't she? She deliberated for a moment. Perhaps not. In fact, if Summer took into account what she felt at this juncture in time, and had experienced since being with Doug, maybe she was about to get an entire pay-back package for every single iota of pain she had ever inflicted.

Bring it on, she said to herself. A new resilience seemed to have taken charge of her thoughts and emotions. It was familiar to a point but Summer sensed this might be a totally spontaneous defence mechanism, just to get her through the next few minutes. And maybe, just maybe, she could spring a surprise or two for Doug Delany, standing there, looking sorrier for himself than anything or anyone else. The water works were effective but didn't wash with her. He was giving this miserable performance to an actress.

The stupid thing was, despite all these vengeful feelings, Summer was still desperately in love with the pathetic old ham.

Doug suddenly broke the sticky silence.

'We have to end it... no... that's not strictly true. I have to end it. I have no choice.'

'No choice? Life's full of choices, Doug,' Summer replied in a dark monotone.

'Well, that's as well may be for other people, Summer, but not for me.'

Summer released a little derisive laugh, head still back, not wanting to look at him yet.

'Just another play thing for your summer season, Doug? Time to put your toy back in its box?'

'You know that's not true,' Doug said in a slightly offended tone. He sat on the other sofa and poured himself more wine, immediately taking several gulps. 'Summer, we have to face the fact that our time has come to an end. It was a wonderful... beautiful thing we had, but I can't give up my children.' He saw a frown pass over Summer's face but she didn't move or attempt to speak. 'If I give up my wife, I give up my children. It's as simple as that.' Doug downed the last of his wine. 'Perhaps when you have kids of your own, you'll understand that.'

'Sooner than you think,' Summer said quietly, almost under her breath and up to the ceiling.

Doug's breath caught. 'Pardon?'

'Sooner than you think,' she repeated slowly, for added effect, then lifted her head from the cushions and looked directly at him. A cold hard stare that penetrated to his core.

'Just what exactly are you saying?' Doug asked, his voice less than friendly.

'I'm pregnant,' Summer announced while reaching for her glass and tasting more bitterness. Nothing like the fetid bile that was rising up inside her.

Doug had to put a steadying hand on the coffee table. He was shaking quite violently. In an instant his mind was filled with so many thoughts that it overloaded and was then rendered completely blank. He might have even heard a pop in his head as everything seemed to implode. He realised he hadn't taken a breath for several seconds, his chest rigid to the point it felt as though it might never expand again. Slowly, Doug inhaled delicately, though it stuck somewhere between his throat and windpipe and reduced Doug to a fit of choking.

Summer stayed where she was and didn't make a move to help him.

'How far gone are... you...' he spluttered. 'When did you... find out?'

'A few days ago. I've been waiting for the right moment to tell you,' Summer said matter-of-factly and without blinking as she continued her relentless icy stare. Then she added with a smirk, 'And before you bestow the indignity of your next question... yes... it's yours. So! What are you going to do about it, eh? I think I'll let it sink in and call you later.' With that, she got up, slung the strap of her bag over her shoulder and walked out of the room. Doug hurried after her, managing only to see Summer open the front door and slam it thunderously behind her. He stood in the soundless hallway just looking at the door, listening to the sound of Summer walking to her car. Another door slammed shut and an engine revved, then the car seemed to speed away at a dangerous rate. Doug heard a high-pitch squeal as she left rubber on the road.

The walls seemed to close in on him and Doug sank to his knees, finally letting himself be swept away by the tide of horrendous emotions that needed to break free. He began to sob uncontrollably, beating the floor with his fists, again and again, tears and saliva dripping in unison as he screamed incoherent words into the carpet.

Eventually, Doug curled into a foetal position and just lay quietly, still weeping until, utterly drained both mentally and physically, he fell asleep.

CHAPTER THIRTY FIVE

Giancarlo sat motionless, fingers in the shape of a steeple, tips pressed against his chin. His gaze fell nowhere in particular on the other side of the office. Imaginary hands had taken a vice grip of his insides, slowly constricting and twisting them into a huge knot, tighter and tighter, until Giancarlo felt he might break in two.

He just concentrated on his breathing that had become very shallow, inhaling deeply and holding the air in his lungs for moment, then carefully exhaling on a measured breath. Each time he released the spent air, he allowed a fragment of his seething fury to float away with it. Eventually, Giancarlo began to feel calmer and it was only then he would let himself consider what Alessandro had just told him.

So Summer had strayed. Given herself to another man. Again. Dismissed their relationship as something not worthy of her loyalty. But what bit into Giancarlo like a tenacious toy poodle on an unsuspecting ankle, was that between Alessandro leaving and returning, he could never really know how this had happened, how often, and how serious the problem was. Whether it was a direct threat to his plans for her. Them. Even though the head screamed to finally let Summer go, deliver himself from what could amount to much trouble in a future made with her, the heart would not comply. She was the only woman for Giancarlo now and there was nothing he could do about it. Whatever she had done, was doing, if not already, would soon be at an end.

While he mentally paddled about in circles like a manic duck in a round pond, Giancarlo could feel uncomfortable boxing jabs from the fact that he too had sought carnal pleasures from someone else. But he was a man! It was different for him. The woman eventually becomes the

327

mother, therefore must remain untouched. For him, it was merely a process of switching off and soothing a man's mind at the end of a busy day. Nothing wrong with that, was there?

I've been in London for too long, he sighed to himself. *How could he ask such a question?*

The internal stranglehold was fast subsiding and Giancarlo considered that for all his righteous disgust directed towards Summer, they had never really discussed marriage. Skipped around the issue sometimes, even made passing jokes about it, but neither had ever said any heartfelt words on the subject. They were not betrothed and in truth, Giancarlo had not given Summer any reason to believe she meant anything of great importance to him. Oh, they had often said that they loved each other, although, in the light of this new information, he could not be sure whether Summer could ever really mean it, never solemnly or with the gravity that real love demands. Thus, he found himself in this dire situation.

It was just that it seemed Summer had orchestrated their separation of the last few months. Had used his moment of petulance on the telephone so many months before as an excuse to act like she obviously had. A point that did not sit well with Giancarlo, however much he loved her, because it meant that, once again, she had played him for a fool. How many times was he going to allow this behaviour and then forgive? He should never have given in all the other times and this occasion would be no different. He had no choice.

Giancarlo would have to pardon Summer one more time.

God only knew what his papa would think or have to say on the matter. Well, Giancarlo could almost hear the fiery lecture, though that didn't necessarily always indicate Paulo's true thoughts accurately. Perhaps there lay the downfall of his son in respect of the woman he wanted... would have... as his wife.

Giancarlo had strenuously resisted giving away any of his innermost feelings for fear of appearing weak as a man. Instead, he had practically given Summer nothing of his emotional depths and now it seemed he had made a terrible misjudgement. But he was not a man of change, for him, it was not even included in his gene package. Though in the face of everything he had instinctively known since birth, been strictly taught by his father and generally picked up along the course of his life, Giancarlo would have to somehow change for Summer. It would be an unusual compromise for one to whom such things were an anathema. But he sensed she craved a different kind of Giancarlo to the one he truly was and had been quite honest in his giving of. Maybe one who was more... new English man. Perhaps with a few subtle alterations here and there, he might penetrate her defences, find his way through the intricate labyrinth to where her stubborn English heart would be waiting.

Giancarlo allowed himself a modest smile for the first time since the call. Of course, such changes would only have to be temporary, would they not? Just until she had surrendered and he had secured for himself the woman he had decided would bear him a son and heir.

The phone on his desk rang.

It was Summer.

Silent line, then... thought you should be made aware of someone called Amanda Jacobs and you might want to ask your husband about her... click.

Maybe, but Jayne had been there, done that and worn the tee-shirt until it was ripped to shreds. Then gone back for more of the same. So, required now was a different kind of action. Strong and decisive. The kind of response she should have made the first time, or at the very least, when the second time arose. But no, Jayne had let herself wait until there was yet another obnoxious phone call in the middle of the night that had come nearly two months before. And she had no reason to suspect the cowardly covert voice was telling her an untruth. Everything fitted. Like it always did by the time these slippery bulletins made their way to her from out of the murky darkness.

Over the weeks that had passed since, Jayne had thought longer and harder about her future than ever in her entire life. She had been a lone debating society, considering all her options, if, in fact, there were any to choose from at all. The process had been horrendous, so alone and hurting desperately. Encased in her own feelings of failure and inadequacy, it was impossible to ease her burden by breaking free and maybe telling a sympathetic friend, who might simply let her pour it all out and just give Jayne a comforting hug afterwards without trying to get involved. So Jayne had protected her solitude away from work, which in itself had provided some welcome relief to her otherwise anguished mind, so that she could finally settle on what would be her best route forward.

During the days after Adam had left for Blackpool and an inappropriate introduction to Ms Jacobs, Jayne had actually started to let herself believe that Adam was really trying to turn over a new leaf, despite breaking a promise about Daddy's birthday. It occurred to Jayne that perhaps her husband had never been taught the importance of keeping one's word. Then again, having met his delightful parents, he probably had but decided the virtue was surplus to his requirements as a man.

She recalled the way they had made love and his adoring words before he left. Quite stupidly, Jayne had seen them for what she had wanted to see them as, not for what they truly had been, Adam up to his usual tricks.

Like some mindless door mat, Jayne had fallen for it all over again.

Dear old cantankerous Daddy had always been right about Adam. Even before the car arrived to take them both to the church, Trevor had tried earnestly, and with as much love as possible, to make Jayne see beyond her rose-tinted view of her fiancé. See the reality of the marriage that awaited her after the fairy-tale nature of this auspicious day had faded. Most likely as quickly as his agonised false smiles. He had almost pleaded with her, to no avail. Jayne had obstinately said that she was quite prepared to walk down the aisle by herself if he continued in that vein, and Daddy knew when it was time to shut up. But it had made Trevor sick to his stomach to have to act as though he was willingly handing over his precious daughter to the son-of-a-bitch who stood at the altar, a picture of smug triumph. Cock-a-hoop at having defeated a formidable foe.

Trevor and Adam's eyes had met for an edgy second as the vicar obliviously asked the ceremonial 'Who giveth this woman to this man?', Trevor nearly choking on his required reply of 'I do' while reluctantly holding Jayne's hand out to the enemy. Both men knew in that instant they would loathe each other for the rest of their lives.

In the middle of her painful thought fest, Jayne had weakened to a point where she simply had to speak with someone. Not anyone, someone who would make good honest sense, be pragmatic and get her to refocus on the problem. Her mind had become so mixed up with conflicting wants and needs and what ifs, that Jayne knew she had to turn to the only person who would help her see the wood for the trees again.

Daddy. For all his barking and bluster, straight-to-the-point opinions and don't-fuck-with-me attitude when required, he was still Daddy and had never given her the wrong advice. But it wasn't easy. She lost count of the times she would pick up the phone and put it back down again. It progressed to actually dialling the number but then hanging up when it connected. Eventually, her need for his guidance was so desperate, Jayne finally managed to hang on long enough for Trevor to answer. When he did, whilst he remained the model of constraint and fatherly understanding, soothing with calm words and affection and interjecting a few of his crass Aussie jokes to try and lighten her mood, Jayne was in no doubt that all the while, her father would have a vision before him of looking Adam straight in the eyes for the full drawn out and grievous duration of his torture and death.

Somehow, something about this last instalment in the sorry excuse that was her marriage had been the catalyst she had subconsciously been waiting for. The one with enough power in its mighty wallop to wake her up to the stark truth about her damaged union with Adam. In a remote part of Jayne, she had always known the marriage was doomed from the start, but hey! there was always divorce... Well, she was at that ominous threshold now and it didn't seem like the easy and unlikely ever to be required solution it had as she victoriously said her vows to the man she knew she would be with for the rest of her life. Jayne wondered, if everyone knew in advance what traumas lay ahead for them due to their decisions in life, would anyone ever venture out into the unmapped and chaotic world called experience? Rather, stay in their cosy, dark places of safety, never peeking out to sample what good things might be on offer.

And STILL Jayne loved Adam. Was there no end to the pathetic sick love she felt for the low life? Would it ever subside, at least? When their marriage was legally ended, or 'dissolved' as it is always so charmingly put in black and white on a nondescript piece of A4 representing her decree absolute, would she be happy or sad, or a combination of both? Maybe have one of those New Age divorce parties, or slink away and crawl under a rock to hide for a while until her feelings of embarrassment and humiliation wore off?

How the hell should she know? But at least when that seemingly now-inevitable moment arrived, Jayne would be in the love, care and emotional shelter of her parents.

Far away from this devastating world of Adam Nash.

Her flight on Qantas was booked, Daddy having kindly upgraded his daughter to first class. There was no going back from here. All that remained was for Jayne to tell Adam. She looked at the telephone for the longest while, planning her speech, weighing up whether she should approach it with quiet dignity or the poison she was well within her rights to drip down the line.

Jayne settled on the form of her delivery and reached for the phone.

Adam hung up. He stared down at his hands that rested in his lap, where a thumb and index finger slowly turned his wedding band.

He had always sensed this day would eventually come. In a strange way, Adam couldn't really understand why his clever producer wife had managed to put up with him for so long. Why she had forgiven him so many times. And why in God's name he had screwed around on such a wonderful person. But though she had finally broken, or perhaps he had broken her, Adam was in no way relieved. He was utterly shattered. His wife had struck the hammer blow harder than he had imagined she would on the day of reckoning and he sat there reeling from it. Apart from the fact he had no fucking idea who the scum bag was that seemed to have nothing better to do than spy on him, Adam wasn't prepared for life without Jayne.

She anchored him in his sycophantic world of show business, where he was allowed to wallow in the dreamlands of imagined future successes and where people gave enthusiastic praise and encouragement and were stabbing you in the back at the same time. A world where intelligent minds become contaminated by the possibilities of greatness and where the opportunities for reaching it, even for the very talented, were few and far between.

Jayne kept Adam Nash grounded. Sadly, it just didn't run to keeping him away from the constant availability of arse in the theatre.

In a nauseating twist of fate, Adam had already tired of the once-luscious Amanda. Had already made the decision to end their affair, this time certain that his wife would never know about it. Amanda had become like all the rest, tiresome and clingy, always the time to say goodbye and get rid. He was going to tell her on the final night, just as he was leaving the theatre. Easier that way, a quick word or two and then a speedy exit before they could create a nasty little scene. He remembered with dismay the frightful drama he endured in the full sight of the whole company when he had given another girl the old heave-ho.

He'd thought she was the biggest mistake of them all, but Amanda Jacobs may just have stolen that dubious mantle. She would also be the last one to wear it.

Adam knew he had been a twenty four carat prat and was on the brink of losing the one woman who had ever loved him. The only woman Adam had ever loved. It was time to prove that to her. Show her she was wrong. Their marriage could work, be strong again and flourish. The marriage they had set out to prove would endure to all the doubters who drank their champagne and ate their wedding breakfast with them. The same people who, he had since found out during a particularly spiteful spat with Trevor, were actually taking bets with each other on how long the marriage would last. It was of little comfort now, but at least Adam had the satisfaction that he and Jayne had beaten even the most generous term given.

'Well, we can still show them!' Adam suddenly said aloud. 'It ain't over till the fat lady sings, is it, boys?' he asked of Floppy and Rasher who looked at him from their respective cases. Faces ever set in their individual expressions and answering him in the way they always did. Never saying anything Adam Nash didn't want to hear. Forever smiling, huge brightly painted eyes held permanently in a theatrical look of surprise, even during his darkest moments. This being the most sombre of all. Yet still Adam's boys watched him in irreverent fashion.

As he now mutely regarded his little guys, something in Adam suddenly snapped, seemed to break out and be expunged. His obsession with them, perhaps? An overwhelming self-obsession, maybe. Whatever it was, he began to cry.

'What the fuck have I been doing?' he almost screamed at himself, spittle flying. 'They're nothing but stage props... latex and foam, paint and material. Puppets!' Adam was sobbing now, shaking his head in a new dumbfounded disbelief of himself. 'The only real thing in your whole sorry life has been your wife. Now she's gone...'

Adam abruptly stopped his rantings and pondered that

fact for a moment, sniffing and wiping his face with his sleeves.

No, she hadn't, not yet, anyway. He had one chance. A single opportunity to salvage his marriage and the best part of himself. Show Jayne and in a sense, himself, that he was no longer that cowardly twit of years gone by. The funny thing was, he'd never felt so scared in his life, but having finally realised what he had to do, Adam was astounded at just how much he was ready to make the leap from being someone who avoided confrontation to being a person who would face up to real life. Nothing else mattered. From this, for him a novel prospective, Adam could see clearly how he would be able to prove it to Jayne.

She had to sit down on the bed, still sweating from a sudden urge after her call to Adam to throw herself into an aggressive workout with her female-friendly free weights. Coloured in accordance with their weight by a plastic coating. The 3 kg weights she had favoured for this session of therapeutic reps were a delightful shade of purple.

Jayne could only listen. She simply didn't have the words to make the call a two-way conversation.

'... and so I'm coming to Perth with you, Jaynie. You never know, the television station where Trevor found you a job might even have a bit of work for me!' Adam laughed softly. Yeah, like they were going to need an ageing cheesy vent. After all, that's what he was, wasn't it? But this wasn't about him, for a change. It was about his wife and what she wanted, needed. There would never be another chance to let Jayne know how much he had always loved her. Maybe putting his own personal needs and career to one side, she would believe just how far he had come in realising what a pig's ear he had made of their relationship and was set on making it up to her. '... and as far as Trevor's concerned, I promise...'

Jayne smiled to herself. A sad sceptical little smile.

'... I will sort things out. Even if it takes the rest of my life, Jayne, I'm going to make this work.'

Adam knew he was beginning to sound a bit desperate, but he didn't care anymore. One chance.

There was a strained pause while Jayne searched for the right way of saying what she was about to say. How on Earth was she supposed to put this, in the light of Adam's totally unexpected spiel? Straight and to the point seemed the most fitting, and in keeping with her newly found emotional strength.

'Adam...' She stumbled for a moment then said, 'The thing is... I don't want you to come to Perth...'

'What?' His response was as much swallowed as spoken.

'Going to Australia is a new start for me. The beginning of another life. One that doesn't include you. I'm sorry.' Jayne suddenly wondered why she had said 'sorry'. Habit, probably.

'But, Jaynie, please, hear me out...' If she had been there with him, Adam would have got down on bended knees and begged.

'No!' came the short sharp reply, ejected down the line like the lethal venom of a disturbed death viper in the Australian outback.

Not again. Not anymore. Not this time...

'Good-bye, Adam,' Jayne said with a distinct air of finality and put the phone down. She looked across the bedroom to her travel documents sitting on a bureau. She knew Adam would make a hurried journey home, driving through the night after the final performance, probably bearing some ridiculously expensive gift as a peace-offering. Like all those other unsavoury times. Her dreadfully misguided husband full of contrition, falling on his knees again, clasping her legs, doing another one of his well-practised performances of pleading for mercy with the soul-wrenching despair of an innocent man about to be hanged.

Shame.

What Jayne... *oops!*... had forgotten to tell Adam was that by the time he got home, she would already be in Australia.

CHAPTER THIRTY SIX

Doug had woken with a scant ninety minutes before curtain up. It took several of those precious moments to shake off his groggy head and the shrill whining in his ears from a trauma-induced deep sleep. He made sure he was moderately *compos mentis* before jumping in his car and going to the theatre, but Doug was still in a disorientated state. He was of the opinion, though, that it would be better to try and collect himself while in the safety of the theatre and privacy of his dressing room, rather than remain longer at the house and make a mad dash later on through rush hour traffic.

In any case, the house now felt like a hostile environment, the walls sniggering at him having watched the awful spectacle of earlier. He knew how to be within the welcome confines of backstage, and yes, she would be there too, but they would only see each other during the show and not to talk to. Doug would make sure of that. If there was one overriding thing that he was sure about, and confident would be steadfastly in place despite the personal whirlwind he had just been sucked into, was his professionalism. As Doug Delany, comedian extra-ordinaire, many years of experience of treading the boards through thick and thin, with fanfare, lights and applause, he could deal with anything that bastard called life felt like chucking at him.

The following morning, Doug took himself off for a long drive, letting the car find its own way to somewhere quiet where he could decide what the hell to do about Summer and the news she had just dumped on him.

During the show the previous evening, Doug had taken refuge in his dressing room, door closed, only making the brief walk to and from the stage. During the finale, he had managed to keep his eyes either on his feet, the stage or out into the audience, never once did he chance looking at Summer. Stage crew noticed his unusual reticence but being consummate professionals themselves, remained discreet and kept out of his way. A star with a sore head bore an uncanny resemblance to a Grizzly... they tended to react the same way as well, when disturbed. While making a quick exit from the theatre at the end of the show, Doug found a moment to thank Clive for keeping calls and visitors away from him. He even managed a strained smile, after all, it wasn't Clive's fault Doug was knee deep in all this unmitigated shit.

After driving fairly aimlessly for about an hour, Doug found himself parked and overlooking a southern stretch of Morecambe Bay. It was a particularly sparkling sunny day, at odds with his mood, and the tide was completely out. A huge field of sea bed spread out before him, sunlight glistening on the wet muddy sands, shimmering in places where the outgoing tide had been caught as pools by natural depressions, giving the scene a mirage-like quality.

If only Doug's dreadful dilemma were simply an optical illusion, some frighteningly realistic dream, instead of the living nightmare now playing performances night and day in the dilapidated theatre of his mind.

He sat staring out across the bay, noticing a few experienced fishermen digging for cockles, the bay famous for them and lug worms, to use as bait out at sea, for catching mackerel and other fish on a line. Homing in on the squiggly sand domes that indicated where they might find them. The fishermen reminded Doug of his dad. Simple, hardworking and proud, ordinary folk. Damned proud. There were no distasteful dramas in their lives because they lived in a manner that prevented such things, but to an aspiring performer, it had seemed like a dead-end existence and stifling for a free spirit. Doug knew it would slowly diminish the artist in him and it was his determination to break out that had brought him to that fateful stag night.

Now sitting with a burden so heavy he could almost feel the weight bearing down on his shoulders, pressing into his flesh as he struggled to keep them straight, the strain on his heart felt as though it might just take its toll. Perhaps a massive coronary would end his problems. But his wife and children would be left with a worse ordeal than he himself faced at that moment. It was time to take responsibility. Time to make the most difficult decision of his life. Either own up to fathering Summer's unborn child or take the same route he had all those years ago. Strangely, and somewhat disturbingly, on another sandy beach.

Things had been different then. The Doug in Scarborough had looked upon life through the eyes of a bachelor and career junkie. Well, he wasn't a bachelor any more. He had looked to his future with the point of view of someone with places still to go and explore, with huge goals to achieve and the all-important fame to be had. Okay, so he'd been to all those places and beyond, achieved every type of success he could possibly have dreamed of and his name was probably known by every household in the land. Where did it leave him now? Somewhere so complex and dire that it might exceed his ability to cope.

Think! Think! he urged of himself.

If Summer was adamant about keeping the baby, then she would be making the decision for him. And then there would no chance of keeping their child under wraps. He would have to tell Gabrielle, his agent, the press...

Oh, Christ!

Sasha and Phoebe would probably be able to grow up in the knowledge of having a half-sibling without too much disruption to their lives, but Alexander...

'Oh, Alex...' Doug said out loud as his whole body seemed to heave with an alarming regret. This would most likely damage their relationship beyond any kind of suitable repair but even worse, it could destroy his son forever.

If Doug had not already done so.

Should Summer opt for a termination, then there might be the tiniest possibility that the situation could be retrieved. It seemed Gabrielle was once again willing to let the affair go for the sake of the children. He didn't deserve her, now more than ever. He never had.

Doug Delany would do anything to keep his family together, and let's not forget the bloodbath in the tabloids. Anything.

But what all these strenuous mental gymnastics were, in fact, ultimately deliberating, was the fate of a human life. Another unborn child. Whatever it might lead to in Doug's future, and that of his family's, surely he couldn't let such concerns interfere with this baby's right to live? Just like he had done before? Look what it had transformed the genuinely sweet and lively girl who had been carrying their child, into. Was Doug really prepared to see Summer disintegrate into another butch tyrant like Cynthia? Strip Summer of who she truly was to the extent that it would be impossible for that Summer to exist any longer? And all for the sake of this pathetic pillock who was only looking out for himself?

Doug was in no doubt that Cynthia retiring from performing and setting up as an agent was in direct response to his callous dismissal of her as a lover, a woman, and as the mother of his baby. Now when he thought back to sitting in the car park of the abortion clinic, like some vile pimp keeping watch over one of his streetwalkers as she satisfied another degenerate punter down a seedy alleyway, waiting for Cynthia to walk out after they had ripped a life from inside her, Doug knew it had been an evil decision. One that had never allowed for what Cynthia might have felt or wanted. He had used her weakness for him as a tool to construct a thought process in her frantic mind that would eventually come round to his way of thinking. Make Cynthia take the only course of action that would set them both free. Free to still pursue their dreams.

It had worked for Doug. But for Cynthia?

Did Doug have a cold enough heart to manipulate another young girl's life so that it did not impede his own?

And what of Gabrielle? Which woman would be able to endure the most pain? The younger more energetic woman with time on her side? Or the older woman with a full experience of life, though maybe now with a depleted resolve? It was an impossible question. One that would only ever be answered when Doug had made his decision and the play was acted out to its conclusion. Only then he would know whether he had chosen wisely, the woman upon whom to bestow the ultimate betrayal. But hadn't he already betrayed everyone he loved? Were they not already in a stinking pit of constant despair because of him?

What kind of man was he, for Christ's sake?

Think! Think!

Doug bowed his head and sighed like a man who couldn't take much more, but there was no time to wallow in self-pity, only this stolen interlude to consider his options and whether the embryonic offspring now growing inside Summer would be allowed a chance at life.

As he pulled the car to a halt outside Summer's flat, he saw her car in the driveway. Doug looked up to the first floor and felt about as brave as someone with bare feet faced with walking across a carpet strewn with tacks. He was more scared than ever before. Not so much because of how he would be with Summer, more, due to the decision he had finally made.

In the end, Doug had realised he had no option. Only the right one for everyone, in the long run. People dear to him were going to be desperately hurt and there was nothing he could do other than try his best to ease their suffering.

He didn't relish the task and it would be of no comfort to them, but Doug's soul was already racked with more pain and guilt than they could ever imagine. He had to do this. The whole thing had seemed preordained when the truth of his situation dawned as the tide had started its roll back into the bay, putting a full stop to his wandering about in a mental wilderness. A clarity had instantly befallen his dishevelled mind and Doug could almost feel the soothing hands of calm that can only follow the right decision.

He stood for a minute, took a deep breath and pressed the intercom button.

Summer opened the flat door in a fluffy pink robe, with a towel on her head fashioned into a perfect twist. She said nothing and simply indicated for Doug to go through to the kitchen. He also remained mute, trying a modest smile, but Summer had already turned away to close the door. Doug obediently walked into the ultra-modern kitchen with all its stainless steel and polished granite work tops.

'Wine?' Summer said in a perfunctory tone as she entered the room without looking at him.

'Yes... thanks...' Doug replied a little hesitantly, perching himself on a stool by the breakfast bar.

'I've only got white, that okay?' Her voice was still somewhat stern and clipped.

'Yeah, that'll be great.'

As Summer passed Doug to fetch glasses, he caught the sensual aroma of her freshly showered state. The perfume was so powerful he had to restrain himself from going over and grabbing her, holding her close to him and telling her everything was going to be all right.

He stayed seated on the stool, sensing she needed this physical and mindful space between them. Doug was already walking a fine line along a very uncertain road and didn't want to take a wrong step so soon along the way.

Summer handed him a glass full of a wine so clear, it almost had no colour, just a hint of a creamy lemon hue. She saw him studying it.

'Frascati,' she said simply, then, 'But a decent one.' Summer took a long sip of her own. It was actually Giancarlo's favourite tipple on a sultry London evening, sitting out at a table on the pavement in front of Carlo's.

Doug tried the wine. It was very light and crisp, quite pleasant, in fact.

'Very nice,' he said.

Their eyes finally met.

'So, what brings you here?' Summer asked in a voice and manner somewhat nonchalant.

An ephemeral wrinkle crossed Doug's brow.

'Should have thought that was obvious!' he replied with mild incredulity. What kind of question was that?

'Obvious?' Summer said in a way that suggested she really had no idea.

Was she doing this on purpose? Doug regarded her for a few seconds, trying to read into her strategy.

'Summer, you told me you were pregnant,' he eventually said, slowly, coldly, then took a deep swig of his wine. Now it tasted decidedly tart and he quietly shivered.

A tiny expression of recollection passed over Summer's eyes, but was immediately replaced by one of remorse.

'Doug...'

He dived in. No time like the present.

'Before you say anything, let me say what I've come here to say...'

'No,' Summer cut in. 'You don't understand...'

But Doug pounced on her words.

'What?' he snapped, voice icy. 'What... is it that I don't understand?' His eyes scorched a path to hers.

Summer looked away and slammed her glass onto the dark grey counter with a clang.

'I was pissed off!' she replied, flapping her arms in a wild gesture, causing the towel to loosen on her head. She pulled at it and discarded it next to her glass. Her hair fell in long damp strands across her face and she flicked them back with an angry swipe. 'I was just trying to make you feel like I did. I don't know... scare you, I suppose...' Her words trailed off into a whisper.

'What are you saying, Summer?' Doug asked in a voice that was low and menacing. It didn't seem as though it had come from him at all but some dark dank chasm, hidden deep inside that had not been opened for a very long time.

Summer found herself holding her breath momentarily at the sound of it, before saying, 'I'm not pregnant. I never was. Look... I'm sorry if...'

Doug ignited...

'SORRY!' he hollered. 'FUCKING SORRY!'

'Yes...' Summer responded timidly, trying to back into the counter but with nowhere to go. 'I... it was... Doug, please, I know it was a stupid, hurtful thing to do...'

'You evil BITCH!' he screamed and lunged his arm across the breakfast bar in fury, his glass flying off it and down to the laminate wood flooring with a resounding smash, shards of glass and Frascati spread over a wide area.

'Doug...'

His glare stopped her as he stood up from the stool. It was full of absolute hatred. Summer had never seen eyes like it. Even on Giancarlo. She was terrified.

'Just go!' she screamed nervously at him as he started to approach her. 'Get out, Doug. Just leave me alone!'

But Doug was already upon her, taking hold of Summer's shoulders, the grip brutal and she winced in genuine pain.

'Doug, you're hurting me!'

His hands squeezed harder until his knuckles were white, tips of his fingers now digging through her robe into muscle and ligaments.

'Hurt you?' he spat into her face, an inch from his. 'You don't know the meaning of hurting. You couldn't BEGIN to understand the concept of hurting someone, you stupid STUPID little girl!'

Summer was trembling and started to cry, blabbering like the child Doug had likened her to.

'Doug, for God's sake!'

'Fuck God! This is me... MY life you're screwing with. How could you?'

'I... I don't know!' she replied, now shaking uncontrollably and snivelling through tears that streamed down her reddened cheeks.

Inside, Doug was a torrent of emotion that raged like white water rapids through his veins on a terrible loop. After each circuit of his body, it seemed to gather strength. He was looking into the face of Summer Laine but all Doug could see was the face of Cynthia Hersh, full of despair and hopelessness. Defeat.

He had destroyed a lovely girl that day on Scarborough

beach. Put her through a heinous experience and changed her life forever. And Doug had never even found it in himself to say sorry.

Now I'm here with this... this... Doug looked Summer up and down with utter revulsion. *This... spiteful little piece of shit...*

All Doug's regrets, all his self-loathing, welled up like a boiling geyser, travelled down his arm and congealed at the centre of his hand. Every pain he had inflicted, and probably continued to inflict upon Cynthia, the devastation he had so nearly brought to bear upon Gabrielle and his children by telling his wife about the baby, all the anguish he had somehow managed to survive over the last twenty four hours, everything... was balled up in his fist as it connected with Summer's jaw.

She let out a dull groan rather than a yelp or scream, slid violently across the polished granite counter and caught her head on the corner as she crashed to the floor.

There was a terrible silence as Doug gasped inwardly, horrified at what he had just done. She lay very still. Too still. He fell to his knees beside her and gently touched her face.

'Summer?' he whispered.

Her head tilted to one side and Doug suddenly saw the bright red blood oozing from her ear.

'Oh God, no!' Doug wailed and started to shake her. 'Summer!' he shouted. 'Summer!'

But she remained out cold and completely motionless. It was this stillness that filled him with unbelievable panic.

Think! Think!

Doug ran to the phone.

CHAPTER THIRTY SEVEN

Gabrielle sipped rose hip and orange tea and munched on a celery stick while waiting for the maintenance chap to finish cleaning and covering the pool for the winter. It was probably a bit early in the year but although heated by a state-of-the-art system, the air temperature was simply too cold for Gabrielle to contemplate even taking a quick swim to relax tense muscles. It wasn't being in the water itself, it was the getting out afterwards. No thanks. Now that Alex and Sasha were back at school, the pool was further rendered rather redundant until the following year.

Of course it had been of much value during the summer months, assisting Gabrielle with her various garden parties for some of the charities she and Doug supported. The attraction of a dip after whatever 'afternoon' Gabrielle had laid on was a good crowd puller and produced more readies in the coffers at the end of the day. Her wealthy ladies that lunched, particularly for charity, thus making them feel remotely useful, thought it was 'wonderful, dahling!' and it seemed to loosen their purse strings somewhat, as well.

If only they knew the problems Gabrielle had put up with during the installation of the pool! Poor old Jim. She had grown quite fond of him in the end. He was a good honest worker, once her ground rules had been understood by all. He had taken himself off to one of the English encampments on a Spanish Costa for a break afterwards. Gabrielle was in no doubt he would need every bottle of San Miguel and huge jug of Sangria that he could manage.

A knock on the open utility room door brought Gabrielle back from fond memories of a fun girlie holiday she had taken with several friends to Nerja on the south east coast the year before she got the job in Bournemouth. The year before she met Doug. Happy days...

'All finished, Mrs Delany. I'll just show you what I've done and get you to sign the form for me, then I can let you get on.'

'Okay, do come in, won't you?'

The pool man carefully wiped his feet several times on the mat before stepping into the utility room and then again on the mat at the kitchen door. Word had indeed got around!

Alone again, Gabrielle started to potter around the house, getting ready for Doug's return later that week, when Valerie drifted into her mind.

Dear Val, she thought. They hadn't spoken since that dreadful day her friend had rushed out of the house. The two women had briefly acknowledged each other when meeting their daughters from school, but even during the long holidays, neither had called the other. Gabrielle considered whether it had been her responsibility to make contact, concluding that it had. After all, it was her snide remarks towards Valerie that had caused the rift in the first place. She had dishonestly dismissed the whole Tarot thing and Gabrielle should have been sensitive to her friend's feelings. She thought about those damned cards and recalled the strong woman. Was that her? Hard to tell. And the mysterious dominant man. Gabrielle still wasn't sure, just that it couldn't possibly be her husband. The death card continued to trouble her, though she knew Valerie had said it really meant the end of something and starting afresh.

Gabrielle smiled to herself, she still wasn't convinced. But should she have allowed that opinion to hurt Valerie and damage their friendship?

It had been quite lonely sometimes without the sparky Val to brighten things up, though with everything Gabrielle had been through mentally and emotionally over the last few months, it was probably best that Valerie had kept her distance. Still, Gabrielle hoped at some point they might get back together. With Doug coming home and all that could lead to, she may be in need of some moral support.

Ah Doug, Gabrielle thought. *Darling Doug.* Her wayward husband and prize shit head. Coming home to play happy families. How lovely. How sick.

The descent of her thoughts to Doug's base level brought Gabrielle to a halt. Nothing was going to change for her or the children until she actually found it within herself to do something about it. And that was that. End of story.

For now.

When the children are old enough... she promised herself.

The phone rang.

'Gabs!' came a shaking breathy voice. It was Doug's voice, but what the hell was wrong with him?

'Doug? What's...'

He cut in sharply.

'Shut up and just listen...'

Gabrielle's brow shot up but she remained silent as ordered.

'I've done something terrible...' Doug said through a couple of sobs, then regained an element of teetering control. 'I don't know what to do.'

Gabrielle had involuntarily stopped breathing while waiting for the punchline.

'Gabs?' Doug said in a wildly desperate tone in response to his wife's reticence.

'I'm here, Doug. What on earth has happened?'

Her voice was purposely poised and calm. Not how Gabrielle felt at all.

'It's Summer...' Gabrielle's chest suddenly felt confined and her heart thumped like a busker's drum. What was coming now? 'She's... Oh, Gabs, oh God!' Doug seemed to be fast disintegrating into a blithering wreck. She and God in the same breath. This must be serious. She needed to get to the bottom of it quickly. Doug in this unstable state wasn't capable of much.

'Doug... calm down,' Gabrielle said sternly like those strict hospital matrons of old. 'Tell me what's happened. Take a deep breath and speak slowly.'

There was a pause and she could hear Doug trying to compose himself, sniffing and clearing his throat. The next time he spoke, Doug told his wife everything.

Gabrielle's blood turned to ice as she listened. When Doug had finished his shocking tale, she had to swallow away the onset of horrified fear before she could speak.

'We need to stay calm, Doug, and think.' She drew a faint breath. 'Have you called an ambulance?'

'No.'

'Police?'

'No, you're the first person I've called. HELP ME!' Doug sobbed.

Gabrielle began to sense waves of utter panic beginning to hit, then, quite out of the blue, Angelo Maldini popped into her head. She rewound a mental recording of him saying how he could help them...

Gabrielle! That's the most stupid... Was it? If Angelo had been serious, would it not be the perfect solution? If, in fact, he had indeed meant what Gabrielle had hesitated to believe he had? Could she really make that call? Her mind was rushing here and there, this way and that, up and down, side to side...

Concentrate!

Then something from Gabrielle's youth seeped into her thoughts. A speech, words from a play... *Come, you spirits that tend on mortal thoughts, unsex me here; And fill me from the crown to the toe, top-full of the direst cruelty. Make thick my blood...*

With increasing consternation, Gabrielle also remembered in great detail the comment she had made to Valerie about the three witches, their menacing faces staring her out... and tears rushed into her eyes.

Was this a folly of both Doug and Gabrielle's making that the cards had been trying to warn her of?

'Doug?'

'Mmm?' he replied, sounding somewhat calmer.

'Listen to me and listen carefully.'

Like the cold-hearted ambitious queen in Shakespeare's

bewitching story, Gabrielle seemed now to have an extremely cool and collected head on her shoulders. She didn't know why or from where she had drawn this Machiavellian asset, but whatever it was, Gabrielle knew with it, she would make the right decision. For her. For Doug. And for the children.

'Doug, there's something I've got to tell you...'

And she told him about the favour that Angelo had offered them both. Just the favour, not why.

Doug was completely silent for a while afterwards, then said with an air of disbelief, 'You're not serious?'

'Totally, and I think with the problem before us, it's inspired.'

She had never felt so sure of anything in her life. Perhaps she was that woman in the cards, and if that was so, how did that bode for the rest of them?

'Are you honestly suggesting... Gabrielle... I've got a dead woman...' Doug was off and rambling again. There was little time. Gabrielle had to act quickly if this was to work. She pondered whether she should chance a prayer to God that Angelo would be available, then felt under the circumstances it might not be advisable.

'Are you sure she's dead?' Gabrielle asked Doug as if she were asking about the weather.

'Yes... quite sure... she's not breathing... hasn't moved at all... and the blood... Christ Almighty! Oh Gabs..!'

There it was again, her name and His in the same sentence. Was He playing with her? Or was it an ironic little game born of the other one? Seeing as she was most likely heading for his place, anyway, Gabrielle thought she might ask Old Nick when she got there.

Now to the business at hand.

'Doug, I'm going to hang up. Don't move or do anything... do you understand me? DO NOTHING. Do you hear me?'

'Yes, I hear you... but... Gabs, you can't...'

'Oh, shut the fuck up, Doug. I'm going to try and get us out of this mess. So, sit tight and wait for me to call you back. Where are you?'

'At her flat...'

Oh great! thought Gabrielle. *Just to make my life even more difficult...*

'Okay, where is that and what's the number?'

In a very small and wobbly voice, Doug gave his wife the information.

Gabrielle hung up.

Doug stared at the phone. What had Gabrielle turned into? He didn't recognise the woman he had just spoken to. Who was she? Could it be that this was the foul hybrid he had created through their years together? Can someone change that much? Be a loving wife and mother and at the same time be about to commit...

He didn't want to even think about what Gabrielle was going to do. Or himself for that matter. And anyway, who the hell did Gabrielle think the flirty obese restaurateur was? Don whatever his bloody name was in *The Godfather*?

Doug was shaking like a leaf now and couldn't seem to stem the flow of tears. He wanted to vomit but fought back the urge, just wanting to run out of the flat and away from all this. But that would never be possible because Doug couldn't ever run away from himself and there was no theatre, studio or show on Earth that would take away the evil he had done.

The evil that he was.

Suddenly, a delirious little laugh escaped from him.

His wife was named after the archangel. Funny that. Must be the comedian in him. Even at a time like this.

Doug began to laugh out loud, then caught sight of Summer through the doorway and stopped. His heart pounded and with legs that felt like they wouldn't support a feather, walked gingerly into the kitchen again. It was odd being so scared of something so lifeless but he forced himself to go over to the body and look down upon its face.

In death, as in life, Summer Laine was as beautiful as ever.

Angelo sat with his hand resting on the telephone as he slowly digested Gabrielle's call.

He had always known something of this nature would come to him at some point. Angelo just didn't think it would be so soon or from this particular source. Most difficult of all for him, it also involved Giancarlo. How was he supposed to break this to his cousin? Then it occurred to him that if he handled this matter with maturity and professionalism, he might go up in the family's estimations. His cousin would see he was not just the bumbling idiot Giancarlo sometimes thought Angelo to be.

Get this right and it could be his moment of glory.

Angelo dialled a number.

'Si,' Giancarlo said brusquely as he answered his private line.

'Cousin...'

'Ah, Angelo... how you doing?'

'Giancarlo, just be quiet for a minute...' Then considering an image of his cousin's face at that moment, quickly said, 'Forgive my disrespect, but you must listen to me.' There was an uneasy silence. 'Is our friend still in place?' Angelo asked. A coded question.

Giancarlo knew instantly that he had meant Alessandro, and yes, he was still in Blackpool. But what of it? 'Si,' he said simply with a shrug.

Angelo closed his eyes and allowed himself an inaudible sigh of relief before saying the next with trepidation.

'Giancarlo... it's Summer...'

CHAPTER THIRTY EIGHT

Present Day

That all now seemed like a lifetime ago. In many respects, it was. In another, his memories were so vivid and still incredibly precise that those nightmare events could have taken place only yesterday.

It was strange how the passage of time and a personal journey through it over a few years can melt away to nothing when faced with a memory of extraordinary proportions. As though a life built from and lived beyond the aftermath was only a brief respite between the actuality of a past and the instant one chose to revisit it.

Doug was now alone in the studio. Bob Welsh had been an excellent guest. Far more open than all had expected. Doug had warmed to the poor sod in the end, after all, he without sin...

The e-mails and calls since the show went on air had been extremely favourable and it augured well for the continuation of the show with Doug as its presenter.

He had even managed to pass a few pleasantries with Cynthia before she whisked Bob off for a debriefing prior to his carefully planned interview in the *Mail on Sunday*, the tabloid that had exposed him in the first place. Cynthia was good. She knew her stuff. Bob Welsh could look forward to his role as Jimmy Newgate for many years to come. Just as long as the evil drink didn't get him again.

Doug had found himself asking Cynthia if she was happy these days. There had been a calculating look in her eyes and a loaded pause before she just gave him an ambiguous smile and took a long drag on her ever-ready fag, blowing smoke just past his right ear. Doug sensed he might have raised the shutter about an inch before she brought it crashing back down.

After Cynthia left, Doug recalled the deep lines around her mouth that hadn't been there when he knew her, no doubt due to years of chain smoking. He pondered whether contrary to the startling physical changes, deep down, Cynthia Hersh was still the same person. Then Doug considered his wife and decided that the Cynthia now was probably far removed from that girl in Scarborough.

As he gathered his belongings together, including the proposed script and questions for his guest the following week, Doug also picked up a CD and put it in his briefcase. It belonged to Gabrielle, her favourite album of all time, Supertramp's *Breakfast in America*. She had insisted he play one of the tracks on his show for her. Or was that ordered? It didn't make a lot of difference, he had played out that week's broadcast with her most-played track. Duty done. Until the next one was issued.

It was just another small way of paying her back. Redressing the balance after Gabrielle had been there for him when he had needed her most. She had a little help from Angelo Maldini, but even so, Doug's wife had saved him from God knew what. Though, it still bothered Doug that Angelo would have made such an offer in the first place. Gabrielle was less than forthcoming on the matter and although something didn't fit, he had long since given up trying to piece it all together.

Doug would never know what actually took place after he was called at the flat by some rough-sounding Italian bloke who told him to 'Leave like everything is normal, say goodbye before closing the apartment door and look happy as you leave the house.'

Doug had simply carried out his instructions, it was about all he could manage at the time, his mind and body working on some shock-induced autopilot. Nature's famous 'fight or flight' mechanism. Do what you have to and then contemplate 'what ifs' afterwards.

When he had somehow dragged himself to the theatre that evening for the penultimate show, Doug had quickly learned that a call had come in to Phil Beauchamp from

Summer's boyfriend in London that she had been taken quite ill with seafood poisoning, probably some mussels she had eaten for lunch. With only two shows to go, it wasn't a catastrophe and the adaptability of talented professional dancers was second to none. Doug had been impressed with how efficiently they had reorganised the routines.

Summer wasn't missed.

But standing on the stage, cracking jokes while some faceless thug was scraping her body off a blood-stained floor took its toll. As he gave his all to the audience, the woman he had loved beyond measure and then snuffed out in an appalling moment of madness was being summarily disposed of in whatever fashion it was that those people favoured.

Even now, Doug would immediately want to throw up every time he stepped back to that horrendous day. Normally he tried not to and had been quite successful up until now.

It was just that bloody song...

There had been no suspicions, no investigations, nothing. And so the Delanys had gone forward with their lives. Very changed lives.

Gabrielle insisted that Doug give up any lengthy shows or those that took him away from the family. So he had turned his hand to writing material for others. Doug had been rather good at it. Learning about the particular comedian involved and working closely with them. He was also asked to assist in scripting several satirical radio plays. It was how the offer of his own chat show had come about.

Of course, initially, people had questioned his motives and reason for changing direction at a time in his career when he was king, but Doug had enough front left in him to get away with his explanations. Gabrielle had done the rest for him and continued to so.

A massive shift had taken place in their marriage. Gabrielle now called the shots where their careers were concerned. It seemed to Doug his wife called ALL the shots now, but he let her. What else could he do? Even from the grave, he would be repaying his wife.

Doug had also taken on the challenge of being a hands-on father. To his utter amazement, and to much extent Gabrielle's, he had loved it. Like one of his son's ducks to water. Their mother had become a teacher of jazz and modern at a London dance studio. It was gradually taking up most of her time. She often stayed in central London overnight. Doug didn't mind. Gabrielle more than deserved her success. There was even talk of opening her own studio. He would just plod on with his little weekly radio slot and occasional writing of scripts. Doug figured that he still held the most important job. Looking after their three children.

Well, that said, Alexander was now a typically difficult teenager, full of himself and opinions on everything under the sun. He was always right, of course and no one understood him. And Doug mused that if Alex said those confounded words 'wicked' and 'respect' just one more time...

Sasha was fast growing into catwalk model material, but with the brains to go with it, thank God. It seemed she had also finally discovered boys and Sasha knew exactly how to use them to wind her father up.

Then there was little Phoebe, who was no longer so little, a bit of a tomboy and quite a handful at times, but she had become 'Daddy's girl' quite unexpectedly. Maybe because she was the youngest and at an impressionable age, she was getting the best access to her father. Whatever the explanation, Doug adored his rough and tumble mate.

He smiled at these thoughts as he yawned and stretched. He was completely shattered. Not just because of the intensity of the interview with Bob, and seeing Cynthia, but his sudden trip into a past he thought he had boxed up and safely hidden away.

Memories; distant and near, transient and permanent.

Just as he stood to leave, the internal phone rang. Doug's shoulders sagged.

'Yep?'

'Oh, sorry, Doug,' said Flick when she heard him trying to stifle another gaping yawn. She was the studio suite's young pretty receptionist and general production runner. 'I've got the Italian agent here.'

Doug's brow furrowed for a second. Italian agent? Perhaps Pete, his producer, had mentioned it and Doug had forgotten. Not a rare occurrence these days.

'Mr... Scar... latti?' Flick said to try and help Doug along while reading from the agent's business card.

Doug thought for a moment. The name seemed familiar and yet, not.

'Okay, Flick, love, send him in,' Doug finally said with a tired sigh. He'd speak to Pete later.

As he went to open the studio door, Doug accidentally knocked his briefcase and all the papers fluttered to the floor in a heap. He reached down to start collecting them and became aware of someone standing in the doorway. Doug's eyes settled on extremely expensive shoes, they must have cost hundreds of pounds. or was that euros? He looked up to find a tall, strikingly handsome man standing watching him with dark Latin eyes. He was impeccably dressed in a faintly pinstriped tailored suit. Doug stood and held out a hand, feeling somewhat shabby in comparison.

'Doug Delany, pleased to meet you, Mr...?'

The man half smiled lifting one corner of his mouth, and without breaking eye contact, took Doug's hand in a firm grip.

'Giancarlo Scarlatti, Mr Delany. It is good of you to see me.'

Giancarlo... Giancarlo...

Doug suddenly felt uneasy but couldn't put a finger on why.

'I'm sorry, Mr Scarlatti,' Doug said with an embarrassed smile as he indicated the mess at his feet. 'Just give me a minute.'

He crouched down to quickly gather up the copious typed sheets and Gabrielle's precious CD. As he did, Doug saw another pair of feet emerge from behind Mr Scarlatti's, also exquisitely adorned in Italian leather. His eyes wandered up to perfect ankles and toned legs, a sludge coloured cashmere dress and coat ensemble touching at the knees.

Something in Doug stirred.

Then he saw a neatly swollen stomach. From his experience with Gabrielle, Doug would have said about five months. A cream silk scarf completed the outfit. It all screamed of Milan couture.

Doug slowly stood up. He was shaking now.

Natural blond hair was shaped in a blunt bob-cut, held back from her face by large Gucci sunglasses delicately edged with gold detail, strands of hair teasing the lobes of her ears.

Ears he had once kissed and caressed with his tongue. A silky-skinned neck that he had once nuzzled as they had made love. Luscious lips, now shaded in a startling deep red. Same unforgettable eyes that now gazed into his. Cold and unreadable.

Summer.

Suddenly for Doug there was no air to breath, no power to pump his heart, his whole body just seemed to dissolve into non-being, while his life was held suspended in some ghastly frozen moment as time for him appeared to be terminated.

A man's voice echoed from a faraway place and his words slithered into Doug Delany's frenzied mind as he stared hopelessly into the abyss.

'I'd like to introduce you to my wife...'

ABOUT THE AUTHOR

Darcy Drummond was born to show business parents and grew up surrounded by it. Although she chose not to follow them into the business, it remains a fundamental and cherished part of her life to this day. Some of the wonderful and talented people she met as a child remain her dearest friends. After having several successful careers, Darcy now concentrates on writing. She is married and lives in the south of England.

ABOUT THE PUBLISHERS

Saron Publishers has been in existence for about ten years, producing niche magazines. Our first venture into books took place in 2016 when we published *The Meanderings of Bing* by Tim Harnden-Taylor. *The Ramblings of Bing* is due out in time for Christmas 2017. *Minstrel Magic* by Eleanor Pritchard came out in June and tells the phenomenal show business story of the George Mitchell Singers and the Black and White Minstrels. Further publications planned for 2018 include *Every Woman Remembered*, the story of the Newport women who died in service in the First World War, *From Heart and Soul,* a collection of poems by John Marshall, and *Jackie*, the second part of the successful *Life and Soul* trilogy by Julie Hamill.

Join our mailing list info@saronpublishers.co.uk. We promise no spam.

Visit our website saronpublishers.co.uk to keep up to date and to read reviews of what we've been reading and enjoying.

Follow us on Facebook @saronpublishers.

Follow us on Twitter @saronpublishers.